THE
KEYS
OF
PERSEPHONE

The Keys of Persephone
Copyright © 2025 by Kate Gray Glass
All rights reserved.

First published in the United States by Contrarian Publishing

contrarianpublishing.com

Summary: Lane, a ghost, has been falsely accused of turning ghosts into shades. Shepherd, an unwitch, is searching for her sister. When the two reluctantly team up, they stumble upon a secret so big that it might be the end of Life as they know it.

Library of Congress Control Number: 2024917402
ISBN: 978-1-965422-01-4
ISBN (ebook): 978-1-965422-04-5

First Edition

Cover illustration by Jora Lemon
Book and cover design by Jamie Ryu

THE KEYS OF PERSEPHONE

A Novel

KATE GRAY GLASS

CONTRARIAN
PUBLISHING

Brooklyn, NY | Est. 2024

CHAPTER ONE

Lane could never seem to get the landing right no matter how many times she jumped between worlds. After falling through the air, through the darkness that separated *nothingness* from *somethingness*, she hit the cold ground and landed hard on her back.

A string of curses flew from her mouth as she pushed herself up.

The unfamiliar street swallowed her. The sun here was too bright, the air too hot, reminding her just how different this world was. And yet, there was something about it that kept pulling her back—even when she didn't want to come.

At least no one had seen her fall on her ass this time.

The houses on either side of her became clear as her head stopped spinning. She couldn't tell where they had been sent on this assignment—not that they were supposed to know. And that was fine with her. But, of course, she tried to figure it out anyway. The town was full of color and sound, the opposite in every way of The Academy. Townhomes of every color surrounded her: yellow, red, green, black, as if each was a living thing with its own personality. The alley was empty, but cars honked in the distance as a bright red double-decker bus passed her on the street. She still wasn't used to it. She tried to think of the details Tripp had taught her, in secret, about Life. Red bus, small houses, signs all in English—she supposed they might be in England, or maybe in a smaller city in the US.

"There you are." Tripp's gruff voice called from behind her. As she stood, she rubbed the gravel in her palms against her pants, trying to erase the evidence of her fall.

She wouldn't hear the end of it if her classmates noticed, that was for sure.

Tripp and Perry walked toward her down the narrow brick path, fresh and unbothered by the jump between worlds. Neither of them fell when they Blinked. Or if they did, they never admitted it to their younger, less adept friend.

Tripp adjusted his backpack on his shoulders, his hand covered in scribbles of tattoos.

"Thought you might have gotten lost." He grinned. "I was worried you would be up a tree again."

She crossed her arms as he rubbed the top of her hair. The more Tripp teased her, the more she wanted to punch him.

"I was only in a tree because I was very inconveniently chased by a pack of ghost wolves, and you know it." She pointed a finger at him. "And this time I landed closer than either of you. You both know what that means. Pay up. An ampere each, both of you."

Perry raised an eyebrow, her expression saying, *You'd better be joking*.

"I'm sure The Academy will be *so* impressed by your progress," Tripp teased. "No wolves this time, at least."

Tripp snorted as he handed his ampere to Lane, the coin shining in the blinding daylight sun. Lane held out her other hand to Perry.

"Don't think I don't see the gravel all over your pants." Perry turned away. "We can talk when you can actually Blink properly." Perry pulled up the sleeve of her jacket. "Can we please just get this over with before time runs out? I have another class after this."

Their uniforms were simple—protective jackets, dark pants, mission backpacks. The first priority of their uniforms was utility. The second was to blend in. The third was protection, which must have been some kind of sick joke.

The dead were not particularly easy to kill.

Most people expected peace in death. Some expected there to be nothing at all. Lane didn't know what she'd expected when she was alive, but it was certainly not this. She doubted that anyone ever expected to spend their afterlife at a school for ghosts, taking classes in death magic and going on assignments to retrieve escaped ghosts.

"We only have an hour." Perry pointed across the road. "We better split up. Remember what The Academy says—negotiation comes first. Force is only to be used as a last resort."

The sharp stare Perry gave her said it all. Lane held up her hands, as if she was being falsely accused. Which she wasn't.

"Victor already went through the mission details. He doesn't like being shown up." Tripp looked up at the sun. "And it can't be any worse than our last run."

"Oh yeah." Lane sucked on her teeth. "The wraith. That was rough."

"Or the shadow wolves before that."

Perry pressed a finger between her eyebrows as if she might banish their presence like a migraine. Her sleeve was folded up to the elbow, exposing the thin, bracelet-like tattoo that encircled her wrist, identical to the ones they all wore. Their obols, branding them as students of The Magistrate Academy.

"Do you two ever listen to anything? This ghost is dangerous. He was a witch." Her voice was flat. "He could have escaped and gone straight to Haven Hall."

Lane's typical sarcastic retort died in her throat. She was used to Perry keeping them in line, but even Tripp wouldn't play around when it came to witches. She'd heard stories of witches and their violence, of the way they used their living magic to torture, to prey on others. There were not many of them left, but that only made the leftovers even more radical. Especially those at Haven Hall.

Lane had never met a witch, but even she knew to be afraid. Still, she placed her hand on her friend's shoulder. "Don't be too worried, Per. If they thought he knew anyone at Haven Hall, they wouldn't have sent us. They would have sent someone better."

Tripp snorted.

Ignoring her, Perry flicked her wrist for them to spread out. "I'm just saying, be careful."

They turned in three different directions. She always went left. Tripp always went right. And Perry, always determined, moved straight ahead.

It was just like any other assignment, any other test. But Lane couldn't help but look over her shoulder, watching Perry walk away.

"What's the worst that could happen? We're already dead."

She passed a group of students, laughing in their school uniforms as the bell chimed in the distance. Humans were not supposed to be able to see ghosts, but they still took every precaution. It still surprised Lane that they were even corporeal enough to bleed, to breathe, while being dead. Some called it being undead. The Academy picked a very select few students who could retain their corporeal form with the help of death magic. It was purely selfish, of course—how else would they be able to fight and capture their targets? And, of course, it kept the students in line. If you were kicked out of The Academy, you lost the ability to retain a physical form, relegated to eternity as a purposeless, drifting ghost. Or worse, a shade.

Lane wasn't about to let that happen because of some witch, that was for sure.

She passed another row of houses, the spaces between them closing in until they touched, the street becoming more dilapidated as she went on. The gardens were overgrown and unattended, but beautiful. Creeping vine crawled across cold stone like spiderwebs. It reminded her of The Academy and its ghost-filled woods. The town was almost as empty, almost as abandoned.

Sometimes it seemed like there were so few differences between dead and alive.

Had she lived someplace like this when she was alive? Each trip to Life was a needle pulling at the invisible thread of who she had been. It was better, she thought, that their memories were removed when they joined the school. She knew exactly how fast she would unravel if she did remember.

But she couldn't think about that now. She needed to focus. The time limits they were under were strict.

Her boots echoed in the empty streets as she paced a perimeter around the houses. It was mid-afternoon, and there was laughter in the distance. She imagined the ringing of a school bell, the rustle of uniform skirts as the students hurried back inside for class from the courtyard. She could almost see their faces, smiling, sticky, red from playing in the sun. That's what she imagined a normal school to be like. The Magistrate Academy. . . was not. She didn't imagine that Haven Hall was either, based on what she'd heard. The Academy might have been a shadowed place, full of whispers and the wisps, but Haven Hall was a dark place for even darker magic.

Lane shuddered. And then she felt it. The call of living magic. It drifted toward her, enticing like a lover's kiss. Butterflies danced across her insides as the honey warm glow of it sank into her skin like sunshine. The air around her became tighter, full of the pulse of electricity that radiated from the magic.

She spat on the ground and shook her limbs as if spiders crawled against her skin.

Disgusting.

Living magic was a manipulative force. It knew what it wanted, and it wasn't afraid to take it—by whatever means necessary. It always felt like a deception to her, as if the magic itself was made of lies.

She stomped toward the magic, frowning as she tried to shake the feeling, even as she got closer to it.

Perry stood in front of a dilapidated house, staring at its broken-down roof with her arms crossed tightly across her small chest. With broken windows and an overgrown yard, it looked like no one had lived in the shack for decades. But the energy around the house sizzled.

Her hairs stood on end.

"What's wrong with you?" Perry asked. She must have noticed Lane's nauseated look.

"Nothing," Lane said. She averted her eyes from Perry's gaze and back to the house.

The girl turned away from her, indifferent. Lane exhaled. That was a close call.

She wasn't supposed to be able to feel the magic of the living, being dead and all. When she had first realized, she'd asked around The Academy, as gently as she could. She'd gone to Victor, who knew everything, and he'd just looked at her. The dead couldn't touch living magic. It was lost to them. And the witches who played with living magic weren't able to use the magic of the dead, although they'd tried for centuries to capture it and put an end to death for once and for all.

Lane didn't hate them for the thought. But because of The Academy, she knew better. There was no way to end death. Not without ending everything else with it.

"Any run-ins with humans?" Perry asked as Tripp arrived behind them, his slow jog coming to a stop.

Tripp raised his pierced eyebrow at her. "We *are* human, you know."

"Not anymore."

Lane snorted. In a lot of ways, being students at The Academy made them almost indistinguishable from the living.

Until you tried to touch them. Lane could touch Perry and Tripp—but if a living, breathing person were to walk by the shack, she would walk right through them. They wouldn't even see her.

Still, Victor always made them report if they saw humans. They could never be too careful, not with the witches and Haven Hall up to their tricks.

All three of them jumped as something slammed against the front of the house. Shadows passed by the windows, flickering as if someone was pacing angrily, just out of sight.

"He's getting stronger," Tripp said.

Lane watched the shadows inside the house as another object hit the wall with a crash. The ghosts at The Academy could move things too, but this was different. Violent.

"Let's get started. Guard duty?" Perry asked.

Tripp smirked as he planted himself at the gate. Lane rolled her eyes. She didn't know why Perry bothered to ask. Tripp was just as good at shirking their school responsibilities as he was at partying.

Perry met her eyes and Lane nodded, slowly following her classmate toward the front door. It opened with a shrieking creak, as if the wood would fall apart beneath Perry's touch. Perry didn't look back as she stepped into the darkness of the house, leaving Lane outside, alone.

With a heavy exhale, she stepped inside.

The room was pure darkness as her eyes adjusted. The shack seemed to be barely standing, held together by the humid air and pure will. It was small, one room in the style of the early century when most families slept in one bed. Rotting floorboards led to a decaying, empty kitchen and a set of stairs climbed to a second-floor loft. Abandoned furniture littered the floor: a small dining table, two broken chairs, an oven toppled over on its side.

There was no sign of the ghost, but Lane could still feel him. The warmth of his magic brought beads of sweat between her eyes.

Lane paused as Perry walked toward the stairs. The room was full of this ghost's power—but not the kind he was supposed to have.

"Wait, Per—" Lane grabbed at her friend's sleeve.

Perry stopped, scowling at her, one combat boot already on the broken stairs.

"If he's a witch—he can't use Vis anymore, right?"

The word felt like a curse in her mouth. *Vis.* In the old language, it meant the force behind living magic—the kind that ghosts like them weren't supposed to have. The kind that Lane could feel coating her skin like paint.

"Not that I know of. Unless the professors are right and the witches are coming for us," Perry snorted. "They aren't supposed to be able to, no. We'll be fine."

Perry pointed up toward the loft, moving to climb the stairs. Her footsteps were light but left deep prints in the grime-covered floor.

Lane nodded, following. She couldn't tell Perry about the magic. And Perry was probably right. It was fine. This was nothing new.

A crack split through the floor. Floorboards snapped toward them, splinters flying.

Perry hurried up the stairs, jumping over the crack. She held out her hand and made a motion for Lane to be quiet. She rolled her eyes in response.

At the top of the stairs, the familiar smell of uncontrolled magic crackled. Power radiated through the air in blurred lines, like the horizon on a summer day.

Lane crouched as she reached the landing. The entire second floor was one room, barely large enough to be called a bedroom. And it was completely empty.

"Anyone home?"

Another violent tremor rocked through the house, turning the floor beneath their feet to water and sending cracks up the walls. She fell to her knees, gripping the ground with tense fingers to keep upright. Perry landed beside her with infuriating ease.

"We know you're here." Perry pulled a pouch of bone dust from her belt.

A shadow whirled in the far corner of the loft.

"What did you do to me?"

The ghost stepped out of the shadows, his gray form eerily thin. A chill traveled across Lane's skin. Like the ghosts at home, his outline flickered, the shadows around him moving and defying the rules of light. But unlike the ghosts Lane knew, his eyes were completely black, staring at her like twin voids.

Something was not right.

His voice was metal scraping the floor. "They said it wouldn't hurt—"

Whatever had once been a ghost was no longer there. His body seemed trapped between corporeal and shadow—half in this world, half in the other. His form snapped back and forth between black shadow and silver wisp, and in between, he stopped looking like a man at all.

Lane had no idea what that meant.

"It hurts."

It seemed like he was reliving something, maybe replaying a memory from his life. His eyes were hollow and vacant.

"Look, there isn't an easy way to say this." Lane cleared her throat. "You're dead. We're dead. So whoever hurt you. . . they're probably long gone. And they can't hurt you anymore."

At least death promised that, if nothing else.

"Who are you?" The words stretched for too long, his mouth gaping into a black oval. "I thought. . ."

He reached, fingers turning to black wisps.

Perry emptied the pouch of bone dust into her hand. They needed to get him back to After Life.

"Something is wrong with him," Lane hissed.

Perry glared back, *You think?*

An unearthly wail erupted from his throat as his stare landed on her. His mouth stretched from ear to ear, sucking the air from the room.

Her breath was yanked from her lungs. Clawing at her neck, Lane gasped for breath, thinking over and over that she didn't *need* to breathe—she was dead. But it certainly felt like she did. Her lungs ached against her ribs, threatening to collapse.

Perry crawled across the floor, the veins in her neck popping as she dusted ground bone onto the floor. They needed to create a bone circle around him, trap him inside.

Lane's head pulsed from the lack of oxygen. They were going to run out of air before Perry finished.

They needed more time.

Lane pushed through the pain in her lungs and rushed to her feet, launching herself at the ghost. As her foot connected with his chest, his energy blasted outward into the wall. Whatever was wrong with him, it hadn't affected her ability to hit him, at least.

He tilted his head back with a groan. Behind him, the window exploded. Shattered glass flew across the room like arrows. Air from the outside rushed into the room and Lane collapsed, gasping.

Perry cried out, a gravelly groan that sent Lane's heart racing. She shot around at the sound.

A piece of glass jutted out from Perry's leg at a harsh angle, ripped through the muscle of her thigh. Lane watched Perry as she gritted her teeth, falling to her knees. She clutched at the wound with desperate fingers. The bone dust fell to the ground, sticky with blood.

Without thinking, Lane rushed toward her, reaching for the wound. There was too much blood. Too much for a small shard.

Too much for a dead girl. They could be injured when they were in Life on missions, as part of the trade for traveling between Life and Death. But this?

Perry tried to speak, but only the sound of wet blood came out.

Too late, Lane realized what she'd done. The ghost's attention followed Lane's line of sight to Perry—and the previously unnoticed bone circle she was trapping him in.

The black voids of his eyes blazed. He erupted with a thunderous wail, his outline flipping violently between wisps of smoke and shadow.

Like lightning, he shot through the wall.

Before Lane could get to her feet, he was gone, screeching as he disappeared into the night.

Perry groaned, struggling to stand. She ripped the glass from her flesh, dropping it to the ground in a pool of her own blood. On missions, they were slightly more corporeal than in After Life—but only just. Just enough to breathe, for their hearts to beat. Just enough to bleed.

Lane stared at the window, shattered glass surrounding it like a starburst.

She could let him go. She could go back to The Academy, get Perry back safely so she could heal, and get another team of students to finish the mission. She should drop it, and definitely not try to get revenge for hurting her friend.

But was she going to?

Absolutely not.

"Lane, don't you dare." Perry reached out.

It was too late. She jumped out the window.

Lane smacked against the ground, knees screaming as she tried to land gracefully.

"Good thing I have so much practice falling," she muttered.

Tripp watched, eyebrows raised, as she ran after the ghost.

She was going to find him, and figure out what was going on with his magic, before the mission ended.

Her boots thundered on the pavement as she ran, eyes trained on the black smoke that the ghost had left in his wake. She followed him as he flew around corners, down alleys. Following him through the streets, she narrowly avoided a crowd of people, hoping she hadn't gotten too close. She didn't need another reason for Eurydice to hate her.

A forest, not unlike the one that surrounded The Academy, filled her vision. It was a large city park, filled with trees as far as the eye could see, she realized.

As if laughing at her, the ghost's form disappeared into the leaves, hidden among the dark foliage. The sun hung high in the sky, casting shadows everywhere. In the distance, there was a footpath, where people walked, pushing strollers. But the ghost had disappeared into the untamed thicket, far away from the living.

She called out as she slowed to a halt, searching the branches for his outline as she stepped onto the soft, warm grass.

"I know how you feel," Lane said. "Believe me. I know you just want your life back. I know, better than most."

It wasn't a lie. Lane didn't want anything as much as she wanted to be alive again. Not a ghost, or whatever in-between version of ghost and undead she became on these test missions. She wanted to be alive. And that was what The Magistrate Academy promised, after all. Not everyone could be a student there. Only those who might one day be able to return. And when she graduated, that was exactly what she would get.

She wanted it so badly she could feel it down into the roots of her teeth.

That promise was everything.

A roaring cry filled the air, full of betrayal and pain. Her ears rang. She spun on her heel toward the noise as a whirling, blurred shape rushed toward her, knocking her off her feet. Her skull hit the ground with a heavy smack, blurring her vision.

Everything turned black.

She was in the woods. Her woods. White trees, their trunks turned and bent like broken bones. The branches hung around her, some naked, some with the dead foliage of winter. Somehow, she was standing, her feet crunching against the white, dried grass.

The forest surrounding The Magistrate Academy was as silent as secrets and filled with more than trees. It housed the dying breaths of the forgotten, the spirits and ghosts of those who could only wander. She walked between them, ducking under the branches that reached for her like hands. Like everything, the air was gray. A thick, wintery fog laid over her, over the trees, over After Life.

The spirits followed her, clinging to her. They circled around her, their gray forms floating.

"Hello," she called to them, even though she didn't know their names. But she could swear she saw them smile. One drifted forward, her white hair in wisps as she reached toward Lane, brushing translucent fingers against her face like she meant to cup her cheek. The gray-white of her form glowed against the brown of Lane's skin, making it seem even darker.

"They like you," Victor said from behind her. Had he been there the entire time? She didn't remember.

"I'm the only one who talks to them," Lane chided. "If you came out here, they'd like you too."

He stepped into view, his inky-black hair hanging in his eyes. He tucked a piece behind the gold frame of his glasses.

"You should be in class."

"And you should be teaching," Lane said. "I just wanted to make sure they're okay."

"You don't want them to be forgotten."

The air around them grew colder as they drifted away. Lane waved them a sad goodbye as their shadowed forms disappeared into the black of the distance.

"Of course I don't," she said. "No one deserves to be forgotten."

"Is that why you asked me to meet you here?" Victor asked, taking a step back. "You aren't going to graduate for years. But if it means so much to you, I promise I will keep checking on them. At least they're quiet company."

Lane shook her head. "No. I needed to talk to you—away."

Her eyes traveled behind him to the cold outline of the school, its stone walls and turrets glowering down at her.

Victor stepped toward her expectantly.

Lane inhaled. The foggy scent of After Life filled her lungs, and she wished the ghosts hadn't left. Being near them gave her a kind of strength.

"Victor," she said. "I'm remembering things. Who I was. Who I am."

Lane awoke with a start, her hands grabbing at the too-green grass. Her vision filled with spots as she looked up. The sun hung lower in the sky, settling the city in a dusky glow.

She spat onto the grass, her tongue thick and metallic.

It had happened again. She'd blacked out. Where was Tripp? Where was Perry?

She tried to remember what had happened in the time she was knocked out—it must have been hours. But she could only find pieces, fragments of images. She recalled The Academy, and Victor. But that was nothing new. Was it a memory? Like a dream, it drifted away from her the more she tried to remember.

How many blank spots did she have now? She'd lost count. She hadn't told Victor—nor had she told him that she thought she was somehow seeing pieces of her memories when they happened. She wasn't sure if she could.

She pushed herself up and stumbled toward the small clearing of trees. Thick, unnatural smoke billowed toward her as she ducked under the brush, the clouds dense and hotter than steam. Small, tiny cracks of lightning shot through the smoke, as if she'd walked into a storm.

Sulfur filled her nose, mixing with the smell of wet grass. It was strange and familiar, and not entirely unpleasant.

She stepped hesitantly into the tendrils, searching with her hands outstretched. The fog singed at her eyes as it began to clear, revealing her hands, the air, and then the dirt beneath her feet.

A smoldering pile of dark gray ash sat alone in the middle of the grove, smoke floating away from it in lazy circles.

She looked around, confused, the smoke and fog blurring her vision. And then she saw him.

The outline of the ghost moved toward her, but he was no longer flickering. His form had turned black.

He opened his mouth, but no words came out. Lane took a step back, stumbling away from him, from the void that was his face. The pile of ash sat at her feet, smoldering.

The ghost motioned at her, his arms moving. He pointed at her, at the pile of ash.

"You're trying to talk to me," she said. But he kept motioning. Her face scrunched in confusion, but she followed his arm movements as he frantically pointed toward the pile of ash.

She crawled toward it, reaching into the sandy texture. Grit and grime burrowed itself under her fingernails as she dug through it, the ghost hovering over her.

She clawed until her fingers hit something hard and cold. She yanked it from the smoldering ash, trying to hand it to the ghost.

But his form was flickering again—his face frozen in a scream.

With a flash of darkness, he exploded, filling the grove like the night itself. She was surrounded, submerged in his form, struggling to breathe as the ink of him sunk against her skin.

In the blink of the moment, the darkness disappeared, as if sucked back into itself. The sun glared in her eyes, its sudden appearance too bright.

He was gone.

Some people thought there was nothing worse than death. Some days she might have agreed with them, trapped in After Life. But they were wrong.

Dying when you were already dead was worse.

When you met your final death, you were obliterated. The last remnants of you, of your ghost, disappeared, and your soul died, until there was nothing left at all. The final end.

Lane crawled backwards across the ground, knowing what was coming.

With a scream, a dark shadow shot out from the pile of ash.

The shade screamed as it rocketed into the sky. Lane braced herself, waiting for it to turn back and come for her—but it shot past her and into the horizon.

She turned and dry-heaved onto the grass.

The ghost had turned into a shade.

What had he been trying to tell her?

Lane turned, searching the grass for the object. She must have dropped it as she'd scurried away from him.

Laying in the grass was a key. Old-fashioned, the handle thick, long, the kind they made for antique iron locks. It was the color of pure ivory, some pieces of it stained yellow. She picked it up, twisting it in her fingers as she brought it closer to her face.

Teeth, human teeth, jutted out where the locking ridges should have been. It was made entirely of bone.

"Lane!" Tripp was yelling at her in the distance. "We're over time! Blink back!"

Looking up, she saw him running toward her in the distance, pointing at his obol. Perry wasn't far behind.

She closed her eyes, grabbing her wrist and holding the key tight with her other hand, but before she could push herself back, something pulled her away.

CHAPTER TWO

Dead leaves, dead trees, gray sky, gray ground. Lane stretched her fingers, finding blades of dying grass between them. Her back was cold against the hallowed ground, the lifeless dirt crunching beneath her as she moved. The air was cold, and she rolled over, wrapping her jacket tighter around her.

After Life.

She didn't need to open her eyes to know she was back. The difference was obvious in the thinness of the air, the whispering wind that seemed to carry voices from some far-off place. They weren't cries or screams, but breathy words that she could barely decipher, like a shadow humming a dead girl's lullaby.

The trees cast willowy shadows across her legs, the branches like fingers trying to grasp her thin ankles. No, it was not like Life at all.

There was no hot, golden sun blazing between the leaves. There was no breeze. Only the strange, traveling wind that whispered across her skin. The voices in the distance weren't of laughing schoolchildren, but murmurs of what had been, and what would never be.

Still, it was home. And it welcomed her like a strange friend, the kind that no one but her understood or cared for.

Lane glanced around her, looking for the ghosts that wandered. She hadn't visited in days; her schoolwork and mission assignments had kept her away.

Something bit into the flesh of her palm as she pushed herself up to stand.

The strange piece of bone was still in her hand, jagged edges of broken teeth scraping her skin. She'd never seen a key made of bone before—not that she could remember.

And she was pretty sure she would remember such an eerie thing, memory problems aside.

"Skeleton key," she whispered to herself, flipping it over in her fingers. Whoever made this had a twisted sense of humor. It didn't seem like the ghost could have made it while he was in Life. It was too old, the bone too stained.

And why had he tried to give it to her? All they had in common was trying to kick the other's ass. And both being dead, of course.

Lane shook her head. No questions. She'd learned that the hard way.

Don't ask about who you were, who you are, what your name was, why and how you came to be at The Magistrate Academy.

The last thing she needed was to get her graduation delayed.

"You certainly cut it close."

She spun around, expecting to find one of the ghosts.

But ghosts were translucent, shadowy white, like casts of marble. And Victor was a Renaissance painting, done in full color.

He stood over her, hair like black ink that fell over his silvery eyes. His hand was outstretched, his tan and warm-toned skin contrasting the wintery forest surrounding him. His emerald Teacher's Assistant uniform made the forest seem almost alive.

Almost.

She stood, ignoring his hand. "You pulled me back."

"I've no idea what you're talking about."

"Your obols are still glowing orange."

He tucked his hands behind his back. "I don't see anything."

She rolled her eyes. "I was going to handle it. You didn't have to pull me back early."

"Early?" He snorted. "You were seconds away from the mission end. You know—"

She waved her hand in his face. "Blah blah, you can't get stuck there or you'll be obliterated, turned into the ash your skeleton left behind, blah blah."

She hoped he hadn't heard her stumble over the word *obliterated.* Her mind flashed to the ghost, disappearing into nothingness.

"Not to mention that Headmistress would bring you back to life just to skin you alive and murder you again," he said, holding out his hand for her.

Lane smacked it away again. Leaves crunched under her feet as she turned to walk through the dead woods and back to the school.

"You'd never let that happen though, would you, Mister Junior Professor?" She smirked at him. "Being her protege must have some advantages."

Junior Professor wasn't quite right—technically he was a student, the same as the rest of them. But he'd been passed over for graduation so many times that everyone saw him as a teacher—including the Headmistress herself.

"If it did, I wouldn't waste them on protecting your ungrateful behind."

"I'd certainly hope not," she said. He stifled a chuckle as he stepped to match her stride. "I can handle myself, you know."

No longer trying to be subtle, he rubbed at the obols on both his wrists where they still burned red. It wasn't as painful as other death magic, but it still stung.

"I'd never be so obtuse as to imply otherwise." Victor looked down at her from behind his glasses, eyes twinkling. It was hard to say when—or where—he was from. He had a thick accent that was vaguely European and spoke like a gentleman from a regency romance novel. She knew that he'd given up on trying to pretend he was like the other students—he was too smart, too unique, too good at what he did. After centuries of seeing others move on, he was still held down by this place.

Victor was special, and they weren't about to let him go.

"Although," he started as they neared the edge of the trees. "You could do with paying a bit more attention to your assignments. And your studies. And your homework. . ."

Lane pushed his arm. "And you could have pulled me back to the check-in point instead of the middle of the woods. Not so perfect, yourself."

"I didn't have a lot of time to manage the precision. My apologies." He didn't seem very sorry at all. "How was the mission, anyway?"

Her breath caught in her throat. She paused, one foot in front of the other. "Fine. Just fine."

"Well, now I know it was anything but fine."

Lane chewed her lip. Victor was her only constant. He had been there when she had woken up, obols freshly tattooed into her skin. He'd been the one to explain that she was dead, and that she had been selected to attend The Magistrate Academy. A school for ghosts who might get a second chance. As long as you managed to graduate. She hadn't noted the tone of bitterness in his voice back then, and it was still hard to think of him as resentful. He was the only person at the school who seemed like they genuinely wanted to help her.

"Has a ghost ever recognized you?" she asked, squinting up at him. He was at least a foot taller than her, but most people were. The sky was blindingly gray behind him, a shadowed twin of the sun.

His expression flickered. "Well, the professors and other students do pretend that they at least remember my name."

"I'm serious." She crossed her arms. "Not, like, the Headmistress or the other professors. Not even the ghosts outside the school."

Victor turned toward her, branches framing the edges of his sharp-angled face.

"Did something happen?"

"No, no, not at all," she said. "I was just wondering. . . what would happen if a ghost happened to know us? You know, before?"

It seemed to be the only thing that made sense. The ghost had been angry, but once they were alone, he'd tried to speak to her. Could they have known each other?

But no. He had been a witch when he was alive. And Lane was a lot of things, but she certainly wasn't some asshole witch.

"Laney, we've been down this path before. There is no way to know who you were before." Victor placed his hand on her arm, just lightly enough that her skin prickled.

"I know." She rolled her shoulders. "Let's go inside."

She stepped out of the woods into the shadow of the school.

The Magistrate Academy itself seemed lost to time. It was like an artist's rendition of a medieval castle, black stones piled into towering turrets and long, thin cathedral windows. But the lines were stretched too thin, pulled apart, so that the castle itself looked like its own shadow. Anything that wasn't stone was hewn from the white wood of the surrounding trees—the window frames, the balustrades, the support beams. The Academy was the only structure for miles, surrounded by the woods and the mountains of After Life.

There was no front door for them to enter through. Or any door at all, for that matter. In its place, there was a clean wall of straight black and gray stone.

It wasn't the strangest thing, not to Lane. The castle with no doors. Ghosts rarely needed those, anyway. The only thing that bothered her about The Academy was that it seemed to be the only building in After Life at all, as if it had been stolen from somewhere else and placed there. But she knew they weren't alone in After Life. Once a year, all of the dead were invited to visit.

So where was everyone else?

Lane twisted her face, exhaling. It wasn't any worse than Blinking to Life on an assignment, but she still couldn't bring herself to do it without closing her eyes. With another breath, she pushed herself forward. The barrier resisted, and for a split second, she was neither inside or outside, but in some strange, empty space in between.

And then she was back inside the school, as if she'd never left.

It could have been any regular boarding school. Other than the ghosts.

The halls were hung with banners and tapestries of historical accounts she didn't recognize or couldn't remember. Victor's steps echoed beside her like dripping water, the sound carrying down the cold, empty hallways and back to her ears.

Two students walked by, wearing identical mission uniforms to Lane's. Heading to their assignment or maybe returning from it. Fable and. . . she couldn't quite remember the boy's name. There were barely twenty students in the school, as far as Lane could tell, so she should probably remember all of their names.

A school with only twenty students was barely a school, really. But no one had asked Lane, and she was well-practiced in keeping her mouth shut. Except with Victor. She'd been able to weasel out of him that it was typical for there to be so few. Whether it was because they were special or expendable, she didn't ask.

As they turned around a corner blanketed in a red tapestry, one of the professors glided by, his milky white form appraising Lane and Victor. Lane recognized him as the ghost that was supposed to teach death magic—or *Nil* in the old language. Victor had started taking on the students' magic lessons as the professor faded more and more year after year, getting closer to being forgotten.

The hall opened into the wide mouth at the center of the school, where four corridors led to a spiraling staircase that wrapped around the wall, up and up and up to the dormitory turrets. Beneath it lay the door to the library, where Victor spent most of his time. Lane rolled her shoulders, still aching from the mission. She'd rather be anywhere than the library right now.

She took a step back from Victor's side, slowly backing away.

"Somewhere to be?" he asked her, turning with his hands clasped behind his back. His face was smug and smirking, and it made Lane want to hit him. "Class?"

"Yes," she said. "I'm supposed to be in. . ." She did not have class, as a matter of fact. She tried to think of the class that would interest Victor the least. "History and Worlds."

The double doors to the library opened behind him, revealing dark rows of shelves and candlelit tables that stretched as far as the eye could see. Chandeliers hung from the steepled ceiling, unlit and covered in cobwebs. Their crystals glittered in the dim orange light, casting skeletal shadows across the floor.

"We'll debrief on your assignment later," Victor said.

They both knew she was lying then.

Nodding, Lane turned away from him just as she heard the crashing sound of someone falling. Heavy footsteps sped toward them. Fear pulsed through her. Instinctively, she reached toward Victor, her arm stretched across him—whether to protect him or for him to protect her, she wasn't quite sure. Victor was much older and more practiced in magic, but they hadn't let him in the field in decades. Together, maybe, they would be good in a fight, but separately. . .

Behind her, Victor lifted an eyebrow, smirking at her as she grabbed his sleeve. His face was the perfect picture of calm. It made Lane's heart settle. He didn't have to say a word; his expression said it all. This wasn't Life. There were no dangers here, not at The Academy, not in After Life. Nothing could hurt the dead.

Tripp bounded around the corner, red dreadlocks swinging around his shoulders. His freckled face was flush with fear.

"Victor!" he shouted.

"What is it?"

Lane looked between them as Tripp slowed to a stop, hands on his knees. He must have run the entire length of the campus.

"It's Peregrine," he gasped.

Victor tilted his head, questioning.

"Something is wrong, I don't know. She was hurt on the mission." Tripp struggled to catch his breath. Even though they were dead, their bodies remembered being alive and acted as such. They breathed, they ate, they slept, they bled.

Lane's memory flashed. "She was hit by a piece of glass. She was bleeding. But she should have healed by now."

"She's hasn't. She's bad. I took her—I took her to Deryck."

"Deryck?"

Tripp stood. "I didn't know what else to do. We don't exactly have an on-site doctor."

She nodded. Deryck was a demon, the only demon allowed at The Academy outside of the celebration on All Hallows Day. She had only ever met Deryck, but she knew that all demons, ghosts, and anyone else who resided in After Life came to The Academy for All Hallows Day, when the border between Life and Death was thinnest. Eurydice threw a huge party under the pretense of celebrating, but really, the Headmistress wanted to make sure she had a close eye on anyone who thought they might pop over to Earth for some autumnal haunts.

Deryck ran The Academy Union, commonly known as The Bar. Most institutions of higher learning had them, Victor had explained.

But the important thing was that, unlike everyone else, Deryck was alive.

"He might be the only person who can help her if she is injured," Lane said. "He cuts his hand on broken glasses all the time."

Victor stared at Tripp, scowling. In the entryway of the library, neither of them moved. The high ceiling seemed to swirl over their heads like storm clouds.

"What are you waiting for?" Lane pushed Victor. "Let's go!"

Without warning, she broke into a run.

The school corridors echoed with her footsteps as she turned corners and ran down flights of stairs to the basement. They had been at the very epicenter of the school and The Bar was at the far end of the longest basement corridor, so far beneath ground that it might have once been a dungeon.

Ghosts drifted through the hall like snow, the cold trailing as she ran past. Sprinting around their whisper-white forms, Lane smiled. Sometimes The Academy felt truly dead. The hours of quiet, of sitting, of waiting. But then there were the moments of running, of the missions chasing ghosts, where she believed that she was once alive.

It was almost enough to forget her friend might be in real danger.

The door to The Bar came into view at the bottom of a dark staircase. The heavy, metal sliding door was locked shut.

Trying to catch her breath, she banged her fist against the metal, striking so hard that it shook. "Deryck!"

Tripp and Victor fell in behind her. Tripp gave the closed door a puzzled look. It had clearly been open before.

Lane shouted Deryck's name again, giving the metal a hard kick. In the distance, she heard grumbling, the shuffling of feet.

The door swung open with a metallic song.

Deryck stood in the doorway, pants hanging around his hips, threatening to fall off. His eyes were closed, his pale chest bare except for a tattoo over his left breast. She averted her eyes away from his pale chest, crossing her arms.

"I do not like to be interrupted." He ran his hands through his grassy hair, yawning.

Lane huffed, placing her hand on his chest and pushing him inside. His eyes shot open as she shoved him into the wall.

28

It still shocked her to see his completely white eyes. No irises, no pupils. Their blankness stared, somehow recognizing her.

"Hello, little Laney," he said, looking her up and down. Noticing Victor, he said, "Oh, it's you."

Victor opened his mouth, likely to complain about Deryck's state of undress or some rule he was not following, but Lane waved her hand.

"Let's skip the *I hate you* part. Where is Perry?"

Tripp stepped forward. "I left her in the kitchen with him—"

Deryck held out his arm, blocking his entry. Tripp stared down at him, inhaling so that his broad shoulders widened.

"Did you? I don't remember that."

"I must insist, if she is back there, we certainly do not have time for this—" Victor stepped forward, but Deryck didn't move, his blank eyes twinkling.

"Don't play this game," Lane said. "She's in danger. Please."

He smiled. "Oh, I like that, say it again."

"Please," Lane said through gritted teeth. "We would owe you. All of us."

Deals in After Life—and especially with demons—were more valuable than any currency. And Lane was already deeply in his debt.

With a grin, Deryck stepped to the side, motioning them to follow. "Right this way, love."

He brought them through the empty bar and into the kitchen. The room was plain, no sign that it was the site of his seedy activities—a dirty prep table, a large refrigerator, and an antique desk. Ominous-looking magical vials scattered across the surface, liquids varying in color from blood red to milky white.

Perry lay across the table, blood covering her leg. Her eyes fluttered open at the sound of their footsteps.

"She's certainly lost some blood." Deryck shoved a finger inside the gaping wound on Perry's thigh. Lane and Tripp both grimaced. He pulled a wheeled chair underneath him, his finger still inside the gash. "This is surprising, considering your little obols. It's good you came to me. I would hate for our angry friend to meet her final death so prematurely."

Lane sucked in a breath. For a moment, she'd almost forgotten about the shade.

Deryck slid a threaded needle between his fingers and stabbed it into Perry's leg. Perry barely stirred.

"I would advise you ensure that doesn't happen," Victor said, looking down at Deryck under the rim of his glasses.

"Or Eurydice will hear about it, I know." Deryck rolled his eyes. Or Lane thought he had. It was hard to tell. His hand wove the needle back and forth through her skin. "How is the headmistress? Still trying to protect you all from the things that go bump in the night?"

Victor's scowled, but he said nothing. Lane's mind shot to the witches.

"They don't understand," The Headmistress had said. *"Death is not something you conquer. It conquers you."*

"Like you?" Lane snapped.

Deryck snorted in response. Turning, he grabbed a bottle of liquid and poured it over Perry's thigh. It seeped into the last remaining opening in the gash. Deryck sealed it tightly with a final sling. He snatched a small, velvety pouch from his desk and turned it upside down. To Lane's surprise, a thick gel crept out, dark yellow and smelling of diseased mucus.

Lane traced her fingers over the outline of Perry's obol. They came away coated with blood.

"What happened?" Victor asked her and Tripp as Deryck slid across the room on his stool. He reached into a low drawer in his antique desk and pulled out a small, wooden box. Something inside made scratching sounds, and Lane frowned.

"You're not going to—" Lane started to ask, ignoring Victor's question. But before she could finish, Deryck moved and opened the box, dropping milky yellow maggots onto Perry's thigh. Beside her, Tripp gagged, spit sticking at the corners of his mouth.

"That should do the trick." Deryck pulled away from the table. He rubbed his hands, stained with Perry's blood, across his trousers. The maggots crawled toward her wound like moths to a flame, ravenous. "Good thing you all came to me, since none of you are technically corporeal. She'll need to rest for a few days."

Tripp nodded. She gave him a look, trying to tell him he did the right thing, but he looked away.

Lane watched Perry's unconscious body, feeling Victor's stare in the side of her face like two pinpricks. She held her breath, watching as Perry released a sigh, as if she was drifting into a comfortable sleep. Finally, Lane let herself relax, knowing that Perry was safe and that her death would not be her fault.

Not today, anyway.

"What happened?" Victor repeated.

Deryck stood from his stool.

Lane bit her lip. Victor would find out one way or another. Better it be from her.

"The drifter. . ." She paused. "Something was wrong with him. He was powerful. And he was using magic. Not death magic."

Deryck spun toward her, eyebrows furrowed.

She continued, "He blew out a window, and it hit her in the leg. He tried to get away, and I chased him. But when I found him—"

When I found him, I blacked out. And then he tried to talk to me, but he was already turning into a shade.

"And then I found him and sent him back to After Life."

Silence fell heavy on the room.

"She just didn't heal?" Deryck asked.

A wrinkle formed between Victor's eyebrows. "Thank you for your help."

Deryck smiled. "Don't worry, Lane will square the bill."

Lane traced the concern in Victor's muscles as she turned toward him. There was more on his mind, something that she was missing. And it didn't make her feel better that he wasn't saying what it was.

Deryck raised a bottle of alcohol in the air, motioning to the bar door behind him. "Well, she'll be sleeping for a while. Fancy a drink?"

CHAPTER THREE

Lane took a deep breath before tossing back a glowing green shot. Deryck claimed it was absinthe, but she seriously doubted it. Next to her at the marbled counter of Deryck's bar, Victor swirled his finger over a glass of dark, smoking liquid. He had been silent since they'd left Perry in the kitchen. On her other side, Tripp inhaled his drink and raised a hand to order another round.

"Don't think you're drinking free all night," Deryck growled. "You're only increasing Lane's tab."

The Bar was buzzing. Behind her, a group of The Academy's guards went through motions that seemed almost life-like. . . sitting at the table, raising invisible glasses to one another. Another group of students, still in their black uniforms, sat in the corner, their eyes downcast.

Victor stared into the mirror mosaic behind the bar, his slate-colored eyes vacant.

He didn't speak, so she didn't ask.

Victor turned his finger around the rim of his glass. Finally, he said, "So, how long do you want to sit here, not talking?"

"I don't know what you mean."

He turned on his stool to face her. He held his goblet loosely, with too-casual fingers. Lane worried it would drop and shatter across the floor.

"We both know you didn't tell me everything."

"If you already know everything, I guess there is nothing to say, is there?"

Victor laughed icily, rubbing his wrist as he placed his glass back on the counter. Someone turned up the music and the bass grew louder, until she could feel it vibrating in her bones. Victor looked around, and his eyes flicked to the door. He motioned for her to follow him outside. She hopped off her stool, almost glad at the distraction. Maybe outside, away from prying eyes, she'd be able to admit that it was her mistake that caused Perry's injury.

In the back hallway, the music became more and more distant, the words turning to pure rhythm. Victor glanced at her over his shoulder.

"You remember what you said to me when you woke up?" He pushed his fingers against the door. "I'd just told you what happened, why you couldn't remember anything. You looked at me and said *eff that and eff you.* It's one of the things I admire about you."

He looked away quickly and swung the door open. A cool wave of night airbrushed on her skin.

She raised an eyebrow as they stepped outside. "And?"

34

He shrugged. "I'm just trying to say—"

"That I'm a stubborn ass."

"Actually, I was going to say—no one has ever been able to make you do anything you didn't want to do." He smiled and warmth flooded Lane's skin.

"I do love a challenge."

A dry breeze swirled through the alley as he leaned against the brick wall. She shoved her hands into her pockets, her fingers landing again on the key. It hummed beneath her fingers, the image of the shade flashing across her mind.

"There was something so off about him. The ghost. It was like he was deteriorating but getting more and more powerful at the same time. He wasn't undead. He was something else. Caught in between. And his magic. . . I can't explain it." She paused. "Tripp thought he was using both his witch magic and death magic. Maybe that was what killed him."

Victor pinched the bridge of his nose. "There's still so much we don't know about Nil, Vis, the energy that makes it all tick."

"He was after something, wasn't he? Like Eurydice says."

Victor leaned toward her, as if afraid someone might hear. She could feel his hot breath on her cheek, smell the scent of old book pages and crackling smoke on his skin.

"It's possible." He glanced over his shoulder again. "He might have found a way to work with the witches, to communicate with them from After Life. Maybe he was working with the Haven."

A curl fell from her bun. She watched the strand bounce, conscious of the growing tension in Victor's shoulders. "And somehow, I'm lucky enough to be who they attack."

"If they did something to him so he could access both magic . . . he would have been very dangerous indeed." His eyes were full of worry as he looked down at her, his fingers tapping along his leg. "You should have never been in that situation. I'm sorry."

Witches, Lane knew, used predatory magic. To wield it, they stole energy. Usually from unsuspecting victims.

Death magic was different. Whatever sacrifice it was that magic required, the dead had already given it.

She tried not to think about what it meant that she could sense both like static electricity.

"What usually happens to witches when they die? So that they can't access their magic?"

"Lane," Victor warned.

They weren't supposed to ask for information that could reveal something about their past—or ask questions at all, really. It didn't seem to bother the others, especially Victor. The Academy was his life.

For Lane, it was different. Memories haunted her— dancing at the edge of her vision, slipping through her fingers, just out of reach. Each time she blacked out, it seemed their edges became a little clearer, a little more solid. If only she could look a little harder, reach a little further, she might catch them.

As the blank spots increased, so did the dreams. It was always the same. She saw a school not unlike The Magistrate Academy but, at the same time, nothing like it at all. It was red stone, manor-like, surrounded by fields of green grass. She saw doorways, opening and closing. Mostly, she had the feeling that she was not alone. There was a presence with her, the twinkle of an old man's laughter.

But when she reached for the man, he was gone.

Victor looked at her, his eyes full of something she couldn't read. "If I promise to look into it, do you promise to stop asking? Before you really get in trouble?"

"Yes, yes, absolutely, I can do that." She nodded. "Not a word from me. But Vic—"

Why would you break the rules for me? She didn't finish the question.

His mouth was a crooked smile. "You know I'd do anything for you."

She turned away, his eyes burning holes in her scalp.

There were so many things she wanted to say, but instead, she did the same thing she always did. She left it unspoken, sitting in the air like an unfulfilled prophecy. "Let's go back inside."

Other students filled in now, some with library books across their laps, reading. Lane never brought a book to The Bar—she was more of a drinker than a reader.

Deryck handed her a shot as they sat down at the bar, his eyebrow raised. Her face must have looked as nauseous as she felt, she realized.

"I lied," she said to Victor. "Before, when you asked me what happened. I didn't send the ghost back like we're supposed to."

Victor laughed. "I know."

"You know?!"

"You did say that I know everything," he said. "The staff get reports on all of the missions. They told me that no target was sent back from your run."

Heat filled her cheeks. "Did you also know that when I caught up with him, he turned into a shade? He's gone. Dead. *Dead* dead."

The words came out like venom, spitting toward him. She hated that Victor always made her feel off-kilter, as if she wasn't doing enough, wasn't doing the right thing.

His eyes darkened. "Tell me."

"I ran after him after he injured Perry, thinking that—well, that I was going to make him regret hurting her, and that we'd get our asses kicked if he got away."

To her surprise, Victor didn't scold her. He snorted.

"When I found him. . ." She paused, skipping over her blackout. "He was already turning. Someone did something before I got there, hurt him. And then he died."

Turning to a shade was a fate worse than death. It was nothingness. The soul, your consciousness, died, leaving only the husk behind. A shade. They were impulsive, acting only on instinct.

"Laney." His fingers brushed against hers. She let her gaze drift to meet his. "It's not your fault. It's—"

Before he could finish his sentence, the floor shook beneath their feet. Lane jumped as her chair tipped from beneath her, clattering to the floor. Around the room, students stared up as the music cut out.

Lane turned to the room as Victor leapt from his stool. The Bar was as still as the forest as everyone stood, unmoving. The floor shook again, walls swaying.

A scream split through the night. The sound broke the room in half. Lane slapped her palms to her ears instinctively.

The trance possessing the room snapped like a twig. Everyone pushed and shoved into each other, fighting for the door that led back into the school.

Chairs, tables, and drinks were knocked onto the floor.

Victor grabbed Lane's shoulder, his spine straightening as he watched the room. None of the other students or professors seemed to notice him as he tried to shout at them to stop. Lane looked up at him. His fingers were pressing into her shoulder. There was nothing he could do, she realized. Not in this chaos.

Her insides turned cold. She didn't know what was happening, but she knew enough to be afraid of anything that scared the dead.

In one swift movement, Victor pushed her forward, shoving her into the crowd and guiding them through broken glass and the flurry of bodies. Ghosts drifted through the walls, disappearing like smoke.

Guiding her with one hand, Victor led her to the kitchen door, away from the crowd. It swung open as her body collided with it, his feet on her heels as they tumbled into the room and onto the floor, a crumpled pile of limbs.

The linoleum was cold against the heat of her skin, and for a moment, Lane wanted to stay there. Her ears rung, strange screams ringing in her ears even over the roar of the crowd.

Victor leapt to his feet as she struggled to find her footing. The floor still seemed to sway beneath them. Or maybe that was her swimming headache.

"What's going on?" Tripp appeared out of a dark corner, lipstick smeared across his freckled chin. Epps was nowhere in sight. Another scream traveled through the air, further away this time, as if the source was moving from inside the bar to outside.

"I'm not sure yet," Victor asked. "It's coming from the forest, I think. We need to get you both back to the dormitories. Then I will—"

Lane tried to clear her throat, her vision tunneling. Neither of them noticed. Her hand shook as she pointed at the table in the middle of the room, empty and covered in blood.

"Where is Perry?"

CHAPTER FOUR

Shepherd slapped a piece of paper onto the table, her choppy hair falling in her eyes.

"Let's not play games," she said to the man on the other side of the table. "You know who I am, and I know who you are, so we can skip to the part where I agree to your price, and you agree to tell me what you know."

The witch leaned forward, crossing his dirty sleeves over his chest. He pushed his large tankard of beer out of the way. Around them, the sounds of the Night Market buzzed, completely undisturbed by Shepherd's little show.

Maybe it was because of the hat, she thought. She needed to work on being more intimidating.

"I would, if'n' I knew what yer were talkin' about."

White spittle collected on his lips as he spoke. Shepherd tried not to gag, if only because he wouldn't appreciate the humor. She'd known what to expect when she came looking for the Tracker. Very few witches had the Tracking skill, and McWhateverhisnamewas was the best.

Shepherd flipped the poster over, revealing a "missing" poster. Addie's tan face and white teeth shone up at her. It was almost enough to make her grab the poster and run out of the tavern, leave this conversation behind. She could imagine the look on Addie's face if she knew that Shepherd—of all people—was the one searching for her. After everything Shepherd had done, it would certainly be a surprise. What had Addie called her? Selfish, criminal—

"This is my sister. She's been missing for almost a month. None of her friends have seen her, her school hasn't seen her. Something happened to her, and I need to find her." Shepherd pulled the photo away from McWhatshisface. "And people say you're the one to go to if you need something found."

He leaned back in his chair, running a finger along his pock-marked nose. His oily skin almost glowed under the orange light of the tavern. "I've heard the same about you."

Shepherd lifted an eyebrow. "So you have heard of me."

The man grabbed the photo. "Is this all you got?"

Reaching into her pocket, Shepherd pulled out a strip of paper with a slew of numbers and letters written down. "These are all of her passwords to her social media, her schoolwork—"

The man took the piece of paper. "This 'ent enough, darlin'." What was his accent, anyway? Irish? Scottish? Oafish?

"Well, that's all I have," Shepherd said. She reached for the paper, grabbing it back from the man's hand. "Are you a witch or not? How much do you really need to work your magic?"

McSomething scowled at her, running his hand along the edge of the table. He picked up his tankard of ale and drank two large gulps. His throat bobbed up and down.

Shepherd did not have time for this. She had a shift at the bookstore later, and a meeting after that, and at some point she needed to text her ex-girlfriend and remind her that they were broken up.

Oh, and her little sister was missing.

"It's true what they say, then," McStubble said. "You really don't—"

"What else do you need?"

The man picked up Addie's photo, running it between his hands. "Something of hers to do the Tracking with. A photo won't work. You'll need something that belonged to her."

Her hand went instinctively to the necklace hanging from her neck, dangling against her chest. She had started wearing it after Addie disappeared, after she'd pilfered all the information she could from Addie's bedroom in the three-room apartment they shared with their parents.

"Something like DNA? Or more like something important to her?"

He scoffed. "DNA? Get outta here with that human crap. O' course something important to her. The closer, the betta. The more time she spent with it, the betta."

Shepherd nodded, dropping her hand from the necklace. "I'll need a day or so. I can bring it by here tomorrow night, same time."

McKinley, she remembered. That was his name.

He stood up, towering over her as he reached across the table with an open hand. "And yer payment?"

Internally, Shepherd sighed. Not for the first time, she wondered if she would ever be able to get out of this game.

"Tell me what you want, and I'll find it," she said, matter of factly, as she turned away. The crowd was thin, but it usually was in the Night Market, or anywhere that witches traveled. There just weren't that many of them. Shepherd could count the witches she knew on two hands, and most of them were her relatives.

"Just like that?" he asked. "And yer not a Tracker?

She nodded as she pushed on the door, leaving the voices of the pub echoing behind her.

"I'm not anything."

She looked at the time on her phone. Just under an hour until her shift started.

It was just enough time.

The basement of the bookstore was dark, dank, and overcrowded, books lining the walls and threatening to fall on her head as she worked. It smelled of yellowed pages and mildew, but it was exactly what Shepherd needed. Private. And Eileen, her boss, didn't mind that she used the space as a make-shift apartment. Eileen didn't like to pry, and Shepherd wasn't big on sharing. Her tiny cot was shoved next to her tiny desk, with a little orange light hanging overhead. Shepherd yanked on the metal chain, bringing the space to life.

Her family's apartment was too small—big by city standards, but too small for things to go unnoticed. Living like that, they had no secrets. It was physically impossible. It was part of the reason she knew Addie hadn't just run off.

She'd been over all the details with her parents, the police, had done all of the things a person was supposed to do when a loved one was in danger. She'd answered all their questions. Yes, Addie was a wonderful student, studying at an advanced private college even though she was just sixteen. No, there was no reason for her to run away. No, she wasn't under too much pressure, hadn't turned to drugs. They had labeled her a runaway anyway. Eventually, their parents had asked Shepherd to stop badgering the police, even though she knew there was more they could be doing.

More that *she* could be doing. It wasn't like the police were going to help. Shepherd knew no one was looking for a mixed teenage girl, even one as smart as Addie. And they certainly weren't going to be friendly to Shepherd, the community college dropout turned black market lurker. Not that they knew that part, of course. To know that, they'd have to be witches.

When Addie had disappeared, they had decided it was best that Shepherd be the one to interact with the police. She was the obvious choice. Out of all of them, she was the most normal. To everyone else at least. Among their family, she was the outlier. A genetic outlier, a black mark.

Shepherd's family wasn't like the other families at school, or like any of the other families the police investigated.

They were all witches.

Except for Shepherd.

As far as Shepherd knew, there was no one else like her. She'd just been born different. Her family had tried to treat her and Addie the same, running them through all the same magic lessons, having them apply to the same magical schools. Shepherd had never been left out. When their mother's father died, Shepherd had been left magical heirlooms the same as everyone else, even though she couldn't use them.

To their credit, her parents had really, really tried. It just hadn't made a difference. There was a certain prophecy in being born an outcast.

But for once, they had needed her.

It hadn't taken long for Shepherd to realize that she couldn't just be her family's emissary to the police, making sure they were on the right track. They just didn't have the complete picture. If magic was involved in Addie's disappearance—and Shepherd was pretty convinced it was—then they would never find her.

And that was what had driven her here, standing in her "bedroom" in the basement of the bookstore, in front of the poor excuse for an altar she created. Her desk was littered with Addie's belongings—her journals, schoolbooks, a candle from her bedroom, the objects she'd inherited from their grandfather. Behind the knick-knacks, tacked to a cork board, Shepherd had collected articles on other missing teenagers, but she was never able to find a connection between them.

Her phone buzzed in her pocket, and she flipped it out.

Will you come home for dinner tonight? I know Papa said he was mad, but he isn't. He's scared.

And then: *We love you.*

Shepherd shut her phone with a heavy sigh. She hadn't been back home—not since Addie's disappearance. And she certainly couldn't go now. Her parents and grandparents would never let her leave the house again if they knew what she was doing.

She clutched her fingers around Addie's necklace as she opened one of her schoolbooks, the margin full of her handwritten notes on enhancing the spell, changing the ritual.

"You know I don't care about this BS," she said to the room. "And I know there is about a zero percent chance of this working.

But if I have to make a fool of myself and try some stupid spell for the first time in ten years to find you, I'll do it."

She ran her finger down the spell she had been hesitantly planning. It seemed simple enough, although she'd learned from McOilyFace that Tracker magic was anything but simple. Plus, Shepherd was. . . Shepherd. She was just as likely to electrocute herself as she was to actually get the ritual going properly. More, actually.

She took the candle anyway, flipped a pencil between her fingers, and carved Addie's name in it upside down, backwards, forwards.

She lit the candle and held her fingers over the fire, her skin stinging and her eyes filling with smoke. At least the pain blocked out how stupid she felt. She wrapped Addie's necklace around the candle and said the words on the page, some language she didn't understand and hadn't tried to translate. A red, shining welt appeared on her hand as she blew out the candle.

And she waited.

And waited.

In the darkness, her heart beat like a prayer.

"Well, now I look stupid, and my hand is burnt." She fell back onto the cot with her hand to her mouth, sucking on the burn.

Disappointed, she put the necklace back on and tucked it under her shirt, the texture cold against her skin. It was an odd object. It was a key, the color of bone, with strange carvings like human teeth on the edge.

Sometimes, if she held it and closed her eyes, shutting out the sounds of the city, she swore she could hear it sing.

CHAPTER FIVE

Lane stood frozen as Victor stared at the empty table. Perry's absence was like a blackhole, pulling them in and sucking all of the air out of the room.

Victor closed his eyes, blinked once, blinked again. Lane went to reach for him, but without warning, he sprinted from the room.

Grunting, Tripp grabbed her arm, pulling her along.

The back hallway of The Bar was empty. The rest of the students and professors must have run toward the main entrance, back into the school. But the back hallway led outside, toward the haunted woods that surrounded The Academy. Tripp threw open the door and Lane gave a fleeting glance to the stone wall where she and Victor had been speaking only seconds before. It seemed an eternity away now as another earth-shattering scream rang through the foggy night.

There was pain in it, something almost animal as it howled. But she knew it was human. Between the cries, she swore she could feel a lifetime of sorrow.

Victor ran for the woods, some of the other teachers flanking beside him as their willowy forms disappeared into the white branches. Lane called after him, but he ignored her. Or maybe her shouts were drowned out by the sound of the screams.

The cold of the first ghost hit her skin like a splash of water, awakening all her senses and filtering the alcohol from her blood. She shook her head, banishing the dream-like daze. She could no longer hear the song of the whispering breeze, the scratching of the branches as they rubbed against one another, or the distant sighs of the ghosts. All of it was drowned out by the screaming.

Cracks ran through the ground toward Lane, jutting out from the center of the grove she'd landed in after her mission. She and Tripp ran through the crowd of students and toward the source of the screams like a starburst. On the edges of the circle, the ghosts floated, pale expressions full of concern. And something like. . . anticipation.

The branches of the grove reached toward them like the fingers of death itself.

Lane shoved one out of her face, groaning. "Why is everyone going toward the bloody sound?"

Most of the small population of The Academy usually stayed away from the woods. Too haunted, too eerie, too much of a reminder that they were really and truly dead.

Except for Lane. Lane couldn't stay away. It was discomforting to see the trees crowded with the others, like coming home and finding someone new living in her bedroom.

"What does he think he's doing?" Tripp asked.

"I would tell you if I could see." Lane jumped on her tiptoes but could only see the shoulders of the students around her. "Just wait here."

Making herself as small as possible, she pushed through the crowd, ducking under the elbows of a few other students and pushing through the ghosts, ice traveling her skin as she walked through them. Victor was at the middle of it all, holding the other students back with his arms spread like wings.

Right where the danger was.

"It has to be Haven Hall," Fable said. "Only those *witches* could do something like this."

She spat the word *witches* like a curse.

The few students of the crowd formed a circle, the ghosts surrounding them as if they were afraid to get any closer.

Another scream split her eardrums as she followed the crowd's stares toward the center of the grove.

A woman stood in the middle of the crowd. And she was smoldering.

Her edges were pixelated with red and black, like a stoked fire, and her veins were black, a spider web of darkness painted across her skin. A cloud of black fog surrounded her, as if whatever was happening to her was staining the woods beneath her feet.

Two voids replaced her eyes, hollow but still seeing. A line of black ink dripped down her chin, a twin to the poison that seemed to run through her veins.

The flickering intensified as she screamed again, and Lane's stomach dropped. The other students around her gasped in surprise, but she knew.

She was becoming a shade. This person, whoever she was, was dying.

As the woman flickered, her face appeared in the darkness, features barely visible.

The world dropped out beneath Lane's feet, her knees buckling. It was Perry.

Lane cried out.

For a moment, Perry was there, a look of horror strewn across her pixie-like face. And then she was gone, replaced by the blackhole eyes and the flickering shadows of the dark.

Perry screamed again as the darkness overtook her. Inside the thrashing shadow, Perry's thrashing outline dropped to her knees.

Victor took a step toward Perry, arms cautiously outstretched. Lane reached for him, trying desperately to yank him back, but her fingers just missed the fabric of his coat. And suddenly he was alone in the center of the crowd with Perry.

"Please." Victor's whisper toward Perry was drowned out by the screams and the whipping of the woods around them as the forest pushed back at the evil invading their home.

Without thinking, Lane held her breath, following Victor into the circle. They could do something. They had to do something. There was still time to stop Perry from becoming a shade.

The black voids that replaced Perry's eyes landed on Victor, and he stared back. They were magnets, drawn to each other. He spoke again, something Lane could not hear. Her disappearing hands clutched at her face, realizing that she was disappearing.

Perry's eyes didn't leave Victor's, even as the last pieces of her human form disappeared.

Some part of Lane thought if she could just reach Perry, just grab her, wrap her arms around her. . . she would be solid again. She could grab her, and they could get away from this place, graduate and truly live. Perry was so close, so close to graduating, to leaving death behind.

With each step, the wind forced Lane back.

Victor shouted something at Lane over his shoulder, and then the crowd separated like a river as someone stepped through.

Headmistress Eurydice stepped through the crowd, knee length white jacket flapping around her in the growing wind. Despite her dark skin, she looked almost like the ghosts that surrounded the school. Her steps were smooth as water as she joined Victor in the middle of the crowd. Two of the other professors who still retained their corporeal form followed in behind her.

Eurydice smiled at Victor. The other students took several steps back, retreating away from the Headmistress and back to the school—out of fear of her or of Perry, Lane wasn't sure.

Lane turned back to Perry's flickering form. With each second, the thing in front of her looked less and less like her friend and more and more like something from beyond the nightmares of the dead.

With a flash of darkness, Perry's form cracked. She erupted, gray wisps of smoke and translucent hands reaching out toward Lane. A shade hovered in her place, volatile, empty, black. A haunting of her former self. The shade flew into the trees, thrashing as she shot toward the sky with a furious scream.

Perry was gone, the anger of an empty shell left in her place.

But it wasn't just anger. It was hunger. Lane knew that shades would feed on the living if they came near, but she'd never seen it. The shade lunged from the trees toward Victor, black tendrils snapping at him. Lane flung herself at him, shoving him to the ground.

"So graceful," Victor grunted into the dried leaves that filled his mouth. His glasses laid on the ground beside him, broken.

The shade lunged at them as Victor grabbed Lane, pulling her to her feet and throwing her toward the trees. All of the remaining students left, leaving only the haunting of ghosts surrounding them. They tilted their heads to the side almost in unison, white eyes curious.

"Get out of here!" Victor shouted at her.

"That's what I get for saving your ass? How about a thank you?"

The shade barreled back toward them as he grabbed her again, throwing her out of the way. She turned to snark at him again, but it wasn't Victor.

Eurydice held the collar of Lane's uniform jacket, dark eyes gleaming.

"Troublesome child," she purred. "Of course, it would be you who stays."

Apparently, Lane's reputation had preceded her. Even though The Academy had few students, she'd only ever interacted with the Headmistress a handful of times.

"Get her out of my sight." Eurydice gave Victor a feline smile as she tossed Lane in his general direction.

Lane blinked at Victor, not knowing what to do. Behind him, Perry's shade growled, screaming as black shadows erupted from its center, like the explosion of a dying star.

"Get out of here," Victor repeated, glancing over his shoulder at Eurydice. She was holding her fingers out, shadows curling around them with death magic. What was she planning to do? Wouldn't she try to save Perry?

"I can't." Lane forced herself to turn her attention to Victor. "We have to help her."

But he was already walking away and toward Eurydice.

"We have to help her!" She wrapped her fingers in the velvet of Victor's coat. The two other professors stepped toward her, their expressions stern.

Her lip curled, daring them to come at her. She wouldn't leave Perry, not for them, not for The Academy, not for a second chance to live, no matter how badly she wanted it.

Victor held up a hand, a silent request for them to stop. It looked like an order.

"You need to go. I will stay." His fingers clasped hers tightly. "Blink back to The Academy."

She knitted her eyebrows together. That wasn't possible. They only ever Blinked on assignments, and never without Victor's precise coordinates, without the magic of The Academy at their back. She couldn't just go wherever she wanted, whenever.

He must have seen the doubt in her eyes. The two professors stepped closer to her, the threat in their faces clear.

"Yes, you can," Victor said. He pulled her closer, his breath hot on the part of her hair.

He shoved something into her fingers, squeezing her hand once as he pulled and walked away.

The light around her shuddered as she opened her hand.

It was a shard of bone, smaller than the strange key in her pocket—yellowed, hollowed out, and cracked.

Like the key, it seemed like it was calling to her.

As she clutched her hand around it, a sound rang in her ears, tinny and metallic, like a harp off-key.

With a gasp, she was yanked away, the world disappearing beneath her feet.

CHAPTER SIX

Lane was used to traveling between both worlds, popping out of one place and into another. The shock of being vacuumed out of her surroundings and spat out had lost its effect on her, even if she usually fell on her ass.

But this was different.

Every student at The Academy, and everyone that knew anything about death magic, understood the principles of Blinking. The obols contained enough energy for them to get where they needed to go, and sometimes even any magic that the mission might require. The power in that thin, tattooed line allowed them to cross the boundary between Life and Death.

It was an exhausting process, and not one that she had learned overnight. The magic and spellwork required was not like taking a step off a staircase or into a closet. It was not like closing your eyes and appearing somewhere else, like some fantasy story. Each student taught their muscles to make the perfect movement like training for a marathon. They learned to teach their bones to re-arrange themselves, and then their organs, and then each cell, and then their very selves.

Even after all of that, after all the lessons, she did not understand it clearly. Because this was not supposed to be possible.

She lay on the floor of The Academy's dormitory corridor, right outside of the main rotunda. The hallway to her left was a maze of doors, leading to their private rooms—hers, Fable's, Tripp's. . . Perry's. She turned to the right to the main rotunda, the walls floor-to-ceiling glass.

Her breaths heavy, she walked toward the glass and pressed her forehead to the cold surface. Stars glinted on the surface, like ghosts crossing into the afterlife across the night sky.

The forest wrapped around The Academy and into the distance as far as Lane could see, snaking around the expanse of After Life like a blanket of snow. Past that lay mountains, and miles of nothingness. The desolate expanse of rock and fields where the greys floated, listless, teetering on the edge of existence. The shadow of the mountains in the distance covered the horizon, their snowcapped tops barely visible against the glittering gray of the night sky. Always gray, no matter the time of day or night. And past all that, The Nether.

Victor had told her once that when someone became a shade, their soul went to The Nether. Not After Life or Life, but nowhere at all. A return to nothingness.

The emptiness of it called to her, an ache in her core.

Whenever she Blinked, there was a moment in between when she was truly *nowhere*. Faded into the dark, disappearing and reappearing after going through the last place in the world.

Was that where Perry was now? Nowhere?

Pulling away from the window, Lane looked at the broken shard of bone in her hand. She could feel the key in her pocket, a slight pressure against her leg. Two pieces of bone in one day. A ghost turning to a shade. And then Perry. . . Lane couldn't even bring herself to think it. It was one thing to be dead, and to find out that the afterlife did exist. It was another thing to have that taken from you, yanked from your grasp.

The death of death itself.

Lane didn't know much about Nil. She tried to pay attention in classes, but she preferred studying on her own in the library, looking for things that might be useful on their missions, or things that interested her. But she knew enough to know that something was very wrong.

She walked aimlessly toward the library. She was not much of a student or a reader—that was Victor's domain. But there was something about the books, the towering shelves, the dark shadows, and warm orange candles that filled her with a sense of comfort. Even being in the room, which was an almost cathedral-like cavern at the epicenter of the school, seemed to warm her. Like a blanket and cup of coffee against the chill of winter that awaited her outside in the wilds of the afterlife.

She stepped into the room, wrapping her arms tight around herself. Maybe she could find some information about shades, or even about these strange bones. Not that she even knew where to look.

She hoped Victor would be back soon.

Crossing between the stacks, she ran her fingers across the spines of books. She had no idea how they had gotten there, or when. It didn't seem likely they had been taken from Life. They only ever went on missions to capture the dead that had escaped, not to steal from life itself. That was more of the witches' thing.

Maybe it was the library of the dead, of the ghosts themselves.

The spines were ordered alphabetically, and she followed along by candlelight, unsure what she was looking for.

"Lane?" someone called from the distance.

She looked up, squinting. Tripp stood in the doorway of the library, only his red hair visible beneath the shadows of the shelves and the vaulted ceiling.

"Are you okay?" he asked. "What happened? All the other students left and—"

He didn't know.

Lane stepped toward him, hands reaching up to retie her black, curly hair in a knot on her head. She yanked on it, trying to find the words.

Neither of them said anything, Lane's sad eyes answering Tripp's own. He didn't really have to ask. Perry had been missing. And now she was gone. Tripp was made of jokes and laughter, not books and seriousness, but he still knew.

"She's gone."

Lane nodded.

His fists opened and closed like he didn't know what to do with his hands.

Lane wanted to say she was sorry. If she hadn't jumped out the window, if she hadn't chased the ghost-witch. . . but there was nothing to say. She'd never experienced loss before. She didn't know what you were supposed to say when someone died—when they were wiped from existence entirely. She didn't know what the ghosts said to each other as they faded and were no more.

"But how?" he asked.

"I don't know," Lane said. "She turned into a shade. She's. . ."

Lane wanted to say *gone* but knew it would not help to say it out loud.

"Tripp, I think something is wrong," she said. "Someone did this. You know the dead don't just become shades. It requires something violent, like murder. And on the mission—"

His face made her stop cold.

"Really?" Tripp asked. "You can't even wait ten minutes? You've already forgotten about her and moved onto conspiracy theories?"

The muscles in her chest seized like she had been stabbed.

Without a word, he turned on his ankle and stalked away, his footsteps echoing with anger until the sound was swallowed by the walls of the school.

She didn't try to follow. She knew he was right. She should have been thinking about Perry, not worrying about herself.

The library echoed with silence the way only books could. Turning back to them, she stared out across the room and its empty tables, the lamps slowly burning their last oil. All of the other students must have gone straight to the dormitories. None of the ghosts even floated through the walls, leaving the library and the school itself in an eerie silence that reflected the barren world around it. Lane pulled her arms tighter around her chest, leaning into one of the nearest bookshelves.

"Why are you even here?" she asked herself. Even in a whisper, her voice echoed through the stacks.

What had she thought was going to happen? She would find a book on shades in the library and the answer would magically reveal itself? That somehow, she'd find the answer and be able to help Perry?

Perry was gone. There was no saving her. But there still could be answers. She just wasn't going to find them here, in this haunted library.

Turning away from the shelves, Lane left the library with slow footsteps, as if not to wake the sleeping castle. She saw no one, and the hallways appeared darker than usual, the shadows playing games with her. No matter the time of day, the school was usually consumed by the eerie white-fog glow of After Life, so it never really achieved the blackness of night.

Victor's bedroom and office sat just around the corner from the library, almost adjacent. If there had been a secret door at the back of the room, he would have been able to step right into the stacks of the Historical Magic section. Instead, a fireplace filled the wall, dying embers red in the still warm hearth. Lane paused in the doorway, staring at the back of Victor's head. It had been less than an hour since he'd sent her away, but somehow, the distance between them felt wider.

He stood squinting at the large map that hung above his fireplace, his black hair jutting out from his head at all angles. It was a small room, dank and dark, with a fireplace and two burnt leather chairs flanking his desk.

"Victor."

Lane cringed internally. Was the relief in her voice as obvious as it felt?

Finally noticing her, he looked up in surprise, still squinting. He rubbed a hand across his face, leaving a trail of dirt on his pale cheek.

Taking a step into the room, Lane leaned over his desk and opened the top drawer, revealing his spare glasses. Wordlessly, she handed them to him, not moving her eyes from his face. His eyes stayed on her like she was a puzzle he hadn't solved.

"I forgot about those."

"Obviously."

She pulled her hand away before he could respond, their knuckles brushing. Victor turned back to his fireplace, looking lost in thought. Lane scanned the titles on the books that lined the shelves, the doorway to his bedroom that she had never opened, a wardrobe full of clothes he never seemed to wear.

After several minutes, she realized he wasn't going to say anything.

She sighed, breaking the silence. "You can go to the crows, you know that?"

He spun toward her.

"You asked me to leave you behind. You asked me to leave her behind." She paused. "And then you *Blinked me away* because you knew I wouldn't listen."

Victor tucked his hands behind his waist, exposing his untucked shirt. Something seemed to wash over him as he stared at her, steel eyes behind steel frames.

"I know." He opened his mouth and then closed it again, as if he could not find the right words. She picked at a stray string that was fraying on the leather armchair.

"Did anything else happen on the mission?" he asked.

"I already told you everything."

Except for the blackouts.

He turned, grabbing a pen off the table, and scribbled something along the inside of his arm. He was always covered in hastily written notes like that.

"What's going on with the map?" she asked. He didn't respond.

"On the mission, the ghost. You said it seemed like he was using Nil and Vis. But did it seem like he was doing it intentionally? Like he was in control?"

Lane shook her head. Nothing about that ghost had been in control. "Whatever happened, I don't think he knew what it was. He seemed. . . scared."

Like Perry. Neither of them said it, but Victor's eyes flashed, and she knew they had thought the same thing.

She looked at him, finally realizing what he wasn't saying. "You think that something is wrong with After Life's magic. That's what's causing this?"

Victor paused, shaking his head like he was trying to banish a thought.

"Victor," she demanded, rising to her feet.

He turned on his heel, the map behind him casting an eerie glow across his face.

"The balance of death magic and living magic is temperamental. Over the centuries, people have tried to harness both, to manipulate power to their own liking. It never ends well."

Lane knew this. It was one of the reasons the school was charged with tracking down escaped ghosts. Each one was a tiny leak of death.

His eyes traveled around the room, to the map, to his books, to the dark ceiling. Anywhere but to her. The hair on her arms rose.

She replayed his words in her mind. It wasn't just that something was happening to After Life, to death, to magic.

"Someone is doing this," she realized.

She thought of the white key in her pocket and reached into her jeans, feeling the cool teeth under her fingers. What if the key meant something? What if it did something?

"Intentionally? Maybe. Accidentally? Maybe. But it doesn't matter what I think." His gaze flickered to her, the gray steel in his eyes suddenly soft. He took a step toward her. "Laney. . . They will blame someone for this. She will blame someone for this."

"Who?" Lane asked. Her mind went to the witches, although that didn't make sense. They had never breached the line between life and death, not in a millennia.

"This school has rules, responsibilities," Victor said. "Ones that Eurydice must uphold."

Lane was too aware of that. She'd been lectured too many times on the importance of The Academy, of their missions, and of their responsibility to uphold the legacy of death magic. She knew the rules. Don't ask questions, especially about life. Do what you're told. Don't go near the witches, or Haven Hall. Don't play with magic.

A silence stretched between them, his silver eyes glistening.

Slowly, she realized what he was trying to say.

He'd told them what happened on the mission. That was why he'd wanted her to leave the woods. Not because he was worried about her, but so he could report to Eurydice.

They believed it was all connected—Perry turning to a shade. The leak of death magic into life. The ghost, dying, trying to warn Lane of something.

Someone was purposefully doing this.

And they believed that person was Lane.

"No," she said. "They can't think it was me. I'm no one."

Footsteps echoed down the hallway. Victor looked at Lane, his eyes full of something unreadable, torn between panic and regret.

"Do you think I had something to do with this?" She stepped away from him, toward the door. He didn't answer. "Victor, do you?"

He shook his head as the door opened behind her.

"Please, sit," Eurydice purred as she entered the room. Two of the school guards flanked her at either side, their black uniforms the perfect match to her midnight skin. "We have much to discuss."

CHAPTER SEVEN

Trapped. Lane was trapped in Victor's office, with Eurydice and her guards blocking the door. The fireplace cracked, the room growing warmer as they filled the small space.

"Thank you, Victor," Eurydice said. "You may leave."

He didn't move.

"You really think I have something to do with this?" Lane snapped at Victor, angrier at his betrayal than at what this meant for her. "How long did you wait to tell her? How long after Perry died?"

Tripp had said something very similar to her, she realized.

She watched his face, hoping she was wrong. There was no way Victor really thought she was connected to this.

"You're a coward," she spat.

"Lane, I didn't know— I just wanted to protect the school."

"What did you think would happen?" She stepped backwards as the guards reached for her, trapping herself in the room.

Eurydice sighed, stepping between them, flat boredom painted across her features.

"Please, don't argue on my account," Eurydice said. Victor stepped out of her way into the corner. Lane's hands balled into fists at her side as she watched him stand to the side. As if there was nothing he could do. Nothing he would do.

Eurydice stood with her shoulder pointed at Lane, her white cape spilling behind her. Her eyes met Lane's, her already thin eyelids narrowing.

"You have no idea what you have done," Eurydice said. "You have put us all at risk. You have skirted your lessons, disobeyed orders, and played with magic you do not understand. Do you know how precarious our position is? How important? Of course not. Because you do not care. The role this academy plays in the protection of death, of magic everywhere, is bigger than whatever game you are playing."

Lane took a step backward, stumbling. The guards caught her, pushing her forward with rough hands. She caught her balance on the chair, her fingers digging into the leather. There was nothing she could say, she realized, that would change their minds. She tried to find words to prove she hadn't done anything—that she didn't even know *how* someone might do what they were implying—but instead, rage exploded inside her.

"How could I know? None of you tell us anything!"

Victor pressed his fingers to his temples.

Eurydice turned toward her. "Is that so? Victor tells me that you can sense magic—both Vis and Nil. And I am supposed to believe that this connection is completely innocent?"

Her mouth opened, closed. She hadn't told him she could sense magic. She hadn't told anyone.

"That's not true," Lane argued. "I don't know anything more about magic than any of the other students."

"I knew I should have been keeping a closer eye on you." Eurydice sighed. "As of this moment, you are stripped of your status as a student at this school. You will never graduate. You will join the other useless spirits in the wastes."

Lane's heart dropped. The school gave her the blood and body that separated her from the ghosts in the woods, gave her some semblance of life. She would be forgotten, lost to time.

Against her will, a cry escaped her throat.

Eurydice snapped her fingers, binding Lane's arms at her side. Lane cried out, her muscles frozen and aching as she fought against the invisible bonds. She pushed against them, but her arms remained tight at her sides.

Eurydice took another step toward her, a lion circling a wounded bird. "Tell me, this witch that turned into a shade." She brought her face close to Lane's, her breath surprisingly cold. "What do you claim happened, exactly? He did it to himself?"

"Of course not," Lane spat. It was a fate worse than death itself.

Lane's arms went slack at her sides. She tried to hide her fear, but from Eurydice's smile, she knew she had failed.

"That's what I thought."

The guards grabbed for Lane's arms as Eurydice's hand fell, dropping the spell-crafted bonds. Lane's vision blurred as she lashed out, ducking as they reached for her elbow. She kneed one in the stomach and kicked the other in the side. Her hair fell out of its bun and into her face as she slid under the desk. She reached for a bag of coin amperes, throwing them in a guard's face as he lunged for her.

The guards stared at her from either side of the desk, huffing as they tried to decide how to grab her in the small, hexagon-shaped room. Eurydice rolled her eyes, waving to urge them forward. Even with Lane fighting back, she was bored.

"Please." Victor stepped between them. "Eurydice. Lane would never hurt Peregrine. There could be something much more serious going on here. Something bigger than her or the students at this school."

Eurydice held up her hand, silencing him again. Her thin, red lips curled to reveal the sharp points of her teeth. "I'm surprised, Victor. Would you really risk your position after all these years? On one mediocre student?"

Lane's hand tightened around the remaining amperes. She knew she was missing something in their conversation, but her mind couldn't focus.

"That's not what I am saying. The evidence might show that something else is going on."

"Don't be foolish. She was the only one present at both murders." Lane wanted to argue, but it didn't matter. Eurydice didn't care. It wasn't about what made sense. She would do anything to protect the school. "Would you prefer I punish you instead?"

Victor looked over his shoulder at Lane. His jaw was tight.

There was nothing he could do.

The guards took another step forward, each of them approaching on either side of the desk. Lane tightened her grip on the heavy bag of amperes. She could already hear the crunch it would make when she hit the guard in the face.

She closed her eyes as the guards separated, rounding the room on either side of the desk. It would be a tough fight, and Victor would not help. Fighting would only delay the inevitable. She knew she couldn't take both of them and Eurydice and get out of there unscathed.

But she would sure as hell try.

She opened her eyes and they landed on the map behind the guards, lit up like the night sky.

"The witches," Lane whispered, almost too quiet for anyone to hear. "What if they did this? What if they have finally made their attack?"

Victor dropped his arm, tilting his head to one side in thought. Sweat beaded on Lane's brow as Eurydice stared at her, the warmth of the room crawling up Lane's neck.

"It is possible," Victor said to Eurydice. His voice was calm, as if ignoring the situation unraveling around him. "You have always been wise to be wary of them. The witches could have targeted the drifter, or worse—they may have been plotting. Just as you always suspected, Headmistress. It only makes sense that you were correct."

Eurydice's gaze circled the room, flicking between the guards and Lane. Victor took a step toward Lane, his pale hand neared hers, their fingers almost touching. She wanted to reach out and grab his hand, even if this was his fault. Old habits died hard, she supposed.

"Yes." Eurydice traced her hand down the column of her throat. "It's possible."

Lane's shoulders fell, a small sigh escaping her throat against her will.

"Go ahead," Eurydice urged.

Too late, she realized her relief was premature.

One of the guards pounced. He grabbed Lane by the neck, yanking her toward the desk and hitting her head against the wooden surface. Her vision blurred, surrounded by a sea of stars. The guard dragged her across the room.

She tried to shout, but his grip pushed against her windpipe. She could hear Victor yelling—at the guards or at Eurydice, she did not know. The second guard grabbed one of her arms, pushing her toward the door. She twisted in their grasps. The room was destroyed, papers scattering on the air.

"I must protect The Academy and After Life," Eurydice said. "We will continue our investigation and take you into custody. For the time being."

Lane kicked harder. She could guess what would happen once she was in custody. She knew Eurydice's history. How many people had been arrested who managed to prove their innocence?

Lane would never be seen again.

She shoved at the guard's legs, pushing against the grip on her throat. Every time she moved, the air was knocked out of her, the guard tightening his grip on her windpipe. They carried her between them like a corpse, dangling in the air.

She managed to free one of her hands and lashed out, scratching for his eyes. But he was too clever for her. He pulled his head back, bending her other arm backwards. She was only able to kick and scratch at them, even with her months of training. Their grips were too tight. In front of them, Eurydice opened the door to her rarely-used office.

Lane could hear Victor's footsteps clacking, chasing after them. Lane twisted toward him, her arm grazing along the side of her thigh as she turned. His gaze flicked to her pocket, then back to her eyes, then back to her pocket, as quick as a hummingbird.

The bone.

She wriggled her free hand into her pocket, wrapping her fingers around the shard. The bone key was still in there too, grazing her fingers with its familiar hum. Her hand closed around them both until she felt the skin break on her palm.

She closed her eyes, imagining herself somewhere else. Anywhere else. In her hand, the bones seemed to burn, heat traveling up into her arms.

She would track down every Vis wielder, every drifter on her own if she needed to. She would find out what had happened to Perry.

She would not let them take away what little she had left.

Someone would suffer for what had happened.

And it sure as Hell wasn't going to be her.

CHAPTER EIGHT

Shepherd had spent most of the day at the Night Market, listening for any whisper of Addie or anything that could be connected. Mostly, she heard whispers of other missing people—kids, teenagers, adults, and even magical creatures. What was left of the Night Market was buzzing with fear over what was happening to their friends, which was saying something, considering there was barely anything left of the market at all.

Other than that, she had come up empty. Most missing persons cases were like that. Eventually, people stopped caring. Except the people closest to them. They never stopped.

Her phone had buzzed all day. Her friends, wondering where she was. Her ex-girlfriend, texting her to hangout. Her mother, asking her to come home.

She had ignored it, and at some point, had mindlessly walked to the police station, even though she knew there was no way they had any new leads.

But they had found something, she discovered.

It was a photograph, fuzzy and out of focus, lifted from CCTV. Addie stood in the street, her arms outstretched as if she was angry. And she was not alone. A man faced her, his face pointed away from the camera. Addie was blurred in the black and white static, but the man's outline was solid, stark. As if she was running from the frame and he was frozen in time. In the corner of the image, the timestamp showed it was taken hours before Addie disappeared.

There wasn't really a choice, and Shepherd was used to making bad ones. So she grabbed it and ran.

She looked over her shoulder as she turned between two row houses, the street steadily curving into an uphill slant. She wasn't sure who she was afraid was behind her.

The police? As if.

Whoever had done this to Addie? Possibly.

As she walked up the hill, her phone rang mercilessly in her pocket. Probably Eileen, wondering where she was. She was missing a closing shift, but she couldn't go to work. She needed to go back to the Night Market and find McKinley.

Having the photo wasn't enough. The man's face was obscured, his pale hair and pale skin blending with the gray of the image. She needed to know where to find him.

She stopped at the edge of the market, photo in hand, her face turned toward the cold night air. It was autumn in the city, which meant it could be freezing or scalding hot, whichever way the fates willed it.

It was both immediately obvious and not clear at all that the Night Market was a thing all its own. The air stiffened, the sky darkened. Anyone who happened into the Night Market might have thought it was an older part of the city, a remnant of a bygone era of architecture. The roofs were beautiful clay tiles, not the clinical gray of the city. Dirty pavement turned to cobblestone in a single step. The windows were rounded rather than square, although most of them were boarded up, garden boxes long abandoned.

No one lived there. Not anymore.

The Night Market had bustled when Shepherd was a child—she still remembered clinging to her mother's jeans as she treated minor wounds, walking around the pub with her father and Addie. Now, only the pub and some small shops remained.

She glanced up at one of the signs, the small shop where McKinley was known to do business. She'd done plenty of deals in the shop herself. It was the kind of place that bought and sold artifacts, no matter where they were from. Magic, non-magic, Night Market, black market, it was all the same. A rune was carved over the door of the shop, the strange curling tail of a letter and the slanting slash through the top. "Vis." Witches had stopped using that word for their magic a century ago, stopped using the language of magic that it came from. There just weren't enough of them left to keep it going. Shepherd's father had made her learn it, as a matter of principle, even though she would never be accepted into Haven Hall. It had worked out for her. The ancient language came in handy with her line of work.

A tiny bell clanged as Shepherd stepped into the store. It was dark except for a single kerosene lamp on the counter, the flame sputtering blue and orange. In many ways, the store was similar to

Eileen's. Stacks of books scattered across the floor in piles, creating a cityscape of towering books that threatened to teeter and fall on her as she maneuvered around them. The walls were wrapped in shelves, blanketed in dusty, magical objects that she couldn't begin to identify. Her heart skipped a beat as she realized how many magical objects there were in one place, ripe for the picking. But she couldn't lift them. Not here. She'd delivered some of them herself.

"Hello?" Shepherd called out. The gas lamp cast shadows on the walls.

The man who ran it was well known for being the kind of shady person who could get you whatever you needed, when you needed it. Even if he made you pay a hefty price. She was used to that.

"Tracker?" She called out. Her voice echoed off the shelves. The place was empty. Through the thickly stacked shelves, she could barely see the back of the store except for the flickering light on the ceiling. Something whistled, eerie and low, and she turned to her left, coming face to face with a ceramic sculpture of a child. Its porcelain head was cocked to the side, glass eyeballs staring, and Shepherd shivered. Around her neck, Addie's necklace seemed to quiver in response.

"This." She pointed at the glass doll. "This is why I hate magic."

Well, one of the reasons, anyway.

She walked to the back counter, smacking her hand against the small bell that sat there. No response, as she'd expected.

Behind her, a stack of books toppled over, sending objects rolling in every direction. Shepherd jumped. She must have hit them as she walked by. Except she knew she hadn't.

She was imagining things.

The dark shop was unnerving even when it was not empty, with the strange magical objects that tried to manipulate her into touching them. But empty, it was too dark, too quiet.

She shoved her hands into her pockets, walking toward the back room.

Itssssss itssss itssss

Shepherd turned on her heel as a shelf crashed toward the ground.

"These damned magical objects." She kicked at a golden cat statue that rested near her foot. She braced herself, placing her hand on the brass handle and opening the door. The metal was unnervingly cold, covered in a strange frost.

Black shadows swirled in the room like ropes. Black ink leaked from the walls, pouring onto the floor and toward the door. In the center of the room was a dark shape, the outline of a man made entirely of smoke. Against her better judgment, she reached out a hand, fingertips brushing through the smoke.

"McKinley?"

The shadow lurched toward her, wrapping around her wrist. Her flesh stung with cold. The darkness in the room expanded, reaching toward her. A dark tendril shot toward her, and she stumbled backward out of the room.

Without looking back, she sprinted through the store, jumping over fallen shelves as she aimed for the front door. She clutched the photo in her hand as the shadows raced after her, extinguishing the gas lamp and knocking over artifacts.

She reached for the front door, kicking it open and filling the room with the crisp night air.

Noo, nooo. Staysttstaayyystayyy. Don't you want to know what happened to your sisterrrr?

She paused, her hands clenched into fists as the door swung back toward her. She could still leave, pretend this hadn't happened. It wouldn't be the first time she'd walked into something and immediately seen her way out.

But no, of course she couldn't. Not when Addie depended on her.

"Damn it all," she cursed, unsure if she was mad at herself or the collection of shadows.

A shadowy tendril of fog slithered across the store. She took a step back across the carpet, hand outstretched. The fog swept toward her, rings forming around her ankles like the exhale of pipe smoke.

"My sister?" she asked the fog, feeling ridiculous. Either she was talking to shadows or she was standing in the middle of magic that shouldn't exist. Both were bad options.

The strange, hissing voice did not respond. Shepherd blinked, shaking her hair as if she could wake herself.

But it wasn't a dream. It wasn't even a nightmare.

The tendrils of fog weaved and wrapped until they formed the shadow figure of a man again. Or maybe it was a woman, a nondescript figure of black smoke with legs and arms but no face.

"Look, I'm a very busy individual. And you clearly want to tell me something, so let's just get on with it." She crossed her arms. Did she know better than to provoke people who were clearly more powerful than her? Absolutely. Had it ever stopped her? No.

The shadow laughed, the sound of wind in an empty house. The hair on Shepherd's shaved neck prickled.

The shadow didn't have a mouth, but it was speaking.

The thing cocked its head to the side. It almost seemed to smile, as if it could hear her thoughts.

It lunged for her, wrapping its shadowed hands around her throat.

"I . . . thought . . . we . . . were . . . friends," she choked out as the dark thing tightened its grip on her windpipe.

The room quaked with the sound of shattered glass as the front window broke, exploding across the store. Shards flew through the shadow's form. With a pained screech, it dropped her. Shepherd fell, tiny pinpricks ripping through her shirt as she hit the floor.

A pair of boots stood in front of her on the carpet.

Shepherd looked up.

A girl had jumped through the window.

Without pausing, the stranger lunged for the shadow.

The girl struck out, her leg kicking through the black smoke. The light from the street ebbed through the broken window, flickering a warm glow through the room.

The thing screamed as the girl shot forward, her hand out-stretched with a strange pouch. She tossed something into its dark shape—a gray, powdered substance. Shepherd raised her eyebrows. She'd never seen anything like it. The monster recoiled, screeching.

Shepherd rose to her feet, ducked half behind a bookshelf. Whatever that substance was, it would probably fetch a pretty penny at the market . . . Shepherd had seen most kinds of magic, but she'd never seen anything like this before.

"Can you behave?" The girl smirked, her eyes glinting like black fire.

Hurtttss.

The girl crossed her arms impatiently, the pouch still in her hand as she tapped it on her arm, the dust falling in front of her in a line.

Youuu can'ttt.

Shepherd shook her head, as if she might shake the voice out of the inside of her skull. The creature's mouth didn't move, but Shepherd could tell they had both heard it. The girl smiled. She didn't seem to notice that Shepherd was there, her attention completely on the monster in front of her.

"Who did this to you?" she asked, her hand still tapping dust onto the ground in a circle. The shadow laughed again.

The smile fell from her face, replaced by something unreadable as she lunged for it. The thing seemed to go back and forth between solid and shadow, arms, legs, an almost human face, and then back to the dark amorphous darkness. The girl slammed it into the wall, pinning it with one hand.

"Tell me," she said through gritted teeth. "Did you do this to yourself? To Perry? Were the witches involved?"

Shepherd tilted her head. The witches? The girl said it with disdain. If she wasn't a witch, what was she?

The shadow screamed a hollow cry. It was the sound of a thousand deaths. Instinctively, Shepherd's hand went to Addie's necklace.

"Tell you what," the girl said. "Tell me the truth, and I won't send you back. I'm that nice. You can haunt here forever for all I care."

The shadow shrieked, its human form disappearing into an explosion of inky darkness. Against all physical sense, the girl still held onto it, the blob captured inside the clutch of her arms. Shepherd tried to think through the girl's words despite her pounding heart.

Send it back.

The shadow might know something about Addie, although Shepherd doubted that was true. It was some sort of mind trick. Still, she needed to find out before this girl sent the thing back wherever it was from.

The girl raised her hand, white dust falling between her fingers like sand.

With a deep breath, Shepherd jumped toward her, tripping over a pile of fallen books.

"Wait!" she shouted as she fell, catching herself on a broken shelf.

The girl whipped around, seeing her for the first time. Her eyes were green and brown and hazel, the color of rain in the forest.

The girl shoved Shepherd out of the way as the shadow lashed out toward them.

The shadow hit the girl across the face with a dark tendril. It wrapped itself around her neck, throwing her across the room. Her back hit the wall with a crack, and she toppled to the ground. Shepherd winced, rushing toward the girl, but the shadowed figure reached for her. Shepherd braced herself, holding up her arms to shield herself and the girl.

It stopped short as it reached the line of dust the girl had laid on the ground. Shepherd stopped, stunned, as the shadow swirled, almost like it was trapped in a glass vase.

She turned back to the girl, who was rubbing her head and hurrying to regain her footing. She was small, petite, muscular, and probably no older than Shepherd herself. She had naturally tanned skin and angular features that Shepherd couldn't place. She was beautiful, with a heart-shaped face and mouth and dark curls piled in a bun on top of her head. Beautiful and dangerous. Where Shepherd was wearing jeans and a trench coat, the girl was dressed like she'd come straight from battle—cargo pants, a military-grade vest, black combat boots, and a toolbelt at her waist that held more of that dust.

This girl was going to be trouble.

"Are you all right?" Shepherd asked. She held out her hand to help the girl stand, but she looked right past Shepherd toward the trapped attacker.

"Marvelous. And yourself?" The girl's voice was saccharine as she rolled her eyes. Shepherd pulled back her hand and shoved it into her pocket, her lips pinched.

So that was how it was going to be.

She followed the strange girl as she walked back to the shadow figure, navigating around fallen bookshelves and the remnants of the destroyed shop.

The girl held her hand outstretched as she reached him, as if holding a talisman. Shepherd took a step backward, wary of whatever this girl meant to do.

"This is your last chance," she said.

"Do you know where my sister is?" Shepherd asked the shadow.

The shadow laughed.

Before Shepherd could stop her, the girl lashed into the darkness and stabbed, her hand aiming for the core of the shadow.

Everything went still. The shadow flickered, and for a moment, the black, inky web of tendrils disappeared. A man stood in its place. His features were more silhouette than human, entirely black. Shepherd could just make out his features. Strands of hair that fell around his ears, the hollow alcove at the base of his throat, pointed ears. His expression was pure surprise as his black eyes looked down at the shining, white object sticking out of the center of his chest. His dark fingers reached for it as if he recognized it, and his eyes filled with something like longing.

The key. . .

His voice faded as he spoke, disappearing as he tried to get out the words. Whatever he wanted to tell them, warn them about, died in his throat. He disappeared completely.

The room filled with an eerie stillness. Shepherd hadn't noticed how cold the room was until a slow, comfortable warmth sank onto her skin. With a heavy exhale, she leaned over, placing her hands on her knees like she was trying to catch her breath. Addie's necklace swung around her neck like a pendulum.

The girl turned back to her, eyes narrowed and head cocked to the side. Shep fought a smirk. Now was no time to flirt, especially not with this Buffy wannabe.

"What an introduction," Shepherd said, glancing back at the broken window. "Nice to meet you. And, well, thanks for getting rid of that thing."

The girl lunged for her, grabbing at the collar of her shirt as she threw Shepherd to the floor. Shepherd was taller than her, but lankier, and the girl's well-earned muscle showed. She shoved her knee between Shepherd's ribs.

The girl's lips formed a thin line as she stared down at Shepherd and wrapped her hand around Shepherd's necklace.

"Where did you get this?" she hissed.

CHAPTER NINE

It couldn't be a coincidence that Lane had found this girl fighting a shade. Not with a key around her neck.

The girl struggled as Lane tightened her grip on the chain. She'd turned the damned thing into a necklace. The key seemed to scream beneath her hand, pulsing with magic. The shard of bone and the other key were unusual, but this one was full of so much power, it made her head spin.

"Where did I get what?" The girl asked, her tone annoyed. She was taller than Lane, thinner and less muscular. She should have been able to fight back, at least, but she laid still beneath Lane's grip.

"Do you know what this is?" Lane tried to ask it like she herself knew, even though she was desperately waiting for her answer.

The girl raised an eyebrow. "If I did, do you think I would tell someone who is currently kneeing me in the lung?"

Lane looked down at her knee and then looked back at the girl's eyes, staring at her. This shouldn't be possible. Humans couldn't see ghosts, and witches could only sense them. But they were touching.

She jumped away from the girl like she'd been bitten.

"You can see me," Lane said, the words spilling from her mouth.

The girl raised a dark eyebrow. "And? Is invisibility your skill or something?"

Her skin was the color of summer sun, with short, spiky hair curling around her ears. Her eyes stared at Lane, dark brown and questioning.

This girl could see her. Touch her.

Lane grabbed her own wrist tightly, as if the pain might make it any less real. But no, this girl was watching her.

"What. . . are you?" Lane asked.

There was only one explanation. They had been taught wrong. Witches could see ghosts. Or at least, this one could.

Lane took a step toward her. She needed to change the subject. If this witch-girl didn't know about ghosts, she'd already revealed too much. She reached for the necklace again, tugging it from the girl's neck with an unmerciful yank.

"Where did you get this?"

The girl's eyes flashed from her to the necklace and back, full of anger.

If this witch knew about the keys, then she probably also knew about what happened to Perry. She might know everything.

Lane bit her lip.

If this girl knew something, she wasn't just a regular witch.

She was dangerous.

Lane's fingers itched to reach for the knife she kept at her belt. The necklace was wrapped around her fingers like brass knuckles.

"I'll tell you what," the girl said, a trace of a smirk dancing on her face. "I'll tell you if you tell me what that thing was. And how you knew how to fight it."

The girl was smirking, hands in her pockets. If she was rattled by what had happened, she certainly didn't seem it.

Lane's brow furrowed. She didn't know what to make of this witch. "You first."

The girl shook her head, hair falling into her eyes. Her smile widened.

Lane rolled her eyes. "Fine." She pursed her lips. She could say a little without giving too much away. "It was a shade. But not a typical one. Something was. . . done to it."

None of the three shades she'd encountered in the past day were normal. Shades were usually violent but driven by instinct. They were slow and empty, usually harmless. But these were different.

They weren't just violent. They were angry.

Vengeful. Driven to kill.

The girl didn't flinch. If anything, it seemed like nothing Lane said even registered to her.

"So not a ghost?" She nodded appreciatively. "Well, I thought I'd seen everything, but magic never ceases to surprise me."

"Are you a witch?" Lane's voice cracked. It was a dangerous question. If she was a witch, then Lane had just revealed she was vulnerable. If not, then she had opened an entire other can of worms.

She snorted. "No, no, I'm not. I work with witches. My family are witches. But I'm not. I'm nothing. No one."

Lane froze, surprised. She had never heard of such a thing, a witch born without magic. So she knew things about magic, but had no power.

At least, not that she was aware of. Lane reached toward the girl, and her eyes followed. The girl could see her, touch her. What if that was some kind of magic, and this girl had simply never met a ghost before?

"Aren't *you*?" the girl asked. Lane felt her eyebrows raise. "I've never seen that type of magic before, though. Whatever you did with that powder to the shade thing."

"Ashes," Lane corrected. "It's not powder, they're ashes."

The girl stared at her, tilting her head to the side.

Lane didn't answer her question about being a witch, taking two steps backward. There was no good answer without revealing Nil, and she'd clearly said too much already.

Lane dangled the key between them. "Your turn."

"It's my sister's. She's missing." Her voice trailed off as she looked at the store, at the fallen objects, crashed and broken. She looked back, glancing at the necklace. "It isn't just a necklace, is it?"

Lane shook her head.

"I should have known." The girl shook her head, almost laughing to herself.

"You came *here* to find your sister?" Lane gestured to the store. Even though the room had warmed, the place sent a chill up her spine. They both knew the kind of place it was. It was filled with too many competing magical objects, some surely stolen. Their energies mixed in the air. She could feel the distant song of some charm, calming and neutral, against the wall of something darker, more sinister, threatening to eat the smaller magic alive.

"I quite like it here, actually," the girl said, picking an enchanted dagger off a shelf and tossing it between her hands. She caught it, frowned, and put it in her pocket. "I'm Shepherd. My friends call me Shep."

Lane pursed her lips, giving a polite nod. Shepherd didn't seem to know anything about the necklace or about death magic at all. She could have been lying, but unlike the rest of the store, nothing radiated off of her. Lane was used to the radiofrequency of magic, a constant shrill hum in her ears. Shepherd was a dead radio in a sea of static. Against the chaos, she was silence.

Lane took a step toward her, wanting to be closer to it. In her chest, her heartbeat seemed to relax.

Still, she had very little reason to trust Shepherd. She was still a witch by blood, even if she was one without any power.

"I'm Lane." She did not reach out her hand. Shepherd continued down the shelf, perusing through the magical items. This place would have made Victor scream. "Just Lane. So how did you end up getting attacked?"

Shepherd shrugged, lifting a small statue of a broken doll's head into her palm. "It was here when I got here."

"I'm supposed to believe that?"

Shepherd tucked her hands into her pockets again. Must have been some kind of nervous habit. She swung her hips back and forth, whistling out of the corner of her mouth. "It's not like the thing was after me. I'm no one. Believe me, don't believe me. Doesn't really affect me either way."

Shepherd shrugged and then motioned to Lane with a flourish of her wrist. Her turn.

"Shades are what is left of a person after the soul dies. An empty husk. Ghosts retain some characteristics, because their souls are still intact. But shades are usually mindless. That thing," Lane paused, thinking of Perry, the way her shade seemed to recognize Victor, "it *spoke*. Before you got here, was there anyone else here? Or maybe something happened with the necklace?"

Shepherd could have been lying about the necklace being her sister's, Lane knew. She could have taken it, or stumbled upon it, the same way Lane had.

Shepherd leaned down, picking up books from the floor and stacking them neatly on the shelves. Lane grabbed the key from where it had fallen, shoving it in her pocket while Shepherd wasn't looking.

"I like books," Shepherd offered, as if that was some kind of explanation. "And no, there was no one here when I got here. I was looking for this Tracker. . . but didn't find him. And the key has been with me since my sister went missing. She got it when our *eduda* died," she added. She must have seen the lack of recognition for the word on Lane's face. "It means grandfather in Cherokee."

Shepherd turned toward Lane, clapping a book shut. The sound made Lane flinch.

"Why do you think the thing was after me, anyway?" She took a step toward Lane. "For all I know, you sent it here, and I'm just an innocent bystander. You're the one that knows what it is, and how to fight it."

Lane couldn't argue with that. It seemed she was raising everyone's suspicions lately.

"Where did you say you're from? I've never met a witch with magic like yours," Shepherd said. "And I've seen all the specialties. Healer, Warrior, Tracker. . . but Ghost Hunter? Never."

Lane's mouth twisted, puzzled. Witches had specialties? She had never heard the professors mention that. She would have to ask Victor when she got back. *If* she got back.

Shepherd snapped her fingers and grinned, her white teeth glinting against the dark tan of her skin, as if she had discovered some secret.

"Aha." She pointed her finger into Lane's face. "You're from one of those nomadic Necromancer colonies, aren't you? Which one are you from? Mongolia? Chile?"

Lane didn't respond, but Shepherd only grinned wider, a look that made her want to smile back. A part of her was excited by the idea. But that would mean she was a witch, and that just wasn't possible.

Lane reached up, retying her hair into a bun. The key still dangled between her fingers.

Shepherd raised an eyebrow. "What did it say to you, when you killed it? It looked like it almost recognized you."

She shook her head. "I didn't kill it, I sent it back."

"Back where?"

Lane smirked. "Where it belongs."

"I was just wondering. Before you broke through the window," Shepherd half snorted, "It said something about my sister. And it asked me to stay. Like it. . . wanted me? Do you think it was going to drain my blood?"

Something about the look on Shepherd's face said that she was a little excited about the idea. Lane tried to hide the judgment on her face.

"Why would it know anything about your sister?" she asked. "Do you think that's why it was here? For her?"

The key had belonged to her sister. It made sense. Shepherd might not know anything, but this sister might.

Shepherd reached up and held the back of her head with her palms, which lifted her t-shirt and exposed a sliver of tan skin. "I don't know. I thought we were close, that I knew everything about her. But now I realize how little I really knew about her. I was hoping that the shade-thing might tell me where she is. . ." Her voice trailed off, and then suddenly her eyes snapped up, glinting with the strike of a thought. Shepherd pulled a photograph from her pocket and pushed the glossy paper toward her. "This man was the last person to see her. He could know something about where she is, about the shade and why it was here. I came here to get the Tracker to try and find him, but—"

Lane held the photo up to the light. It was a grainy, low quality still taken from an even lower quality video. There was a girl, a little younger than Lane, reaching toward a man in a black coat. She was beautiful and looked very much like Shepherd. They both had a look that said they were up to something, some plan, some trick up their sleeve. Lane looked at the man and his triangle shaped jaw, his dark coat. There was something vaguely familiar, something she couldn't place.

"I think he might know where she went." Her voice was soft, sad.

"Is he a witch?" Lane asked. "Or something else? A demon maybe?"

Shepherd's eyebrows disappeared under the shaggy angle of her bangs. "Demons? There are demons? Now, this is why I told my parents I didn't want anything to do with magic—"

Lane shook her head, smiling to herself, and ignored the question. "And you don't think he sent the shade to stop you from finding him? To. . . well, kill you."

Shepherd took a step back, eyes wide. It clearly hadn't occurred to her. She was poking around in dangerous places that she didn't understand. "That's possible?"

Lane didn't want to tell her all the things that were possible. Some things were better left as nightmares. And she didn't know what these new shades were capable of, if they were being controlled or just attacking randomly.

Lane wasn't sure if the man in the photo had sent the shade or if he was even a witch.

But it was all she had to go on at the moment. She needed some way to find the witches—ones who actually had magic. They were behind this, and she needed to find them. Before Eurydice found her.

Well, thanks for the chat, lovely to meet you, Lane thought as she slowly backed away from Shepherd, taking small, half-steps to the door. Shepherd took a single stride toward the door, slapping it closed beneath her palms.

"Oh, no you don't." Shepherd's hands were on either side of her face against the surface, trapping her. Their faces were so close they were almost touching. The muscles in Lane's neck tensed as she stared into Shepherd's honey-brown eyes. They were flecked with black. Her breath smelled like coffee and cinnamon. "You're not going anywhere with my necklace. Or that photograph. I only stole one copy."

"And you're going to stop me?" Lane smirked, tilting her head to the side. Quick as a feather, she jabbed her hand into Shepherd's ribs, ducking beneath her elbow and spinning away in one fell swoop.

She grinned as Shepherd coughed, turning toward her. She was between Lane and the exit now, blocking her.

"Hear me out," Shepherd said. "I'll help you if you help me. Help me find my sister, and I'll help you figure out what's up with these shade things. Why they're different and what they're after."

Her lips pinched together. "What makes you think I care?"

Lane hadn't exactly been forthcoming with her reasons for being there, but Shepherd had clearly realized them anyway.

She shrugged. "If you weren't after those things, I don't think you would have broken through that window and saved my life. You don't seem like the saving-a-damsel-in-distress-just-for-fun type."

"How can you help me? You don't have any magic, and you thought this was a *necklace*." Lane held up her hand, but the key was gone from her fingers. Eyes wide, heart racing, she looked across the ground for it.

Shepherd dangled it between two fingers, holding it out to Lane with a devilish smirk.

"Looking for this?" She laughed. It was deep, and hoarse, like her voice. "Don't underestimate me. I have skills."

"Clearly," Lane grumbled.

"And you are clearly not from here," Shepherd continued, pocketing the necklace. "I've lived here my entire life. I can help you."

Lane looked up at her, eyes wary.

"I don't see how you have much of a choice," Shepherd said. "I'm the one with the necklace and the photograph."

Lane's hand flew to her pants. Shepherd had somehow stolen it from her pockets. Damn.

She shouldn't be speaking to humans, let alone working with a witch. But she'd already been kicked out of school, at least for the time being. What did she have to lose?

"Do you know where to find her?" Lane asked, gesturing to the photo.

Shepherd shook her head.

Figures.

Lane looked up at her with a dark grin. "We're going to need a body."

CHAPTER TEN

Shepherd found herself breaking into the university's cadaver lab with the modern-day Buffy behind her. Just a totally normal day.

"Can you explain why we're here?" she asked as she knelt.

She was beginning to worry that she had made the wrong choice. Not that she didn't enjoy a little breaking and entering. Maybe being attacked by that shade had scrambled her brain. But. . . whatever it took to find her sister.

"We're going to track the man from your photo," Lane answered.

"That didn't really answer the question."

"You'll see." Lane smirked.

Shepherd sighed internally. So far, she had learned a few things about Lane. One: she took no bullshit and could probably beat her up, or at least send her to whatever hellish dimension she had sent that ghost. Two: she was one of the few people that could spar verbally as well as Shepherd, which was more irritating than exciting.

And three: she was hiding something.

Shepherd pressed the two bobby pins that Lane had removed from her hair into the lock.

"You aren't some kind of criminal, are you?" Lane asked, leaning toward the door. "Or do all witches know how to pick locks?"

Shepherd put her ear to the door, jiggling the pins around and waiting to hear the signature *click*.

"Don't ask questions you don't want the answers to," she said. "And I'm not a witch."

"By blood, you are." Lane stared pointedly.

"By blood? What are you, an eighteenth-century duke trying to marry off his daughter?"

Shepherd turned to face her. They were only inches apart as they both pressed their ears to the door, waiting. She could smell the faint residue of ash on Lane's skin, like an autumn campfire. It reminded her of winters by the fireplace with her family, roasting smores and eating *kanuchi*.

Lane rolled her eyes. "Criminal or not, you are exhausting."

"I'm not a criminal," Shepherd said through gritted teeth. "But it doesn't hurt to have skills."

The lock clicked open.

She pushed on the door with an overly large flourish of her arm, smirking at Lane. A small sliver of light flooded under the threshold.

Lane patted her on the shoulder. "Maybe you aren't useless."

Lane reached for the light switch, flooding the room with sterile fluorescent light. The room smelled of formaldehyde and bleach, a sickening mixture of science and the macabre. It was the kind of smell that stuck to your clothes for weeks.

"You know there are people here, right?" Shepherd hissed, pointing at the lights. "Are you trying to get us caught?"

Lane shrugged. "They won't see us. What are you, afraid of some regular humans?"

Shepherd shook her head, watching Lane as she crossed the room. They had more to worry about than campus security, sure. But more than most people, Shepherd knew exactly how high the price was when you thought magic solved all your problems.

Shepherd imagined the room would be like a morgue, which in all honesty, she had only seen on television. When Lane had asked where to find a body, she'd immediately thought of the university. She'd taken the occasional course, trying to figure out what to do with her life, but had never been inside the lab. She had imagined cold, locked doors hiding the sleeping bodies of the deceased, and maybe an examination table.

Instead, the room was lined with sterile tables like cots in a boarding school. Rows of corpses, each more grotesque than the last. The first still had all its skin and could have been alive if it weren't for the gray-blue tinge of his skin. The second's face had been peeled off. The third's chest was cracked open, lungs missing. The last was a map veins and muscles, organs torn from it.

"Science," Shepherd said, unenthusiastically as she held out her arms. She whistled, the smell of medically preserved flesh filling her nose. Lane approached a table and reached into her pocket, pulling out a small, velvet pouch. She ran her fingers nervously on the fabric as she contorted her mouth in thought.

Shepherd was aware of most types of witches, or at least she had thought. Each witch was born with a certain skill, usually inherited from the parents, although that wasn't always the case. There were Healers and Trackers and Warriors and Botanists and Mentalists. There were witches who could start fires with their minds and who could walk through dreams. There was still so much about Vis that they didn't know. Especially Shepherd, who had stopped paying attention once it was clear she wasn't magically gifted.

In the ancient runic language of magic, Vis meant force—although there was some debate whether it really meant "to force" or "life-force." Depending on the person, the distinction vastly changed how they viewed their magic. Some thought that magic required an action of force to work, something that provided energy, while others thought that it fed off the very energy of life itself.

But magic that needed a corpse? That was new.

"What type of magic are you doing, exactly?" Shepherd asked as Lane turned away, spilling a pile of coins into her palm. They must have been hidden in that utility belt. "I would guess it would be some kind of Tracker magic, but you aren't a Tracker. And I've never heard about any Trackers using a dead body."

Although, Shepherd thought darkly, it wasn't a terrible idea. She'd have to recommend it to McKinley the next time she saw him.

"Maybe you just don't know as much about magic as you thought." Lane tossed the coins from hand to hand, her eyes far away. She pointed across the room. "Can you figure out which one of these is the freshest?"

Shepherd tried not to make a face. If she had known tagging along would mean playing mortician's assistant, she might have sat this one out. She weaved around the tables, holding the sleeve of her shirt up to her nose. Each body had been assigned a number, but there was no indication of date.

She motioned to the table closest to them, the body with the least surgery and most skin. The man's lips were pulling back from his teeth, shriveled and dry.

Lane tied her jacket around her waist as she walked to a nearby sink, exposing olive-smooth skin that led from the straps of her tank top to two delicate tattoos around her wrists. She filled a metal bowl of water before opening the velvet pouch again. She poured a small amount of ash into her hand, like at the store. She dropped the grains into the water, mixing with her fingers as the water swirled. Shepherd told herself that she wasn't interested but found herself leaning in as Lane poured a small amount of the mixture onto the corpse's torso. With two fingers, she drew runic symbols across his chest.

"How does it work, then?" Shepherd asked. "Other than the part where you desecrate a body."

Lane didn't look up. "You're not as funny as you think you are, you know."

"And you're not half as clever, ghost girl." Shepherd placed her hands on the metal table as she arched a brow at Lane. "So, how does it work? Does it pull energy from the body, somehow? Or do you use your own?"

She leaned as close to the body as she dared. The smell stung at her eyes, and she pulled back to see a dark look on Lane's face.

"I told you—this magic doesn't work like that. It doesn't steal energy." Her voice was sharp, resentful. "It uses death itself. It isn't forced or drained. The sacrifice has already been made."

Lane looked at her pointedly, as if she personally went around draining people's energy like some witch-vampire hybrid.

Shepherd tried not to think about how cool that would be as she took two steps away from the table, rubbing at her stinging eyes and getting increasingly irritated.

"But it does have to be closely contained or it can get out of control. So we have these." She pointed to the coins and then to her tattoos. "And these."

"Your tattoos?"

"They aren't tattoos. They're obols."

"Obols. Like the Greek coins?" she asked. She wasn't a complete dumbass, after all, despite what Lane clearly thought.

Lane nodded. "It's hard to explain. They look like tattoos, but they're more like an implant. They go deeper than a tattoo. They're a type of ampere, a magical battery that stores—"

Lane cut herself off and bit her lip, looking down at the corpse again. Whatever she had been about to say, she had clearly decided against it. Which only intrigued Shepherd more. What was Lane hiding exactly?

"Sorry." Shepherd shrugged. "I didn't know there were different types of magic out there. I've always tried to stay away from it. And I didn't exactly get to go to school."

"School?" Lane asked, but Shepherd didn't answer. Lane's expression softened, her green eyes appraising Shepherd in such a way that Shepherd looked away. She glanced down at the swirls and strange symbols on the man's blue skin.

"Is that Cyrillic?" Shepherd asked, changing the subject.

"The Theban alphabet," Lane finally said. "Non-Phoenician alphabets work best. Anything symbol-based is best, like Runic or

Egyptian. Greek, Cyrillic, even Mandarin would work. I've never tried English, although that would certainly make things easier. . ."

Shepherd's head buzzed with the hum of the fluorescent lights, and the formaldehyde was starting to give her a headache. "So, you'll use the energy in your obols to find the man in the photo?"

Lane shrugged as she finished a symbol. She wiped her dirty fingers across her black jeans, leaving the fabric stained with dust and water. "More or less, actually."

Shepherd smirked. "That sounds like Tracker magic."

"It's not."

"You're using magic to follow something, to find it. The only difference is that your energy source is contained in some kind of battery."

Lane reached into her pocket, her hand cupped over it so that Shepherd could not see, before placing something on the table with a quick, clearly unapologetic glance at Shepherd.

It was Addie's key. Frantically, Shepherd tapped her pockets and around her neck. She hadn't even noticed she had taken it.

"How did you—"

Lane only smirked, ignoring the question. "What I do is much safer. "What I do is much safer, more easily contained, and rarely results in anyone's death."

"Because everyone is already dead."

Lane stared, dark green eyes glinting. Then, she snorted.

She turned away to gather her coins from the side of the table, cupping them in her hand. They were different in shape and color, some rusted red, others shining silver, and none were any currency she recognized. Whatever the value was, it wasn't in the metal.

"Where did you learn all this?" Shepherd asked. She wondered if she was just trying to distract herself from the stomach-curdling chemicals with the question, but she knew that wasn't it.

Lane was a mystery she wanted to solve.

"Someone taught me."

Shepherd saw Lane's half-smile. She was teasing her. Fine. That was fine. It was certainly an improvement from disinterested annoyance.

What did she know about Lane, anyway? She was hiding something, always obviously avoiding where she was from and what kind of witch she was. She was beautiful, with dark hair, olive skin, and green eyes like wintergreens. She definitely did not like Shepherd, and it seemed like she had something against magic despite being a witch, which was something they had in common, at least. She was unusual and intriguing, but Shepherd couldn't put her finger on why.

Like a car crash, she couldn't look away from her.

Lane reached for the body and then paused and then reached for it again, as if she was unsure whether she wanted to move forward.

Or that she was unsure how, Shepherd realized.

"Have you done this before?" she dared to ask. Her chest fluttered, waiting for Lane's biting remark.

Lane reached up, tying her hair as she raised her eyebrows. "Have you?"

That was a no then.

Something glinted in Lane's eye as she swung around, stomping across the black linoleum. She opened cabinets and peeked behind shelves, a black mark in the white of the classroom. She made a small, excited noise when she found what she was looking for, before scurrying back across the room.

A blade glinted in her hand. It was sizable for a scalpel, and scarily sharp. Shepherd took a step backwards as Lane flipped it between her hands.

Before Shepherd could ask what she was going to do with it, Lane sliced the blade across her palm. She didn't so much as flinch as she placed the blade down next to the cadaver. She held her hands out over the corpse, letting the blood collect in the lines of her palm.

"Okay," Lane announced. "I'm ready."

"Are you sure? You don't seem sure." Shepherd glanced from the red blood to Lane's face as bile filled her throat. For a black market dealer, she had a surprisingly weak stomach.

"Yes, I'm sure," Lane said. "Now, should we hurry up before someone realizes you've broken in and desecrated this body, as you put it?"

She'd almost forgotten about the threat of security guards. Perhaps it was the dead bodies and the blood, but a part of her felt like she'd left the world of non-magical threats behind.

"All right, let's get this over with," Shepherd said. She wasn't sure what came after slicing your own hand, but she was about to find out.

Lane squeezed the palm of her hand. A droplet formed, the size of a pearl, running down the side of her hand. Like a raindrop, the surface broke and the blood fell onto the man's chest. Lane held several of the coins in her other hand and held both her arms over the body like she was praying. The blood continued to drip, splattering across the dusty symbols and collecting in the hollow of his rib cage.

After several minutes, she said, "Something should have happened by now, I think."

Shepherd needed this to work. She needed to find the man in the photo. And she knew Lane needed this too, although she hadn't shared why.

"Well, try not to blow us up, whatever you do. I don't want to end up like our poor friend here." Shepherd patted the man's calf and then regretted it almost immediately. The cadaver's flesh was cold and surprisingly dry. "Fred, we barely knew ye."

Lane didn't laugh. A heavy sigh whistled between her teeth. The blood on her fingers seemed to be drying and her hand was shaking slightly—from pain or frustration, she couldn't tell.

Lane closed her eyes.

"Should we try something else. . ." Shepherd's throat dried out as the air around them grew hot. It crackled. Lane's tattoos began to glow.

The tattoos emitted a soft orange light, like the warm glow of candles. Her mouth went slack as she watched it grow stronger. Lane's eyes were still closed, but a victorious smile twitched at the corners of her mouth.

"Is that supposed to happen?" Shepherd asked.

"Whatever works," Lane said under her breath.

The blood on the body's chest began to move, slithering across the corpse's pale flesh like a worm. It rolled toward the symbols, turning them red as the blood touched and filled each letter until there was no blood left.

Shepherd's breath hitched in her throat. The ice-cold room grew hotter, and beads of sweat formed on her forehead. She worried, somewhere in the back of her mind, that Lane would burn herself with the warm light coming from somewhere within her—but the thought was fleeting as she watched Lane stand meditatively still, a priestess guiding an ancient ceremony.

There was a flash of black. It exploded outward like a wave, crashing away from them, and then it was sucked back before exploding again. It was an orb of darkness, ebbing and flowing around them before rushing in a dark bolt of lightning toward the corpse.

Lane opened her eyes, blinking. She hadn't seen it, the dark orb, the light, the glow. Shepherd's jaw hung loose, her muscles aching from how tightly she had been clenching.

A shadow floated up out of the man's body. It sat straight up, a black fog in the outline of a person. It was like the shade when it had revealed its human outline, but more translucent, an actual shadow cast upon the wall. It sat up and pulled itself free of the body, suspended in the air.

Shepherd swallowed hard and forced herself not to run away.

The thing stood in front of Lane, cocking its head to one side. Shepherd looked at the outline of the body and back to the man and realized their features were the same. It wasn't quite what she expected a ghost to look like.

"This is what you meant to happen, right?" Shepherd asked, but Lane was already walking toward the thing, holding Addie's photo in front of his face.

"Find him," she ordered.

It vanished.

Handing the photo back to Shepherd without looking, Lane smiled to herself, white teeth flashing brilliantly against the olive of her skin, tiny freckles across her flushed cheeks. She started wiping the body down, erasing any sign that they were ever there.

"Do things always disappear around you?" Shepherd asked.

Lane was still smiling as she raised an eyebrow, as if there was some secret Shepherd was not in on. "He'll be back any minute."

"Was that another shade?" Shepherd asked, walking up next to her.

"No. It's a ghost. A grey, we call them sometimes. It's more like. . . a faded spirit."

"And how exactly is it supposed to help us?"

"You ask a lot of questions for someone who claims to want nothing to do with magic."

"Point taken. It's just . . ." She couldn't find the words. She was used to feeling out of place, but between the shade, Lane's secretive demeanor, and the body, she was starting to wonder if she was out of her depth. "Weird."

Lane reached over her head and untied her hair, letting it fall around her shoulders. It was long enough to cover her collarbone in loose, black curls, hiding the base of her throat for just a moment before she reached up and retied it. She was stunning but mostly terrifying.

"There's nothing weird about death," Lane said, shooting that same fiery look. "What's weird is the witches using magic that takes more than it gives."

The grey floated up through the floor. Shepherd, surprised, stumbled backwards, catching herself on the table.

"Shepherd, meet Fred." Lane waved.

It rotated its head in eerie slowness, raising the hairs on Shepherd's neck, until its gaze landed on Lane. It raised its arms slowly, as if it was dragging them through deep water.

It motioned for them to follow.

CHAPTER ELEVEN

The grey disappeared in and out of sight as he moved from shadow to shadow, a whisper on the breeze. Lane hurried as he vanished into the dark umbrella of a building and then reappeared on the other side of the empty sidewalk. It was the middle of the night, and any pedestrian they came across didn't notice the dark figure, or the clip in Lane's step.

Shepherd trailed behind her. Lane knew there was more to her story—something she wasn't saying. A witch born without magic, one that could see ghosts? That could see *her?* For all she knew, Shepherd was playing dumb about the key, waiting for the moment to trap her.

Lane herself was layering on lie after lie. Whether or not she wanted to reveal the truth about who she was didn't matter—she couldn't trust Shepherd.

She paused, waiting for the grey to reveal itself. Shepherd stumbled into her, hitting Lane between the shoulder blades. Both of them mumbled awkward apologies.

"So, can you control all ghosts with your magic? Tell them what you want, and they do it?"

Lane snorted as the grey appeared on a street corner, hiding in the shadow of a stop sign. She could barely make out his arms and legs.

"No, of course not," Lane said. "And even if I could, the spirit might not listen. They have their own motivations."

Shepherd smirked, her teeth glinting like a wolf's. "You know what it sounds like? Tracker magic."

Lane flashed her best imitation of Perry's *you-are-so-annoying, don't-push-me* look.

Lane was still grappling with the new knowledge that witches each had a specialty. A skill, Shepherd called it. At The Academy, they'd only ever been taught about witches as a monolith, who drained, stole, and even killed others for their magic. Vis and Nil were opposites. Vis required the energy of something, or someone, to work. Witches drained victims to fuel their magic, or themselves. Nil was fueled by itself alone, by the ever-moving cycle of life and death.

"It's not."

"But you still won't tell me how it's different?"

Shepherd looked down at her, the streetlights illuminating her black hair in a golden halo. Her brown eyes were nearly black in the darkness, but there were tiny flecks there, like stars in a sea of night. Looking at her sent a strange thrill down Lane's spine, and she looked away.

She refocused her attention on the grey as he disappeared into a woman's shadow, piggybacking as the woman waddled down the sidewalk. Lane grabbed Shepherd's sleeve and followed.

The spirit started to shift, reappearing and disappearing in shadows quicker now, like a flickering candle. Lane tightened her grip on Shepherd's wrist as she broke into a run, chasing the grey as he disappeared from one shadow to another, between car doors and apartment windows. Sweat formed on her brow as she bolted after him, and Shepherd's fingers found her own, tightening around her palm.

The grey disappeared. Lane stopped, cursing.

"I think you've got magic all wrong," Shepherd said as Lane searched the street. Where their fingers touched, Lane's skin was warm against the chill air. "It doesn't have to be taking or stealing. I've always thought of it like a circle. What goes around, comes around."

"Or you could not take anything at all," she said. She knew that wasn't how it worked. The witches couldn't use death magic. They hadn't made the sacrifice. Not yet. And when most of them did eventually die, they would never be chosen for The Academy. "But you're the expert."

Lane turned just in time to see the grey disappearing around the corner.

They caught up with him as he stopped and disappeared into the shadow of an abandoned building. Shepherd dropped her hand, out of breath.

"Go on, ask me," she panted. Lane tilted her head, questioning. "I know you want to. I'm an open book."

Shepherd stood up, shoving her hands into her pants pockets with a rolling shrug.

Lane felt her face tighten. There were plenty of things she wanted to ask. About magic, about witches. She just didn't know how to ask it without revealing she wasn't one herself, and that her magic was not witch-like at all.

"Your family are Trackers?" Lane asked, finally.

"No, not Trackers. My mom comes from a long line of Healers. My dad . . . well, a little more complicated."

Lane arched her brow. So she *was* hiding something. Or at least didn't want to get into it with a stranger. Lane could understand that. She couldn't imagine explaining her complicated relationship with Victor to anyone.

"And you're the only one that doesn't have magic?" *A long line*, she had said. How many witches were there? Headmistress Eurydice had always made it sound like witches were rare.

"I have other talents." Shepherd smirked, running her fingers through her straw-like hair.

Lane rolled her eyes. Out of the corner of her eye, she saw the grey stop.

He was standing in the middle of the sidewalk, alone and hidden in the darkness of the street. His bleary edges blended in with the shadows of the night, dark outline barely visible beneath the illuminating streetlamps. Slowly, he lifted a wispy hand and pointed.

"I guess it worked." Shepherd whistled.

They stood in front of a Victorian-style brownstone, the bricks painted black and the trim painted a faded gray. It seemed abandoned, the windows blacked out with spray paint and wooden boards. The front door took up most of the front of the house, almost castle-like. It was a dark, red wood, looming before them at almost ten feet tall.

The house was beautiful and eerie, with a haunting familiarity. The hairs on her neck stood on end.

Magic.

"Here?" Lane asked.

He nodded. A moment passed, and another. She looked back and forth from his empty expression to Shepherd, trying not to feel unnerved as he continued to stare into her. She could almost feel the pressure of his cold stare, even though he didn't have eyes.

With a jump, she realized he was waiting for her to set him free.

"Oh, sorry. Thank you for your help, you can go back now."

She hoped that would do it.

A sigh drifted on the air, and before she could look back at the phantom, he was gone.

Shepherd bobbed her head. "I'm impressed. It just disappeared. No bibbidi-bobbidi boo at all."

"Am I supposed to know what that is?"

Shepherd laughed. "Bibbidi-bobbidi-boo? Are you kidding? Have you never seen *Cinderella*?" Still laughing, Shepherd walked up the front steps. "What do you think we should say when he answers the door? 'Excuse me, do you know where my sister is?' 'Did you send a shadow monster to kill me?'"

To be honest, she hadn't thought that far ahead.

"We'll play it by ear." Lane climbed the porch, grazing the black metal handrail. The large, double door was oversized, with arabesque loops of metal. In the dead center of the door sat an ornate, brass knocker. It was similar to the one on the door of The Academy, but where their knocker was a ring through an animal's mouth, this

108

knocker was a collection of ornately intertwined carvings of vines, flowers, and ivy.

"Well, go ahead. Knock."

"Really? We're just going to knock?" Shepherd asked.

"What's the worst that could happen?"

"He could send another shade after us. He'll know we're here and he could run. He could open the door."

"Ugh, you sound just like Victor." Lane groaned. "Fine, go try to look through a window or something. I'll walk the perimeter around the house and see if there are any wards."

Shepherd started to protest, but she must have seen the look on her face. "Fine, have it your way. But I'm going to haunt your ass if we both die."

Lane laughed. She really had no idea. "Unlikely."

She watched as Shepherd lumbered down the stone steps, her hands outstretched on the back of her head. She took a deep breath before shoving her body into the bushes, struggling against branches to get to the window. Lane tried not to laugh as she heard Shepherd maneuvering through the thorns and brambles.

She couldn't imagine what Tripp or Victor would say, seeing her laugh at a witch. Every second she spent with Shepherd and not finding the witch who killed Perry made her look guiltier and guiltier.

Shaking her head, she turned to round the house in the opposite direction.

There was only a thin space between the rowhouses, too small for even two people to stand side by side. The ground was entirely concrete, with weeds and patches of grass bursting through cracks, as if someone had planted a garden between the houses once upon a time before promptly deeming it too much work. She reached into her pocket and pulled out a small ampere coin, engraved with a woman's face. Holding it in her palm, she reached out for the stone wall of the house, searching for any source of magic.

She could feel eyes staring into the back of her head, like the wicks of two burning candles. Chills ran across her arms in goosebumps. She held her breath in her chest, listening.

There was no one there. No sound at all.

She spun on her heel, her boot squeaking against the concrete. "Lane."

Victor stood before her in the alley, his arms crossed and fighting the smile at the edges of his mouth. His hair gleamed in the light of the night sky, shining dark brown and gold.

She rushed toward him. "How are you here?"

Hades, it was good to see him. She pushed down the thoughts of his betrayal. He had saved her, after all.

He smiled as she reached for him, but her hand went right through him.

Confusion wrinkled her face. She passed her hand through him again. There was nothing but air.

His lips curved in a half-hearted smile.

"Sorry about that—astral projection," he said. "I would have come in person, but. . . no one can go in or out right now. Eurydice has the school locked down."

She crossed her arms. "Of course she does."

He reached toward her, even though they both knew his hand would pass right through. He placed his palm near her cheek, hovering. She felt nothing, no warmth, no pressure. It was like being touched by the faded ghosts of the woods—less than that.

"I didn't know you could project yourself."

He rolled his shoulders, cracking his neck. "I've never had to before. I had to. . . do some extra favors for Eurydice to get the extra amperes."

His voice trailed off. Whatever he had done, she knew better than to ask. Something always changed in his expression when he spoke of Eurydice, like someone was walking over his grave.

"What are you doing here?" Crisp wind blew through her hair in the small alley. "Are you. . . following me?"

She wasn't sure how to feel about it. On one hand, he could easily reveal where she was to Eurydice, even accidentally. But on the other hand, she was so happy to see him.

He smirked at her, his tongue running across the bottom of his teeth. "Oh, besides making sure you're okay? I needed to make sure you didn't get yourself killed—again."

"I'm fine." She took a step away from him, leaning against the rowhouse wall.

"So, where are you? What are you going to do?"

"I don't need any more of your help, Victor."

Victor looked down at the ground. "I'm sorry, Lane. I didn't know that Eurydice—The Academy—would blame you. It was a mistake. I thought that the truth would help them find whatever happened to Perry." He looked up at her from beneath his dark brows. "I was wrong."

Lane pursed her lips, leaning toward the Victor that was not really there. "It's not like you to admit you're wrong."

He smiled. "Am I really so terrible?"

Lane laughed. "Oh, in every way."

A part of her wanted to stay angry with him, but she knew it wasn't really his fault. They were both beholden to The Academy and what it asked of them. Eurydice held their lives on a string—literally.

"I went looking for the witches," Lane finally said. Victor's face flashed with alarm. "They have to be behind this. And I found another shade. But this one was somehow in control. Not like Perry, or any of the actual shades we've seen. He could speak, and he was angry."

Victor pushed his glasses up his nose, his face pinched with worry.

She exhaled. "I think someone is doing something to them."

"Where was this shade?" Victor asked. "And promise me you're being careful."

She nodded absently as her mind ticked through the possibilities. She didn't answer his question, distracted. "What I don't understand is why. Why would someone murder Perry? And these other two men. Why would someone do that?"

"Maybe they were targeting The Academy, and Perry was the first student they saw. She did die right after your mission." Victor closed his eyes, thinking. "Or maybe it's a coincidence. Random. Maybe she was collateral damage."

"I just wish I had something, anything, to go on."

He reached his hand out tentatively, but dropped it back, as if remembering he couldn't touch her.

"I'm doing everything I can to look into it," he said, clearing his throat. "Speaking of which, I didn't have much time, but I looked into your past like we talked about. I don't want to get your hopes up, but. . ."

A buzz ran through her. "What? What is it?"

Her heart thumped in her neck, her fingers tingling in excitement.

She hadn't actually thought he would look into it at all. She didn't want to know what he had done to find it.

"It seems like you might have a brother." He looked down at her. "That's as far as I've gotten. He could be dead or alive, and I haven't found much else. It's hard, without your true name."

She started to ask him more questions, her mind racing, but a whistle traveled in the air as Shepherd turned the corner.

"Someone's coming," she hissed, shoving him away. Her hands fell through his chest.

Victor couldn't know about Shepherd, that she was working with a witch. It would only make things worse. But somehow, she was more worried about Shepherd seeing Victor.

He gave her a quick smile before disappearing, only a small zap of static electricity in the air to show he had been there at all.

"Lane?" Shepherd called as she stepped into the alley. "Find anything?"

Lane wiped at her face, hoping Shepherd couldn't see the color in her cheeks. She shrugged, trying to look apathetic and unbothered.

"Nothing through the windows, either." Shepherd shoved her hands into her pockets, tilting back and forth on her heels. "Should we just try knocking?"

Lane glanced over her shoulder. Invisible lines of magic streaked the air where Victor had stood. Shepherd said something, but she barely heard.

A brother.

Her mind raced with the possibilities. She imagined them being close, thicker than thieves. She imagined him with the same dark hair as her, the same dark skin. She imagined they both looked like their parents.

She hoped they were all alive. With everything that had happened, she'd almost forgotten the blank spots and the strange dreams that filled them.

"Lane? Are you okay?" Shepherd waved her hand in front of Lane's face, as if trying to wake her from a trance. She swatted at it, pushing past her and back toward the house. Shepherd grinned. "What now? I could try to pick the lock again. Or we could break a window—"

Trying to focus, Lane reached up to let her hair down and retied it, then let it down again, retying it, then once more, hoping to clear her mind.

"Do you hear that?" Shepherd asked. Lane shook her head and turned. Shepherd's ear was tilted toward the street as if straining to hear something. "I swear I just heard—"

A wolf's howl echoed off the buildings, guttural and screeching like an animal thirsting for blood.

Lane's eyes went wide.

Another howl echoed in the distance, and Shepherd reached for her arm.

"Look, I know you're not from here—but that *is not* normal." Shepherd didn't have to tell her that. Lane knew exactly what it was. She yanked Shepherd by the wrist toward the street, keeping one arm across Shepherd's chest so that the girl was safely behind her.

Another roar broke through the quiet of the approaching dawn.

She looked to the top of the hill and saw it bounding toward them, claws not even hitting the ground as it stormed down the street. White eyes glowed against the darkness of its black fur.

"That's not a regular wolf?" Shepherd asked, not really a question.

"No, it's not," Lane said. "It's a hellhound."

Four rows of jagged teeth jutted from its mouth in every direction, dripping saliva into its fur. Its hair glistened with wetness. Blood.

"Run."

Their fingers locked as they ran back toward the house. The hellhound launched itself toward them, leaping through the air. Lane pushed herself to go faster, her muscles screaming. Her feet flew up the stairs, Shepherd barely holding on as Lane yanked her toward the door.

"Open it!"

"How?" Shepherd shouted back. Both of them were screaming in panic. The sound of the jackal's growl grew closer. "I can't pick a lock under this kind of pressure!"

"Figure it out."

Lane shoved Shepherd toward the door as she pulled a handful of amperes from her pocket.

She just needed to buy enough time.

The hellhound stopped at the bottom of the steps, gnashing its teeth as spit dripped from its mouth to the sidewalk.

"I don't want to hurt you," she said. She'd spent enough time around Eurydice's pet hellhounds to know they weren't animals, not really. It still bothered her.

The hellhound's shoulders were almost as broad as Lane was tall, veiny with muscle under its matte, black skin. It twitched its ears and bared its teeth at her, its gums gray like ash.

The beast hurled itself at her and she tucked into a roll, hitting it in the stomach as it leapt over her. With a growl, it turned, skidding on its claws and completely ignoring Shepherd, who was banging her shoulder into the door, her hand twisting manically at the doorknob.

Lane backed down the steps as the hound lunged for her again. Its teeth snapped as she jumped out of the way, rolling across the concrete. Its claws grazed her leg as she slid underneath it, her pants ripping.

"The door isn't opening!"

"I'm a little busy!" Lane shot back.

The jackal threw its entire body at Lane, claws digging into her skin. It sliced through her shirt like it was water. Searing heat traveled across her skin as it tore into the soft flesh of her stomach. Fur filled her mouth as it trapped her, grabbing her between its front paws and throwing her skull into the stone steps. She cried out, her vision blurring.

She could only see its snapping teeth as the world around her spun. Spit and blood filled her eyes. The hellhound was torn away from her. A row of teeth scratched across her cheek as she broke free.

Lane scurried to her feet. Shepherd grabbed her, standing between Lane and the beast. She had pulled it off of her.

"Are you insane?" she screamed at Shepherd.

"The door!" Shepherd yelled back as she raised her fists. The hellhound growled at her, spit flying.

Lane turned around. The door was still locked.

The beast lunged for Shepherd, leaping over the steps and jumping into the air. It was going to crush her. Without thinking, Lane grabbed her by the wrist, pulling Shepherd into her chest and wrapping an arm around her waist.

Please work, she thought.

In the fraction of the second as the hound leaped for them, Lane reached into her pocket and grabbed the shard of bone. She imagined them on the other side of the door, safe. She begged whatever power was in the strange object to save her again.

Holding Shepherd closely, she threw their bodies backward into the door. She expected a hard smack, a crack as her skull hit the wood, but instead—

They went right through it and into pure darkness on the other side.

The inside of the house was a void, as if she was looking down into space itself.

The hound's howls were muffled, sounding further and further away, and suddenly they were falling through the dark, speeding through the blackness toward some sort of invisible crash.

She was still clutching Shepherd's shirt when they hit the ground. Their landing was too soft, too cushioned. The door was gone, no splinters covering the ground around them. Her cheek pressed against the cool dew of grass.

They were outside.

"I am so sick of falling."

Beside her, Shepherd was flat on her back, eyes wide as she stared up at the piercing blue sky, the sun shining down in soothing rays.

"Where are we?" she asked.

They sat on a great lawn, fields of grass and woods surrounding them. Birds chirped, and she swore she heard laughter. At the end of the grass, underneath the orange ball of sun, sat a large, sprawling mansion.

"I have no idea."

Lane turned, scrambling to a kneeling squat as she sensed someone staring at them.

Behind them stood a red-haired woman, her skin the color of earthen pottery. To her left stood a man in a knee-length, emerald green coat. He was oddly familiar.

"Pip!" the woman called out, over her shoulder. "Someone broke through the protection ward. We're going to need a new door."

The man and woman stepped toward them, the woman crossing her arms as she stared down at them. Behind them, two more people approached, their dark forms blurry as salt and pepper clouded her vision.

Lane's ears rang. Her vision tunneled. She thought Shepherd might have said something—to her or to their growing audience, she wasn't sure. She couldn't take her eyes off the man in the emerald coat, even as her vision spotted. He looked back at her with a devilish grin.

His eyes were completely white. Her vision blacked as she tried to stand up.

"Hello, little Blinker."

"Deryck?" she asked.

Her vision blotted to nothing as she fainted.

CHAPTER TWELVE

Lane jolted awake, her body aching as she tried to sit up in the unfamiliar bed. Silky soft sheets were against her skin, and the soft mattress beckoned her to lay back down. But she pushed herself to her elbows, scanning the room. It was a small space barely big enough for the mattress and small frame, like a boarding school dormitory. The small table to her right held a basin full of water and bloody bandages as well as a plate of cold food.

Deryck and Shepherd sat in wooden chairs against the wall, staring at her. Both crossed their arms in tense silence.

Deryck. It was him, but it also wasn't. The same white eyes, but his hair was smooth, shoulder-length and brown. The Deryck she knew had dry blond hair that stood up like lake reeds. At The

Academy, he always looked like he was tired, thin. But this man was all round, freckled cheeks. He'd taken on a new form, a different body.

"How are you here?" Her throat was dry, her words sticking in her throat like the jagged edges of razor blades. She coughed twice, a sharp pain traveling up her rib cage where the hellhound had attacked her. "Why?"

The Academy was extremely selective about its students and their missions. They would never let a demon leave After Life.

"I suppose I'd ask you the same thing, Blinker." His sharp teeth glinted in the light as he smiled.

Avoiding the question, she sat up, pulling her knees to her chest. She glanced at Shepherd. Her hands were shoved tightly in her pockets, her shoulders tight around her ears. The veins in her thin, muscular arms seemed to pop with stress.

"What happened?" She coughed. Shepherd leaned toward the table, grabbing a glass of water and handing it to her. She gulped it down greedily, coating her sandpapered throat.

"You've been out for almost an entire day," Shepherd said. "Must have been some nap."

"A whole day?" Her spine straightened in surprise, sending another tearing pain through her abdomen. She should have healed by now. . . although she had been away from After Life for longer than she'd ever been.

She looked again to the basin of bloody water. Her stomach dropped.

"It's very impressive, really, that you came out so unscathed." Deryck leaned back in his chair, propping his feet up on the bed. "It seems that you portaled into the portal that hid this place, breaking through all the wards at once. It must have taken an exhaustive amount of magic. And attacked by a hellhound?"

She wasn't even supposed to be able to Blink alone, let alone through some sort of hidden portal. The shard of bone—and the keys—had some sort of hidden magic in them that was helping her do this. But what was it?

She looked down at her waist, tentatively lifting up her shirt to reveal a clean bandage covering her ribs. There was no more blood, but the soreness told her she was not healing.

Just like Perry.

"I patched you up, if you're worried." Deryck smiled. She wanted to glare at him, knowing what he was implying. Only the two of them could know what she was.

"Young Shepherd and I have become best friends." Deryck continued, pointing his chin at Shepherd who sank deeper into her chair. "Though she isn't very talkative. At least, not at first."

"We aren't friends," Shepherd snapped.

Lane raised her eyebrows. Shepherd, not talkative? She glanced at Deryck, then back to Shepherd, her mouth twisted to the side.

"Yes, once she realized we knew each other, and that I had even been to your *isolated Necromancer colony,* we had plenty to talk about."

The corners of Deryck's mouth tilted upwards in a smirk.

"And I learned that you're *friends* with demons," Shepherd interrupted, her tone accusing. She glared at Deryck, darkness in her brown eyes.

"You told her that you're a demon?" Lane asked before breaking into a coughing fit.

Deryck crossed his legs and placed his pale hands behind his head. It was odd to see him in a different body—brown, silken hair— but every expression, every taunting smirk was unmistakably Deryck.

"Oh no, Shep worked that out for herself. So clever. You should keep her. Or I might take her for myself." Deryck winked at Shepherd. "Although I don't usually prefer women."

Lane rolled her eyes. Shepherd shrunk away from Deryck, crossing her arms protectively over her chest.

"Tell me he's joking," she said to Lane.

Lane shrugged.

"Other than that, she's been silent. The people in charge are quite frustrated."

Lane shot Shepherd a questioning look, her forehead wrinkling as she coughed again.

Shepherd only shrugged.

Lane smiled. She'd underestimated Shepherd, she realized. If Lane had been awake, she would have told Shepherd to keep her mouth shut about what they were doing and who they were until they knew who these people were. It seemed Shepherd didn't need that warning.

Deryck interrupted her train of thought. "So, now that we have come full circle, care to tell me why you are here?" He seemed on edge, and Lane was surprised.

"Why are we here? Why are you here?" Lane angled her body toward him on the bed. She was glad that they had left her clothes on as she kicked out her legs, forcing herself out from under the warm sheets. Her pants stuck to her skin, caked in blood. "And where are we?"

His blank eyes rolled as he leaned back against the wall.

Lane glanced between Shepherd and Deryck, raising her eyebrow as silence filled the room.

Shepherd stood up with a sigh and motioned around her. "Welcome to Haven Hall," she said. "The most elite and elitist school for magic known to witch. Or what's left of it, anyway."

Haven Hall.

Lane put her hands on her knees, letting a dark curtain of her hair hide her face as she felt herself turn white.

Her blood pulsed with fear. Or maybe excitement. She wasn't sure.

"What's left of it?" she asked, her voice cracking.

Deryck grinned as he sat up, putting his feet back on the floor. They were clad in black leather boots much like Lane's, except his extended up to his knees in rows of buckles. They thwacked against the ground as he stood up. He tucked his hands behind his back and turned away from her, looking toward the door, as if he were staring out a window only he could see.

"The walls are still standing, but the school is barely running. It's mostly a safe house for witches and magical creatures now. Anyone and everyone on Earth who is being hunted."

"Hunted?" Lane pulled back her chin in surprise.

He responded with a curt nod. He was not supposed to be sharing this information with them, she realized.

She shook her head. "But the witches, they're. . ." She stopped herself as Shepherd smirked.

"Dangerous?" she asked.

"Well, yes." Lane placed her hands in her lap. "Everyone knows that magic is dangerous."

"You know less than you think," Deryck said.

Lane hissed at him.

"Addie was invited to go to school here and decided not to. . . probably because of me," Shepherd paused, as if this was a new realization. "But we had no idea about this safe house, or that witches are being hunted. If my family isn't safe, I need to know."

Deryck ignored her. Shepherd seemed worried, her brows knitted together and her hands shoved into her pockets. She would feel the same way if it was her family, Lane realized. Hell, she was risking her graduation to find Perry's murderer. She wanted to reach for Shepherd's hand and squeeze it, to comfort her. But none of it made sense. The witches couldn't be in danger.

"Shepherd, can you give us a minute?" Lane asked, hoping she wouldn't argue.

Shepherd seemed too lost in her own thoughts to protest, and she pushed her chair back angrily before stalking into the hall, slamming the door behind her.

"Well, someone's cranky," Deryck said.

"What is going on here?" She threw her legs over the side of the bed, standing up. "The truth, this time. Everyone knows the witches are dangerous."

"What is it they say? History is written by the victors."

She took a step back, leaning against the nightstand for support. A sharp pain traveled through her ribs, peppering her vision with stars.

What was he trying to say?

"Don't be ridiculous," Lane said. "I know how magic works. Their magic drains them if they don't choose to drain someone else's energy instead. They're either a danger to others or a danger to themselves."

Deryck just shrugged, as if to say, *Have it your way.*

Lane growled. "Fine. Let's assume you're telling the truth and they aren't dangerous. Who is hunting them in this fantasy world of yours? Other witches?"

He still hadn't explained why he was there. It was all too convenient. Too strange.

He had been there, she realized, when Perry was murdered, turned to a shade. The muscles in her neck tensed.

Deryck sighed. "It's probably easier if I just show you."

Lane groaned as Deryck turned on his ankle to leave the room.

He swung open the door, and Lane struggled to follow him into the hallway, the pain in her side forcing her to limp. His long jacket and skirt swung around his knees as he swaggered up to Shepherd, who stood at the top of a spiraling staircase. Lane held the wall for balance. Every exhale threatened to knock her over.

"Keep your heads down," Deryck said as she finally reached them. Shepherd ran her hands through her spiky hair. "They're going to look for you now that you're awake."

"Who?"

"You'll see," Shepherd said. She had been here an entire day while Lane was unconscious. What did she know?

Deryck smirked as he sauntered down the stairs.

They walked slowly through the dark passageway, lit only by frosted glass sconces on navy blue wallpaper. Up close, she realized the walls were covered in thin lines of stars, barely perceptible in the dark. She ran her fingers across it, surprised to find that the wallpaper was a soft, textured velvet.

There were muffled voices behind every door like the beating of hidden hearts, drumming out of tune with her own. On a landing, they passed the open door of an abandoned classroom. The desks were pushed to the sides, the floor covered in blankets and cots.

Lane struggled to follow Deryck down the stairs, the dark, ebony steps creaking beneath their feet as she grasped her aching abdomen.

A man spoke to another in hurried tones in an alcove. One of them was a witch, but the other had skin like bark. Lane tried to stop and stare, but Deryck disappeared around another corner. Shepherd placed a hand on Lane's arm and helped her down the steps.

At the bottom, the stairs opened into a large room with high, cavernous ceilings strung with chandeliers. It was the kind of room that could have fit the dining table of a king.

The long, rectangular room was empty of all furniture. A mass of candles lay strewn across the floor, collected in clumps of differing heights, their once-white wicks melting wax onto the dark oak floors. Flower petals crushed under her feet, some still fresh, red and pink edges bright with life.

"Here." Deryck's voice held a somber tone that Lane did not recognize. He motioned toward the far wall. Shepherd inhaled a breath like a hissing candle.

The entire wall was covered in photos. Some were aged and torn, others were freshly placed and pinned as if they were from that very morning. A young woman smiled, black and white, her hair flowing in the wind. There was a hand-drawn photo of what looked like a pixie with green wings in mid-flight. In another photo, a man looked solemnly over a bottle-covered bar, his eyes hovering just above where the camera would have been. There were creatures she recognized and ones she didn't, and one where a mermaid-looking woman hugged two human children, her body half-submerged in a glassy pool, her hair made of reeds.

But mostly, there were pictures of witches.

On the floor, there were small shrines, the collections of candles surrounded by well-loved objects left behind—a locket, a handmade doll. Prayers and notes were written on bits of paper in languages she couldn't read. A child's slanted, crayon-drawn writing read, "I miss you."

Something inside her cracked.

"What is this?" Shepherd asked, over her shoulder. Her voice was suddenly hollow, as if something inside her had fallen and she couldn't pull it back to the surface.

Deryck leaned against the opposite wall, one foot on the ground and the other kicked up to his side, knees exposed under his skirt.

"There is a reason there are so few witches today." His face was hidden as he picked at his nails. "There are people who will do anything to get rid of them."

Lane stared at the wall.

"That can't be," Shepherd said. "I know the Night Market has lost vendors. Things have closed down, but witches can't just be disappearing. There can't be some secret war that I don't even know about. It's not possible."

"Perhaps your family wanted to protect you from it, since it was unlikely anyone would be coming for you."

Shepherd's face fell. Lane wanted to say something to comfort her. . . but what? They weren't friends, not really. Lane had no right to be the person to comfort her, and she tried to ignore the feeling that she desperately wanted to be.

Lane swept a hand across the photos, too many of them for her to count. Thousands of eyes stared back at her. So many people. So many faces. "Who could be behind this?"

But she already knew.

The witches were the most powerful magic users on Earth. More powerful than any other magical creature, more dangerous than humans. There was no one that would dare take them on. No one alive.

But dead?

The Magistrate Academy had taught her that the witches were dangerous, that Haven Hall was their rival in every way, ready to destroy them and capture Nil for their own use. She had been told that the witches wanted to conquer death, master its power and avoid their own mortality.

But could it be the other way around?

Her hands trembled as she crossed her arms over her chest, as if she might hold in the pieces before she fell apart.

"They would never do something like that," she tried to reason. "They won't even come on missions. They don't. They can't."

"They can't. They don't. They won't," Deryck mocked. "But they can, can't they? We're both here, after all. Their borders aren't as secure as they pretend."

Lane shook her head, her hair falling out of its bun and around her face.

"Why? Why would they do this if you're so sure?" She dropped her hands to her side. Shepherd stood icily still next to her, as if she was frozen beneath the stares of the photographs.

"You haven't seen what I've seen. Done the things that I've done. It's only been a year for you. It's been *hundreds* for me." Deryck paused, pulling Lane to the side and lowering his voice so Shepherd couldn't hear. "She will stop at nothing to stop this imagined threat against The Academy."

Eurydice was honest about that, at least.

"So what is your part in all this? I know you. I know your game. There isn't enough coin in the world for you to risk yourself in the middle of some war."

"Oh, you couldn't be more right, little Lane. They couldn't pay me enough. You could say I'm a sort of undercover agent." He laughed, his voice a little louder. "Who better to easily blend in? I can change faces whenever I like. I'm quite useful."

Lane looked at his face, so different from the one he wore at The Academy. She had known that his ability as a demon was to move from body to body. She'd just never seen it in action.

Shepherd broke from her trance at Deryck's booming laugh.

"You can wear any face," she said, as if she was reasoning it out, mentally writing it on some chalkboard. "So you go out in the world and find people to bring her. Meet people they want to hide. There's less risk for you—because no one can figure out how to find you." Shepherd took a step toward him, shoulders tensing.

Deryck turned to Lane, his expression all smirk. "I really do like this one. Maybe we replace Victor; he's too condescending."

She rolled her eyes, but next to her, Shepherd's hands balled into fists. She'd stopped listening.

"You're the man in the photo." She turned to Lane. "I didn't show it to him while you were asleep. But it's him, isn't it?"

Shepherd reached into her pocket and pulled out the glossy paper, wrinkled and folded into squares.

Lane didn't even look down at the photo as she grabbed it, shoved it into Deryck's chest. She didn't have to ask. She already knew if the man in the photo had been facing the lens, his eyes would have been white.

"Say it. It's you."

They'd found exactly who they'd come for. And he'd distracted her by telling her some story about the witches, making her feel bad for them. Making her want to help them.

The shades. Perry. Addie. It all led back to him.

Cold, unfeeling anger washed through her. It was the only thing holding her in place as her mind threatened to spin out of control.

Deryck took the photo from her hand. He looked down at himself, wearing yet another man's skin.

"What did you do to her?" Shepherd's voice shook.

She stood eerily still, hands at her sides, her muscles tensed. She didn't look relieved.

"Yes," Deryck said. "I remember this. The man I possessed was very stylish. He was almost too excited to meet me. A movie producer, I think. Sometimes my friends aren't so happy about being possessed and I have to help them forget afterwards. You know how it is."

He shrugged as if they should both know what it was like to possess another person. Shepherd's square jaw was wired shut.

Lane felt her blood heat and rise under her skin.

She pushed forward, shoving both her palms into Deryck's chest. "Where is she?"

Deryck straightened his sleeves, smoothing the fabric.

"Although my services here do occasionally involve looking for those who need help, I did not do so with your sister. She found us."

Shepherd turned to look at Lane, wrinkling her forehead. "Why would she do that?"

Deryck lifted a hand, twirling it as if to brush Shepherd's question from the air.

"This is what I know," Deryck continued. "Your sister was worried that she was too powerful and that she couldn't control it. She'd chosen not to study here, correct?"

Shepherd nodded. Lane motioned for Deryck to get to the point.

"Somehow, she knew that powerful witches were being hunted.

She was afraid they were alerted to her presence by a particularly large-scale bit of magic she did. She wanted protection."

Addie wasn't just afraid, Lane thought. She was afraid of herself.

If Addie wasn't in control of her powers, what was she capable of?

She looked over and saw that Shepherd was as surprised as she was. Her mouth hung open, head tilted to the side. She blinked twice.

"Then what?" Shepherd asked. The candles across the room casted a haunting glow on her sharp cheekbones. "Did you protect her?"

She'd calculated it much faster than Lane. There were only two options: Either Addie had gotten protection, and she was here in this house at this very moment. . .

Or they had gotten her.

Lane looked at the wall of photos.

"No." Deryck's voice was flat, devoid of emotion. "I gave her the key and invited her to join us, and then I never saw her again."

Addie wasn't here. She never had been. They had run in a completely pointless circle.

"What key?" Shepherd asked.

Lane spun toward her, surprised. Of course.

She stepped toward Shepherd, pointing at her pocket. Slowly, Shepherd reached to where Lane knew the key was and had been since Shepherd had stolen it back from her.

Lane held up a hand to wait as Shepherd pulled it from her pocket. Someone was coming toward them. Footsteps tapped across the floor above their heads.

Shepherd moved in closer, her height blocking them from the view of the hall. She smiled at Lane, as if she could sense her thoughts. Their bodies close together, Shepherd held out the chain between them, the chain dangling between her fingers.

Deryck's eyes turned into circles, wide and white as twin moons.

"Where did you get that?" Deryck asked, reaching for it. Shepherd snatched it back, clutching it between her fingers. "Is that—"

Deryck shook his head, running his hands through his hair. "Lane, that's not the key. It's not a key at all—not to any door, anyway." He leaned in, his face haunted and dark as he whispered, "That's a Key of Persephone."

Lane raised her eyebrows at him as Shepherd opened her palm. The strange, toothed bone laid across the lines of her hand. Lane could sense the small, electric hum buzzing through it even though she wasn't touching it.

"Someone is coming," Deryck said.

Shepherd dropped the key into Lane's hand, and she closed her fist tight around it, hiding it as quickly as she could.

Voices and the thundering of footsteps grew closer behind them.

"There you are."

CHAPTER THIRTEEN

Deryck stepped in front of them, his height obscuring Lane as she hurried to shove the key into her pocket. She didn't know what a Key of Persephone was, but she knew the witches couldn't know she had one. It didn't matter if she'd agreed to work with Shepherd, she still didn't trust witches. With or without magic.

"Hello, boys," Deryck said. "Don't you all look the perfect picture of overzealous brutes? We were just coming to find you."

His words dripped with sarcasm as Lane and Shepherd stepped out from behind him. She took in the guards. There were three of them in total, but only one of them was a witch as far as she could tell. She wasn't sure the other two were even human. The first to step forward had skin as black as night, with yellow eyes that seemed to glow in the dimly lit room. The other was covered in bark, small leaves sprouting from his joints.

"You're finally awake," the dark-skinned one said as his eyes landed on her. "She wants to see you in the classroom."

They could see her. Lane looked down at her arms, confused. She had thought Shepherd had some strange power that made Lane visible. But now these men could see her as well? Fear trickled across her skin. It shouldn't have been possible. Was her connection to After Life and the magic that protected her fading?

The other guards moved toward her, and Lane took two steps back.

She'd been grabbed by enough guards this week; she wasn't about to let it happen again.

"And who, exactly, is *she*?" Lane asked, tightening her fists at her side. She felt for the utility belt around her waist, her knife and amperes safely tucked into the fabric. Besides her, Shepherd subtly shook her head.

"We can't fight all three of them," she whispered as she grabbed Lane's wrist. Lane scowled up at her.

"Speak for yourself." There were three of them, and three guards. She liked their odds.

The bark-skinned guard smiled. "Seren. She's the de facto leader of Haven Hall. She was—is—a teacher here." He paused. "And I'm Yarrow. This here is Korvu," he pointed to the dark-skinned man, who took another step toward Lane. "And this is Ewan." He tilted his head toward the salt-and-pepper haired witch. "She just wants to ask you some questions."

So the tree-looking man was the nice one, then. Good cop, bad cop was a game Lane knew all too well.

"Not Headmistress?" Lane asked sarcastically. "You would think a school of such renown would have a headmaster."

Korvu reached for Lane's elbow. Up close, she saw that his skin was not black, but tattooed so closely together that it was no longer possible to see his skin. Interesting. She wondered if it was some sort of ritual, or maybe a spell. If she got the chance after fighting him, she would ask.

"The headmistress died," Korvu said flatly as he grabbed her, digging his dark fingers into her skin. His nails were sharp, biting into her flesh.

"Is this really necessary?" Deryck waved his arms.

Korvu tightened his grip on her. Her fingers twitched at her side, but she saw Shepherd side eyeing her.

"Let's just hear them out," Shepherd said. Her expression was almost pleading. "You can beat them up afterward."

Lane snorted internally. Fine. She could do that. On one level, she knew Shepherd was right. They had come too far to leave without answers, and they wouldn't get any if Lane knocked everyone on their ass. Even if she really wanted to.

"Your friend here has not been very forthcoming while you slept," Korvu nodded toward Shepherd as he grabbed Lane's other arm. "Hopefully you will be."

"And what makes you think I'm going to help you? Between the two of us, Shepherd is clearly the nicer one."

Shepherd rolled her eyes, but Lane caught the edge of a smile at her lips. If only she knew it wasn't exactly a compliment.

Yarrow motioned to Shepherd and Deryck to follow as Korvu pushed Lane out of the room and into the hallway. Only she needed to be restrained, apparently. She'd been unconscious, and they still thought she was the bigger threat.

She could work with that.

They turned past the winding staircase and into an even darker hallway. Crumbled stones kicked up beneath them as they walked, the passage clearly falling apart from disrepair. It opened to another large foyer on the opposite side. Above them, high ceilings opened to the sky through red and gold stained glass. It was patterned like a rising sun, emerging from the darkness of the stone. It was beautiful. She hated it.

Voices in the distance made Lane's ears perk up as Korvu pushed her into another hallway. She tried to listen to the words, but the stone muffled them into mumbles. Korvu stopped in front of a wide door with slash marks in the wood and pushed Lane through the opening with a single, unceremonious shove.

Hushed whispers traveled across the room as Lane stumbled into the class, the others entering behind her. At first glance, it was not unlike the classrooms at The Academy— the same stone, same desks, same four walls. Except for one thing. This room was packed, wall to wall, with witches.

Lane's breath caught in her throat as their eyes turned to her. She'd only met her first living witch that week, and now more than twenty stared her down as if she was a fly on their window. They could all see her, and they were taking in the olive of her skin and the dark waves of her hair. Her hand went instinctively for her knife as Shepherd stepped up next to her, placing her fingers on top of her own. She held Lane's hand tightly, and Lane realized she was holding herself to the ground as much as she was holding Lane back.

Shepherd was scared.

"As I was saying," said a voice from the front of the room. In a single turn, the room forgot Lane and turned their attention back to the woman standing before them.

Shepherd's grip around her hand tightened.

Seren was the most beautiful and ethereal woman Lane had ever seen. She had the heart shaped face of a cherub, but thinned out, as if she'd gone too long without proper food. Her hair was white as spider's silk and tied tightly in a bun, still damp. Seren wore dirty, second-hand cargo pants that hung off her body and a matching military jacket, holes patched across her chest with red thread. She looked more like a rebel than a teacher.

Her eyes traveled the room as she spoke. "There is still so much about magic we don't know. I was a teacher here, and I would have never imagined that we would be here today. Whoever is behind these attacks uses different magic from ours. They don't require an energy charge, so they can attack much faster. Their power doesn't drain them, and it seems that they are almost invisible. So many of us have been taken, so many of us are gone, and no one has seen anything. We had no way to fight back, because we didn't know who we were fighting. Until now."

Seren turned to a broken chalkboard that faced the back of the room. Two witches stepped forward and grabbed it from either side, slowly moving so that the room could see it.

If Lane were alive, her heart would have stopped beating.

The board was covered in a chalk drawing. It was a shade, but it also wasn't, like what Perry had turned into, but worse. Whoever had drawn it had captured the wisps of its form, the billowing movement as it struck forward. Claws burst from the shadows of its body, as if it had been morphed into something even further from human.

"When Ivy was taken. . ." Seren's voice trailed off. Lane's brow furrowed at the sadness that filled her voice. "There was nothing I could do. This thing attacked us, but it wasn't working alone. Whoever took Ivy was controlling this thing. We believe it's some kind of ghost."

The silent room erupted in whispers as the witches turned to one another, shock on their faces. Lane felt frozen in place.

"The history between ghosts and witches is long and full of violence," Seren continued. "We can't ignore what happened in the past, even if it was centuries ago."

There was scattered laughter across the room. Lane felt herself leaning forward, Korvu's grip on her arm digging into the flesh of her bicep. On her other side, Shepherd dropped her hand, her eyes surveying the room. It wasn't just full of witches, Lane realized. There were others there as well. She followed Shepherd's line of sight as it landed on a satyr, hooves barely visible beneath his long pants. A sprite flitted around his head like a lightning bug.

"There are only a few ways to fight off a ghost. I know it's hard, but we have already lost so many—I don't want to lose any of you. First, you must trap the ghost—"

"That's not a ghost," Lane said. She meant for it to be a whisper, but the people directly in front of them had clearly heard. They turned in their seats to look at her. Korvu yanked on her arm, pulling her back toward him as he grabbed her other arm.

Her interruption did not go unnoticed by the room.

"What was that?" Seren asked. She took two steps forward across the front of the classroom.

Her ears rushed with blood.

"That's not a ghost," she croaked out. Hundreds of eyes burned into her like needles in her flesh. "It's a shade." She paused. "Or something worse."

Seren turned to the room, ignoring Lane's words. Beside her, Shepherd whistled beneath her breath, low and worried.

"Thank you, everyone. We will have to reconvene tomorrow at the Council meeting. Please come find me if you have any questions."

Korvu grabbed Lane's other arm, pulling her toward the far wall as the witches began to file out of the room. Lane could see them more clearly as they walked past her, and there were more magical creatures than she had originally thought. The Academy's lessons had included plenty of lessons on the various creatures they could encounter in Life and in Death, but she had never expected to see so many in one place.

The Academy, Victor, and Eurydice had been clear. Witches were dangerous. To use their magic, they went to dangerous and unnatural lengths, draining humans and even other witches until they died. Their magic required it or else they would be powerless. But these witches? They didn't look dangerous at all. Many of them were injured, arms in casts and scratches across their faces. They were all disheveled, their faces in a daze, as if they were only going through the motions of living. Some of them wore no shoes, as if they had run with only the clothes on their back. They had lost something, and it seemed it took everything in them to keep moving forward.

Korvu let go of her as the room cleared. Lane rubbed at the spot on her bicep where a bruise was already beginning to form.

"So you're awake," Seren said. "I was beginning to wonder if you were staying unconscious on purpose."

Lane raised an eyebrow. "That would be quite the trick."

Shepherd shifted uncomfortably.

"Good to see you again, Ms. Silva," Seren said. "We were so disappointed when your sister chose not to attend school here."

Lane's eyes flashed. She bit into her tongue, refusing to look at Shepherd as she shoved her hands into her pockets. Shepherd knew these people? She had been to Haven Hall before and hadn't said anything?

She pushed down her surprise. She knew Shepherd had been hiding something, but she had never imagined it would be this. What else did she know? What else was she hiding? And why would a magicless witch ever go to Haven Hall?

"It's probably a good thing, considering how the place turned out." Shepherd waved her hand at the broken chalkboard and Seren's own destroyed clothes.

"We'd like to ask you both some questions," Seren said, still ignoring their sardonic retorts. If it phased her, she didn't show it. She was a perplexing person. She had an air of propriety but held herself in a slouch that said she had lost touch with that side of herself long ago. "Do you think you could do that for an old friend?"

Shepherd snorted, her nostrils flaring. "That's a very loose interpretation of the word friend. You told me I was worthless and that my family should abandon me to human society because I would never have magic. I don't usually do that to my friends. Do you, Lane?"

Lane tilted her head. Shepherd's face was placid, but Lane could see the hurt behind her words. How old had she been? Twelve, thirteen? She was worthless to them because she had no magic.

Lane narrowed her eyes.

"Some of the students tell me that you portaled through our portal. Very interesting," Seren said as she leaned onto a desk. "Where did you say you're from?"

"I didn't say anything."

"How did you find this place?" Seren asked, looking at both of them. Shepherd crossed her arms, sitting on the corner of a desk. Clearly, she was not in a talkative mood. And in Lane's limited experience, Shepherd was almost always in a talkative mood.

"I get it," Seren said. "You don't want to answer our questions. And I can't make you. But if you want to stay here. . ."

Her voice trailed off. She looked down at the ground, glancing up at Lane from under her thin, pale eyebrows. A knowing smile drew across her moon-like skin.

Lane opened her mouth to retort but stopped herself. She still needed to ask Deryck about the Keys of Persephone. She needed to find the witch who was behind Perry's murder and the shades. Shepherd needed to find Addie. And now, questions about the witches swirled in her head. She needed to know more about them, and whatever was going on with this war.

She needed to be there, and Seren knew it.

"We found you by accident." Lane shrugged. "We were looking for something and somehow ended up here."

"We were looking for my sister, actually." Shepherd stepped forward. "She's been missing for over a month."

"And you thought she would be here?" Seren's eyebrows raised behind the platinum blonde wisps of her hair. "Addie chose not to go to school here."

"Well, this is a safe house now, isn't it? For witches."

"For everyone," Yarrow interrupted. "Everyone is welcome here. As you can see."

He drew a hand along his body, the bark of his skin, the leaves that grew and twisted from his ears.

"Not everyone," Shepherd mumbled. "If this place is supposed to protect people, why didn't my family know about it? Know about this war?"

Yarrow turned to Shepherd, his brown-green eyes empathetic. The bark at the edges of his mouth moved as he spoke. "We try not to alarm people that aren't in immediate danger. It would only put them further in harm's way."

Seren's face softened. "You might not have been welcome as a student here, Shepherd, but your family is welcome to join us if they need to." She stepped away from the desks and walked toward the window.

"As if I could get my *sidanelv* to come to a boarding school." Shepherd rolled her eyes. Korvu furrowed his brow.

"Understandable," Deryck interrupted. "Especially with your history with this school."

Shepherd exhaled, as if she had been holding in her breath in anger. Her cheeks turned pink, her choppy black hair falling in her eyes. Haven Hall had treated her as an outsider, had picked her apart and told her she wasn't good enough, that she could never earn their approval. It was too late for them to go back on that, even if they meant it.

Lane understood how that felt. Ever since joining The Academy, she had felt like she was on the outside looking in—like she didn't truly belong there, or anywhere. The only piece of her identity that she could cling to was that she didn't have one.

Lane let her eyes drift to the blackboard drawing of the corrupted shade, unable to look at Shepherd any longer. Seren had asked for them to come to the classroom. She had wanted Lane to hear her. But why?

"Are you a Traveler?" Seren asked. Lane looked up, startled. A what? She felt her confusion scrunch into a wrinkle between her brows. "An Ianitor? I thought it was you, but based on the look on your face, now I'm not sure."

Her tone was casual, condescending, with the light lilt of humor that meant the joke was at Lane's expense.

Deryck shifted uncomfortably. His thin limbs crossed and uncrossed as he stared at her, his eyes trying to speak something into existence that he couldn't say out loud.

She was talking about Blinking, Lane realized. She wasn't a Traveler, just able to Blink between Life and Death. She tried to keep her face neutral. Seren couldn't know that Lane was connected to Nil, to the shades she was so worried about. And she definitely couldn't know she was a ghost.

"Why do you want to know?" Shepherd interrupted. "We already told you we fell through your little ward-portal by accident."

Yarrow glanced at Korvu, whose eyes shifted to Seren. Lane did not take her eyes off the older woman, noticing the small changes in her movement. Her eyes were too still and her muscles too tense, as if she was fighting the urge to shift the weight between her legs.

"It's because you need something, isn't it?" Shepherd interrupted. Shepherd turned to Lane, a smirk dancing on her face. The sight sent a jolt through Lane, and she found herself smiling back, as if they had both won some silent battle. "They need something, otherwise they never would have let us stay here."

The implication was clear in her words: Haven Hall only cared about people who were useful. Shepherd had not been useful, so they'd cast her aside. Now, she suddenly was.

What they needed, though, was the question.

At The Academy, no one did favors for free. Except for Victor. They did what they were ordered to do, and past that, magic and amperes were currency. Lane had traded far too many of her precious magical batteries to Perry and Tripp for their help studying, or to bribe them to take her on another mission.

Haven Hall, it seemed, was not any different.

"Everything has a price," Lane said, looking at her fingernails as if she was bored. "Name it, and we will think about helping you."

Shepherd raised an eyebrow at that.

Seren collapsed back on the desk behind her, either because she had given up or from pure exhaustion. Lane wouldn't blame her for either. Besides her tightly bound hair, she looked like a broken doll fraying at the seams, ready to fall apart at any moment.

"It's true," Seren said. "We are in need of someone with a particular set of skills. Someone who can get into places that are supposed to be impossible."

Like Haven Hall.

She gestured at the chalkboard and the drawing of the shade, which somehow seemed to move beneath the shadow of her hand.

"There is a man who we think may be connected to these. . . things," Seren said. Shepherd and Lane raised their eyebrows almost at the same time. "He was a witch, once. But he was cursed with immortality and trapped in a prison. He's known for his interest in death magic. In. . . experimenting."

Seren's face fell, and she ran a hand across her face as if wiping something away. "My wife, Ivy. . . she was one of his experiments. She was a human, and he found a way to make her. . . something else."

Lane's teeth bit together, her jaw tightening. This was exactly the kind of thing The Academy had warned them about. Taking magic past its natural limits, hurting people.

"And she's missing?" Shepherd asked.

Yarrow stepped forward. "Everything we do at Haven Hall is by committee. We call it the Council. You don't have to decide now. We will present our plan to the group tomorrow night, and if they agree, you can let us know then. Take the day. Think about it."

He placed a hand on Seren's shoulder, but her eyes had grown distant and faraway. Lane had never seen Eurydice look that way. Like she cared about something.

Lane turned to Shepherd as Yarrow led Seren out of the room. Deryck and Korvu followed slowly behind. Shepherd gave her a shrug and a small smile, as if she was saying, *Well, what can you do?*

But all Lane could think about was the look in Seren's eyes. If Seren could love someone like that, love someone so deeply. . . could all witches? Could she?

CHAPTER FOURTEEN

Lane didn't sleep. She tossed and turned, dreaming of thousands of eyes like pinholes in her skin. The witches staring at her, sensing her, knowing she didn't belong within their walls.

Her skin began to feel like it belonged to someone else. She had been taught that witches would do anything to have death magic, to destroy The Academy, to destroy death itself. But it seemed like that very thing was happening, and the witches were also trying to figure out who was behind it. It didn't make sense for them to be making it up—the wall of photos was enough for Lane to realize they were truly suffering. The crumbling school walls around her only further proved it.

As the sunlight began to pour through the tall windows, Lane crossed the room toward a neatly stacked pile of clothes. She'd been

"Well, at first. . . but no, they don't," Shepherd said. "They asked me to work with the police, me being a *normie* and all. We have a. . . complicated relationship. Me being magicless was hard for them to accept, and I don't think being gay helped much. I can't imagine how shocked my dad would be if he saw me now, here." She motioned around her. "But I'll do what I have to do to find her."

It didn't even seem like a question—it wasn't even second nature. Her family was part of her, even after everything that had happened between them. To Lane, it was foreign. She felt like she could see what tied Shepherd to the world—threads that connected to her family, to everyone and everything she cared about. For Lane, those threads had been cut. When she reached, she found nothing there at all.

Shepherd shrugged, shoving her hands awkwardly in her pockets as they both trampled onto the grass. "I'm sure you'd do the same. You're the one that jumped through a window to save a total stranger."

Lane laughed.

"It wasn't like that," she said. "I was just doing what I had to do."

Shepherd turned toward her, a dark eyebrow arched as if to say, *Exactly, dumbass.*

But Lane didn't think she would do what Shepherd was doing if their roles were switched. She cared for Perry. She was one of the only friends Lane had. And because of their lost memories, she was really one of the only friends Lane had ever had, period. But would she be trying to solve Perry's murder if her own afterlife wasn't on the line? If Eurydice hadn't tried to blame her, would she have tried to figure out who had hurt Perry or would she have just let it go?

Shepherd reached for Lane's arm, her fingers skimming the underside of her elbow. It was a light, questioning touch.

"Come on, it's just over here." Shepherd wrapped her fingers around Lane's wrist, her long fingers laying delicately across the tattooed flesh of her obols. Lane bit her tongue, forcing herself not to say that she didn't need to be dragged. Instead, she let Shepherd guide her gently into the forest that surrounded the school grounds. She was too mentally tired to hear Shepherd's taunts about how much Lane was enjoying her company.

They stepped into an open area surrounded by a grove of trees. A bench sat in the middle, surrounded by cut tree stumps, and Lane realized it was an outdoor classroom. Based on the size of the small trunks, it was made for very little children. The trees bent toward each other and stretched toward the sun, as if they might hold hands and dance in the warm air. It was still early enough that the grass was wet, tiny droplets of dew refracting the bits of sunshine that made their way through the leaves. Shepherd pulled her across the glen as Lane tilted her head toward the warm sun.

"This is where they teach the Naturalists," Shepherd said. "Or at least, I'm assuming. It could be Healers too, or another skill I'm not familiar with. Cool, right?"

Lane nodded. She couldn't help but think of the woods that surrounded The Academy, the white trees twisting toward her like claws and the grass lifeless beneath her feet. And the spirits, fading and silent, that were hardly echoes of the people they had once been. She had always loved those woods, even with the haunted feeling they left in her gut.

But this forest? It was something entirely different. Something settled inside her. For the first time in days, she finally felt safe.

She peeled her eyes away from the trees to look at Shepherd. She had dropped her hand from Lane's arm, shoving it back into her pocket.

"So, you portaled us into another portal and somehow we ended up here?" Shepherd asked, leaning against a thick tree rich with branches. One brushed against her ear, but she didn't seem to notice.

Lane hadn't really had a moment alone with Shepherd to explain, or to ask what she had learned while Lane was unconscious. She wasn't sure if she should tell Shepherd, either way. Their friendship was knitted together by threads of lies.

Maybe this one thing wouldn't hurt. Especially with what Seren wanted her to do.

"I guess so," Lane said. She tried to sound nonchalant, even though she didn't understand it herself. The list of things that had been impossible only days before was getting longer and longer.

Shepherd's eyes lit up. She hadn't expected Lane to answer at all, Lane realized. The thought made her smile. Even after just three days, Shepherd could read her just right.

"Did you know you could do that?" Shepherd asked.

"No. Well, yes and no," Lane said. She shrugged again, pacing around the grove and enjoying the way the fresh grass felt beneath her feet. "But I'm not whatever they think I am. A Ianitor or a Traveler or whatever. I'm not a witch."

Lane's stomach fell. The words slipped out, and now she had no way of taking them back.

Shepherd straightened, her expression unreadable. "I had a feeling that was the case," she said. "But if you aren't a witch, what are you?"

Dead. The undead. A ghost. All of the above. None of the answers sounded quite right, and the last thing she needed was for everyone at Haven Hall to realize she was basically exactly what they were looking for. What would they do to her? What would Shepherd think of her?

"I don't know," Lane said. "I don't know what I am."

Shepherd ran her fingers along a branch as she gave Lane a questioning look. Exhaling, Lane reached up, tightening the ponytail on top of her head.

"I don't remember who I am. I lost my memories." Somehow, she found herself telling part of the truth. "I don't even think Lane is my real name. So whatever I am, whatever I did. . . I just don't know."

She closed her eyes, bracing herself for questions she couldn't answer.

"Well, whatever you did, it worked," Shepherd said. "And here we are."

She turned toward Shepherd, surprised. She seemed completely and distinctly unbothered by Lane's gut-wrenching and anxiety-induced revelation. She had just accepted it, like it was nothing.

Lane's eyebrows furrowed, the corners of her mouth twitching into a smile.

"For what it's worth. . ." Shepherd looked over her shoulder as she continued through the clearing. "I like Lane. It suits you."

Lane laughed. "Thanks."

A small bee floated by, circling Shepherd's arm.

"Do you know anyone like Seren is looking for? A Ianitor, or whatever?" she asked, surprising herself.

Shepherd shook her head. "It's not like they keep an encyclopedia of all the different skills. New ones are discovered every time a new witch comes into their abilities." She paused. "Seren probably does, though. They said the Haven was hidden by a portal? Someone had to have made it, right?"

She ran a finger along her obol. She wondered if Eurydice and Victor knew. They always said Blinking was only for the select few chosen by The Academy. Lane almost felt special. Selected. Even if it was for a task no one wanted.

"So, what do you think you'll have to do if you agree to find this guy? Bank robbery?" Shepherd asked.

Her train of thought had pulled her so far away, she had almost forgotten the mission Seren had asked—or really, forced—her to go on.

Lane raised her eyebrows. "They'd better hope not. We both know you're better at break-ins."

Shepherd scoffed, shoving her hands into her pockets as she rocked on her heels.

"Come on, we'll miss it," she said suddenly.

Shepherd bent a branch out of the way and ushered Lane to her side so that they were on the edge of the clearing, partially hidden by a wide tree.

Shepherd held out her arm protectively as she poked her head around the oak. Reaching back, she pulled Lane close to her so that Lane could also see the clearing, her face comfortable against the edge of Shepherd's arm and back. She tried to ignore the heat that spread across her face as she felt the fabric of Shepherd's thin t-shirt, the muscles underneath. Lane had been close to others before—women and men—even though the selection at The Academy was scarce. But it was never like this. There was a comfort in the way Shepherd held her arm out, the way Lane tucked against her, her pulse quickening even as she felt completely at ease.

Lane shook her head, banishing the thought. She couldn't think like that. Not about Shepherd.

Shepherd held up her hand, one finger to her lips as she gestured past the line of trees.

The forest opened to an explosion of flowers blooming in every direction. The field was lit up with the sun—red, yellow, blue, green, gold, orange as far as the eye could see. Petals danced on the wind as the stems and stalks swung in the light breeze. Like the mosaic window, the garden glittered a thousand colors, shone like a thousand gems.

Lane let out a long, awestruck breath.

Barely a length away stood a group of children gathered in a circle around a woman with shockingly red hair. Her dark skin gleamed in the sunlight as they chattered and tumbled around her. Even at this distance, Lane could see them reasonably well. They couldn't have been older than twelve—younger than Haven Hall's usual students, she assumed.

The children waved their hands over the grass, back and forth, as if they were kneading dough. One girl stood over a small seed, cupping her hands above it over and over, until it burst into a small sproutling, green leaves reaching toward her. Then, it shot up, growing into a small tree, branches twisting and popping with white-pink flowers. The tree towered over her, nearly four feet tall in only a moment. The woman walked over with a basket and garden clippers, snipping the flowers into the basket.

"What is she doing?" Lane watched as they plucked the freshly sprung flowers from the tree. It seemed sacrilegious to destroy something so beautiful so soon.

Shepherd looked over his shoulder at Lane with a knowing grin. "This is what I wanted you to see."

The child smiled as the woman patted her on the head, handing her another seed. The girl got to work again.

Lane watched as two more students held their hands out, plants spurting beneath their palms. One of them bloomed into the long stalk of a sunflower, towering over even their teacher. The boy next to her coaxed a pumpkin to pop out of a seed.

"You said that magic steals. I wanted you to see that it can be more than that," Shepherd said. "You know how my mom is Cherokee? Well, she taught me that it isn't our job to control or rule over nature but to maintain our place as a part of it. She believes that if you listen hard enough, you can hear the spirit of the plant—the spirit of nature itself—and it will guide you and tell you how to best honor it."

She pointed at the children, gathering their seeds and blooms. "Healers used to drain themselves, their own energy, to save others. They were abused and taken advantage of for their gifts. . . especially people like my mom and our ancestors."

She paused, sadness washing over her face. Lane leaned closer to the crook of her shoulder, trying to listen as Shepherd whispered.

"But magic doesn't have to be bad. Like all nature, it's how you use it—who is using it. These children draw on the energy of the Earth and grow something new in its place. And then their magic is woven into the trees, into those flowers, and even given to the Healers to make tonics. And as they say, the circle of life continues."

She smiled, a silent joke that Lane didn't understand. "Magic isn't something that disrupts the balance of the world. It's a part of it. And it's our responsibility to honor that and maintain harmony.

"At least, that's what my mom says." Shepherd shrugged awkwardly as a flush ran across her cheeks.

Was she. . . embarrassed? Lane couldn't help but snort. The cocky, sarcastic Shepherd, embarrassed.

"What?" Shepherd asked.

"Nothing," Lane said. "I think I would like your mom."

She turned back to watching the class of children, a line forming in her forehead. This wasn't what Vis was supposed to look like. She watched the first girl bend to the Earth and kiss the ground. The rest of the children followed suit as clouds passed over their field, the sun disappearing as cool air fell over them.

"What are they doing now?"

"They're thanking the Earth for providing the energy. It's part of the cycle to show thanks for what you have been given. And then, you give back what you have taken."

Lane wanted to take a step back, to pull away, but she couldn't stop watching as the children smiled and laughed, their hands digging into the Earth. Their tiny laughter was infectious.

"How do they give it back?"

Shepherd's eyes shone as she spoke. "There are lots of ways. If you chop down a tree, you plant a new one. Or they can find a way to use their magic to help another, and add to the cycle that way, like helping the Healers with their tonics. And one day, just as they have taken from it, they also return to it."

She said it so plainly that Lane almost missed it. She cocked her head.

"You mean when they die? That's part of the cycle?"

Shepherd turned her body to face Lane, her arms across her chest as she smirked. "Probably the part you're the most familiar with."

Lane started, but then realized—Shepherd still thought she was some kind of Necromancer.

Lane felt her mind turning, her eyebrows furrowed.

"What kind of witches do you think they are?" Lane asked as the teacher moved the children away from the clearing. It was nearing midday, so it seemed their lesson was over. "I mean, what's their skill?"

She stepped into the clearing as the children walked away, a ray of sun across the dark tan of her skin. "Who knows? Naturalists, probably. Not really my area of expertise."

Lane took two steps toward her. The ground slanted, exaggerating the height difference between them. "Right. Because you don't care about any of this stuff. You hate magic."

She raised an eyebrow at her, motioning with her arms to the grounds of the school surrounding them, and Shepherd laughed.

"All right, you're right," Shepherd said. "I guess you can take the magic out of the girl, but you can't take the girl out of the magic."

They both laughed.

"What does that mean?" Lane asked.

"It means. . . it means that as far as you run, you can't run away from yourself."

Lane pursed her lips. If there was one thing she understood, it was that.

"Come on," Shepherd said with a grin as she grabbed Lane by the hand, pulling her into the garden.

Time ticked by as they lay on the grass amongst the flowers, the sun moving slowly, setting and warm on Lane's skin. As they waited for the Council meeting, Shepherd told Lane about Addie and her powers, how she had broken a vase during a temper tantrum as a child with a single thought. She told Lane about growing up without magic even though both her parents came from strong, magical families. She talked about growing up with her mother, visiting their relatives on the reservation, but spoke scarcely about her father.

And Lane, even though she knew she shouldn't, shared stories right back. She told Shepherd about Victor, and how she thought they might have got along—they were both stubborn as hell. And she told her about Tripp, about Perry, and how she was gone.

"That's why I'm here," Lane told her. "I need to know what happened to her."

For a moment, it felt like nothing else existed. Not The Academy or Eurydice or the witches. For a moment, she had nothing to lose.

If only she could find a way to forget the things that haunted her instead of the things she wanted to remember most.

When dusk hit the horizon, they set off across the lawn toward the house. As Shepherd laughed, oblivious, Lane steeled herself for what was to come.

She had never been to a gathering at The Academy. There weren't that many of them, for one thing, and it always seemed harder to wrangle the professors who had gone full ghost. They liked to float around, slowly disconnecting from reality. The only time they really gathered was for All Hallows Eve. Lane had been looking forward to it—drinking with Tripp, dancing with Victor, and meeting the dead from all across After Life. It sounded like a party to remember, but Lane was starting to worry she wouldn't be back for it. It was only in a few days.

Whatever this Council meeting was, she didn't think it would be anything like that. She swallowed hard.

They walked into the Haven side by side, and both she and Shepherd stopped short.

The room was full of laughter. Seren sat at the large table, laughing as two guards spun her in her chair. The three of them downed shots of alcohol before switching places, placing the tattooed guard in the chair. Music whisked across the room, a song of summer. Lane noticed a man with green skin in the corner, his face pressed against a strange-looking violin that he picked at with claws instead of a bow.

Yarrow approached them and Lane tensed, but he only smiled, handing them two glasses of wine. Shepherd smiled in thanks as Lane pressed the glass to her lips. Her eyes were trained on the room like an eagle stalking its prey. But all around her, the witches, the magical creatures. . . they seemed like they didn't have a care in the world.

The drink was honey on her tongue, the taste of peaches and rich fruit, of sunshine and the refreshing tickle of bubbles as she swallowed. She'd never tasted anything like it. At The Academy, everything tasted like ash—but they drank anyway, just to feel alive.

That wasn't what this was. This was *because* they were alive.

The sweet taste turned bitter in her mouth.

Shepherd elbowed her in the side. "I don't think it was like this when I tried to go to school here."

Lane rolled her eyes, pouring the rest of the drink down the back of her throat. She wanted that harsh burn, but the honeyed wine only soothed her.

"People can be more than one thing, you know. Just because they're scared doesn't mean they can't have fun. And just because someone does one bad thing doesn't make them bad." Shepherd's face faded into a frown. "Things aren't so black and white."

"In my experience, they are." And gray, she thought.

Shepherd snorted. "You're impossibly stubborn, you know that?"

Lane looked up at her, holding her glass against her cheek. "Funny, I was just thinking the same thing about you."

She turned toward the large table where the crowd started to gather. It wasn't that she didn't agree—she knew Shepherd had a point. But she needed to think about herself and whatever mission they wanted to send her on, and how she could use it to get out of this mess with The Academy. She couldn't worry about whether these witches were one thing or another. She needed to focus on finding her way back to The Academy and graduating to a new life.

She was not one of them. And she never would be.

The meeting began so casually that Lane wasn't sure it had started at all. Everyone packed into the room in rows like a children's choir, gathered around the table. Although Seren was the clear leader, the others at the table all appeared to be older than her by at least a decade.

The room seemed to grow silent as Seren's gaze drifted to Lane. They locked eyes across the crowded room, and Seren tilted her chin, the movement barely noticeable. It was the only signal they would get. Lane nodded her head once in return. They didn't have to tell her not to interrupt. She knew how these things worked.

Seren rose to her feet, placing her palms on the table.

"I've told you all before about the man who was cursed with immortality, and how I believe he may have answers about the creatures that are hunting us—and who is controlling them. I've told you about the things that he has done." She paused, her thin eyelashes fluttering as she blinked. "But we didn't have a way to get to him, behind the wards of his curse. Until now."

Murmurs exploded across the room.

"How?"

"Do we even want him here?"

"Is it the same witch that broke our wards?"

Lane wanted to protest. She wasn't what they thought she was. But she couldn't tell them what she truly was either. They would obliterate her on the spot, and she wasn't ready to die. . . again.

Seren lifted her hand, and the whispers halted. She glanced at Korvu before settling her gaze on Lane.

Dozens of eyes turned to stare at Lane. They blinked at her like bats in the darkness, their stares burning into her like the heat of burning candles on her skin.

Shepherd's fingers wrapped around her palm, hidden behind their legs in the crowd as she squeezed her hand. It was a small thing, but Lane felt the tension in her shoulders loosen.

"I hope that he has the knowledge we need. But if not. . . he is still dangerous." She looked at Lane. "You understand."

"If you agree," Yarrow interrupted, "we will put it to a vote. Everyone gets to decide if this is the right path for us."

"But remember." Seren glared at him. "We are fighting a losing war. We don't know who is attacking us or how. If he can help us, it could make all the difference."

There were nods across the room. Beside her, Shepherd dropped Lane's hand, crossing her arms.

"And if he doesn't want to help you?" Shepherd asked.

Everyone went silent.

But Lane already knew the answer. It seemed simple enough. They wanted her to get whatever information this man had, and if he fought back, they wanted him eliminated.

It was like any other mission, really. Not that Seren had said how *exactly* she was supposed to eliminate an immortal man.

Silence stretched across the room. They were waiting for her to respond.

"Oh," Lane said. Seren tilted her head to the side and seemed as if she was making every effort not to roll her eyes. "You want me to just. . . pop over there and talk to him?"

"Yes."

Seren and her guards answered in unison. Lane was beginning to think that they weren't guards at all, but some kind of triumvirate.

There was something they weren't saying, something that made Lane's hair stand on end in warning.

Shepherd broke through the silence. "You're hiding something. Tell us what he can do. We can't go in there blind."

Seren smirked. She'd expected this, Lane realized, but she hadn't expected it to come from Shepherd. She had underestimated her.

And so had Lane. Shepherd's jaw was tight as she stared at Seren, brown eyes glinting with fire. Her hair was tucked behind her ear, revealing a raw, red scar that ran along the length of her neck. Lane hadn't noticed it before, and wondered what it was from.

Seren looked back at Lane. "He was cursed with immortality a long time ago, trapped in a prison of his own making. He's not only a gifted witch, but a gifted warrior."

The muscles in Shepherd's arms visibly tensed.

"He has used his skill—and time— to alter magic as we know it. He's found ways to expand it, nullify it, remove it, amplify it. You all know what he did to Ivy." Seren did not look up as she said this, as if it was something she couldn't bear to speak of again. "She isn't the only one. If anyone knows what these creatures are—what has been done to them—it will be him."

Shepherd's face darkened as she twisted her mouth into a thin line. "You want someone like that here?"

She waved her arm across the room, gesturing to where families and children gathered. They all turned to each other, still mumbling amongst themselves.

Lane didn't hear a word of it. She'd already decided.

Whoever this man was, he knew how to change magic, alter it and use it to hurt others.

Just like the shades.

Her voice echoed across the room as she locked eyes with Seren. "When do I leave?"

CHAPTER FIFTEEN

"I told you, you aren't coming."

"And I told you, I'm not listening." Shepherd held herself back from winking at Lane as she crossed her arms. It was almost cute.

Whether it was stubbornness or a trauma-induced, lone-wolf mentality, Lane seemed to think it was better that she go on this suicide mission alone. And Shepherd was not having it. She needed to go. And it had nothing to do with wanting to be with Lane, making sure she was okay. Definitely not.

Lane stomped away from her across the main hall, and Shepherd followed, hands in her pockets.

"Admit it. I've been great back up so far. We fought off that hellhound together, and we've—"

Lane pivoted on the toe of her combat boot, her chin tensed up at Shepherd.

"You. Don't. Have. Any. Magic." Lane hissed.

Shepherd smiled. They'd been repeating this argument since the night before, and she hadn't gained any traction. At this point, her strategy was to wear Lane down until she was so exhausted she wouldn't argue.

Shepherd scoffed. "I don't need magic, never have. There are other ways to get things done. I have my personality and my good looks."

One of the professors—a small woman with broken wings on her back—had given Shepherd a fresh change of clothes. She'd tried not to take offense at it. Her jeans had been replaced with green cargo pants that hung loose on her thin waist. They'd given her a high collared men's shirt that was loose in the waist and tight against her arms. She'd thrown her own trench coat over it, and somehow felt like a mix between herself and the witch she might have been.

Seren had asked them both to meet her at the memorial wall, probably to get some last intel on the mission. Shepherd knew Lane was plotting to lose her sometime between now and then, so she followed closely behind her as they entered the hall. It was nearly empty, the sun sitting low so that no rays shone through the stained-glass window.

"I've got a few tricks you haven't seen," Shepherd said. If only Lane knew. "Plus, you'll protect me."

She rolled her eyes. "They said he was dangerous, Shep."

Shepherd tried not to smile. "Are we on a nickname basis now? Does that mean I can call you Laney?"

Lane glared.

Shepherd knew it was dangerous, probably more than Lane did. Lane might have fought ghosts and demons and who knows what else, but they both knew she didn't know a single thing about this man. And she certainly didn't know much about magic—at least, the kind most witches used. The kind he used.

Shepherd had to go with her.

"Lane." She stopped, reaching for Lane's elbow. Lane half-turned toward her, her dark brown curls swinging around her face. It reminded Shepherd of the first time she had seen Lane—terrifying and beautiful and strong all at the same time. "You don't know anything about this guy. At least let me come and ask him about Addie, see if he knows anything. " Her voice was a whisper although only Deryck was around. "We could ask about the Keys."

"I think you just like arguing with me," Lane said, rolling her eyes as she pulled her arm away.

"And *I* think you just like the sound of your own voice."

They both smiled.

To their left, Deryck grumbled. "*And I think* that if you two don't stop, I might have to ask someone to make me deaf as well as blind."

They had met with Korvu, Seren, and the other teachers-turned-Council-members—Yarrow and Una—earlier that day to lay out their plan. Not that Lane was going to follow their plan, Shepherd knew, but at least she was going through the motions.

Korvu had laid it all out simply. Lane would do her thing and take them to a location just outside the immortal's wards, and then she would need to get through them, just as she had done with the Haven. That was how they knew she would be able to help them. The setup of the school's wards were based on his prison. The irony was not lost on Shepherd.

She sat quietly as they described his house, on the back end of the Night Market, on the top of the hill. No one seemed to know if the Night Market had been built around it, or if it was the other way around. Shepherd assumed that it was the former, although the market was known for being pulled out of time. It could have been thousands of years old, for all she knew.

Lane didn't stop her as Shepherd followed her into the long dining room. Seren stood at the far end of the room, her hands clasped behind her back as she stared at the photos. Her straight blonde hair was in a tight bun on her head, similar to Lane's, but far less messy. Shepherd's own hair was a hacked-up bed of straight, grassy hair in comparison, and she vowed to never cut her own hair again.

Shepherd watched as Lane's eyes drifted from photo to photo. Shepherd had shoved the grainy, black and white photo of Addie among them. Lane reached toward the photo, her hand brushing across the corner of the printed paper.

"I didn't know you put this here," Lane whispered. There was something about the room, the staring faces, that required it.

"It seemed like the right thing to do." Shepherd shrugged. She knew that Lane had her own reasons for going on this mission, for being at Haven Hall at all, but for Shepherd, it was so much more. She had to find Addie.

"You think you're going to find her?" Seren asked. The edges of her voice were rough.

"That's the plan," Lane said, rocking casually back on her heels. Shepherd chewed on her cheek.

Seren dropped her hands from behind her back as she took a step toward the wall.

"You know, it's odd. I've never met someone who knew so much about ghosts, or shades. . . whatever you called them. And I have certainly never met anyone who was both a Necromancer and a Traveler. How rare is it for someone to have two abilities?" Lane rolled her neck, not meeting Seren's gaze. Seren continued. "It's not just rare. It's impossible."

Seren looked out of the side of her eye at Lane, the stare of her blue eyes hard and cold as an ice storm. Shepherd thought she might drown in it.

"I already told you, I'm not a whatever you call it. A Traveler. Some-one who makes portals," Lane said. There was no tone of defense in her voice. She sounded almost irritated.

"We just want to help," Shepherd said. But Seren wasn't looking at her. She might as well have been invisible. She was used to that. The Haven had always made her feel that way.

Lane turned to face Seren's cold gaze. "I want to help you. I want to find these people. I want to find Addie, and I want to figure out who is behind all of this. Not just for you. But for me. I have to know the truth."

Lane glanced at Shepherd, her green eyes glinting with flicks of gold like the bottom of tide pools in the sun. Shepherd wasn't sure if she'd taken her lesson to heart, but at least Lane wanted to help the witches now, whatever she thought of them aside. And she wanted to help Addie. At some point, their conflicting goals had merged into one.

The thought made Shepherd grin.

"And if I have to," Lane said, "I will burn everything to the ground."

They stared at each other, ice and fire, as silence filled the space between them, both of them waiting for the other to make a move. Shepherd was tempted to break the silence with an awkward joke, but it didn't seem like either of them were in the mood.

After several moments, Seren smirked. "See that you do."

Her hand drifted out in front of her, her fingers lingering on a single photo—a woman with mousy brown hair, with glasses too large for her face and a stack of books beside her. The photo was faded sepia, but she could still see the light brown-red of freckles dotting across her nose. She seemed to be laughing at the person behind the camera.

Seren's mouth puckered, as if she wanted to say something but was holding herself back.

"The man you're going to see, Baltus," Seren said, "she was close with him. Worked for him. She never fully recovered from the things he did. Sometimes she still wakes up at night, screaming."

"Then why do you want him to join you so badly?" Shepherd asked.

Seren straightened her spine, shaking her head. Something rolled over her, erasing the person and replacing her with the warrior she had become. It reminded Shepherd too much of her father, who could flip between loving family man and dedicated soldier like a light switch.

"I don't have the luxury of putting someone I love before the needs of everyone else. I must do what is best for everyone."

Seren glanced over her shoulder, her eyes barely pausing as they drifted over the photo of Ivy. Then she looked at Shepherd.

"You probably noticed there aren't very many students left, or professors either. The Headmistress is gone," Seren said. "They were all attacked by those things. Shades, you call them. We've been calling them *nochtra*."

Shepherd didn't recognize the word, although she had wondered about the other students. She wondered where Addie would be if she hadn't convinced her not to go to school here, if she would have been any safer.

"*The corrupted ones*," Lane said. "In the old language."

"It's exactly the kind of experiment Baltus likes to play with," Seren said. "I might hate him, but if he can help us, I'll live."

Shepherd forced a swallow. This was going to be interesting.

"Here are the coordinates," Seren said stiffly, handing her a slip of paper. "I recommend getting there before dark."

Her eyes sparked with the secret threat before she stormed out of the room.

Lane shoved the piece of paper into her pocket, barely glancing at it as she walked out of the room. Shepherd didn't bother to look. She already knew where they were going. Probably too well.

They stepped out onto the main veranda where stairs cascaded down from the large double doors that had once been the formal entrance. Lane chewed on her lip until it turned pink.

Shepherd's chest tightened as her stomach tied itself into knots.

"You don't have to do this, you know," Shepherd said. "We could just leave."

Lane cocked her head at her, messy pieces of hair falling into her eyes.

"You shouldn't come," Lane said. "For one thing, we know almost nothing about this guy except that he's dangerous. And for another, I'm not what they think I am. You could end up in pieces all over the floor, and I'm not sure Seren would ever forgive me for the mess."

Shepherd snorted as she rolled her eyes. "Oh, I'm sure they have plenty of magical ways to clean up blood."

"I hope so," Lane said. "It sounds like we're going to need it."

Shepherd felt her own smirk fall. "My dad always says, '*Nothing worth fighting for is easy*,'" she said. "Cliche, I know. But whatever happens, I'm with you. We've got this."

Lane pulled the coordinates out of her pocket, unfolding the crumpled piece of paper. "All right then. We're going to the Night Market."

Shepherd tried to force herself to breathe, hoping Lane couldn't see the secrets written across her face. Lane grabbed her hand, wrapping her other around the shard of bone that she was always fiddling with.

Shadows swirled around them as they fell into the nothingness between worlds.

The darkness disappeared with a flash, replaced by the city square and cobblestone streets. The street was empty. Lane wondered what kept non-witches away from the Night Market. Was it the old-timey, misplaced buildings that told them to stay away, that something was out of place? She had never had the chance to explore the dark trading place, although the other students told tales that if you knew who to ask, you could find anything there.

Looking out across the empty streets of the Night Market, Shepherd let out a low whistle.

Lane set off up the road, ignoring her. Shepherd's face had gone pale, but she hurried to match Lane's pace.

Night was approaching, the sun bathing the world in an orange red-glow. The sunset reminded her of the red sky of After Life as the rays landed across the tops of buildings, brightening and darkening the city at the same time. Across the horizon, lights started to blink to life as evening took hold, like glittering stars beneath their feet. It was like standing at the top of a mountain, the whole world lay exposed before her. Beyond the orange horizon, the sky was still blue, a painting of bleeding colors.

"This is why I want to live," she whispered. She hadn't meant to say it out loud.

Shepherd half-laughed, smiling at her as she looked out at the sunset. "Should I be worried that you're already preparing for our doom?"

She thought Lane was worried about the mission. Lane laughed, relieved. "Only a little."

It was getting harder and harder to keep secrets from her.

Shepherd reached for her arm. "Lane," she said, more formal and urgent than her usual tone. "I have to tell you something."

Lane imagined how this conversation would go. Shepherd would tell her some secret, something she had been hiding from her. And then Lane would tell her the truth, about The Academy, about Deryck's suspicions that they were behind the nochtra, and Hades knows what else.

No, she couldn't tell Shepherd the truth. Not now. She had no doubt the lies she'd told Shepherd were much worse. For one, Shepherd thought Lane was alive.

At the end of this, even if they ended up on the same side of this war, they would be on different sides of life and death.

"Why?" Lane asked. "Why now? Because we're friends? Shepherd, we barely know each other. It's been less than a week. That's not exactly enough time to know each other."

Shepherd's hand fell sharply away from her, as if she'd sent a static shock across her skin.

"Clearly, you've never had a one-night stand," she said. Always with the clever lines. "But really, I should tell you—"

Lane stopped her. "Shepherd, don't. You don't owe me anything. If everything goes well, we might find Addie tonight, and then we probably won't see each other ever again."

The expression on Shepherd's face was unreadable, and Lane's forehead wrinkled as her stomach sank. She knew she was doing the right thing, even if it felt wrong. Their friendship was built on lies, and nothing good ever came from that.

"It's better this way, trust me."

"Yeah. You're right. No need to complicate anything," Shepherd said, shoving her hands in her pockets. She turned away, her boots louder against the sidewalk as she hurried away and up the hill.

It wasn't easy to say no to Shepherd, but Lane had to. She had Victor, and Tripp, and the chance at a second life— a real life. A life where she could have parents, and choose what she wanted to be, and who she loved. She couldn't sacrifice that for one person.

At the top of the hill, the house finally came into focus. It was as if someone had dropped a cliff on top of the hill they had already struggled up. An iron gate wrapped all the way around it, obscuring the entrance in a dark forest of trees.

Stepping closer, Lane could feel the strange hum of magic surrounding the fence. Her ears rang as she held out her hands, feeling for the invisible ward. It had been silent for the past hour. The sudden sound was like a snare drum in her ears.

"Ready?" Lane asked. They had arrived at the Night Market relatively unscathed—but whatever wards this guy had, they were likely to be worse than Haven Hall's, meant to keep something in as well as out.

Shepherd shook her head. "Only if you are. Let me know if you need me to find a hellhound to chase you again. That seemed to work last time."

Lane snorted. "Don't push our luck."

Shepherd smirked, but turned away as she held out her hand. Reluctantly, Lane took it, afraid to hold too tightly. She put her other hand into her pocket, wrapping her fingers around the pair of bone keys, feeling their own song battling against the harmony of the fence.

"Close your eyes."

"Why?" Shepherd asked, closing one eye and peeking out through the other.

Lane glared up at her. "Because I don't want you to throw up. And you're making me nervous."

"I'm making you nervous?" She laughed. "You're the one that's about to yank me through a hole in the universe."

"Do you want to mess me up?" she asked. Shepherd shook her head emphatically, black locks flying around her ears. "Then close your eyes."

She took a deep breath.

The darkness surrounded them, heat creeping up her fingers from the keys to the obols on her wrists. She could feel them glowing, even with her eyes closed. She had no idea how they had jumped through the wards at Haven Hall—she just hoped she could do it again.

Cold rushed over her face, like storm winds on a beach. Her feet hit ground sooner than she expected.

"I think you might actually be getting better at it?" Shepherd said.

Lane swatted at her.

It was hard to believe a house of this size was hiding in the middle of the city. Pillars towered over them, made entirely of ivory. The house was dark and a strange mixture of old and new—glass windows, metal walls, but stone everywhere, as if it had been part of an ancient temple and slowly rebuilt.

"Thank you," Lane said, looking at Shepherd out of the corner of her eye. "For coming. For helping when you didn't have to."

Shepherd was staring up at the expansive door of the house, the frame of her face in profile against the light of the moon. It made her square jaw seem even more refined, darkening the hollows of her cheekbones. She looked like a painting. She could have been an ancient warrior or a princess, her features so androgynous and beautiful that she could be anyone she wanted to be. Except for her hair. It looked like she had hacked at it in the dark, the straight black pieces fraying at the edges in the humid air.

It was so very Shepherd. It was Lane's favorite part of her.

Shepherd looked down at Lane and *tsked* out of the side of her mouth.

"You might regret that thank you in a minute," Shepherd said as she knocked on the giant, black door. "I'm sorry."

Lane took a step back as the hair on her neck stood on end.

"For what?" Lane asked, her voice cracking. The churning in the pit of her stomach turned to fear as the door swung open with a snapping creak. A man stepped into view, slow and graceful like a ghost bride. Scars stretched around his mouth as he smiled.

"Shep. I didn't know you were stopping by."

CHAPTER SIXTEEN

Shep?

If Lane had asked it out loud, her voice would have squeaked. A nickname. This man—the target of her mission—had called her *Shep.*

They were friends.

The man stepped through the doorway and placed his hand on Shepherd's shoulder, smiling with impossibly white teeth. Lane stood, frozen and gaping. He wore what might have once been a military uniform, an unbuttoned coat covered in ribbons and ropes that hung loosely, revealing a bare chest covered in even more scars.

"Bally," Shepherd said. A simple, familiar greeting. She turned to Lane. "Lane, this is Bally. Baltus."

Lane tried to keep her face blank, but it must have been more of a glare.

"I did *try* to tell you."

"*This* is what you were trying to tell me?"

With his hand in the air and a flick of his wrist, Baltus turned to face her. He looked her up and down the way only a man who was used to getting what he wanted could.

"And what have you brought me?" Baltus asked. His feet were bare, pale against the dark stone. Lane flinched as he reached toward her with a pale hand. "Dark, beautiful, smells of danger. Exactly your type, am I right?"

He grinned at Shepherd. Lane half expected him to elbow her in the ribs, like schoolmates telling an inside joke.

In a blink of shadow, he was at Lane's side, his cheek nearly pressed against hers. She could feel his cold breath, stinking of whiskey and wine as he pulled a curl from her ponytail.

Bally smiled, his eyes shining like a wolf in a cage. His eyes were old and young at the same time, as if he had seen far too much.

Lane pushed his hand away with a glare.

He laughed. "Well, don't just stand there. Come in, come in, have a drink. Someone bring them a drink!" he yelled into the empty, echoing halls of the house.

No one was there. Only the echo of his own voice.

Bally led them through a narrow hall, the tiles an alternating pattern of black and white. Statues stared at them from either side, shadowed carvings of disfigured beasts that seemed to follow their steps as they walked by. Lane eyed every corner, daring to slow her pace behind Bally and Shepherd to check in crevices and down winding passages.

Seren would have never guessed that Shepherd was friends with this man—rejected, magicless Shepherd. . . She could just imagine the look on her face. Lane would pay to see that.

The house creaked beneath their feet, the sounds of wind traveling through the house like screams. Every inch of the house, every bit of dust in the air and every crack in the wall, pulsed with magic. Lane dug her fingers into her palms as it vibrated against her skin, charged like an electric current. Beside her, Shepherd was like a blackhole.

"What did you bring me today, Shepherd?" Bally asked as he stepped to the side, swinging his arm to invite them into the large room.

It was an atrium, the ceiling open and exposed to the dark sky above. Across the floor laid soft, velvet couches and cushions, the room bathed entirely in crimson fabric. Trees lined the corners of the walls, leafless and haunting in the light from the night outside. Birds shuffled in their branches, chattering like prisoners.

"I'm not here to trade, Bally."

"Trade?" Lane raised her eyebrows. Baltus turned his gaze on her in surprise, as if he'd forgotten someone else was there.

"Of course," Baltus said, reaching for Shepherd. "Shepherd deals in the best and most exclusive goods that the magical world has to offer. You know you're my favorite dealer, Shep."

"Only because I give you a discount," Shepherd grumbled.

Lane felt her mouth fall open.

"Just a magicless witch, hm?" she hissed as Baltus turned away from them, grabbing glasses from a nearby glass bar cart that seemed to appear out of thin air. "I don't think that's the same thing as *magical black market dealer.*"

Shepherd grinned at her, and it was not her normal sunny, taunting smirk. It glinted with satisfaction.

"I'm full of surprises." She shrugged. "You were the one who didn't want to know."

Lane ground her teeth until she was worried they might crack.

Bally walked toward them, a bottle of wine in his hand as he flopped onto one of the red couches. Shepherd joined him, sitting on one of the embroidered cushions without a single look back at Lane.

"If you aren't here to trade, I hope you aren't here to ask for your family's weapons back. You know my answer," Baltus said as he lifted the glass to his mouth. It stained his white lips red.

Lane sat on the cushion that was furthest from Baltus, a purple and gold Turkish patterned pillow that was separated from the rest by a low, bamboo table. Baltus placed the other two glasses in front of them, already filled to the brim with burgundy liquid.

"Is that how you met?" Lane asked as she grabbed a glass.

Baltus shook his head. "Oh, Heaven's no. We'd been dealing together for quite a long time before she finally decided to give those up." He smiled at Shepherd. "Strongest Warrior magic I've seen in centuries. I just had to have them, especially considering who Shepherd's family is."

Lane raised an eyebrow as Shepherd grabbed the other glass, dangling it between her fingers as she leaned forward. She looked down at the ground, avoiding Lane's gaze. Good. Lane knew her own face was burning red with blush.

She had learned more about Shepherd in the past five minute than she had since she met her. And she'd regretted not telling her the truth? And she had thought. . . well, what had she thought, exactly?

Nothing. Lane erased the thought as if it had never existed.

"Warrior magic?" Lane asked. Her voice was high, but she forced herself to sound polite, innocent, inquisitive. She could play this game if she had to. "But you said your mother's skill was Healing."

"It is," Shepherd said. "But my father's side. . . he comes from a long line of African witches who specialize in battle magic. Going all the way back to Carthage. It was. . . extra disappointing for them that I didn't inherit his skills." She flicked her eyes to Baltus. "And I have told Bally I regret selling them *several* times and have tried to get them back."

This is what The Academy was afraid of. Warrior witches. Warrior weapons sold to the highest bidder, so that he could do whatever he wanted with them. Shepherd had sold them to this man? Who was famous for toying with magic? That was why her family wasn't speaking to her, she realized. She had sold off their family's prized possessions like knickknacks.

"Finders keepers," Bally laughed. His teeth glinted in the low candlelight of the atrium. There was a single green jewel implanted in his right canine.

"And what do you plan to use them for?" Lane asked flatly, as if she was barely curious.

Bally cracked his neck, leaning across the table. His smirk washed over her like she'd been dropped in an icy lake. "Oh, you'll see."

He leaned back again, resting his arms on the ornate pillows as he moved his glass between his fingers. Lane had the strange feeling that they were at some sort of ancient, formal meeting between lords, as if the rest of the world were beneath them.

The wine suddenly tasted like acid on her tongue.

"So, if you aren't here to trade, and you aren't here to beg me for your swords," Baltus said, "then why are you here?"

Lane felt her pulse rise. The magic in the room was affecting her, beating against her skull like a drum and pricking at her skin like a swarm of locusts. She scooted closer to Shepherd, hoping to get into that bubble of silence that surrounded her. Her jaw tightened as their knees touched, Shepherd's fingers brushing against Lane's thigh as she moved to switch her glass to the other hand. Both of them tensed, even as a calm washed over Lane, loosening the knots in her chest.

Shepherd glanced at her, but Lane looked away. She could answer this one since she and Bally were so close.

"We. . . Haven Hall sent us," Shepherd finally said.

"Oh, Shepherd. How could you work with those vile people after what they did to you?" Baltus curled his lip. His disdain for them was just as clear as Shepherd's. That didn't exactly help his case.

It didn't help hers, either, though.

Shepherd sighed, running her fingers through her messy hair. She pulled at the edges, pushing the longest pieces so that they didn't fall in her eyes.

"Witches have been disappearing, Bally. Magical creatures, too. Not just a few. Dozens. The school is barely standing."

"They're trying to figure out who's behind it," Lane interjected.

His face remained neutral. Behind him, the glow from the skylight made the shadows dance.

"And they sent you to me?" He cocked his head to the side. His thin skin wrinkled like crepe paper as he did, but it didn't make the gesture any less threatening. "I can't even leave these walls."

It didn't seem to be holding him back any, but Lane didn't say that.

"They think it has something to do with these creatures. Nochtra," Shepherd said. The word was awkward in her mouth, like she hadn't practiced the language of magic in years. Lane supposed that was probably true.

"They're like shades," Lane said. "But corrupted. Changed."

"Ah, these I know," he said. "Shades. The poor creatures left after the murder of a soul. Not a thought in their heads. But these nochtra, they are different. Stronger, faster, almost like they understand. Like they are angry."

His accent made every word punctuated. They pricked at Lane's skin like needles.

"So you do know them?" Shepherd asked. "Did you know about the witches? About them disappearing? What they're doing to us?"

So it was *us* now, was it? She'd been so quick to fight Lane that she wasn't even a witch just days before. But Lane's stomach fell as she looked at the cold glare on Shepherd's face. If Baltus had known and said nothing, and Addie had been kidnapped. . .

Baltus only shrugged. Shepherd's knuckles tightened into fists.

"What else do you know about these nochtra? Do you know how they are made, or who is doing it? How they are doing it?" Lane asked.

Baltus laughed. "It's not me, if that's what you're trying to say."

She swore she saw him roll his eyes, but the whites were so full of burst red vessels that it was hard to tell. She wondered if he had always been this hideous, or if something inside him had rotted from the inside out.

"Seren told us what you did. To Ivy. You've been experimenting with power, pushing it to its limits, altering it." Shepherd's voice was flat but shaking. She was losing her patience.

Lane knew that feeling well. She had thought this man was her friend, maybe even someone she could trust. It wasn't that different from what Victor had done when he had turned her into Eurydice. Except that Victor had no choice. Baltus had every choice to help Shepherd and her family and had chosen not to.

Lane's jaw tightened even further. She thought about reaching for Shepherd's hand but clenched her fingernails into her palm again instead.

"My work is about so much more than power," Baltus spat. "These nochtra are child's play. Every few centuries, they pop up again. Do you know what the easiest way to make a mindless slave is? To get a powerful, magical creature to do your bidding? You remove its soul."

He slid back into the couch.

Lane ran her hand across her face as a chill ran over her. And what was the easiest way to remove someone's soul?

Start with a ghost.

"Why would someone do that?"

At the same time, Lane asked, "How?"

Baltus tilted his head back, staring at the skylight that loomed above them. The night was black and full of clouds, so the eerie, reflected light of the moon fell on his face.

"Isn't it obvious? It should be to you, anyway."

He pointed at Lane. She looked back at him in surprise. He knew what she was. Lane's arms froze at her side. She felt the comfort of her utility belt around her waist, the knife hidden there.

"With death magic."

He smirked.

Trying to pull herself together, Lane leaned away, placing her glass back on the table so that her hands were free. Shepherd, beside her, seemed almost unaware. She gave Lane a puzzled look but stayed silent.

"The nochtra are created by the violent murder of someone who is already dead. Obliterating them from all existence. And then taking the creature that remains and infusing magic into it—both death and living magic. The combination would kill someone still living, but there is so little left when someone becomes a shade that instead, it creates something new. Something monstrous," Baltus paused. "They've been used as tools for centuries. It's been a few hundred years since the last time the Living attacked the Dead, but if there is anything I've learned over the past two thousand years, it's that everything happens again eventually."

Shepherd shook her head. "There haven't been any ghosts on Earth since the 1700s. The last war put an end to all that." She blinked twice. "Or at least, that's what my dad said."

The Academy hadn't taught them about any past wars with the witches—at least, not that Lane recalled. She would have to look through the library when she got back. But if Baltus was telling the truth, their warnings had been just as true. The nochtra being back proved that someone was using Nil and Vis, combining them to try and conquer death. But it didn't make sense.

"Is that so?" Baltus raised an eyebrow, looking pointedly at Lane. Imperceptibly, she shook her head, hoping he would take mercy on her. Shepherd couldn't know what she was. He didn't seem to notice. "If someone is using the nochtra again, I would assume it's for the same reason it always is. Power. Control. The ability to bottle death, kill the Grim Reaper, decide who lives and dies as you see fit."

"It isn't supposed to be possible," Lane said. "Death magic and living magic being combined. The magics would fight each other until the nochtra imploded on themselves."

Baltus shrugged. "I didn't say it was a very effective or long-lasting method of war. Sometimes, all you need is more foot soldiers to sacrifice themselves at the front lines."

Beside her, Shepherd gulped. Her eyes traveled across the room. Lane wondered if that was part of the reason she hadn't mention her father's Warrior magic. She didn't agree with the way it was used.

"But if Haven Hall thinks these nochtra are being controlled, maybe someone found a way to stabilize it," Baltus said. He rolled his shoulders, cracking his neck. "I'm growing tired of this conversation. That happens at my age, unfortunately. Perhaps you should leave, unless you have changed your mind about selling me something, Shep."

He let out a sour laugh. Honestly, Lane was surprised he had entertained her inquiries at all. The tension between them hung like a guillotine waiting to drop. But behind her tensed muscles, Lane sensed that Bally didn't mind speaking with them. She couldn't imagine how terribly lonely he was, trapped in the same house for centuries.

Shepherd glanced at her, biting her lip. Her eyes sent a desperate plea. They couldn't leave. They didn't have any more information than they arrived with. They weren't any closer to finding Addie.

Lane reached into her pocket. The bones thrummed against her hand, a silent song that was just for her.

She tossed Addie's necklace onto the table, leaving the key she had found on her mission and her small, broken shard of bone in her pocket. Shepherd's eyes grew wide as she must have realized what Lane was doing, and she leaned forward to grab the key. Lane gave her an almost imperceptible shake of the head.

"What if the person was using these?" Lane asked. "That's what they are, aren't they? Some sort of ampere to control power."

Baltus's eyes slowly traveled from Lane's face to the table, the creped skin around his eyes wrinkling as they widened, landing on the key.

"You have no idea what you have." His voice was a low growl as his fingers clenched and his jaw tightened. His eyes flicked to Shepherd, as if asking for confirmation. Neither of them knew what the Keys were.

The longing in his voice made the hairs on Lane's neck rise. He reached for the key, and Lane snapped it back into her hand.

"How about two?" she asked as she reached into her pocket, revealing the second key. She held both flat on her open palm, raising an eyebrow at Baltus. She couldn't bring herself to take out the small shard. It sang a low hum against her muscle, and it reminded Lane of a small animal, nuzzling against its owner.

She was playing a dangerous game. Shepherd's face said so. But Lane was tired of waiting for answers, parsing between half-truths.

"Tell us what you know, and I will give you one," Lane said.

Baltus cracked his neck, the vein in his throat quivering. "Secrets are the most valuable form of currency. I see you've learned that lesson." He glanced at Shepherd. "You could learn from her."

Lane closed her grip on the keys. "Tell us what you know—the truth. And give Shepherd her things back."

Both Baltus and Shepherd raised their eyebrows at her. Baltus, in what seemed like a mixture of anger and appreciation, as if he was not used to being baited. Shepherd's expression was something like pleasantly surprised.

Baltus leaned back on the couch, putting his arms behind his head. His jacket splayed open, revealing a too-white chest covered in thousands of white scars. Lane blinked, waiting.

"The Keys are particularly powerful sources of energy—and containers. I haven't seen one in centuries. They were once used to push one's magic past its natural limits. But it came with consequences, so people stopped using them. It's possible that someone could use them to try to contain Nil and Vis, combine it, and then use it on these nochtra. It would decrease the risk on the person using the magic significantly."

Lane took the keys and shoved them back in their pocket as she stood up. Baltus jumped to his feet, and Shepherd stared between them.

"If you're going to lie, we're leaving," Lane said. She crossed her arms. There was no way Baltus was saying everything he knew. Not based on the look on his face, the way he couldn't stop licking his lips. The way his hungry eyes glared at Lane, daring her to leave the room with the keys. "Let's go, Shepherd."

Baltus held up his arms. "Fine, fine—fine." He glanced at Lane. "Clever, clever girl. You pretend you don't know what you have, but you know."

He threw his arms up in defiance as he rounded to the back of the couch and back to the bar cart, where he lifted a bottle of deep red wine to his lips.

Lane didn't move, staring straight at him as he began.

"They call them the Keys of Persephone. The Keys of Death. Some call them the Keys of Eternity. They have many names, but only one use." Baltus sighed. "I might as well start at the beginning.

"I was not much older than you when I was cursed. Not that you can tell by looking at me, now." He motioned to the paper thinness of his skin, the reds of his eyes. Shepherd rubbed at her throat uncomfortably. "I was a Warrior, like Shepherd's ancestors. Sometimes I wonder if I fought alongside them. And I was vain. So, so vain. I thought that I could have it all. Power. Glory. And it still wasn't enough. But that was before I was trapped here, in this prison, this body."

Shepherd raised an eyebrow at him. "You had a different body before?"

"No, no. But I do not recognize myself anymore. Thousands of years later, even my shadow is not my own. My children's children's children have died. The city I was born in has burned to the ground. Things tend to lose their meaning. I was a witch and a warrior, and I was a fool. I wanted it all. I wanted the magic. I wanted the world. And I have learned, since then, that desire is a dark mistress. You cannot have what you want."

A shadow fell over his face.

"What did you do to become cursed?" Lane asked, sitting down.

Bally flashed his teeth. "Another time," he promised.

She felt her skin crawl.

"I met them after I was cursed." He flicked his wrist casually toward Lane's pocket, toward the keys, but his face was grave. "The people who created those things. Most of the time, they are simply called The Keys. As if they are one and the same."

So there were others. A group of people who had created these things. Who could be behind the disappearances, who could have created the nochtra. Lane rubbed the keys between two fingers and they released a shrill, high note that only she could hear.

"Are they still around?" Shepherd asked, obviously wondering the same thing.

"Different people have held the title over the years. The Keys have passed from person to person, group to group. I thought that they were lost to time. Like I said, it's been centuries since the last time I heard of someone using them. The Keys of Persephone."

The bones seemed to scream at the words. Behind him, the shadows of the room grew darker, swirling as the moon disappeared in the skylight overhead.

"If they are back, it would be the first I have heard of it. The ones I knew. . . they are all gone. I made sure of it." His eyes flinted in the light, a small devilish upturn in his lips. "They came for me. Like I said, I was vain. Brash. I was trapped here and could do nothing except fight. I had done terrible things, things that thousands of years later, I still regret. But what The Keys did for power. . . it's unspeakable."

He waved his hands toward Lane. "That's all that is left once they are done. Nothing but the person's power, trapped in the key."

Lane tightened her fingers around them as Shepherd inhaled sharply. "They trap a person's power. . . in their own bone?"

Baltus nodded. He looked as if he wished he could fade into the shadows, blot out his memory in the blackness of the room. The candles had all but gone out, leaving the room in near blackness.

"Tell us," Lane said sharply. "Tell us how."

There were pieces that still weren't fitting together.

Baltus leaned forward onto the couch. "All magic requires a source. In my day, if you weren't strong enough, you stole it from others. Or sometimes, you stole it because you *were* strong enough. The Keys took it steps further. They found the most powerful—the immortal, the cursed, the witches who cannot control themselves— and tortured them. Took their bone and trapped all of their power inside. Most did not survive the process. But with my curse. . ."

Shepherd's brows drew together. "They did that to you?"

Her mouth twisted in sadness. Looking at her, it made Lane wish they had never come here. Her heart ached, wondering how Shepherd felt about all of this. Was her friend forgiven now, no matter what had passed between them? And if Baltus could be forgiven, after everything he had done. . . could anyone?

Baltus smiled at her, running his hand around the empty wine bottle. "Don't worry, Shep. It was a long time ago."

Lane took the keys out of her pocket again. "Are these the same keys as back then? Or are they different?"

There was one question scratching at her mind.

Baltus rounded the edge of the couch until he stood in front of Lane, leaning toward her so that he could see better in the light. She felt power ebbing off of him in waves. Whatever The Keys had taken from him, he'd clearly recovered. At least in one way. In every other way, she wasn't sure.

"Originally, there were only seven Keys. I suppose there were only seven people powerful enough to be worth their time," Baltus said. He squinted. "It's hard to say. This one looks rather old, but this one looks almost new. If whoever you are looking for is making new Keys. . . well, I would be very worried indeed."

Lane tightened her grip on the keys as Baltus took a step back, falling back into his couch. She scuffed the toe of her boot into the ground, grinding it as her blood rose.

If these Keys of Persephone had done something to Perry, it might have turned her into a shade. A nochtra. Except they had no reason to target Perry. And their mission, the drifter. . .

It hurt, he'd said.

They didn't seem to be likely targets. Perry was just a student at The Academy, and Lane had never seen her do anything particularly impossible, as smart as she was. The ghost from their mission had just been a regular target, as far as she was aware.

"Did the person have to be very powerful? Or could they use anyone? Any witch?" Shepherd asked.

Lane looked at her. Of course. She was worried about all the missing people from Haven Hall. How many were there, dozens? If they were all being used by The Keys. . . Lane couldn't even imagine what that would mean. And Addie? Deryck had said she was scared, worried about how powerful her own skill was.

She bit her lip as Baltus answered, cracking his neck. "I suppose it's possible, although it would make them much less likely to survive the process. I'd assume the power trapped would only be as powerful as the source, so it doesn't seem very practical."

He rose from his seat again.

"I've told you everything I know. Leave the keys and go," Baltus said.

Shepherd jumped from her seat, her fists clenched.

"Lane." Shepherd's voice wavered as she stepped toward Lane, holding out her arm protectively. Lane almost rolled her eyes as she followed Shepherd's gaze. Her eyes were on the darkness behind Baltus.

She had noticed before Lane had.

The growing shadows of the atrium started to take form.

They were surrounded.

A strange collection of beasts stalked through the darkness, circling the edges of the room and sticking to the shadows. A ghost fluttered in and out of sight in the shadows. A hellhound, teeth gnashing, growled from the wall at Bally's back. A wraith floated to his left, emerging from the shadows, its face removed and a bleeding, black hole in its place.

Bally's grin returned. He lifted his arms and shrugged out of his ragged coat, revealing the pale, scarred flesh of his chest. Scars dotted across his pectorals, ripped through his abdomen, pink lines painted his shoulders.

"Bally," Shepherd warned.

Lane's hand was already at her belt, flipping out her knife. In her pocket, the keys screamed.

Shepherd pushed at Lane, still standing in front of her, urging her toward the door.

Lane elbowed her back, pushing her aside.

"That's fine, we will just stay here and get eaten," Shepherd mumbled behind her. Lane ignored her.

"It *is* you," Lane said. "The shades. The nochtra."

She pointed to the darkness behind Baltus, where the ghost flickered. He was not like the ghosts she knew, her friends in the woods. It was like he was trapped between ghost and something else, like the shade from her mission. Like Perry.

"I cannot take credit, unfortunately, although I wish I could. My friends here are quite different from what you described."

"Baltus. You can't do this," Shepherd said, her voice cracking. "This isn't you. You're. . . my friend. Look at it. It's in pain!"

The hound's eyes flashed red as it looked at her and growled.

Baltus slowly walked away, his white skin glowing opal under the moonlight that filtered through the roof.

"Oh, don't be so sensitive, Shepherd. It's nothing like what The Keys did to me. In fact, you could say they taught me something. I've learned that it's always better to give than to receive."

Baltus turned to Lane, his fingers held taut as if gripping an invisible ball.

"Let me show you."

He disappeared as darkness flashed across the room. Lane could not see—not even her own hand as she held it in front of her face. They were in a sea of black. Shepherd called out for her, reaching for her in the dark. Her hand found Lane's, and she squeezed.

"Run," Lane whispered.

Something rammed into her side. The impact threw her across the couch and sent her tumbling across the floor like a broken doll. A hand closed around her throat as the creatures screamed, howling and shrieking into the night as the darkness imploded.

Shepherd vaulted across the room as the wraith chased her, diving after her like a bird of prey.

Lane blinked as Baltus's hand closed around her throat, his nails digging into her skin. Her veins turned black beneath his grip.

He hadn't just been experimenting with death magic, like Seren thought. He had consumed it, and it had become part of him. The air around him vibrated, and Lane couldn't tell where the magic ended and he began.

Shepherd disappeared behind a pillar, her tan form leaping over another couch and running from the atrium as the wraith and hellhound chased after her. The beast jumped over them as Baltus moved his other hand toward her throat, matted fur and overgrown nails grazing the tops of their heads.

Lane knew better than to waste the moment. As Bally glanced toward the hellhound, she brought her knee into his stomach. His thin skin gave way beneath the force, and he released her throat as she rushed forward, throwing them both to the ground.

"This is what you're doing? Torturing creatures to make yourself more powerful?"

Lane pinned her knee further into his abdomen as she wiped sweat from her forehead. Baltus looked up at her in surprise. People were somehow always surprised when she got the upper hand. It was annoying.

"I'm not torturing them," Baltus spat, the wine-red of his mouth mixing with blood. His body was weak after all these years, after whatever he had done to himself. She felt him relaxing beneath her, already exhausted. "All of my friends, all of us here—we're all immortal. And what does an immortal want more than anything?"

Lane dug her knee harder into his chest. Her hair fell around her face as he smiled up at her.

"To die."

Lane blinked at him.

He had lived thousands of years. The kind of immortality that many would kill to have. And he did not want it. She loosened her grip on his arms in surprise.

"I'm so tired. Tired of all of it," he said. "I just want peace."

The hellhound pounded into the room, its red eyes glaring as it howled in pain. Its left foot limped slightly as it ran.

Bally wanted peace—but only for himself. And he didn't care how he got it.

"It's not all it's cracked up to be," Lane snarled.

He rolled out from beneath her, his arm swinging from under her weight to grab her ponytail. He yanked, pulling against her hair as he kicked her away with all his weight.

Her cheek cracked against the marble floor as she landed. Stars filled her vision as her hair fell from its bun, clumps missing, trapped in Baltus's hand.

"Perhaps you should take a hard look at your priorities, Baltus," Shepherd said from behind her, her voice thick with rage. Lane could only see the floor as she struggled to push herself up. Her ribs ached, her wound reopened from where Baltus kicked her.

"You want to die?" Lane's voice was hoarse as she stood, blood rushing to her head. Her fingers twitched by her pocket, her knife lost in the shuffle.

Baltus glanced at her pocket, the shape of the keys evident against the fabric of her pants. He nodded, his creatures coming slowly toward him at some silent command. He watched Lane as her shoulders heaved up and down with every breath.

"That's all I've wanted for thousands of years," he said.

"Let me help you with that," she growled.

Lane vaulted off a pillar, throwing her entire body weight into a kick that landed squarely in Baltus's rib cage. It cracked beneath her boot as he crashed backwards into the lounging pillows. Unable to catch herself, Lane fell to the floor, her elbow hitting the stone with a matching crack.

Exhausted, she let her head loll against the tile. Baltus struggled to right himself in the pillows.

A hand wrapped around her arm, pulling her to her feet. Shepherd grinned down at her, a long, thin sword dangling from her hand. Her fingers held the hilt with a casual grace that showed she knew how to use it. Another weapon Lane didn't even recognize hung from her belt loop.

"Your heirlooms?"

She grinned.

Bally pulled himself to his feet as the wraith hovered in front of him, its shadows flickering in and out like a scarf in the wind. The dark shape drew shadows to it, wrapping them in a circle of darkness as the hellhound crept toward them, its claws leaving scratched indents in the stone floor. Behind Lane, she could sense the ghost, the rays of death magic radiating off it like a dark beacon.

They were surrounded.

Shepherd squeezed her arm, dropping it as Baltus stepped forward, his hand outstretched. A ball of shadow formed in his palm.

"You might want to move!" Shepherd shouted, pushing Lane to the side as she whipped the blade in front of them.

Lane dropped to the ground at the last moment as the orb barreled toward them. Shepherd's sword swung through the air, slicing through the dark orb like she had been doing it her entire life. Lane looked up at her from the ground, her elbow and side screaming.

"Told you I wasn't useless," Shepherd chided, flipping the sword between her hands.

"Oh, shut it."

Shepherd winked at her.

The hellhound and the wraith closed in on them. Lane's chest tightened as the clear space between them narrowed. Behind them, Baltus tightened his fist again, a wall of light forming between his palms.

"We have to get out of here," Shepherd said. She pulled Lane toward her so that Lane's back was against her chest, both of them inside the reach of the sword.

"We can't just leave them," Lane said. She pulled away from Shepherd's grasp.

"*Now* you want to be virtuous?" Shepherd asked, glancing at the creatures surrounding them.

Bally screeched something at the wraith, pulling it toward himself on some invisible chain. Her knife laid a few feet from him, abandoned among the throw cushions.

"Take this," Lane pulled a pouch of bone dust from her belt, throwing it to Shepherd. "It should trap the wraith and the ghost. And don't let them kill you."

Lane gave Shepherd a grim smile before rolling across the floor toward Baltus, grabbing her knife from the floor. He opened his mouth and Shepherd's sword flew across the room, landing cleanly in Baltus's hand. Behind her, she heard Shepherd groan.

Bally moved toward her with the sword. His movements were graceful but slow, the memory of a warrior lost to time.

"Give me the Keys," Baltus shouted through the chaos.

"I did promise," she said with a smile. She dropped her hand toward her pocket, her knife at her hip.

He saw the opening she had made for him and thrust the sword forward, a needle puncturing flesh.

Heat seared through Lane's wrists as she closed her eyes, hoping this would work one last time.

She Blinked, disappearing as Bally fell, his sword passing through where her chest was only seconds before.

She appeared behind him, surprised as her knees cracked against the floor. She still couldn't Blink without falling. She jumped to her feet, throwing herself at Baltus as he looked around the room for her, confused.

His eyes were wide as she ripped the sword from his hand, pressing the blade against his throat.

"Please." He pressed himself into the blade. "Please."

His eyes watered.

She could not. Would not. He didn't know what it was truly like. He didn't know what he asked. He could never know.

Lane closed her eyes. She would do anything and everything she could to get the one thing she wanted—to live again. Was Bally any different? Lane wanted to live, truly live. Baltus wanted to die, even knowing what was on the other side.

She dropped the blade.

Baltus released a breath, either relieved or angry, she couldn't tell. She closed her eyes again, holding him around the waist as she thought of the darkness between worlds. Of After Life.

And when the smell of dust and ash filled her nose, she let him go, willing herself to return to Life. To Baltus's house. To Shepherd.

It had all happened in a single Blink, a single second.

Tears stung at her eyes as she fell to the floor. The room was hauntingly silent with Baltus gone for good.

Shepherd rushed toward her, reaching as Lane collapsed.

"It's okay," she said, as Lane fell into her arms with an exhausted gasp. Shepherd ran her fingers through Lane's hair as she cried. "It's okay."

"It isn't."

Lane let herself stay draped across Shepherd's lap. Her shirt was slashed open, three claw marks tearing through the fabric. A bite mark was clear in the red skin of Shepherd's neck.

Her own leg bled, a matching scratch deep in the muscle of her thigh.

"That was incredibly stupid," Shepherd said. "You're lucky I don't kill you myself."

Lane laughed through her tears. "You could try."

Shepherd grinned. "Are you okay?"

"Are you?"

"Is he. . . gone?"

Almost in answer, Baltus's creatures surrounded them, calmly and quietly. The hellhound laid down, closing his eyes like he longed for sleep. The darkness disappeared from the room as if the shadows were being called home. Strips of moonlight lit the floor again, sparkling off the sweat on Shepherd's skin.

Lane pulled away. They were both bruised and covered in blood.

"So it was Baltus?" Shepherd adjusted her leg, tearing a strip of fabric from her ripped shirt to wrap around the bleeding wound on Lane's leg. Lane wished she was back in After Life, where everything healed itself. Her body screamed at her, pain in every pore.

"I don't think so," Lane said. "There's something I'm not seeing."

Shepherd stood, grabbing the sword from where she'd dropped it. She tossed it in the air, catching it in her opposite hand and sheathing it in a scabbard Lane hadn't noticed on her other hip.

"Well, we will look together then," she said, extending her hand to help Lane to her feet.

As she reached for Shepherd's hand, the ghost flew across the room, barreling toward her like a bolt of lightning. With a monstrous howl, it knocked her onto her back, surrounding her in the black ink of its tendrils. Shepherd shouted, but Lane could barely hear it as the ghost surrounded her in a cloud of darkness.

Lane screamed as the ghost pushed her to the floor, into and then through it. Shepherd called out, grasping for her hand through the shadows as she disappeared.

CHAPTER SEVENTEEN

Shepherd sprinted away from Baltus's house, her grandfather's sword swinging at her side. The streets were empty except for the cold air and the wraith on her heels. Its scream filled her ears until she could no longer hear the heavy pounding of her footsteps.

Lane was gone. As she disappeared, the calm inside Bally's mansion was split into chaos. The wraith turned, chasing Shepherd from the house as the hellhound howled.

"Should have worked out more," she panted.

Even though she should have been focused on her own survival, on running as fast as she could away from the wraith, Shepherd could only think of Lane.

At least it helped distract her from the stitch in her ribs. She cursed herself for always skipping health class.

Lane might have just Traveled away. She said that she wasn't whatever Seren called her, but she kept doing it.

Another lie.

Shepherd slowed at the bottom of the hill, looking over her shoulder to see the wraith still flying near the rooftops, ready to swoop down. She placed her hands on her knees, panting as the scratches across her chest and stomach throbbed.

She could just go home. She hadn't found Addie, but she did have something. More than she started with before she met Lane, anyway.

But Lane was gone, disappeared into thin air. Shepherd wasn't sure if they were friends, but she couldn't bring herself to leave Lane behind. Maybe it was guilt for lying about Baltus and her black market dealings—the same reason she barely spoke to her parents. Or maybe it was something else. Something she couldn't admit.

She had to get back to Haven Hall and tell them what had happened to Lane. They would be able to help her better than Shepherd could. Seren, as awful as she was, was a powerful witch.

Shepherd picked up her pace, running toward the townhouse that acted as a secret entrance to Haven Hall. She knew the city like the back of her hand, especially this section, so close to the Night Market. What she didn't know was if she would be able to get to the school without Lane's skill.

As the house appeared in the distance, the sun began to rise behind the hills of the city. The building stood out, even among the rows of identical houses lining the street. There was something strange about it, Shepherd realized, as she slowed to a jog. Not just the look, which was completely out of place for the street—Victorian and Gothic at the same time. It was something else, something that felt like a scratch at the inside of her skull.

Magic.

"I hate magic," she groaned, the same mantra she had been telling herself since she was ten.

"It didn't go well, then, I'm assuming," said a voice from behind her. Shepherd jumped, her hand flying to her sword. Her family sword. Maybe her father would forgive her now. She doubted it.

Deryck stood on the sidewalk, hands casually in his pockets, the stringy bangs of his blond hair covering his wide-rimmed sunglasses.

"What, were you following us?" Shepherd asked. She was parched and exhausted, her throat as dry as if she inhaled a plume of smoke. "We could have used the extra hands if you were."

Deryck pulled the sunglasses down the bridge of his nose. His blank white eyes seemed to stare at Shepherd, or through her. It was like looking in a mirror and realizing your reflection wasn't there.

"No, of course not," Deryck said. "Plus, it seems you came out all right, anyway."

He waved his hand in Shepherd's general direction.

"Bally's dead."

Deryck pushed the sunglasses back up the bridge of his nose with an uncaring shrug. Maybe Seren would even be pleased. Maybe she'd known what would happen all along. Lane was just the means to an end.

Shepherd hesitated. Lane was suspicious of Deryck, his role at the school. Shepherd shared the sentiment, although she knew that hers was mostly bias against the fact that Deryck was a demon. She'd never met a demon, had never even known they were even real—it seemed fair to be wary.

The words spilled out of her anyway.

"Lane is gone," Shepherd said. "Just gone, into thin air. One of those things *took* her."

Deryck pressed his lips together, taking two casual, calm steps toward the townhouse.

"Those are two very different things," he said. "Was she taken, or did she leave?"

"Those weird shade things everyone is looking for? One of them attacked her, threw her to the ground, and they both disappeared through the floor."

"Did she have the key on her?" Deryck asked, reaching for the door. There was a small hint of urgency in his voice. "The one she showed me."

"The two," Shepherd said, eager to see Deryck rattled. "She has *two*."

Deryck swung the door to the townhouse open.

"Of course she does!" he said, his voice incredulous and growing higher. "Because nothing can ever be easy, can it?"

Shepherd tried to hide her disappointment as the open door revealed a regular hallway instead of Haven Hall.

Even more surprising, Seren and her two lackeys stood in the hallway, weapons strapped to their backs. Yarrow and Korvu had braided their hair in tight coils, prepared for battle. They were armed to the teeth. To deal with Baltus if Lane didn't beat him, or to deal with Lane? Shepherd wasn't sure, but the surprise on Seren's face said everything she needed to know. They definitely hadn't expected Shepherd to be the one to return.

Shepherd hated to admit it, but she wasn't even surprised.

"You knew."

Seren collected herself, giving Shepherd an icy shrug. "Knew what?"

She looked at Deryck, wondering what outcome they had hoped for. Likely, they had hoped that Lane would somehow free Baltus from his prison with her skill, and then they could interrogate him themselves.

"Well, whatever you were hoping for, it seems Lane was successful. Bally is dead."

No emotion passed across Seren's face as Shepherd said it. She wondered if they knew Shepherd had been friends with Baltus, if that was the only reason they had let her tag along. Always playing games with people's lives. Especially hers.

"It seems that Lane has disappeared," Deryck said, glancing at Shepherd. "Gone into thin air after being attacked by a ghost."

Shepherd's fingers twitched at her side, at the grip of the sword. Even if she wasn't a witch with the Warrior skill, she knew how to use it.

"You have to help her." Her voice cracked, not nearly as threatening as she had been aiming for.

Seren raised her eyebrows, the thin blonde hairs disappearing into her pale skin.

"I don't have to do a single thing," Seren said, peeling her own sword off her back. She placed it against the black and white wallpapered wall behind them, discarded.

"That thing took her!" Her voice rose, carrying through the cramped hallway. "Just like everyone else!"

Korvu smirked as he leaned against the wall. "You poor thing. You *really* think that's what happened?"

Shepherd glanced between them, confused. "Of course that's what happened."

Seren stared at her flatly. Even Deryck's blank eyes seemed to be trying to say something, but she couldn't figure it out.

They weren't there. They didn't know.

"They didn't take her, you—" Korvu stopped himself, biting down whatever insult he'd been about to spit. "She's one of them."

Shepherd dropped her hands. The line between her eyebrows deepened, threatening to become a permanent mark of confusion.

"One of who?"

Deryck placed his hand on Shepherd's shoulder, turning her away from the former professors of the Haven Hall. He frowned at her, his mouth twisting as he searched for the words. Shepherd stared at him with wide eyes, urging him to spit it out.

"Lane isn't a Traveler. She has the ability to go between Life and After Life because they gave it to her. It's highly unlikely she went home unwillingly. She got what she came for."

Deryck's hand fell from her shoulder. Shepherd pulled away, shaking her head, messy hair falling in her eyes.

"Home?" The pieces slammed together in Shepherd's brain. "Your home is Hell."

"After Life," Deryck corrected, rolling his eyes.

"You're saying that Lane went to Hell."

Deryck nodded. "She isn't whatever you thought she was. A witch from a nomad colony with a special skill. She's from The Magistrate Academy. She works for them. Even if she wanted to, she can't. . . she has to do what they ask."

Shepherd racked her brain. The Magistrate Academy? It didn't sound familiar.

"The Magistrate Academy?" she asked.

"They're the ones that are hunting us. They control the nochtra, the shades, whatever you call them," Seren interjected, throwing her hands in the air as if she was tired of their back and forth. "A school, of sorts, in the afterlife where they teach death magic. And teach them to hate us."

Shepherd thought of the drawing Seren had showed the classroom, the nochtra that attacked her the night she met Lane. They had said they didn't know who sent them, but that had been a lie? It was this. . . Academy?

"The people that are hunting us. . ." Shepherd tried to pull her thoughts together. "They aren't even from Earth at all. They're. . ."

She looked at Deryck. He nodded.

"Dead."

Lane talked about her magic as if it was unique, so different from the skills of the witches that Shepherd knew. But she hadn't realized that Lane meant *death magic*. Her hair stood on end as she turned her head, cracking her neck. She knew about Nil, from her studies with her parents before they found out she was an unwitch, and from her dealings on the black market.

"Whether she is part of this Academy or not, we have to help her. I know she didn't go willingly. They must have taken her somehow, like the others. They could kill her."

Korvu rolled his eyes.

"Even if we wanted to help her, we can't go where they took her. And they won't kill her," Yarrow said.

"You don't know that!"

Shepherd looked between them. They were all staring at her as if they were waiting for something, their eyes wide, urging her to catch up. Her thoughts spun around her mouth, but she couldn't catch them. It didn't make sense. Death magic, Lane, nochtra, After Life. . .

"She's dead, you idiot," Korvu said.

Shepherd blinked. Blinked again. Deryck looked at him, his white eyes full of regret.

Dead.

Lane was dead.

Shepherd shook her head, hair flying in her eyes as she looked away. She grabbed for the wall behind her, her fingernails digging into the wallpaper as she steadied herself.

She would accuse them of pulling some kind of cruel prank on her if she didn't know them. Seren and her friends were the last people that would ever joke with Shepherd.

"She can't be dead. I saw her bleed. I saw her collapse. I held her hand, felt her pulse—"

She had felt the warmth in her skin as she grazed Lane's hand, seen the blush in her cheek. She had held her as she cried, real, destroyed tears after she had killed Bally. There was no way she was dead.

But even as she thought these things, she felt herself accepting it. Lane's magic being different, the way she was always hiding something. The things she knew about ghosts, nochtra, shades. . . not remembering who she was, her identity erased.

Lane was dead.

"You really don't know her at all," Deryck said, almost too softly. It wasn't a fact. It was a warning.

Shepherd slid down the wall, her hands buried in her hair. Her grandfather's sword clattered against the tile beside her.

"She's dead." Her mind flashed with all their small moments. Lane, as Shepherd pulled her into her chest, both their hearts beating like rabbits. Her skin underneath Shepherd's hand as she grabbed her by the wrist. The glances they exchanged at each other across the room, almost able to speak without a word.

And Lane had been dead for all of it. Had any of it been real?

The ground beneath her shook, and Shepherd gripped onto the tile with her fingertips. A lamp shattered to the floor, glass shattering, as something threw itself into the front door.

"They've found us," Seren said.

CHAPTER EIGHTEEN

Lane had Blinked thousands of times. She had gotten used to the feeling of being in between, of being neither here nor there, but she had always had the sense that she was pushing herself forward. It was like choosing to launch off a diving board and cannonball into black, unseen waters, not knowing what would happen on the way down. But at least it was her choice to swim.

This was not like that at all.

Something pulled her downward. Invisible hands wrapped around her body, rubbing on her skin and pulling her through the dark. Now that Lane had traveled on her own, not for missions but for herself, she knew that she was being forced back.

Her back hit the ground first, stars of pain shooting through her spine.

"Every damn time."

She blinked at the spots peppering the edges of her vision.

She was in a classroom. Or what looked like one, anyway. There were no desks, but the room was laid out in rows of stadium seating, leading down to a blank wall where a blackboard had clearly been removed. Behind her, stairs led up to a door, but it was not the typical classroom door that she was used to. There was no window, no knob.

The small door had a small, barred window barely an eyehole.

This classroom had been converted to a cell.

Lane didn't need to ask. She was at The Academy.

With a scream, Lane kicked at the door. Her palms and fingers bruised as she beat against it, hoping the wood would splinter beneath her hands, but it didn't budge. She didn't bother to try to Blink. She knew they wouldn't have made it so easy. At least the wound in her abdomen seemed to be healing. One of the benefits of being home.

Home. Was that what The Academy was? It was the only place she had ever known as Lane, but the word no longer felt right.

She dug her nails into the door until they split down the middle, crying out in pain, anger, frustration. She took everything that happened in the past several days, the past year, ever since she had awoken at The Academy, and screamed.

She screamed at being blamed for the nochtra, for the murder of her friend. She screamed for Perry. For Baltus. She screamed at her stupid self for thinking she could fix anything. She screamed because she missed Victor, Tripp, and Perry. She screamed because she knew they had lied. She screamed for Shepherd.

She screamed because she had nothing left. After the scream, all that was left was hollow. She had scraped herself clean.

"Well, I have to admit that I am surprised," said a voice from behind her. "And I hate being surprised."

The Headmistress walked through the wall as if it were air, her hellhound wrapped around her ankles. A slash in its fur was evident. Lane clenched her teeth.

Eurydice's white pantsuit ended just above her ankles, a stark contrast against the dust and ash of the abandoned classroom. The fabric hung loosely around her arms, but still managed to reveal the taut, muscular form underneath.

"But as you know, a deal is a deal."

Lane took a step toward her, but her footing faltered. Even after everything, she was nervous to be under Eurydice's gaze.

"You can't expel me. We both know I had nothing to do with what happened to Perry, or any of it," Lane stopped, recoiling. "What deal?"

Lane would never have made a deal—she knew how dangerous that could be. She hoped it wasn't another blank spot.

Eurydice's smile was sharp teeth.

Victor appeared in the room, walking through the wall like it was nothing. He glanced at Lane before turning to Eurydice, his face a blank slate. Lane's neck prickled. Something was wrong.

"Victor persuaded me to give you a week to prove you hadn't done it and to find the person who did. And of course, as I suspected, it was a witch." She didn't even stumble over her own lie.

Lane furrowed her brow, trying to figure out what she meant.

"You think Baltus was behind it." Lane had thought the same thing, but only for a moment, which only confirmed to her that they were lying. There was no way they really believed that. They were just accepting it as a convenient cover up to hide the truth.

But who were they hiding it from?

Lane laughed, a cackle that tilted her head back. Eurydice snarled. As she lifted her hand to silence her, Victor stepped between them.

"Lane, please." Behind his glasses, his eyes pleaded. *Don't argue. Take what you're being given.*

"What did you do?"

"It's nothing," he whispered.

"Don't be so modest, dear. Deciding to stay at The Academy for another hundred years isn't *nothing*. Men," Eurydice said to Lane with a wink. As if it were a secret joke between them.

Lane's fist clenched as she imagined strangling her.

He'd already been here too long. He didn't deserve to stay longer.

She wouldn't let him sacrifice himself, not for her. She didn't deserve it.

Lane swerved to Eurydice. "We both know Baltus didn't do this. He couldn't have. He was locked in that house. All he wanted was—"

To die. She couldn't bring herself to say it. She hoped that wherever he was, he was happy, and far away from Eurydice.

"So, you've decided to confess instead?" Eurydice crossed her arms, her jeweled hand on her bicep.

Victor placed his hand on Lane's shoulder, giving her a too-tight squeeze.

"Just forget it, Lane. Put this behind you," he whispered in her ear.

Lane's vision blurred. Tears threatened to form at the corners of her eyes. All she could think about was Perry, about the missing witches, about the nochtra, turned and tortured into monsters. Whoever they had been, they didn't deserve this.

She had forgotten so many things, but not this.

She shrugged away from Victor's grip.

"And what about all of the missing witches? What about them? What about the nochtra? Are you going to do anything about that?" Her fists were clenched. "What about The Keys?"

Victor coughed, looking at her with wide eyes that flicked to Eurydice.

Eurydice pursed her lips so thin that they were almost invisible. "I don't know what you're talking about. Missing witches? Nochtra?" Her voice rose, angry and high. "You've been near the witches."

Lane recoiled. Her body went numb. She had just given away that she had done the one thing The Academy explicitly forbade. She was done for. They would never let her back.

"There are people out there kidnapping, killing us! Witches and ghosts alike. These people, The Keys—they're the ones you want!"

Eurydice walked toward the cell door, her cape swinging behind her as she tucked her hands into her waist. For a moment, Lane thought she would disappear through the wall, leaving them behind with Victor staring at Lane helplessly and Lane thirsty for blood.

Victor grasped Lane's wrist. "Please, Lane. Let's just get out of here."

She shook her head, shaking Victor's grip from her arm.

"You're hiding something." Lane took a step toward Eurydice. "You told all of us that the witches were after us, that they wanted to take over the afterlife and destroy The Academy. But it's the other way around, isn't it? You're hunting them."

Victor's hand hung in mid-air, as if he was frozen by Lane's words. Eurydice didn't bother to turn around.

"If you don't find your deal to be satisfactory, both of you can stay here," Eurydice spat, waving her hand in front of the wall. "I believe this cell is more comfortable than some of the alternatives."

Victor shuddered. Lane rattled her head, erasing the thought. She didn't want to know.

"You don't deny it." She stormed toward Eurydice.

Lane's voice rose above the angry whisper to a harsh, vicious snap. The urge to lunge for Eurydice and tear her arm from its socket rocked through her.

Eurydice snarled as she surged toward Lane, her red lip curling and her hand whipping through the air.

Lane was against the wall before she realized she was flying, air erupting from her lungs as she hit the stone. She was pinned there, floating and feet dangling above the ground, all from the flick of Eurydice's wrist. Victor rushed toward her, but Eurydice held up a single, dismissive hand.

"Do not pretend to know what you are talking about, girl. Do not presume that your year here has taught you anything. Do you even know what it means, to be in charge of this school, to have to protect death magic from the outside world? What do you think you would do if it meant protecting all magic? Saving not just you, but everyone—both alive and dead?"

Lane struggled, her feet kicking against the wall. The wolf slowly slunk away from Eurydice, its teeth gnashing at her. If it leapt, it could take a bite into her flesh, and she wouldn't be able to do a thing.

Eurydice took a step toward her, letting Lane fall to the floor as she dropped her hand. Her knees hit the dirt-covered stone, an audible crack running through the room.

Eurydice stepped toward Lane, grabbing her by the sleeve of her shirt and lifting her into the air like a paper doll. The borrowed black shirt tore beneath her red fingernails as her eyes blazed. Lane recoiled, turning her head away as Eurydice brought her face too close to Lane's, so close she could feel the weak, cold breath of someone undead.

"What do you think *I wouldn't* do for that?" She held Lane's chin, the sharp tips of her nails digging into her flesh.

Without warning, she dropped Lane, letting her fall hard on her knees. Eurydice didn't say a word as she disappeared through the wall, her cape trailing behind her like smoke. The wall shuddered like tidal ripples around her before turning solid again.

Lane crumpled to the ground, unable to hold her weight any longer. It was true. It had all been true. Shepherd, Seren, Deryck—they had all been right. Some part of her must have known. But the girl who only knew The Academy—only knew her life here—had hoped that she would prove them wrong.

Victor knelt next to her, placing a hand on her shoulder. His first two fingers reached for a lock of her hair, twirling it between his fingers.

She tried to stop the hitching in her chest as it rose and fell, threatening to collapse into sobs.

"It's all right," Victor whispered, wrapping his arm around her as best he could. "Let's get you back to your room."

She could not force herself to her feet.

They had lied. Victor had lied. The Academy had lied. And worse, she had believed them—had gone looking for the witches to blame Perry's death on them.

"I have to go back."

She struggled to her knees. Victor's fingers slowly dropped the single curl of hair, his eyes confused.

"It's too dangerous. You can stay here now; I worked it out with Eurydice—"

"You lied to me."

He stared at her, stunned.

"You knew, didn't you? That the witches were being hunted. Did you know about the nochtra? About Perry?"

Victor's arm fell as she stood. He stared at her, a thousand emotions flashing across his face.

"Do you know about The Keys? Are they behind this?"

He furrowed his brow, taking a step away from her. Silence stretched between them, a candle that had been snuffed out.

Finally, he spoke. "No, Lane—I didn't know. I knew that Eurydice wanted to eliminate the threat of the witches, but if she's done anything, I had no idea. And nochtra? *The ruined ones?* I've never even heard the term. And what is this about keys?"

Lane stared at him, backing away toward the door. She looked around the edges, searching for a weak spot.

"The Keys. They're this group of people who kill others for their magic and use these keys—like amperes—to control it. Nil and Vis. Just like what you said might be happening with the shades."

She looked back at him. "You must have heard of them. Baltus. . . he thought they might be connected to whatever is happening."

Victor took a step toward her, rolling up his sleeves. His stringy hair hung in his eyes, which looked down at the floor, away from her. His jaw was tight, his teeth grinding, like when he was working out a problem. Maybe he didn't know. His face was all confusion, surprise.

"And why did he think that?"

Lane exhaled. She didn't have time for one of his intellectual exercises.

"You can either help me get out of here or watch me do it myself," she spat, running her fingers along the seam of the door.

"Lane," Victor called from behind her. "Wait. You can't. You're injured. You need to stay here, to heal, before—you've been in Life too long." He paused, and she glanced at him over her shoulder. "And I missed you."

He turned away from her, as if he couldn't bear to look at her while he said it. Something inside her leapt to hear them. The thing between them had gone unspoken for so long, she'd thought she imagined it. There had been moments when she thought he felt the same way, even though hundreds of years separated them. Even though he was basically a teacher, and she was a student. He'd been the only one she could turn to, the only one she had told about the strange things that had been happening to her.

Her mind snapped to Shepherd. With Victor, things had always been quiet, unspoken—a secret that was barely there at all. Shepherd was his opposite in every way. Everything about her was loud.

Lane shook her head. She couldn't think like this. She needed to focus.

She turned back to the door. "Help me or don't," she said, her voice colder than she intended.

Victor appeared beside her, his hand feeling against the classroom wall. Lane shoved her arm through the small eyehole, but barely made it halfway before her forearm muscle blocked her. Victor knelt, reaching beneath the door with his fingers.

At least he was helping, even if he didn't agree with her. But something he said nagged at the edges of her thoughts.

"What is Eurydice planning?" Lane asked.

She stopped feeling the door, looking down at him. To her surprise, Victor's usually expressive face revealed nothing. He didn't even flinch or take his eyes off the cracked wood of the door.

"You said it's too dangerous," she pushed. "Why?"

"I don't know. You think she would tell me? There are parts of After Life, things she knows, that I have never even seen." He looked up at her. "But whatever it is, it's not safe for you. You can't go back."

She looked into his eyes, the glistening of steel gray. They were flat as stone. There was nothing to be found there but the hint of regret. It was the face of a gambler who was afraid to reveal his hand, even at the end of the game.

"You're her right-hand man. Her attaché. Her *errand boy*. Tell me you don't know. Tell me you didn't know about the witches. They aren't evil at all. They aren't even after us."

She tried to hide the accusation in her voice. She felt raw, like the flesh was burned from her body and regrowing, pink and tender.

Victor winced. The stringy locks of his hair hung in his eyes like a broken crow's wing. "I think I knew more than I wanted to admit to myself. But I'm no one. It's not like I could stop her."

They faced each other, both of their hands on the door. Lane couldn't read the expression on his face. Even her own feelings were too complicated, her brain all fuzz. She knew he was right. They were both trapped here—him, more so, especially now. If Eurydice was up to anything, if she had really kidnapped or hurt the missing witches, Victor would have been helpless to stop her. He was a shy intellectual as much as Lane was a pissed off, naive nobody.

He exhaled a long breath, pressing the bridge of his nose. "There is one thing I know. She's called people from all across After Life to The Academy. People like her, I think. Leaders. Demons, even. Whatever she's planning, whatever she's doing, it's not just her. It's bigger than us."

"Other people? From After Life?" Some part of Lane had known Eurydice wasn't the only official in all of After Life. There had to be others. Other schools, even, like theirs. There had to be.

"They're coming for All Hallows, aren't they?" Lane asked him. She had imagined the celebration as a big party, a grand ball. Of course, it was more than that.

Victor nodded.

"Then help me with this door," she said.

She turned back to the cell door, searching the edges again for any piece she could remove or force open. There were no latches, no locks, no screws or hinges. The door was sealed with magic, and it seemed that she had no way to open it from the inside.

Victor pressed a hand to the sand-colored stone as if he might take its temperature. He scratched his nail down the edge, pulling away a small layer of rock. Behind his wire glasses, he furrowed his brows.

He rolled up his sleeves, revealing the black ink of his obols. His hands drifted from the door to the classroom wall, his thin brows furrowed.

Neither of them had used the door, Lane realized. She'd been looking in the wrong place. The ward wasn't weakest at the door—it was the wall itself.

He ran his hands across his obols twice, mumbling some incantation beneath his breath. A small bag appeared in his hand.

He smirked. "A small sleight of hand keeps them guessing."

A series of black beads and gold coins poured into his hand. Lane stopped herself from reaching for them. So many amperes in one place. She and the other students were only given one or two at a time. He easily had fifty. How long had he been collecting them for? There were easily enough to power all of The Academy and still have a good amount leftover.

"You're going to overload the ward," she realized.

Victor grinned at her, the corners of his eyes wrinkling with joy. There was no stopping him when he got a new idea, when he wanted to attempt a new project. It was the only time she saw him truly happy.

"You might want to stand back."

Lane did as she was told, watching as he rubbed the coins between his fingers, feeling their weight. She backed up across the floor, the wound in her leg flaring.

Victor turned to face the wall and raised his arms. There was no incantation. With death magic, he'd taught her, they didn't always need one. Words often had no meaning.

Like power, the meaning was within.

The room spun as a crack blasted through the ward and beneath their feet. Lane lost her balance, clapping her hands over her ears as she fell. It was louder than any sound she'd ever heard, deep and deafening. The crack was inside her, in her ribcage, resounding through her as it traveled through the rock of the cave. A trickle of blood ran from her ear. She cried out but suddenly there was no noise at all, only the feeling of the deep, resounding sound in her bones.

Screams followed, but they were not from inside the prison. Their cries were haunting, eerie and quiet, like a river that trickles until it runs dry. Not of this life or the next. Lane squeezed her eyes tight against the darkness as it swirled around her. The power had pulled her away to some unknown place. She couldn't hear, couldn't see, couldn't breathe.

"Lane." She opened her eyes as buzzing filled her ears, like static electricity. Blood ran down her neck, and her side ached. The wound in her leg seared, hot and close to being infected.

Victor stood over her.

"If you're going to go, go now," he said. She grasped his hand as he pulled her up. "There is no way they didn't hear that."

The door was intact. He'd blown a hole straight through the brick, revealing the empty hallway in the school beyond.

Lane let out a single, delirious laugh. He grabbed her hand, leading her into the hall. It was dark, with no torches lighting the way. It was a part of the school she didn't recognize, and she had the strange feeling that they were underground.

It was now or never.

"Victor." She turned to him. "You shouldn't have done that. You've already been here too long. She was going to let you move on soon. Why. . . why would you do that?"

He leaned against the wall, glancing over her shoulder into the narrow passageway. His eyes were downcast.

"You know why, Lane. I would do anything for you." He paused. "Including, apparently, a prison break."

Her breath caught in her chest. She desperately wanted to exhale but couldn't remember how. Victor reached out, running a thumb down her cheek, his nail scratching against her skin.

"You don't have to do this. Stay. Here at The Academy." *With me,* his eyes said.

"I have to help them," she said, taking a step back. "They aren't like we thought. There are good people. Come with me. I'll show you."

They didn't have enough time to cover all the things she wanted to say, and her words came out rambling and wrong.

She knew he wouldn't come.

"You know I can't," he said. "If you're going to go, go."

"Thank you," she said. She took two steps further into the hallway, hoping she was going the right way.

"Just come back," Victor said. "Before it's too late."

CHAPTER NINETEEN

All Lane could hear was the pounding of her feet as the tunnels bent and turned. Her feet slipped against the floor as she struggled to keep her pace at a sprint.

"Should have asked for directions," Lane mumbled, beneath her panting.

She could have never imagined this many halls existed at The Academy. She knew there were parts she hadn't explored, knew that there were underground passages like the one that led to Deryck's bar, but it seemed like the labyrinth was never-ending. Each path led to a new tunnel, more winding than the last. The ground turned from polished stone to wet cave rock, and she slipped against the dampness, scraping her hand along the wall.

She gritted her teeth, pain shooting through her jaw.

She needed to keep going. She didn't know what she was going to do, if she could do anything. But she had been pulled, twisted, and manipulated until she was nothing but a clump of knots.

If she was going to unravel, she would make sure they all came apart with her.

The wound in her leg had not healed since being back in After Life. It screamed as she ran down the unlit corridor. Her ribs felt like they might split from the strain. For once, she was thankful for the hours she had spent running away on missions. Her vision blurred, black spots at the corners of her eyes.

"Don't black out, not again, not now," she ordered herself. Somehow, her vision held steady.

She turned another corner, rushing water running down the wall, and was met with a door. Without thinking, she swung it open, revealing a spinning set of stone stairs that led down into darkness.

"Down it is," she said, taking them two at a time.

She wished Shepherd was with her, if only to make a joke about hating running, or yelling at Lane for putting them in danger once again. But she was alone with just the beating of her dead heart.

At the bottom of the stairs, she was met with another door. This one was newer, like the ones she was used to at The Academy. It made her pause, the strange, new wood inside the strange, dark cave. There was a black metal handle on it, twisted and welded in the shape of a horse. Whatever the hell that meant.

A hoarse scream cracked through the silence, followed by a *thump. Thump. Thump.* Another thump. Lane paused. It was like someone was hitting a wall.

She needed to get out of there. She had been trying to escape, but she only found herself deeper and deeper in the hidden halls beneath her school.

She followed the noise anyway, swinging open the door with a single kick.

It was a hallway of more doors, ten or twelve of them, identical to the one she had been trapped behind. Each had that same small window, barely wide enough for her arm.

The knocking was weak, but in the silence of the hallway, Lane found it easily enough. The person was still screaming, but their voice had gone so hoarse that it was barely a whisper.

Lane tried not to think about how long they had been screaming for as she put her face to the window.

"Oh, good. You heard me," the woman said.

Lane staggered backward, her breath catching in her chest like a skipping note.

Seren's partner, Ivy, laid on the floor of the cell. Her skin was sallow, her light brown hair caked with mud and filth and blood. The angles of her face were all bones, the hollows of her eyes dark and gaunt. She looked nothing like the smiling girl in the photo, glasses askew on her rosy cheeks. She looked skeletal.

She looked dead.

Overhead, Lane could hear footsteps, slow at first and then faster, as if someone was breaking into a run.

Ivy looked puzzled as Lane moved her tongue in her mouth, working up more saliva so she could speak.

"I was going to complain more about the accommodations, but you're not with them, are you?" she croaked with a weak smile. She held her thin arms across her lap, her bony knees exposed through ripped pants. She'd never seen someone so frail.

She hesitated. "No, I'm not."

It felt good to say it, to make it real.

"You're Ivy, aren't you? I know Seren."

Ivy dropped her head against the stone wall. There was no sign of relief on her face.

"Seren," she whispered, her smile fading. She was too weak to respond any further, the name sounding like a distant memory on her lips.

Lane ran her hands down the frame of the door, looking for any weaknesses. She didn't have a hidden hoard of amperes, but she did have her obols. If she could find a weak spot, she might be able to damage it enough to just pry the door open.

Shouting echoed in the halls behind her, traveling down the staircase.

A stern male voice carried down the passageway. "There's someone down there."

Was it one of Eurydice's guards? One of the other professors? She didn't recognize the voice.

Lane shoved her body into the door, willing it to open.

"There's no time." Ivy coughed. Her eyes met Lane's. Even as weak as she was, they were full of strength. She tilted her chin up, her jaw firm. "Promise me."

Promise what? That she would come back for her? That she would help her?

"I can't leave you." Lane pressed her hand through the small bars on the window. Tears welled at the corner of her eyes, although she didn't know why. She didn't know this woman. But as she saw Ivy laying there, something inside her snapped.

"Well, you're going to," Ivy said. "But come back soon. . . or we won't be here. When they take us away, sometimes. . . people don't come back."

There were others. Ivy wasn't the only prisoner.

Lane dropped her hands from the bar. The shouting was growing closer.

"Is there a girl here? A few years younger than me? Named Addie?"

Ivy blinked at her. She coughed, flecks of blood covering her chin.

She heard the door to the stairs open, footsteps pounding on stone above her, down the hall. They were out of time.

"I don't know. They don't let us see each other."

Lane bit her lip. She pushed her hand further through the small eyehole, as if she could reach her. But they were too far apart. Ivy barely tilted her chin in response.

She forced herself to turn from the window.

The hall was no longer empty.

A hellhound stood in the doorway at the base of the stairs, flanked by two nochtra.

Overhead, the lights flickered, threatening to blink out with a hiss. A low, angry growl slowly curled from within its chest as it bared its teeth at Lane.

But she was not watching the hellhound. The nochtra were almost unrecognizable as shades. The free-flowing shadows that grasped and sucked at the light around them had turned into flesh, or something like it. They stood in darkness, legs and arms made of pure shadow. The tendrils still wisped around them, snaking toward the emergency lights and extinguishing them in a single moment, suffocating the light in darkness. Where the shades had no faces, only the haunting memory of what a face once was, Lane could see these creatures clearly. The hollow sockets where eyes had once been, the empty notch of a nose, the thin, disconnected smile. Their skeletal expressions stared at her as they tilted their heads to the right.

Lane sighed. "This is the longest week of my afterlife."

They shot toward her in the dark hallway, shadows behind them like capes. In a moment, they were on her, their movements fast and calculated like trained soldiers. One of them reached for her with a shadowy hand, grabbing her at the base of her neck and lifting her off the ground. Lane threw her body weight into the wall, thankful for the tight space of the hallway, and shoved her feet against the surface. Falling backward, she pulled herself from the nochtra's grasp, its inky fingers still wisping toward her as she crashed toward the ground and rolled away.

The last of the light disappeared, engulfing them in darkness.

The hellhound leapt at her, pouncing on her chest. Claws dug into her still-healing abdomen. Lane let out a single cry as she tried to wiggle away from its grasp.

"Are we really doing this again?" she asked, gritting her teeth against the pain.

She grabbed it by the scruff of its neck, throwing it to the side as she rolled on top of it. She didn't want to hurt it. Like Baltus's creatures, she knew it was only doing what it was told to do.

Gripping it by the skin of its neck, she threw it overhead toward the second nochtra. Gasping, she jumped to her feet. They were all behind her now, the stairway clear. She just needed to make it there, and then out of The Academy.

Easy. Not a problem at all.

Before they could move, she sprinted toward the stairs. Behind her, the nochtra cried, cawing like hawks in the night.

"The other way!" someone yelled from behind another door.

Lane stopped short. She wanted to laugh, but the wounds all over her body burned.

The nochtra lunged for her as she turned and ran toward them. Her leg screamed each time her foot hit the ground, but she pumped her feet, pushing against the rock. Their billowy arms reached for her, the smoke ending in onyx claws. She dove across the floor, forcing each of her shoulders into their torsos with all of her strength.

She expected them to be knocked off their feet, to fall backward with the wind knocked out of them. But she passed straight through them like clean water.

Her skin was ice cold as she slid across the floor on the other side, her chest gasping in shock. Her body shivered. The nochtra screamed, ripping through the air like birds of prey.

Torn wings erupted from their backs. Lane scrambled across the floor backwards as they spread across the hallway. The rips and tears in the shadows only made their wings seem more nightmarish, like gargoyles carved to appear like stories that keep children awake at night.

They both turned their heads back and screeched. Lane closed her eyes, preparing for them to dig their talons into her neck.

Somehow she forced herself up and pushed herself into a run. The nochtra flung themselves at her, scratching at her shirt, their claws shredding through her flesh like it was butter.

She stumbled with a cry as pain seared through her back. She could feel the heat of the wound and warm blood dripping down her spine. Their ruined wings surrounded her in a cocoon as she fell.

She just needed to get to the stairs. Once she was outside the school, she could Blink back to Life—or so she hoped. It was barely a plan. Shepherd would have laughed at her.

Well, too bad. It was all she had.

The nochtra closed its wings tighter around her as she struggled onto her forearms. Shadows crept around her, wrapping around her waist and ankles like manacles and forcing her to the ground again. The second nochtra snarled, leaping onto her back and stabbing its claws into the still-fresh gashes.

Lane screamed. Struggling against their pulling shadows and the talons at her back, she shoved her hand into her pocket, desperate for something, anything—a bit of bone dust, grave dirt, or if she was lucky, her dagger—but her weapons were all gone.

The cold sang through her bones like a hymn. Her fingers wrapped around the shard of bone, her fingers brushing against the two keys. Pieces of someone's power, tortured and trapped.

The nochtra's claws wrapped around her side, slicing into the soft flesh of her abdomen. Lane let out a single, sharp cry.

Something in the key seemed to sharpen in reply. Its hum changed note to something screeching, lilting, a violin out of tune.

"Please," she whispered.

She felt the hum of power resounding in her bones and her own pain responding in a dark duet. *I, too, am missing something,* her body said to the key. *I, too, have had things taken from me.*

Lane had found no solace from her suffering, nothing to fill the void inside her.

There is potential in your pain. There is power in it. Harness it.

She was not sure whose voice she heard.

The nochtra bit into her neck, teeth made of darkness and shadows that ripped at her flesh nonetheless. She yanked the key from her pocket.

With the snap of thunder, light flooded the hallway. Rays of light and shadow exploded from the bone, jutting out from her knuckles and tearing through the nochtra like they were paper. The wings disappeared from around her with a sputtering exhale—the creatures barely had time to scream as they were knocked away from her.

Lane flinched, squeezing her eyes tightly as the room flooded with light. Her hand burned as it held onto the bone. But as she held it, her heartbeat settled. Something soothed through her aches and wounds, as if the key wasn't just helping her—it was healing her.

Free, Lane scrambled forward across the floor, crawling into a run. She sprinted down the cavern-like hallway, rounded a corner, and was met with a dead end.

A set of heavy doors stared at her, identical to the oversized fortress doors that led to the library and out of place in these strange, cave-like tunnels. It creaked open as she ran toward it, as if sensing her presence. With her last gasp of energy, she threw herself to the bottom of the stairs. The door slid shut behind her with a booming thud.

Silence surrounded her, interrupted only by her own gasping breaths. Pushing herself off the ground, she realized she still held the key. A shining pink burn was imprinted across her palm.

She looked up the stairs, light trickling down the stone steps, and knew she was out.

In her hand, the key thrummed at her, as if it was pleased.

CHAPTER TWENTY

"One for me," Korvu yelled.

"I'm still winning," Yarrow called back.

The house shook as another nochtra threw itself against the door. Shepherd held tight to her sword, unsure what to do. They wouldn't be able to take much more of this. The windows had already shattered, and Yarrow and Korvu had set their bows to shoot through the broken glass.

"Are you keeping score?" Shepherd asked.

They both shrugged in unison, pulling arrows from their quivers.

"Keeps things interesting," Korvu said, over his shoulder.

"You have to do what you can to make your workdays less monotonous," said Yarrow.

The sky had turned completely gray, no sign of daylight. Yarrow released another arrow as Shepherd stepped closer to the window, peering over her shoulder.

Even with her father's sword, there was nothing she could do. She wasn't like Addie, or like her dad, or any of the warriors that had come before them. Her father had taught her and Addie how to fight, probably holding onto the hope that Shepherd was a late bloomer. Or maybe he had known something like this would happen one day. But either way, even with his training, she was still just human.

Their arrows were doing nothing to the nochtra. If they truly were dead, it didn't seem so. There was nothing lifeless about them. They were creatures made of shadow, poised to strike, their forms flickering between beast and man. One second, a ghoul made of shadow stood on the street, and the next, a storm of pure darkness, wings taking flight as they threw themselves against the house.

"It was only a matter of time before they found us," Seren said, her back against the door. "What do you say, Shepherd? Is it a coincidence, or did your friend Lane send them as soon as she got home?"

Shepherd's nostrils flared, but she said nothing. She didn't want to believe Lane would betray them. Sure, she was annoying, sarcastic, a little combative, and she had lied.

Not to mention that she was dead.

"She wouldn't," Shepherd said. "Just because she is one of them doesn't mean she's with them. You trust him just fine."

She pointed at Deryck, who leaned against the wall, his fingers running along the hem of his skirt.

Yarrow released another arrow. It broke through the wing of one nochtra, disappearing behind them on the street. The creature didn't flinch. "Nothing is working!"

"Yes, I noticed," Seren said. She glanced through the window and then put her back to the door again, as if she could hold the house together by sheer strength.

"We've got to do something," Shepherd said as the nochtra screamed, throwing themselves against the wall again. The glass shook, shattering to the ground and across Yarrow's arm. "Can we get back to Haven Hall? Through whatever secret entrance you have here?"

Seren shook her head. "And lead them right to us? Not a chance."

Beside her, Yarrow exhaled.

They were trapped.

Seren pulled her sword from her back, her right hand tight on the hilt as she turned toward the door. It was splitting down the middle, the wood splintering with each hit.

"It's better than doing nothing."

Seren gritted her teeth. "I don't remember asking for your advice, little unwitch."

As she spoke, the door buckled behind her, nearly snapping as another nochtra tried to break through.

Shepherd moved to stand next to her, pressing her back into the door beside Seren.

"Finally, serving my purpose as dead weight," she grumbled. Over her shoulder, she glanced at Seren again. "We can't just let them break in."

Seren's hand clung to the door frame, pressing into the wood with all the force she could muster, her sword in her opposite hand. "That's exactly what I intend to do."

Shepherd blinked at her. "You're going to let them in and trap them."

"A bottleneck," Seren confirmed. "Seems your dear old dad did teach you a thing or two before he kicked you to the curb."

Her words had no venom, but Shepherd found herself gritting her teeth anyway. "He didn't kick me out. I left."

"Whatever you say."

Behind them, something thundered, the boom echoing through the house. Shepherd peered over her shoulder through the window, but could only see the black sky, storming with clouds.

Deryck moved toward the window, somehow finally finding it in himself to care. Shepherd gritted her teeth. When this was over, whether she died or not, she was going to punch him right between his white eyes.

"It's the guards from The Academy," Deryck said.

Shepherd spun to look out the window beside him, leaving Seren alone at her post.

Shepherd looked out the window to see half a dozen guards beneath the nochtra, standing completely still. They did not look anything like Lane. Their skin was gray, their eyes black. If she had to guess what the dead looked like when they walked the Earth, it was this. Not Lane.

As if reading her mind, Deryck said, "There's a reason the students at The Academy are the only ones allowed to travel between Life and Death. It's unnatural, and requires a tremendous amount of energy. The longer the dead are away from After Life, the faster they deteriorate."

Seren snorted. "And turn into ugly buggers like them."

Shepherd counted the days. Lane had been with her almost a week. Had she really taken that risk just to turn around and betray her?

Deryck pinched the bridge of his nose. It was not just the guards' black eyes or the strange, distorted hellhounds at their feet. There was something else surrounding them, some kind of dark energy that made Shepherd turn away.

In the distance, strangled, angry growls filled the street. Shepherd pressed against the window again, straining to see through the dark.

A hellhound broke free, snapping the leather leash and launched forward.

Within seconds, it leapt for the porch, teeth bared as it threw itself at the door. It snapped its jaw at the wood and threw its body again, the wood vibrating against Shepherd's shoulder as she pressed herself in next to Seren.

Yarrow held up his bow. He was out of arrows. The hellhound growled and scratched at the foot of the door.

They were going to break through.

Seren looked at Shepherd. She had realized the same thing.

"Yarrow, Korvu," Seren said "It's time."

They nodded. Yarrow and Korvu unsheathed the daggers and knives at their side, holding one in each hand.

Seren turned to Deryck. "Go warn the others. They will know what to do when we're gone."

Shepherd jerked her head, doing a double take as she realized what Seren meant. "Gone?"

Together, they moved toward the door where Shepherd still stood, her back against the wood.

"We will hold them off long enough for you to get to the Haven. Then, we will trap them in the hall."

Shepherd could see her plan in slow motion. They would fight off the nochtra, hopefully eliminating one or two before they broke through the house, chasing after Shepherd and Deryck. Seren would follow them in, trapping the creatures inside the house. They would take them out one by one, trapped in the small hallway, and die trying.

"Seren, you can't. The school needs you. The witches need someone to lead them," Deryck said.

Shepherd swore she heard pain in the usually aloof demon's voice. He spoke only to Seren, not even glancing at the men at her side.

She shook her head. "Then they'll find someone else."

Korvu opened his mouth to object, but Seren raised her hand, silencing him. "I won't let you do this without me. It's my responsibility." She shook her head. "It doesn't matter anyway. It will take all three of us."

Shepherd opened and closed her mouth, struggling to find words. They couldn't do this. There had to be another way. Shepherd didn't care for Seren. She only knew her as the selfish, arrogant professor who had turned her away. But this was a different person. This Seren had given everything she had to protect her students, to protect all witches.

But Shepherd?

Shepherd shook her head. "No," she said. "I'll do it."

Seren stared at her blankly, as if she didn't understand.

"I'll do it," Shepherd repeated, holding up her hand. "I've known for a long time that no one needed me. I'm nothing. Magicless." She shrugged. "Maybe this is why I'm here at all."

Shepherd had always been on the outside looking in. She had made it work for herself, scrimped and scrounged to make a life in the in-between places. But she had always thought it was unfair. Unfair to be the only regular person in a family of magicians. Unfair to be average in every way. Unfair to fall for a girl who was dark, beautiful, terrifying, and dead.

But she'd been wrong.

Her life may have been odd, living in the gray spaces between right and wrong, magical and unmagical. But she had still found her way. Unfair? It was unfair for Seren and Haven Hall to give up, to lose before they even began.

"I'll hold them off. It won't be for as long as you would, but at least you can get to Haven Hall and get everyone out."

Shepherd pulled her father's sword from her waist, the metal singing as she gripped it with one hand. Thank the gods he had taught her to fight.

Her other hand was on the door, ready.

"You'll have to close down this entrance, afterward," she said.

Seren glared at her, flipping her sword from one hand to the other as she stepped toward Shepherd. "You think I'll really let you have all the fun?"

"Gents," Deryck said. He was the only one still pressed against the window, looking out. "Something is happening."

He reached blindly for Shepherd, trying to pull her toward the window.

They moved away from the door, rushing to the window beside her, Yarrow and Korvu just behind them.

The street was black as ink, the nochtra spreading their wings between the zombie-like guards. They had all turned away from the house, so that Shepherd could only make out the profile of their blank faces. She struggled to follow their line of sight through the ever-expanding darkness of the nochtra.

Shepherd gasped. "Lane."

She stood in the middle of the street, her hand clutching at her stomach, fingers coated in blood. A gash ran down the side of her face, her shirt torn to shreds and revealing red-coated sin beneath.

She swayed slightly, as if she could barely hold herself up.

"I told you." Shepherd tried to sound smug, but her voice contorted her words. Lane might be a ghost, but she looked like she was on the verge of dying. And what happened then? Would she become one of those things?"

"Don't get your hopes up," Seren said, sounding like she was doing exactly that.

Lane's other hand grasped a metal chain from one of the hounds. An empty metal collar sat at the end as she wrapped the links around her knuckles. It hung from her hand like a makeshift morning star.

The ghostly guards stared at her, their faces lifeless. Above them, the nochtra screeched like the tolling of a bell.

Lane grinned. Her teeth were coated in blood.

The nochtra pulled their wings back and dove toward her, the wind whistling as the rain struck against their mottled wings. Lane didn't flinch. Only her white-knuckled grip on the chain gave away what she planned.

Shepherd pressed herself against the broken window, heart racing as the nochtra dove for Lane.

The dark creatures were thrown backwards as a jolt of energy exploded around Lane, crackling in the air as she whipped the chain through their broken wings. Their forms ripped to pieces, the shadows falling to the earth like black rain.

Bolts of white and black zapped around Lane, as if she was in the eye of a storm.

The nochtra cried out. The sound was strangled and guttural, like a dying animal.

The guards stood still as the nochtra turned to ash around them.

"I'm going to help her," Shepherd said, reaching for the door handle.

Seren slapped her hand against the door. "You'll get torn to pieces."

"Those things are going to kill her," Shepherd snapped as she pushed on the door. Seren didn't budge.

"She might have led them right to our door," Seren hissed. "They can kill you. They can't kill her."

Through the broken glass, Shepherd could just make out Lane as the hellhound circled her. She still clutched at her stomach as it lunged for her, only deterred by the whipping of the chain. Shepherd watched as she reached into her pocket with her blood-coated hand.

Shepherd wasn't sure if she forgave Lane—or even if she understood exactly who Lane was or the extent of her lies. But she couldn't stand by and let her fight alone.

"I don't care what she is. Dead or alive," she said. "She might be a liar and a traitor and a ghost, but she's still my friend."

"You have a death wish," Seren mumbled under her breath.

"It's called necrophilia, actually." Korvu smirked.

Shepherd ignored him. Because Seren lifted her hand off the door.

Shepherd rushed onto the porch as the guards finally began to move. They moved toward Lane slowly, almost like they were drifting on an imaginary breeze. Their expressions remained blank, even as darkness began to swirl around them. It was like they were barely there at all, puppets on someone else's strings. Their movements jerked and seized as they got closer to her, speeding up. One broke into a staggering run.

Lane's chest heaved, blood dripping from her fingers.

Shepherd slashed the sword out in front of her, letting its song fill the air as she launched herself into the street.

Thunder cracked as she ran toward the middle of the street, toward the guards, toward Lane.

Lane stumbled as they circled above, the remaining nochtra swooping between them. Blood spurted from her mouth, dripping from her chin. She dropped the chain.

As Shepherd got closer, she could see what Lane held between her fingers.

One of the keys, coated in her blood.

Lane collapsed to her knees. She screamed, tilting her head toward the sky, and around her, the world erupted.

A black cloud exploded out from her, swallowing the street in shadow itself.

Shepherd was knocked back by a blast of cold, ashen air.

The silence was deafening. Everything was pitch black, as if she was at the bottom of a lake made of ink. She couldn't move. Her sinuses popped.

Then, like a tidal wave, it disappeared, all of the shadow rushing back toward Lane.

The sun hung over the street, the red-orange of early morning.

The nochtra were gone.

The guards were gone.

Lane collapsed onto her side in the street, completely alone.

Shepherd had never seen her skill before—Traveling, Blinking, whatever she called it. She had always been inside whatever Lane was doing. Was this what it looked like? An explosion of nothingness around her? Shepherd didn't think so.

Somehow, this was different. Her skill had changed. And she would have bet her father's sword that it had something to do with that key.

But where had they all gone? And why had she and Lane been left behind, completely untouched?

As if waking from a dream, Shepherd ran for Lane, pulling her into her arms like a ragdoll. Her head dangled lifelessly as Shepherd dragged her toward the house by her arms.

When they reached the front door, Seren and Yarrow rushed toward them, lifting Lane up like she weighed nothing. The whites of Lane's eyes showed, her pupils rolled into the back of her head.

Deryck stepped toward them as Seren and Yarrow dropped her against the wooden floor with a clang. Shepherd knelt beside her.

The wood was already painted in blood. Shepherd reached for Lane's stomach, pressing the wound to stop the bleeding.

"Should we even help her?" Korvu gestured, crossing his arms. "She betrayed us. And it's not like she can die *again*."

"She most certainly can," Deryck said. "And trust me, it will be far worse than the first time."

Seren, Korvu, and Yarrow stared down at them, as if frozen.

Shepherd felt her face grow hot. "She just saved all of your asses! Don't just stand there, do something!"

Deryck snorted.

Lane's eyes fluttered. Her hair was strewn across Shepherd's lap in a tangle of knots. "You'd think being dead would mean I wouldn't bleed so much."

She laughed, the sound painful and hoarse. Her eyes closed as sweat beaded on her forehead, her cheeks.

Shepherd shook her. "Wake up," she said. "Wake up, wake up, wake up, you infuriating, stubborn. . . !" Shepherd's voice trailed off, unable to find words.

Her eyes blinked open, their forest green color suddenly murky and dark, like crashing waves.

She smiled, her white teeth read with blood. "That's. . . not nice."

Her eyes fluttered closed again. Shepherd pulled her further onto her lap, pressing harder against the wound. Her golden complexion was as gray as ashes.

Lane grabbed for Shepherd's sleeve with surprising strength, her fingers wrapping in the fabric. Her breaths were wet.

"I'll be fine. I'll be fine," she repeated, as if she was trying to convince herself. "But they won't. They won't.

"They're coming," Lane said as she slumped over.

CHAPTER TWENTY-ONE

Voices surrounded Lane in a swirl of broken sentences. She couldn't
make out what they were saying, couldn't

focus

"We need to leave—"

"Well, we aren't

taking her with us."

"Should we even move her?"

"If she stays here   she'll die."

nononono, not again

"I told you, it doesn't work like that. Do you want one of those
things in here with you?"

Deryck.

She concentrated on him through the dark space, the tunnel she seemed to be trapped in.

She tried to push forward, to get out of it, but

    couldn't move

"We can fight about it later. We need to move."

Shepherd's voice thundered against the muffled cotton of her ears. She could feel her skin—feel it against her face, hear her heartbeat against her ear—thundering, thundering, thundering

Shepherd's arms were wrapped around her. Trapped in the hallway, Lane leaned toward her—pressed into the sound of her heart, feeling it on her skin.

They were moving   upstairs?

A step

  A step

   A step

Pain tore through her. She tried to cry out, but

her abdomen seared with heat, with the stinging of a thousand knives.

She was dropped

  Her face hit something soft, soothing the heat in her skin

  And there was nothing

       nothing

Shepherd stood at the edge of the bed as Lane's eyes fluttered open and closed, as if she was trapped between sleeping and waking. They had moved Lane to the comfort of Haven Hall while she was unconscious through a strange portal, like the one they had originally used to find the school, hoping there would be a Healer among all the refugees. There wasn't, and they were losing time.

Deryck shuffled around the small room, reaching into his strange leather bag and throwing vials of a dozen different colors on the bed next to Lane.

All the color had drained from Lane's face. Shepherd herself felt lightheaded, stars filling her eyes. Everything seemed to be happening in slow motion.

She didn't dare ask if Lane was going to be okay. Wringing her hands, she remembered they were wet with blood, and hurried to rub them clean on her pants, her shirt, her face—wherever she could. It wasn't helping, but she didn't know what else to do.

Lane let out a strangled moan and opened her eyes, her fingers reaching for the sheets as if she wanted to push herself up. Shepherd held herself back from stopping her.

What Lane had done, however she had done it, she had saved them. Shepherd couldn't even process the kind of power and skill Lane had shown. But did it matter? She had still lied.

She was still a ghost. Whatever that meant. She seemed just as alive as anyone else to Shepherd. She was certainly bleeding like she was alive. Her heart pulsed in Shepherd's ears like she was alive.

"Deryck?" Lane croaked out. Her voice was a scratching whisper. "Perry?"

Deryck spun around, pulling a wooden stool up to the side of Lane's bed as he wrapped gauze around the top of her arm.

"Not all of the undead would heal so quickly," said Deryck. "It's a gift from The Academy. They couldn't exactly send a bunch of ghosts to Earth and risk them turning to bloody shades every time—"

Was he telling Shepherd or Lane?

"You're incredibly stupid and incredibly lucky that you even survived this long. You should have stayed at the school. Maybe you'd have healed."

Shepherd watched as Lane grabbed for the sheets with weak hands. Her curls were matted to her forehead with blood and sweat. She opened and closed her mouth as if to speak, but no sound came out—only rasping, wet breaths.

Was Lane going to turn into one of those things? That was what they said happened when a ghost died. But Shepherd couldn't imagine her turning into such a monster. She didn't want to imagine it.

Wringing her hands around the bed's iron frame, Shepherd leaned toward Lane as she opened her eyes. At her side, Deryck pressed one hand to the bleeding wound in Lane's stomach, the other sorting through his vials and tools. Shepherd gulped as Lane's eyes opened, taking in the room with a distant, foggy stare.

"For someone that's dead, you're doing a great job dying. I guess you've had practice," Shepherd said.

She hadn't meant for the joke to sound so venomous. She was still angry with Lane—there were so many things she wanted to say, to ask her. Were they really friends? Had everything been a lie? But it didn't seem like the right time. Not with Lane barely able to speak, dried blood trailing from her pale lips.

"You. . ." Lane tried to sit up, barely moving before collapsing back against the mattress.

"That's right," Shepherd said. "I know."

She shrugged. Now they both knew the truth—of each other, of their lies, of whatever that meant.

Lane's eyes glazed over, focusing and unfocusing, until they landed on Shepherd's face. She could feel Lane studying her—her eyes narrowing in on the shape of her face, Shepherd's hands covered in Lane's blood, as if Lane was using Shepherd as a focal point to stay awake.

Lane tried to speak as Deryck wiped blood from her abdomen, trying to get closer to the wound. As he did, more blood leaked onto her skin.

Shepherd wanted to be mad. She wanted to yell at Lane for lying, for being so stupid, for risking herself. But all she could think was, *She can't die. She can't become one of those things.*

"You need a Healer. Or a hospital," Shepherd said.

Deryck raised an eyebrow, pulling a needle and black thread between his fingers. Lane blinked. Clearly, neither was an option. Not for a ghost.

Shepherd shoved her hands into her pockets, letting the dried blood rub off on her jeans. She felt helpless. Her mother came from a long line of Native Healers, the craft passed down over the generations like an heirloom. But like the rest of their culture, it had struggled and fought to stay alive. Shepherd not having the skill for it was a betrayal in itself. She couldn't carry the legacy—and Addie, who had inherited their father's skill for Warrior magic, didn't care to.

She wasn't sure if it would have helped, anyway. There was no lesson for healing someone already dead.

"Are you qualified to be doing this?" Shepherd asked Deryck as he pulled the thread into the eye of the needle.

"Yes," Lane croaked.

At the same time Deryck said, "Certainly not."

Comforting. Shepherd could rest easy, then.

Lane stirred, her eyes focusing as she stared at Shepherd again. Her teeth were gritted in pain, her fingers tying themselves into knots in the sheets. It was just like her—on the edge of death, and still acting as if she was unbothered.

Shepherd rounded the bed to stand behind Deryck. The demon motioned for her to take over holding the towel in place, and she did as she was told. Crouching next to the bed, she pressed her fingers into the blood-soaked rag, putting as much weight as she dared on the wound.

Lane cried out, her eyes closing as her body twitched. Almost as if it was instinct, she grabbed for Shepherd's hand, squeezing her fingers tightly as Shepherd tried to staunch the bleeding.

Their eyes met.

Unable to stop herself, Shepherd blurted, "Did you know? About The Academy? Did you help them?"

She had to know, one way or another. She wanted to believe Lane would never do such a thing, but she had to keep reminding herself that she barely knew her at all. And what she thought she knew. . . well, it could have all been an act.

Weakly, Lane shook her head.

Relief ran through her body. It could be a lie, she knew. But she wasn't sure Lane could find the will to lie, not in this state. Not when she could barely form words.

"Can you talk about your feelings later? I need to close this wound," Deryck said. He held the needle above Lane's torso, motioning for Shepherd to move. She lifted her hands and the towel from Lane's skin, moving out of the way so he could work.

Lane still gripped her hand like a vice.

Without warning, Deryck shoved the needle into Lane's skin. Her entire body twitched beneath his grasp. Shepherd gripped her hand as hard as she could, trying to keep her in place.

There was a sizzling noise. Lane screamed, flailing away from Deryck. He shot backward in his chair with a yelp, holding his hand like it had been bitten.

Her exposed muscle bubbled like acid. The needle was dissolving. With a wisp of smoke, it was gone, leaving only a sliver of silver dripped on her skin.

"These aren't just ordinary wounds," Deryck said. "Whatever has been done to those shades. . . I've never seen this before."

Shepherd's stomach turned upside down. If Deryck didn't know what to do. . .

Lane's eyes met Deryck's, something unspoken passing between them. Her face turned from sad to stern, her eyebrow furrowing, her shoulders straightening.

As if she was accepting her fate.

Shepherd hurried to place a fresh towel over her wound. "Is there anything else you can do?"

"I don't know," Deryck said. "Whatever this is, it can't be fixed by mortal means. And to fix it with magic? It would require too much power—more skill or power than I have. And you don't have any."

Shepherd glared.

Lane closed her eyes. Silence filled the room, each of them completely still, only interrupted by Lane's gasping breaths. Shepherd remembered what the room had been like when her grandfather had died, a silence so heavy that it pressed onto her, threatening to crush her to pieces.

She tilted her head back, fighting the tears that burned the corners of her eyes.

"Shepherd."

She looked down. Lane was reaching for her hand again. Her green eyes were steel, focusing as if she could only see Shepherd. Her nails dug into Shepherd's palm.

"You have to warn everyone. Get them as far from the school as possible." She paused to gasp, each word a labor. "They're coming."

Shepherd bit her lip, giving Lane a forced, struggling smile. There was no way she was working with them. She had sacrificed herself to protect them. She was fighting to warn them, even when it seemed too late.

"Don't worry, we've got that covered. You warned them. They'll be fine. Well, as fine as they can be, considering."

She grinned at her, almost begging Lane to snap back with her own sarcastic retort.

"I found them," she said. "Ivy. They're beneath the school."

Deryck gasped and leaned back in his chair. Shepherd glanced at him, wondering if that meant what she thought it did. "Bloody hell."

Shepherd looked back at Lane, the blood draining from her face. She didn't want to ask. She didn't want to know the answer.

"Addie?"

Lane shook her head. "I don't know."

Her voice was full of a thousand apologies, for things she had done, for things outside her control.

Shepherd leaned toward her, pushing her own blood-stained hair out of her eyes, and smiled. "We're going to get them. Together. We're going to finish what we started. As if I would let you back out of our deal."

If her words were empty promises, she wasn't sure who they were for—Lane or herself.

Lane furrowed her eyebrows at her, confusion filling her already foggy eyes.

"You think you're going to get out of this that easy? I told you, you need me." Shepherd bit her lip. "And I need you. We've still got work to do. So, you're stuck with me. Dead or undead, neither, both or whatever is in between."

It didn't matter if Lane was dead. Not to Shepherd. She was real enough for her.

And she had to survive.

Lane's eyes fluttered closed, her grip on Shepherd's hand loosening as she drifted into unconsciousness.

Shepherd looked at Deryck. "What kind of power are we talking about? How much?"

Deryck didn't answer her, staring down at Lane. She shoved his shoulder.

"Enough to power a huge amount of Healing magic. More than it would be safe for a Healer to pull. In After Life, it would be dozens of amperes."

Shepherd stood up, her arms tense at her side as she paced. Power. Amperes. Energy. She wished she knew more about magic. She wished she'd been born with the skill.

There were no Healers at the school, and it didn't sound like it would make a difference with this anyway. Everyone thought she was the reason The Academy had discovered their location—and maybe she was. If there was a Healer, maybe Shepherd could convince them to pull on her lifeforce, Deryck's, maybe even—

She stopped pacing. "What about the Keys?" she asked. "They're huge reserves of magic, right? That's what Bally said."

Deryck tilted his head at an almost impossible angle. Behind him, Lane twitched, groaning in her sleep. They were running out of time.

"Do you want to kill everyone on this whole bloody campus?" Deryck asked. "Even if we knew enough about how the Keys work, which we don't, it would be incredibly risky—it could backfire. They could reject her, choose not to help."

Shepherd scrunched her face. "Choose? They're keys."

"You know as well as anyone—maybe better, with your *black market* experience, that magical objects aren't just objects. They're finicky. Picky."

Shepherd exhaled, throwing her hands at her side and resuming her pacing. The small room seemed to close in on her, the two feet of floor growing smaller as she walked back and forth. She clenched her hands into fists and punched the wall, her fingers and wrist screaming at her as she made contact. She hadn't so much as dented the wall, but her hand throbbed.

She spun on her heel. "What about the obols?"

She pointed to Lane's wrists, the dried burgundy blood coating her arms. Beneath it, the dark line of her tattoos was barely visible.

"Lane told me that they gave them to her—that they power her magic. They connect her back to The Academy and their magic, don't they? Like a tether."

Lane hadn't told the complete truth when she explained the obols—she hadn't told Shepherd about The Academy, or that she used them to go between Life and Death. It finally made sense why she kept insisting she wasn't a Traveler. But she had told Shepherd that they gave her power, a connection to magic.

He squinted, spinning on his chair toward Shepherd. "You're right. And I know how they work. . ."

His voice trailed off. Shepherd motioned for him to keep going.

If this was going to work, they needed to do it now. Lane's eyes fluttered and her wound still leaked blood. Shepherd rushed to put a rag on it again while Deryck sat there, thinking.

"Do it," Lane whispered. Her eyes flashed down to her wrists, to the thin black lines that circled her wrists like bracelets. Her face beaded with sweat.

Deryck placed his hand on her shoulder. "Lane, if we remove them. . . you won't be able to Travel anymore. You'll lose the connection to death magic."

Her eyes closed, and she nodded, a shallow breath shuddering through your chest.

"If we remove them, and you stay here. . ." Deryck continued. "You'll slowly die, anyway. You might be buying yourself a week at most, and then you would have to return to After Life. Permanently."

Shepherd placed her knee on the bed, leaning over Lane.

She would die either way. A few days at most. That was all she would get.

Lane lay motionless on the bed, not responding.

Deryck dropped his hand from her shoulder. "But it is likely that they are tracking you through them. It's the only thing that makes sense."

Shepherd looked at Deryck, her jaw hanging open. Of course. Lane hadn't led them to Haven Hall—they had followed her. She had no idea. Shepherd felt the tightness in her chest loosen.

Lane looked straight at him, her eyes burning. "Do it. Do it now."

CHAPTER TWENTY-TWO

Deryck jumped into action, turning to his bag to grab a handful of small, silver tools. Lane grabbed at the sheets, barely clinging to consciousness.

Shepherd held her breath. This had to work.

"You might want to hold her down." A knife glinted in Deryck's hand, a little larger than a scalpel.

Shepherd widened her eyes. She was already half on the bed, her hands pushing into Lane's stomach.

"I have to cut them from her arms. It will be painful. . . the ink, it isn't just skin deep."

Lane reached blindly for Shepherd's hand, finding it where she held the rag. Both their fingers were coated in fresh blood.

Lane nodded, eyes still closed. "I'm ready."

Deryck motioned for Shepherd to hurry, and she swung her leg over Lane, straddling across her waist. She removed the towel, tossing it across the room and leaving Lane's torso bare. Her cheeks burned, suddenly aware of the nakedness of Lane's abdomen, their position on the bed, but she held firm.

Deryck lifted the knife to Lane's wrist. Light reflected off the small jewels on its hilt, sending rainbows across the room. "This is a Healer's knife. The skin should heal itself. You might only have a small scar. . . if this works."

Lane gave him a weak smile. "I was hoping for a gruesome one to impress all the ladies with."

Deryck took a deep breath and plunged the blade into her skin.

Lane cried out. Beneath her weight, Lane flinched, but Shepherd was larger and heavier than her. Shepherd held her arms down, trying to contort her body so that she didn't get in Deryck's way.

"It burns," Lane hissed as Deryck sliced around her hand.

Shepherd's heart raced as her eyes followed the blade, her stomach churning as Deryck peeled the skin away from Lane's arm. It hung from her like a snakeskin, waiting to be removed.

As Deryck moved to the inside of her wrist, Lane bucked in pain, her back arching. Shepherd tightened her grip, trying to keep her as steady as possible.

"It's going to be okay," Shepherd said. "It's going to be okay."

Deryck moved to her other wrist, working as quickly as he could.

Shepherd did the only thing she could think to do—the thing she was best at. Talk.

"After this, you're going to be okay, and we're going to go find everyone. We're going to go down to The Academy and kick their asses for doing this to you, for doing this to all of us. We're going to find Addie, and you can finally meet her. I know she'll like you. The first time I saw you, when you broke through that window to save me from the ghost, I knew Addie would like you. Because you're a badass. You aren't the strongest or the biggest or the toughest or even the most skilled—I know, I know—but you fight as hard as you can, even after everything you lost. We're going to get them back for taking away your memory, for lying to you. And then we're going to go find your family. I don't care if you're dead. I don't care if you're a ghost. If you're lucky, I'll even let you haunt my apartment."

Lane didn't stir as she spoke, but Shepherd didn't know what else to do. It was as much a distraction for herself as it was for Lane.

"We can do whatever you want. You can come with me on my black market hunts, travel the world. I can show you all of the magical places. Hell, maybe Seren will even let us stay here and you can learn magic—living magic. I would hate it, but if that's what you want, I'll do it. Because we aren't done yet. You aren't done yet. You have so much life left to live. . . well, you know what I mean."

Her eyes fluttered. Shepherd wondered if she'd even heard anything.

Deryck pulled away from her. "It's done."

Her wrists were raw and exposed, the top layers of skin completely gone and exposing the naked muscle underneath. Blood soaked through the sheets, and Shepherd's arms were slick with it too. Deryck hurried behind them, jars and glass crashing to the floor as he worked.

With the twist of his wrist, he ground the ink and gore from her wrists into the bottom of a stone bowl, mixing it with a watery substance Shepherd didn't recognize. The liquid glowed the orange-white of a flame, just like when Lane used the obols for traveling, or raising ghost-guides from the dead.

Deryck brought the stone bowl to Lane's mouth, the liquid swirling between black and opalescent white. With his other hand, he opened her mouth and tilted her chin, pouring it into her throat.

Lane coughed and sputtered as she tried to swallow. She'd ceased to move, only her eyelids flinching, as if she was having a bad dream.

Deryck stepped back, the bowl hanging tepidly from his fingers. He rubbed his hand across his face, watching her expectantly like a person jumping to their death, waiting to hit the ground.

Shepherd shifted nervously on top of Lane, slowly lifting herself off the bed as gently as she could. She knew her tan skin was bright red, aware of Deryck watching her, knowing he heard everything she said. She jumped to the ground with a light thump, turning to face Lane.

"Did it work?"

They both looked down at Lane, the pale gray of her skin, the blood staining her arms, the bed. Her wrists had already started to heal, the skin slowly forming raw, red ropes where the obols had been.

"We won't know until we know," Deryck shrugged. "Get some rest. If it worked, she'll be awake when you wake up."

She looked at him. "And if it didn't work?"

He gave her a grim smile. "Then I suggest you keep a tight grip on that sword."

Shepherd glanced down at the floor, where her father's sword laid, hastily discarded. If it didn't work, Shepherd wouldn't be waking up to Lane. . . she'd be waking up to a nochtra.

Her throat bobbed. Could she kill Lane, if it came to it? Even though Lane would no longer be there, not really?

Deryck turned away, cleaning the blood and the mess he had made from the room.

"Shepherd?" Lane asked, a half-mumble in her sleep.

She suddenly felt the exhaustion of the last twelve hours—they had been up all night at Baltus's, and everything since began to feel like a blur. She didn't even know what time it was, except for the dark sky outside the window.

Shepherd slowly climbed onto the bed next to her, watching the rise and fall of her chest as she reached for her hand.

Lane awoke slowly, like emerging from a dark wave—one breath at a time, each pulling her closer to the surface. Her head throbbed. Her hands throbbed. Her abdomen throbbed.

Daylight poured across the room like paint on a pallet, vibrant and yellow against the dark of the room. She peered at it through her eyelashes—she hadn't noticed it the night before. Or if she had, she couldn't remember. Everything was blurred and black, like the dreams she sometimes had when she blacked out.

Shepherd's body was draped across the bed, facing Lane. Her hand rested on top of Lane's as if she had fallen asleep holding it.

An ache ran through her chest, and she yanked her hand away. Her memory might have been fuzzy, but she remembered one thing—the outline of Shepherd's face, the glint of her smile, the feeling that somehow, she had forgiven her.

She had promised they would save everyone together. The words had echoed through the haze in Lane's head, forcing her to cling to what life she had left.

She looked down at the pink scars circling her wrist. Her obols were gone, her connection to The Academy. She had never known herself without them—couldn't remember what her skin had looked like before. Now, two ropey scars stood in their place. Somehow, it felt like something bigger than just a tattoo was gone.

She pulled the sheets back and looked at the gauze wrapped around her stomach, still fresh and free of blood. She twisted, searching for any lingering pain as she flexed her muscles, rotated her wrists. There was nothing. She had expected to wake still in pain, the same sting still lingering in her every pore. But she didn't feel pain. She felt invigorated.

Not only was she healing, but her mind felt clearer, sharper. Her muscles didn't ache with the first moments of the morning.

It was as if she had always been asleep, every cell in her body dormant, and for the first time, she was awake.

Shepherd yawned, eyes widening as she realized Lane was awake. "You're up."

She sounded relieved, but it was tinged with something else. Bitterness or lingering anger? Lane faced the ceiling.

She was awake. She was still here—alive, or something like it.

Shepherd looked down at where her hand laid on top of Lane's, grimacing. "If you wanted to hold my hand, you could have just asked."

"Me? I was on the edge of death."

"I'm irresistible." She shrugged. "But next time you want to hold my hand, there's no need to go and die first. You can just ask."

Shepherd grinned at her, her face half-hidden in the pillow. Somehow, her hair stuck out from her head in more directions than usual. It was caked with blood.

"Good thing I'm already dead," she said. "I don't know what to say, Shep."

She swallowed. Shepherd rubbed her hand across the sheets, not looking at her.

Finally, she asked quietly, "What's it like?"

She wasn't even sure if it was something she should tell her. Shepherd had years to live. "It's. . . quiet."

Shepherd snorted. "I guess I won't fit in then."

"Definitely not."

Shepherd turned to face her, dark eyes meeting her green ones. Lane studied the angle of her face, watched the arch of her side rise and fall with every breath. They had never been so close, their faces only inches from each other.

"I'm sorry," Lane said. "I didn't know what they were doing. I had no idea. I don't think any of the students do, or even the professors. But I did lie to you. I lied to all of you. I wish I could tell you that I'm not that person, that I didn't mean to hurt you, that I would never work with them to hurt anyone. But it wouldn't be true. Because I don't know who I am. I'm no one, really, nothing. But I do want to help. I want to find Addie. I want to save those people."

Her words sat heavy on the air. She felt exhausted, put on display for trying to speak so bluntly.

Shepherd looked at her. Her eyes, usually deep brown, shone gold in the light. "I don't think you're nothing."

"What?" Lane blinked at her.

Shepherd sat up, her hands supporting her weight.

"You might not be who you said you were—or who I believed you were—but you aren't nothing," she said. "And you might not know who you are, but I do. Whether your real name is Lane, or whether you're alive or dead. I know you are good and sarcastic and annoying and imperfect. Everyone has secrets, Lane.

"I know what it's like to be on the outside. I know what it's like to think you have to do anything to get in. I spent a lot of my life not knowing who I was or where I fit in. So I understand better than most. You and me, we live in the in-between spaces. Not quite one thing and not quite another. And I've accepted that about myself. You should too."

She looked down at her hands, glancing up at Lane through the dark curtain of her eyelashes.

"No one truly knows themselves. We all change every day. And I might not know everything about you. But what I do know. . . is pretty great."

The air was thick between them, like a brewing storm.

Lane chewed on her lips, unsure of what to say. Her body felt like it had been healed twice over.

She crossed her arms. "Everyone has secrets? Like selling all your family heirlooms on the black market?"

Shepherd pointed at Lane. "Or pretending you're alive?"

She grinned at Lane, that same infectious smirk. Lane couldn't help but smile back. They both laughed.

"We're going to get them," she promised.

Lane nodded.

She looked up at the ceiling, feeling Shepherd's gaze on the side of her face. She had made her choice when she left The Academy, when she had seen Ivy in that classroom-turned-cell, but somehow it still felt like she was leaving a piece of herself behind. The red scars on her wrists were proof of that. She had been at The Academy for almost a year. She had woken up right after the previous year's All Hallows ball with no memory of her life and a new name. It was all she had ever known, besides the small glimpses of her past she got in her dreams. Leaving it behind was leaving behind everything she was. Shepherd was right, though. She was more than who they had told her she was. The identity they had given her had always sat on her skin like too large clothes, uncomfortable and like it belonged to someone else. It had only made her question herself, everything around her. For the first time, she felt like she was waking up on a new day.

Shepherd motioned at Lane's abdomen. The gauze was blooming with fresh blood.

"We should probably change those. I'll get Deryck," Lane said, turning to roll from the bed.

Shepherd grabbed her hand. "No, let me."

Crawling over the foot of the bed, Shepherd grabbed a pile of fresh gauze from Deryck's bag. She turned to Lane, kneeling beside her on the bed. She seemed to hesitate for a moment, and then she reached for the tattered, dried blood of Lane's shirt, pushing it out of the way. Her fingers grazed the exposed skin of Lane's ribcage. Goosebumps fluttered across her skin where Shepherd's cold hands touched her still-warm skin. Slowly, Shepherd peeled away the old gauze, tossing it to the floor behind her.

All of Lane's torso was exposed now, except for where blood had caked and laid rust across her pale, olive flesh. The wound had almost healed already, driven by the deep magic in her obols. Lane stared down at the pink scar, barely a scratch now. She hissed as Shepherd began to work away the last pieces of fabric, where they clung to the wound, sticky with congealed blood.

"Sorry," Shepherd whispered. As she moved around Lane's waist, her face tilted so close to Lane's that their noses almost touched.

Freckles dotted across Shepherd's nose, dark against her bronze skin, like seashells on a sandy shore. Her breath caught in her throat as Shepherd glanced up at her from under her eyebrow. The golden flecks in her eyes glinted as if there was some shared secret between them, smirking in its silence.

Lane felt all the muscles in her body tighten as the last piece of gauze fell to the floor, Shepherd's eyes still tuned into hers.

"Impressive," Shepherd said, her voice low. Her hand trailed across Lane's stomach, drawing circles around the raw scar with her finger.

Lane arched an eyebrow. "Me or the scar?"

She laughed, her hand laying across Lane's stomach. Her hot breath grazed Lane's cheek. "I meant the healing. When I saw it last night, I thought. . . I didn't think you'd make it. Let alone look like this in the morning."

Her voice trailed off. Lane smiled at her. "It's a pretty hideous scar though. Maybe I'll tell people I was in a fight with a pirate. Or got attacked by a bear."

"The possibilities are endless."

Lane's fingers found Shepherd's resting on her stomach. She hadn't known that it was possible to feel hesitant and sure at the same time. She'd felt like she was living a lie ever since she'd died, the small pieces of what she knew scattered across the floor.

Since she'd met Shepherd, all those pieces suddenly fit together.

Shepherd's fingers lightly rubbed back and forth across her skin. After being in so much pain, Lane's nerves lit at the fragile touch. Her back arched slightly into Shepherd's hand.

"Lane, I—" Shepherd hesitated. "I'm just glad you're okay."

She reached for Lane's hair, her fingers wrapping in the curls.

Her lips brushed Lane's. The softness of her lips pressed into Lane with a hunger that Lane could feel through her whole body. She buried her surprise, clashing her mouth against Shepherd's. She bit Shepherd's lower lip, pressing herself back as Shepherd pressed into her. She forgot the pain in her stomach, sparks running down her entire body, her fingers clutching at Shepherd with a need and a want that exposed the truth she had been hiding since they'd met.

Shepherd's hands buried deeper into Lane's hair as her legs wrapped around Lane's, her hand traveling up the bare flesh of Lane's side to her wrist, wrapping her fingers around it. Lane thought of the jolt she had felt when Shepherd had first grabbed her arm. She crushed her lips deeper against Shepherd's, tasting blood on her tongue and running her other hand through Shepherd's hair.

Shepherd tore her mouth away, flipping away from Lane like she had been shocked. She pulled back across the bed, her face a blizzard of emotions, all of them unreadable.

Before Lane could open her mouth, Shepherd was standing at the edge of the bed.

"Shepherd—" Lane pushed herself onto her elbows, the fresh gauze laying at her side, discarded.

"I'm going—going to tell them you're awake," Shepherd said. With a spin of her heel, she was out the door, her short locks flowing behind her as she hurried away.

Lane collapsed into the bed, her fingers rolled in the gauze.

Even if she hadn't betrayed them, even if they forgave her—she was still dead. And Shepherd, with her golden skin, messy hair, and endless smirk—she was very, very much alive. Had she fooled herself, even if it was just for a moment?

CHAPTER TWENTY-THREE

The sting of Shepherd's rejection still ached the following day when Lane finally made her way downstairs. Everyone gathered in that same classroom, waiting for her. They had only wasted time by waiting for her to heal, but Seren had wanted to hear it from Lane herself.

Shepherd sat between Deryck and Korvu, perched on the edge of a desk. Her pants were cuffed around her ankles and her boxy gray shirt exposed the lower half of her stomach. Her hands were shoved in two of the many pant pockets as she tilted her head back and laughed. Yarrow tossed something to her, and she caught it, smiling broadly.

They had both been outsiders. Together. And now only she was outside, looking at all of them. Even Shepherd. They had discovered who Lane really was, and finally realized who Shepherd was in the process. Someone they wanted on their side. Someone worthwhile.

The thought stung, even as Lane tried to be happy for her.

With a deep breath, she stepped into the room. Someone had left new clothes for her—Deryck, probably. She wore too-tight black jeans and a long-sleeved shirt. Somehow, over the last few days, the cool October weather had finally settled over the school after a humid, long summer. Through the classroom window, the trees had started to turn red seemingly overnight.

The room fell eerily quiet as they all realized she was there. The only one that did not stare at her was Shepherd, who took a sudden interest in the floor. They hadn't spoken since their kiss. Lane couldn't bring herself to track Shepherd down, to ask her why she had run, to ask her if it was really so bad, kissing her. But she knew the answer.

"So you found them," Seren said.

"Yes." Lane shifted her weight as Seren crossed the room toward her.

"And they were underneath your school all this time? The school that taught you that witches were bad, that *we* were after *you*."

"Yes."

"And you believed them? Worked with them?" Seren's face was the calm anger of a flood. "Did you come here to try and help them? Did you tell them where we are?"

Shepherd flinched.

Lane's hands fell to her side. She had no proof, nothing but her word. It wouldn't be enough. And any apology she could offer would fall on deaf ears.

"I'm not one of them. Not anymore." Her voice wavered, but she cleared her throat. She needed to say it. "I don't remember why I chose to be a student at their school, to study death magic, to hunt down other ghosts. I only know what they told me. They took that memory from me. They took that choice. But I did make the choice to come back here and help you stop them. I could have stayed. I could have never found Ivy. I could have chosen The Academy. But I didn't. I chose to help you stop them."

She paused.

"I'm sure Deryck has told you what that choice means for me."

Deryck glanced up at her, his legs crouched beneath him like a gargoyle. They both knew she was running out of time without the obols. She would have to return to After Life. Removing them had only bought her the time she needed to help them.

And once she returned, it wouldn't be as a student of The Academy. She would lose her connection to death magic. She would lose her undead body, and she would be just like the ghosts in the woods. Voiceless. Nameless. Forgotten.

"You can't expect us to just blindly trust you. You have no proof. None of us even knows whether there is really an afterlife at all." Korvu crossed his arms, glaring at her.

"And where do you think I came from? Sunshine and daisies? Or am I lying too?" Deryck asked.

Korvu huffed, his shoulders squaring.

"It could be a trap." Seren said.

Shepherd rose from the edge of the desk. "My sister might be down there. And Ivy is. I'm willing to risk it."

She didn't look at Lane as she spoke, but Lane didn't miss that Shepherd had said *Ivy is*. Not might be, not Lane says she is. Shepherd believed her.

And that was something.

Standing a little taller, Lane said, "You don't have to like me. I've never trusted anyone I've ever worked with. All that matters is getting the job done." She glanced at Shepherd. "Trust me or don't trust me, the facts remain the same. Let me help you. Let me get them out. I think I'm the only one who can."

It would have to be her. Only she could slip into The Academy. Only she could even get there.

Shepherd glanced at her, her arms crossed and her expression unreadable.

"We don't have to trust her. Because she can show us herself." She turned to Lane. "I've traveled with you three times now. And after what you did in the street, I wouldn't doubt that you could take all of us."

Lane held up her hands. "No, absolutely not. It's completely different, going between Life and Death. You could get hurt. You could *die*. I've never taken anyone with me before."

"We all saw what you did to those ghosts," Korvu said.

Lane's memory of it was hazy, but she knew what they meant. Somehow, bleeding in the street, she had Blinked away all of the ghosts the Academy had sent to attack them. She hadn't even Blinked herself. Just them, dozens of them, all at once. But the part that worried her—the part she couldn't tell any of them—was that it wasn't her.

It was the Key.

She'd gotten the idea from Victor, using his amperes to break out of the classroom. With the right amount of energy, she could power almost anything. And she had never felt anything with as much power as the Keys. Baltus had told them what they were used for, how they were made, and it turned Lane's stomach to use it. The decision hadn't been a conscious one. She was on the brink of being obliterated, her wounds fogging her mind. It didn't make sense, but it was almost like the Key had asked her. Pushed her to use it.

What she didn't understand was why.

She shook her head. She couldn't do that again. There was too much she didn't know about the Key. And the way it called to her. . .

"Even if she can take all of us," Seren said, "we still don't have a plan. We can't just go to Death blindly."

"I do it all the time." Deryck smirked.

"Well, what do we know?" Shepherd paced across the room, her hands shoved in her pockets.

Lane fought the urge to protest. Just like that, the conversation had turned from her betrayal to how they would save the other witches—together. And Lane was at the center of their plan.

She just hoped she wouldn't disappoint them.

"We know The Academy has been hunting witches and anyone living with magic," Deryck offered. "Although we don't know if it's just The Academy or if there are others helping them."

"Like The Keys," Shepherd said. "Baltus said experiments like theirs had led to these nochtra things before. And we've found two of their keys—"

"One of them right before a shade turned into a nochtra," Lane said.

"So we know The Academy is behind it, and The Keys might be behind it, but not who they are, or why," Korvu said. "That's not a lot to go on."

"We also know that these nochtra are connected. The Academy has been sending them after us," Seren said. "The Academy is playing with dangerous magic, enough to create these monsters. And they've also found a way to control them."

"Unprecedented," Yarrow said.

Shepherd ran her fingers through her hair. "We know more than that. We know where they are, and they don't know where we are."

"Yet," Korvu grumbled.

"We have two people right here that know The Academy as well as you all know Haven Hall. They know its weaknesses."

Shepherd glanced at Lane again, but it was fleeting as she turned to Deryck.

"What else?" Seren asked.

"We know they killed my friend," Lane said. The room grew silent around her. "They turned her into one of those things. But we don't know why."

"So it's not just witches," Shepherd said. "It's the dead too. Ghosts. Magical creatures. For some reason, they're attacking all of us."

"For power," Korvu said.

"They already have plenty of that," Seren said.

Lane's mind swirled. So many pieces, and still so many missing.

"So what do we do?" Seren said. "Lane almost turned herself into a nochtra getting out last time. They have death magic. We have a ghost girl, a demon, three schoolteachers, and an unwitch."

If she had meant it to be a joke, no one laughed. They stood around the room, staring at each other, answering Seren with silence. Despite her best efforts, Lane's eyes were drawn to Shepherd, leaning against the frame of the window. Behind her, the sun was setting, turning the red leaves into a raging fire of golden light. Tomorrow was All Hallows, the one time of year The Academy was full of color, full of people from across After Life. She would never get to see it now, never get to dance with the demons.

A slow smirk spread on her face.

"How do you all feel about a party?"

CHAPTER TWENTY-FOUR

Overnight, Haven Hall turned silent and empty. The few that remained haunted the halls like echoes, their voices amplified by the silence. Seren had ordered everyone to flee as quickly as possible, and now everyone she had saved was gone. All because of Lane. They were careful not to say where they were going around her. She didn't blame them.

She was weak from lack of sleep. After she had told them her plan, there had not been much for her to do but wait. They helped everyone evacuate, but Lane had been left alone. She'd meant to prepare herself, which obviously meant not getting a moment's rest.

The afternoon sun peeked through the windows as Lane moved through the halls like the ghost she was. There was no sign of Deryck or Shepherd. They both knew she didn't have much time without the obols. She told herself it was because they were busy, but it didn't feel that way to Lane.

Somehow, it felt like she was ticking up to something instead of counting down. The leftover power coursing through her bloodstream only made her feel stronger.

She hoped the feeling lasted long enough to work through their plan. She just needed one more day.

At least they had listened to her plan, trusted her enough to go through with it. She wasn't even sure it would work, but she knew they had to try. And it was all they had. Still, it made her uneasy to think about taking all of them with her to After Life.

Especially because of Shepherd.

She needed to make sure they left Shepherd behind.

It wasn't that she didn't want Shepherd by her side—in fact, she found herself realizing that she desperately, desperately did. But she couldn't risk Shepherd's life like that. They had no idea how losing the power of the obols, the connection to The Academy, would affect her ability to Blink. She didn't even know if it would work, but at least the others had their own magic if anything went wrong.

She found herself in the dining hall-turned-memorial room, standing in front of the photos, flickering in the light of candles that threatened to go out. Even though everyone was gone, they had left this behind, like an altar for their ancestors to find in a thousand years.

Lane ran her fingers along the edges of the photos. So many faces. So many people who would never come back. She hoped they would find everyone, but she knew there was no way. There was no room at The Academy for all of these people, each face that stared up at her, hopeful that she would find them. Some of them were like her. Lost.

One by one, she scanned every photo, not sure what she was looking for. Victor had told her she had a family that she could no longer remember. She was haunted by half-memories, half-dreams of their laughter, of stone hallways and strange doors that were not unlike The Academy's. She had no idea how long she had been dead, if her family was even still alive. But she still found herself searching the photos, hoping. Had she been a witch? Likely not, considering that Eurydice chose the students for The Academy herself. But something still tugged at her memory as she looked at every girl, every boy with black hair and olive skin.

"You look like you've just seen a ghost," Shepherd's voice came from behind her. Lane jumped, glancing back at her. Her hands were tucked in her pockets, like she did whenever she felt awkward. It made Lane smile.

"Wouldn't be new for me."

Shepherd laughed. "I almost forgot."

"Welcome to the club."

Shepherd stepped next to her, facing the wall of photos. Her eyes drifted to the floor, watching the candles flicker.

"They really took all your memories away from you? You have no idea who you were, anything?"

"I have glimpses, sometimes. I'm not supposed to. But sometimes I—" Lane paused. She'd never told anyone about this. "I blackout, and I have these snippets. They're almost like dreams, but they feel so real. But other than that, no."

"So what are you looking for?" Shepherd asked, tilting back on her heels. "I saw you searching through all the photos."

Lane felt heat rise to her cheeks. "It's ridiculous, but I thought maybe I might find a picture of myself. From when I was alive. Or of my family, at least. Not that I would recognize them."

"You think you might have been a witch?"

"No. Maybe." Lane shrugged. "I have no reason to think that. It's more of a gut feeling."

Shepherd arched an eyebrow at her. "Well, you are pretty good with death magic. Maybe some things can't be forgotten."

Shepherd stepped forward, her fingers landing on the corner of Addie's photo. She'd shoved it between two others, so Deryck wasn't visible, only the blurred image of Addie running.

"Do you think they did the same thing to my sister? If we find her, will she even remember me?"

Lane sucked in a sharp breath. She hadn't expected that. She looked down at the scars on her wrists, the red, thin lines that were once her obols.

"I don't know," she said.

"You think she's still alive?"

Lane nodded. She had to believe that. For both of them.

Shepherd opened her mouth, but the sound was drowned out. A crack like thunder ran through the air, as if the Earth had been torn in half. The floor shook beneath their feet as Lane's ears popped, Shepherd reaching for Lane's arm to steady herself.

Lane waited for the sound of screams, but none came.

"We're too late," she said. "They're here."

CHAPTER TWENTY-FIVE

Around them, the walls shook, stones crumbling to the floor and threatening to collapse. Shepherd struggled to balance herself as the memorial's candles fell, rolling across the floor. Before she could steady herself, Lane broke into a sprint, running past her into the school. Shepherd chased after her, even as pieces of the foundation cracked beneath her feet and the ceiling crashed above her head.

Lane seemed to cross the entire school in a single breath. She was a blaze setting off across the ground, unstoppable, as she sprinted outside.

Shepherd stopped short as she ran through the front door, eyes wide. The afternoon sky had turned black as night, storms raging in a mixture of green and black clouds. Lightning jumped between them as an icy autumn rain began to pour onto the front lawn.

She hoped that everyone had made it out before this. She hadn't slept at all, trying her best to get everyone ready to run. But it had all been a blur, her mind unable to focus on anything other than her body pressed to Lane's, their lips touching as if she had been starved for her. And then Shepherd had ripped herself away. She'd barely been able to look at Lane since, her skin aching at the very sight of her. She wanted to be angry with her, and she wanted to be near her. She wanted to forget her, and she wanted to forgive her. She wanted to wrap herself around her and never let go. But she couldn't.

Because she was afraid of her. She was afraid of what it meant that Lane was dead. She was afraid that she would have to go back to After Life and never return. She was afraid of the dark magic they had poured into her. And she was afraid of the way that seemed to draw her to Lane even more.

Shouts echoed in the distance and Shepherd broke into a run toward it, gray fog swirling around her ankles as she crossed the stone patio. Seren, Korvu, Yarrow, and Deryck stood in a staggered line, facing away from the school. Behind them, Lane skidded to a halt.

Shepherd could barely make out their voices over the roar of the storm.

"Stop! Don't!" Lane screamed.

The others ignored her. Shepherd just reached them as Korvu shot an arrow into the darkness. She watched as it disappeared into the downpour, as if absorbed by the night itself.

And that was when Shepherd saw it. It wasn't just a storm. The darkness hid nearly a dozen nochtra, staring forward with their black, empty eyes. Each of them was altered so that no two were alike. Some of them had the same bat-like wings protruding from their backs. Others seemed to float, staring blankly like ghosts.

A nochtra cocked its head to the side slowly, turning at an impossible angle to look at the blade in its chest. Its hollow eyes met Korvu's. In a blink, two arms exploded from its sides, ending in razor-like claws. It lifted Korvu in the air like a broken doll, the jagged edges of its arms ripping into his skin. He cried out as it tossed him into the ground. His body hit the brick with a deafening crack.

He lay still against the ground.

Seren screamed. Yarrow ran toward Korvu, bark-covered arms pulling Korvu into his lap. His head lolled, dangling in unconsciousness.

Lane didn't move, staring out into the darkness. A few feet away, Deryck stood, ghostly pale. Neither seemed to notice as two winged nochtra swirled overhead, even as the claws reached for them.

Shepherd lunged forward, knocking Lane to the ground as a nochtra's talons grazed through her hair. She shouted as she landed on her back and Deryck ducked, surprised at the noise. Shepherd covered them both with her arms, hoping the nochtra left them alone.

Her body pressing into Lane's seemed to wake her from her spell. She stared up at her, her hair splayed across the brick and her eyes wide.

"You're going to get us both killed," Shepherd said. "Or me, at least."

"What did they do to her?" She wasn't asking Shepherd. The expression on her face was a mixture of shock and anger. Above them, a nochtra shrieked.

"To who?" Shepherd asked. "Who are you talking about?"

Lane pushed herself out of Shepherd's arms, scrambling to her feet. Her vision was locked on the nochtra, barely noticing Shepherd at all. The ones that stood on the lawn stared back at her with empty faces, loose jaws, and black eyes.

"It's Perry," Lane said.

She took two steps toward the nochtra as Deryck fell beside Shepherd. Seren fought off two nochtra as Yarrow shook Korvu, still trying to wake him up as rain splashed off their faces.

"It's her schoolmate. Her friend, Perry," Deryck said, as if that explained everything. Probably noting the confusion on her face, he pointed a bony, white finger toward the lawn.

In the rain and the storm and the swirling nochtra, it had been easy to miss. One of them didn't appear like a nochtra at all but like a girl. Like the first shade Shepherd had encountered when Lane saved her, her face was distorted, flashing like storm clouds. She danced in and out of shadow, but the darkness seemed to be solidifying around her. The shadows disappeared, leaving only a girl in their place. She had dark skin, short hair, and a heart-shaped face. Rain poured down her face like tears as she collapsed to her knees.

Lane ran toward her, water splashing around her boots as she knelt in front of her friend.

Everything seemed to slow down. The nochtra flew back, Seren screaming after them with her sword in hand. Shepherd felt every muscle in her body freeze. The air was stagnant with stillness. Her breath seemed impossibly loud, echoing in her ears like roaring waves.

Deryck's eyes flashed. "We have to do something before she gets herself killed."

She couldn't move, her eyes cemented on Lane.

"Lane?" Perry asked. Her voice was hollow and faraway, somehow quiet even against the storm.

"Perry, what happened? What happened to you?" Lane reached toward her, and by the quiver in her voice, Shepherd knew she was crying. Her fingers brushed against Perry's shoulder but slipped through it like it was smoke.

Perry let out a strangled cry. "I don't know," she repeated, over and over. "It hurts, Laney."

Lane tried to grab her again, her fingers grasping at nothing.

"I'm going to help you. It's going to be okay." Lane stood up, still trying to grab her.

"We need to go home, something is wrong," Perry said.

Her face was shadowed and still blurred, as if the shadows hadn't gone but merely paused. The nochtra above began to flap their wings harder at the rain, screeching and extending their claws as thunder clapped behind them. Shepherd took two steps toward Lane.

Something was wrong.

With a sudden crash, the windows of the Haven exploded. Glass fell like snow. Seren and Deryck collapsed to the ground as it shook, the brick cracking. Shepherd stumbled, skinning her hand across the stones.

"Lane, get away from her!" Shepherd screamed, jumping to her feet.

Lane was trying to pull Perry to her feet, her hands moving through her like water.

"It's The Academy. They've been capturing witches, turning them to nochtra—Perry, I'm so—"

The girl looked up at her. The irises of her eyes had turned black.

"No."

In a flash, Perry snatched Lane's arm, digging into the flesh. Shadows erupted from her, but she held Lane like a vice. Blood erupted from beneath her nails. Seconds before, Lane hadn't been able to touch her. Now, she couldn't escape her grasp.

Whatever Perry had been—ghost, girl, witch—was gone.

"It's a trick, Lane, it's a trick!" Shepherd shouted, breaking into a run.

A nochtra swooped toward her as she tried to reach Lane. Its claws scratched at her face, its black shadowed wings flapping as it pulled her into its grip. It wrapped itself around her, pinning her arms to her sides and forcing her to the ground. Shadows forced their way into her mouth, down her throat, stealing her breath and gagging her. Her vision went black.

It was killing her.

She kicked and pushed as hard as she could at the wings, but they pinned her tight, forcing her face to scratch against the stone. Talons pierced her skin, but she couldn't cry out.

A scream rang through Shepherd's skull as the nochtra was ripped away. Her vision dotted with white as Seren pulled her to her feet. Her sword was stabbed through the nochtra's skull.

Shepherd gasped for breath, throwing up spit and bile on her shoes. "Thanks," she managed.

Behind her, Perry had pushed Lane to her knees. The shadows wrapped around her arms like tentacles, chaining her to the ground. A single black arm wrapped around her throat, another around her mouth as she thrashed against it, unable to move more than an inch.

"Go," Seren pointed with her sword. "Get out of here. We'll hold the rest of them off."

Deryck grabbed Shepherd's arm before she could respond, pulling her toward Lane in a sprint. Together, they leapt onto the shadow, Shepherd tearing at the blackened arms with desperate hands, ripping them from Lane's skin. Deryck pulled a dagger from somewhere inside his skirts, slashing at the shadowed ropes that blocked Lane's throat and eyes.

The nochtra that had been Perry screeched, pulling back as Lane struggled away. She scratched at the last pieces of shadow that clung to her face as Shepherd reached for her, pulling her into her chest.

"We have to help her," Lane said, her voice muffled by Shepherd's shirt.

"It's not Perry anymore, Lane," Deryck said. He moved to stand between them as the nochtra got to her feet.

The nochtra's form twisted, Perry's features disappearing and reappearing like smoke rings. One moment, her mouth was crooked and mocking, and the next, it was gone, the snarling teeth of some monster in its place.

"I can't leave her," Lane said, twisting out of Shepherd's arms. She pushed through Deryck as Perry rose to face her.

They stared at each other as the nochtra attacked around them. Seren and Yarrow swiped at them with swords, trying to hold them at bay. Deryck's grip tightened on his knife, his jaw squaring as he stared at the shadow. Around them, wherever the others knocked down a nochtra, another seemed to appear in its place.

Shepherd's heart fell. They were powerless. *She* was powerless. She had no weapons on her, nothing to help Lane. Her hair matted to her face from the rain, her shirt sticking to her skin.

Perry took a step toward Lane, her arm extended. Shepherd held her breath, and Deryck raised his knife.

"Whatever that thing is, it's not your friend. Not anymore," Shepherd shouted. "There is nothing you can do for her!"

She knew she was right. If Lane didn't make it out of this fight, everything was lost. They needed her for their plan, to get to After Life, to save everyone.

But more than that, Shepherd wanted to save Lane. It didn't matter that she was dead, not in the end. She still breathed, she still felt, she still wanted. And Shepherd wanted her.

"There has to be!" Lane shouted back at her. "I need there to be."

"Why?"

"Because there has to be a way back."

She turned to look at Shepherd, tears visible even through the raindrops that clung to her face. Her skin had turned pale as milk in the cold. Shepherd realized that Lane thought that she was too far gone—that the magic was going to eat her inside out, like it had done to Perry. Shepherd wanted to tell her she would never let that happen, that she wouldn't let her become one of those things. But as she opened her mouth, Perry's nochtra tilted back her head and laughed.

Shadows erupted from her, hundreds of tendrils sprouting in every direction. They wrapped around Deryck, pulling him to the ground until he disappeared under the shadowed bonds.

Shepherd tried to hurry backwards as Lane kicked and grabbed at the nochtra, but within seconds the nochtra had pushed them both to their knees. Darkness wrapped around both of them, tying around their wrists and slashing across their skin like barbed wire.

Shepherd toppled to the ground beside Lane, landing half on top of her as the monster's strange arms surrounded them. It wrapped around her legs, around her arms, pulling her tighter against Lane in the darkness until she couldn't tell where she ended and Lane began. She couldn't feel the rain on her back, only the shadows cutting at her skin. The air thinned as it suffocated them, and they both gasped, clawing at the tendrils that wrapped around each other's necks.

"The. . . Key," Lane managed to croak out. Shepherd could barely see her in the swirling shadow, her own arms pinned to Lane's sides.

Elbowing and kicking at the shadow as she strained her fingers, forcing them into Lane's pocket. Her fingers wrapped around the bone, cold and still against her palm.

Lane thrashed back and forth, kicking at the shadows, screaming into the darkness that held them tightly against each other. In the split second that they pushed away, Shepherd shoved the key into Lane's hand.

She closed her eyes, tears brimming at the corners from lack of oxygen. Suddenly, the ground disappeared from underneath her. She gasped for air as cold rain landed on her scalp, her face pressed into mud that calmed the heat in her skin.

Lane had Blinked them away from Perry but only a few feet. They laid tangled in each other's arms on the grass.

Perry screeched into the sky, tilting her head back with a vicious cry that echoed off the walls of Haven Hall. Stone and brick toppled to the ground as the exterior wall collapsed, shaking the Earth beneath their feet.

Deryck ran toward them, still slapping and hitting at the shadows Perry had left behind. Seren followed behind, slashing her sword at the nochtra that followed her and the tendrils that threatened to climb up her leg. She brought her boot down hard on one, breaking it in two, and Perry screeched again.

"We've got to get out of here," Deryck shouted, pulling Lane to her feet.

Lane looked past him, at Perry and the nochtra that collected behind her like an army.

"Go!" Seren shouted. "Before she attacks again!"

Shepherd pushed herself to her elbows, slipping in the mud.

"I can't leave her," Lane said. "Not like this. Not again. We have to help her."

Deryck placed both his hands on her shoulders, turning her to face the school. "And we will. But not like this. You won't be any help to her if you turn into one of those things."

Lane shook her head. "I can't. I don't know if I even can Blink without the obols!"

Deryck shook her, ducking as nochtra narrowly swooped toward them, talons slicing at his scalp.

"Lane, listen to me. They have taken so much from you, from all of us. They took your life, your identity. They have taken and taken and taken." He paused as the storm of nochtra grew louder, closer. "But it's your turn to take. Take what they've stolen from you. Take the ash they ground you into and set it on fire."

Lane's jaw tightened, tears welling in her eyes as she took one final look at Perry. She nodded, placing her hand on Deryck's shoulder.

Fog poured around them, surrounding Shepherd as Perry screamed, the nochtra taking aim for Lane as they plummeted toward her.

Lane closed her eyes. Shepherd cursed to herself.

They were going to leave her behind.

Leaping to her feet, Shepherd ran toward them as darkness enveloped them, just like when Lane had Blinked away all of the shades attacking the safehouse. At the center of the darkness, exploding outward like a black star, she could just make out Lane's outline.

Shepherd couldn't hesitate, couldn't second guess. She leapt into the air, throwing herself into the blackhole. Her fingers grasped onto something in the dark and took hold, refusing to let go as she was ripped from one world and into another.

A single scream followed them into the dark.

CHAPTER TWENTY-SIX

It shouldn't have been possible. With her obols removed, there should have been no connection to The Academy, nothing to guide her back. As the remnants of power faded in her bloodstream, she would get weaker, until there was nothing left of her at all. That she knew for certain.

But at the same time, she knew she had never felt stronger. She knew she would be able to do it, even as doubt clouded her thoughts.

She felt the familiar cold of nothingness as they traveled through the darkness, that invisible place beneath worlds. It seemed to only last a few seconds before her face hit hard ground, but it could have been lifetimes.

Deryck groaned behind her, tangled around her as they both slammed into the floor. Even now, she couldn't land properly.

Her muscles cried for rest, exhausted from fighting and from the heartbreak of seeing Perry. Her mind was a dead signal, the radio waves gone silent and fuzzy.

"All right?" she asked the dark room.

Deryck unspooled himself from where he clung to her waist, rolling across the floor. She squinted, letting her eyes adjust to the darkness. There was stone beneath her hands and something heavy laying on her legs.

Shepherd.

Her body was draped across Lane's ankles, her fingers wrapped in Lane's pants so tightly that she had ripped a hole. Her choppy hair laid across her face, her eyes closed as if she was asleep.

"Shepherd!" Lane cried out, crawling toward her. She tried to shake her awake, shaking her with all her strength.

This is what she was afraid of. She had followed them and now she was hurt, or worse—

"Sorry for crashing your party," Shepherd said, a smile creeping on her face.

Lane shoved her in the arm.

"You stubborn ass! You had no way of knowing that would work—you could have died! You could have been trapped between worlds!"

She shoved her again for good measure as Shepherd shifted to stand.

"Oh, do you want me to go back? I'll just look for the exit then—"

Lane rolled her eyes. "We're just lucky it worked."

Deryck turned around in the dark room.

He flipped his hair, still running his hands along the wall until he found a sconce. He pulled something Lane couldn't make out from his pocket. A box of matches, she realized. The smell of sulfur filled the room as he struck it across the stone and lit the sconce.

The room suddenly became visible in the orange glow. It was a strange shape, somewhere between a circle and a lopsided hexagon. It was completely empty except for the three of them and the torch on the wall. An abandoned closet or office? Lane wasn't sure. The stone certainly looked like The Academy, but Lane didn't recognize the room. She wouldn't know if she had managed to Blink them correctly until they were in a recognizable part of the school.

"What happened back there?" she asked him. "What did they do to her?"

He raised a blond eyebrow. "Oh, you're asking me? Why? Because I'm a demon, so I must know everything there is to know about your silly death magic?"

"Well, I don't know, and she certainly doesn't know." She gestured to herself and then Shepherd.

Deryck sighed. "My best guess? Whoever is creating these nochtra just leveled up and found a new way to make a monster. And they really don't want you to be here."

"Me?"

Why would they even care about her?

"Think about it, Laney dear. They sent Perry. Not some random nochtra, not Shepherd's sister, not Ivy—they sent Perry. For you."

"A trap," she said, looking at Shepherd, who had tried to warn her.

Someone knew that she was helping the witches then, and they had gone as far to torture Perry and turn her into a monster to get to Lane.

"Eurydice," she hissed.

"We've lost the element of surprise then. They know we're after them," Deryck said.

Shepherd scratched at her chin. "Not necessarily. At least, they don't know we're here, as far as we know." She smiled. "And on the bright side, we know they're afraid. Or they wouldn't have bothered."

"I don't know about that," Lane said, tying up her hair. It didn't seem likely that they were afraid of her or getting caught. More likely, they were just trying to torture them before they inevitably failed.

Shepherd turned to her. "So, what now?"

Lane bit her lip. "I don't know. The plan didn't account for Seren and the others being left behind."

"Or for me," Shepherd said with a smirk. Lane jerked her head around in surprise. "What? I'm not stupid. I know you planned on leaving me behind."

Lane scowled. Shepherd was too perceptive. She hadn't even said it out loud to herself. She tried not to look at Shepherd, hoping she wouldn't confirm that it was true.

"It doesn't matter," Shepherd said. "I'm here now, and they aren't. We'll just have to make it work. Which is exactly my area of expertise."

Shepherd turned about the room, her fingers grazing against the wall. "We're really here," she whispered. She turned to them, eyebrows raised. "I'm not dead, am I?"

Only she could joke at a time like this.

Deryck snorted. "No, of course not. At least, I don't think so. There isn't really a precedent for the living coming to After Life the way you did. But not everything in After Life is dead. Like me."

That was something Lane was depending on.

"So?" Shepherd asked, gesturing to the door.

Lane exhaled in frustration. Could they make it work? An unwitch, a demon, and a dead girl up against The Academy and possibly The Keys? No magic against all the death magic in the afterlife, except for maybe Lane's ability, if she could get it to work.

"We need to find Victor." Lane reached for the door handle.

Deryck cracked his neck as he leaned toward her. "Yes, that's exactly what we should do before we attack Eurydice. Inform her personal assistant."

"He'll help us."

"And then what?" Shepherd asked.

Lane smirked as she turned around, stepping backwards into the hallway. "Then we'll really crash a party."

She spun on her heel into the hallway. It was dark and quiet, with only a few torches lighting the way. All of the hallways at The Academy—at least the ones she knew about—looked the same. She took three cautious steps forward, hoping to find anything familiar. Her ears buzzed as she focused on the sounds of the school, the groans of the stones.

Her chest tightened as they journeyed further into the halls, turning corners and rounding bends. Empty classrooms and dead ends lined the way, all looking the same. Shepherd fell into line next to her, her hands shoved in her pockets as always.

"So, what do you have up your sleeve?" Shepherd asked.

Lane raised an eyebrow.

"I know you haven't told us everything," Shepherd said. "I know you better than that."

Lane huffed air through her nostrils. "I've told you everything."

Unlike you, she thought.

"You don't have to worry about me," Shepherd said. "I know you didn't want me here, but I'm fine."

She paused as they rounded another corner. Lane peeked ahead before motioning that the hallway was empty.

"And if it comes down to it, I don't want you jumping through any windows or anything to save me. I can take care of myself."

Lane smiled, thinking about the night they met. She'd never intended to help Shepherd or team up with her or start to like her—but that was exactly what had happened.

"I wouldn't dream of it." Lane smirked.

Voices grew louder in the distance and Lane shoved Shepherd into the wall, squeezing them into a small gap between the stone and a column.

Deryck stopped short, realizing too late that someone was walking toward them. He leaned against the column and looked at the ground, making a terrible act of looking casual and disinterested.

Two people Lane didn't recognize walked by, laughing to each other. They both had drinks in their hand, sparkling champagne flutes filled with a rosy, orange liquid.

"Good evening," one of them said to Deryck. He tilted his chin in acknowledgment. "An excellent celebration."

"Indeed," Deryck said.

They didn't seem to notice Lane as they disappeared down another hallway, and she exhaled a sigh of relief into Shepherd's neck. A flush rose to her face as she noticed how close they were, pulling herself away. She didn't need to embarrass herself again.

"What was that?" she hissed at Deryck. "Who was that?"

His mouth was a thin, crooked line. "Demons."

The party had already started.

"We need to hurry," Lane said.

She rushed toward the center of the school, following the way the demons had come. Music sung through the halls as they got closer, competing voices clamoring to be heard over the crash of violins.

Lane came to a sudden halt, her boots squeaking across the pristine floor. Shepherd slammed into her back. Deryck stopped next to her, his blank eyes taking in the room.

The entire entrance hall of The Academy had been turned into a ballroom. The stone floors had been polished to the smooth shine of glistening tile, gold and ivory woven in a winding circle that led to the middle of a dance floor. The ancient chandelier that hung overhead sparkled with the light of a thousand black candles, bright against the shadowed ceiling. Music echoed off every wall, although there was no stage, no orchestra, no band. Hundreds of pale ghosts circled the room, dancing between the laughing demons. Their white faces seemed enchanted, their expressions as far away as the ghosts that guarded the school. The demons didn't seem to notice.

Lane saw other Academy students amongst them, dressed in formal gowns and suits that were a far cry from their normal uniforms. There were other undead, like Lane and the other students, ghosts who were not quite ghosts. They had been called to The Academy from across After Life for the All Hallows celebration, each of them a perfect mirror of the living person they had been when they were alive. Had they all lost their memories too? Was that the price to pay for not being a voiceless, empty haunting?

As if hearing her thoughts, two of the ghosts closest to them turned, their translucent eyes looking at Lane as they drifted toward her.

"Come on," she said. "Before someone notices us."

With her in her black jeans and Shepherd in her t-shirt, they stuck out like weeds among the glamor of the ball. Deryck wore his usual elegant jacket and skirt, so he could at least pass for one of the demons, if only because of his eyes and peculiar taste.

Lane grabbed Shepherd's arm, pulling her to walk along the entryway wall and down the corridor toward Victor's room.

One of the undead visitors stood outside his door, her heel against the wall as she brushed her fingers through her long red hair. She wore knee-high boots and tight-fitting pants with a black tailcoat covered in swirling velvet. Her chest was bare, exposing the pale skin of her sternum.

Lane inhaled and then shouted, "You! This corridor is off limits. You can't be here."

The woman looked up from her nails, almost bored. "There's no sign."

Trying to look as authoritative as Seren, Lane stomped toward her. "Do you question the rules of your host?"

"How rude," Deryck said from behind her. The demon glanced at him, her face growing worried as she took in his pure white eyes.

"You, you're—" she stuttered.

"Yep," he said.

As he did, her eyes turned completely white. For a moment, Deryck stood completely still, as if transported to a dream realm.

The woman slumped to the floor, her head lolling from side to side as she fell. Deryck shook his head, blubbering his lips as he seemed to come to.

"Grab her arms," he said, motioning at Lane as he stepped over her unconscious form. Winking, he kicked in the door. "What? You need to blend in."

He pushed Shepherd into Victor's room and Lane hurried to pull the woman behind them, holding her by the armpits. Shepherd slammed the door, looking down at the woman.

"Sorry," she said.

They laid a blanket over her as Lane changed into her jacket, thankful that the woman had been wearing a thin undershirt beneath her coat. Deryck flung open the doors to Victor's closet, throwing a uniform jacket and pants at Shepherd's face. She scrunched her face, slamming the door to the closet and locking herself inside.

Lane slid on the woman's boots, tucking her black jeans into them and removing her plain shirt from beneath the jacket. It had a deep V that exposed the middle of her bare chest. She turned to Deryck, motioning to herself with a flourish.

"How do I look?"

"The spitting image," he said. "Really, no one will recognize you. I've never seen you wear anything but a grubby t-shirt."

He walked up to her, reaching up to her head and gently pulling the holder from her ponytail. "Except for this. You always put your hair up when you're upset."

Lane curled her lip as her hair fell, waves tickling her shoulders.

Shepherd stepped out of the closet, pink coloring her cheeks. She wore one of Victor's uniform jackets, buttons crossing her chest in horizontal stripes. It was snug in her shoulders, clinging to the muscles of her arms. She'd even changed into a pair of guard's pants, the black sheen tight on her thighs.

"What?" Shepherd said, almost defensively.

"Nothing." Heat rose in Lane's cheeks as she tried not to think about their kiss or the way Shepherd looked in Victor's uniform. She turned to his desk, busying herself with rifling through the drawers as Deryck fixed the collar of Shepherd's shirt. She found a bag of amperes and wondered if this was where he had been hiding them. She stuffed them into her pocket.

Silently, they shoved the poor undead woman under Victor's desk. Deryck promised she wouldn't wake—at least not until he wanted her to. Whatever his ability was, Lane was glad she wasn't on his bad side.

Side by side, they ventured back into the hallway—Shepherd looking every bit an Academy guard and Deryck his typical demon self. Lane tried to hold her head high, relaxing her shoulders as much as she could as they walked back toward the party.

The music rang from every wall, and in her pocket, the keys buzzed in response. Her fingers twitched at her side, feeling the pulse of magic. She paused as they reached the entryway. There were so many people. She had never known there were so many ghosts, so many undead in After Life. The demons seemed distracted by their revelry, their dancing growing faster and faster, out of time with the beat. Gowns of every color whizzed by them, oranges and reds and the golds of autumn, blacks and grays and midnights, all the colors fitting for an All Hallows feast.

Shepherd stepped in front of her, tilting forward at the waist in a bow.

"Care to dance?"

CHAPTER TWENTY-SEVEN

There was one thing Lane hadn't expected: Shepherd was an excellent dancer. Deryck perched nearby, drinking that strange orange liquid from a triangular glass, as they danced around the room, circling the ghosts.

Lane had never felt more alive.

Shepherd's fingers were interlocked in hers as she led Lane across the dance floor, leading her feet in the steps. They passed other students, who didn't seem to recognize Lane at all as she kicked back her head and laughed into the chiming strings. The tails of her coat whipped around her knees like the skirts of a gown as Shepherd spun her, dipping Lane into her arms.

"Be careful, people will think you're actually enjoying yourself." Shepherd smirked.

It was almost possible to forget why they were there.

As Shepherd pulled her back up, spinning her around again as the violins sang, Lane glanced over her shoulder, peering through the white veil of ghosts that surrounded them.

"Keep an eye out for Victor," Lane said.

"I would," Shepherd said. "If I knew what he looked like."

Right.

"He has black hair, glasses. He's about your height, pale—he won't be dancing so look at the corners of the room."

Shepherd nodded. The spell broken, they both scanned the room.

There was no sign of Victor, or Eurydice for that matter. Lane sighed. She was worried their plan was falling apart, piece by piece. They needed to find their way into the catacombs and get to the cells, find the prisoners, before it was too late. On All Hallows, the veil between worlds was the thinnest. It was the reason Eurydice threw this pretense of a party—so she could keep an eye on all the people from across After Life that she didn't trust. It was The Academy's responsibility, after all, to make sure no one escaped to Life. At least, that was what they had taught Lane. How much of it had actually been true? Either way, it also meant that they would be distracted with the gala, or at least she hoped.

"You're a better dancer than I thought," Shepherd said. "I didn't think you'd have time for lessons, being dead and all."

Lane rolled her eyes. "Careful or I'll think you're complimenting me."

She looked up as Shepherd took her hand above their heads, spinning her out and into her arms.

"I can't change it, you know," Lane said. "Being dead. At least, not by myself. That's the only reason I was ever a part of The Academy in the first place. The promise of living again, of having a life—"

"I never asked you to change." Shepherd spun her around so they were facing each other, her eyes dark. "You know that I know what it's like, wishing you were something you're not. I spent my entire life wishing I was a witch or human, or 100% white or 100% Native, just because I thought that's what other people wanted from me. But all people want from us. . . is us. We can only be who we are, and if people don't like it. . . well, it's their loss. The only person that has to like you is you."

Lane twisted her lips. Around them, the beat of the music changed to something faster, matching the racing of her heartbeat.

"It's fine, I get it. I'm dead, you're not." She tried not to sound bitter.

Shepherd furrowed her eyebrows. "Lane, is this about our kiss, because—"

Shepherd was cut off as someone grabbed Lane's shoulder, peeling her away from Shepherd's grasp with angry force.

"Lane?" Tripp hissed.

He was dressed in his usual mission uniform, unlike all the other guests. She guessed he couldn't be bothered to dress up, although he had slicked back his usually frizzy locks.

His hand was still on her arm.

"Where have you been? I looked everywhere for you after Perry— after she was obliterated. You were just gone."

"No one told you?"

More had happened in the days since she had seen Tripp than she could explain.

"We don't have time to explain." Lane grabbed Tripp by the sleeve, pulling him to the side of the room. Shepherd followed, weaving in between the dancers as they pirouetted to the screeching orchestra. "Have you seen Victor?"

"No, not since this morning," Tripp said. "What's going on?"

He crossed his arms, looking down at her with concern and alarm. Standing on her tiptoes, she peered past him, trying to find Deryck amongst the crowd of other demons. For once, he didn't stick out like a weed in the grass. She cursed to herself. She couldn't find him.

"We need to find Victor and Deryck," she said, pushing up the sleeves of her jacket. She reached for her hair, tying it up in a stressed knot. She could feel the hands of the clock ticking inside her like a bomb. "Can you help us? We'll go find—"

Tripp grabbed Lane's arm, pulling it to his face.

"Lane, what happened to your obols? Are you okay?" His face was full of concern.

Lane hurried to pull down her sleeve, pulling Tripp around a corner and behind a column.

"Eurydice happened," she whispered so that they could barely hear her above the party.

"They blamed her for what's happening to the shades, the nochtra. Your friend Perry," Shepherd finished for her. "They tried to kill her or whatever it is you do."

Tripp looked at Shepherd, who was almost tall enough to be nearly eye to eye with him. "Who the Hades is this?"

He stepped toward Shepherd, veins in his neck tensing. Lane threw her arm across Shepherd's chest protectively.

"This is Shepherd. She's with me. She's trying to help me," Lane said. "I wish I had time to explain more, but Tripp. . . something is really wrong here. The Academy has been lying to us. They're hurting people, imprisoning them. It's not right."

"And you're going to stop them?" he asked.

She nodded.

"Does this have anything to do with the witches and those Keys?"

Lane's neck cracked, she looked at him so fast. "How do you know about the Keys?"

Had she somehow forgotten learning about them? She had been almost positive that they hadn't learned about them at school, but with the blank spots and her memory. . .

"Victor has been mumbling about them all week, ever since they imprisoned that witch who obliterated Perry and created all those creepy shades."

"Nochtra," Lane said. "That's what they're called."

Tripp shrugged in indifference.

"Bally?" Shepherd asked Lane.

Behind them, the music of the party changed again. There was a crash of glass, as if someone had thrown their champagne flute into the ground. Everyone cheered. The night was growing rowdier by the second, the energy turning darker and more electric.

They had done exactly what they told her they were going to do—blamed all of it on Baltus, even when they knew he had nothing to do with The Keys or the nochtra. He had been terrible, but even still, he didn't deserve this.

"Whatever they are saying he did, he didn't have anything to do with it. And neither did I."

"It seems like they'll pin it on anyone," Shepherd said.

Two demons stepped to the side of the dance floor, one of them leaning against the column they were hiding behind. Lane pulled Tripp a few feet further into the hallway, the music growing quieter.

"You're in trouble?" Tripp asked. Lane didn't respond. "You could have asked for help, you know. You could have said anything, said goodbye. I would have helped you. We're friends."

Lane twisted her lips, looking up at him. His expression was a mix of frustration and sadness.

"I'm sorry, Tripp. Believe me when I say it wasn't by choice."

The roar of the party quieted, and Shepherd took a step away, peeking over the shoulder of the closest ghost and into the ballroom.

She leaned in, lowering her voice. "But we could use your help now. There are prison cells beneath the school, deeper beneath ground than Deryck's bar. We need to get down there. Can you help us find the entrance? We might need to split up, find Deryck and search the castle."

Tripp gave her a puzzled look, as if confused by what she was saying.

"What?" Lane asked.

Tripp looked at her and said, "The door in Eurydice's office, it goes straight to the lower levels."

"What? What door in Eurydice's office?" She shook her head, curls falling in her eyes. She hadn't ever even been in Eurydice's office.

Tripp put his hand on her arm, his face full of concern, almost like an older sibling. She felt the color drain from her face as his eyes met hers.

"Lane, we use it all the time. Do you not remember?"

Just as he said it, Eurydice walked into the center of the ballroom, the crowd parting around her.

CHAPTER TWENTY-EIGHT

The music stopped, the room quieting to only the hum of voices as Eurydice crossed to the middle of the dance floor. Around her, the guests raised their glasses, whispering to each other as she smiled at them. Applause broke out, the demons shouting their thanks to her, the ghosts watching her with sad smiles. She turned to her dance partner and they both bowed, the music beginning again as he took her hand, as if the ball had only just begun with her arrival. Lane felt herself stiffen as Eurydice turned the floor with her partner, their faces in forced, tight smiles.

It was Victor.

Lane yanked on Shepherd's sleeve, pulling her away from the crowd as she turned to Tripp. Her heart felt like it was in her throat just from seeing Eurydice's face, and she tried to swallow it. It was now or never.

"Can you take me to Eurydice's office?"

He cocked his head to the side as she continued to hurry down the hallway, his steps easily catching up with her long strides. She hoped they were going in the right direction, or at least that they didn't have to go back through the entry hall.

"You seriously don't remember?"

Lane looked at Shepherd. She shrugged back at her with a gentle nudge. *Tell him*, she was trying to say. Lane chewed her lip, her grip tightening on Shepherd's sleeve as she quickened her pace, from nerves and from fear that Eurydice had seen them.

"I have these blackouts, sometimes. Memory lapses, whole spans of time I can't recall. I think it's a side effect from The Academy removing my memories, like something went wrong."

Her voice quivered. She'd never said it out loud before. She felt tears brimming at the corner of her eyes as she looked at Tripp, who suddenly stopped. She'd been holding it inside for so long.

Shepherd's hand dropped to hers, wrapping her fingers around her wrist.

"Lane," Tripp said. "Perry said the same thing."

A shiver ran through Lane's entire body. She felt outside of and inside herself at the same time, as if she was watching the moment play out like a performance and also feeling every second of it.

"What?" she croaked.

Tripp shook his head. "We didn't talk about it much—you know how she was. But she had been saying for months that she couldn't remember things. Missions, whole spans of time. I thought she was just worried about graduating, the stress. . . I don't know." He paused, grinding his teeth. "Now, I'm not so sure."

Lane took two shuddering breaths. She felt like she was trying to pull her soul back into her body.

"We need to keep moving, Lane," Shepherd said, her voice low.

Lane nodded, almost absently. Her thoughts were stuck on Perry and their joint memory loss. What did it mean?

She shook herself. She needed to focus. They barely had a few hours before the feast ended.

"Take us to her office."

Tripp nodded, motioning for them to follow as he turned down a hallway to the left that passed their mission room and Victor's bedroom, the library, and the kitchens. At the end, there was a small flight of three stone stairs that curved around, ending in an oval, ebony door, nearly the color of midnight.

Tripp glanced over his shoulder as he opened the door, the hinges squeaking like a bat. Shepherd shuddered. Lane stepped into the darkness of the room, her eyes struggling to focus.

She wished that she could talk to Perry about the blank spots. What did it mean? Victor had told her that magic could overload and consume itself. It was what Baltus had said caused the nochtra—the magic became too much, corrupting the shade and turning it into something new. Was that what had happened to Perry?

Was it happening to Lane?

If the magic inside her was somehow breaking down, causing her to forget things, what else was happening inside her that she wasn't aware of?

She wished she knew how long Perry had been blacking out, how long she had felt something was wrong before she had turned into a nochtra.

How long did she have before it happened to her, too?

Tripp lit the sconces on either side of the door, red flames framing his red hair. Lane turned to the shadowed room. It was disused, as if Eurydice barely visited it. There was a desk, smaller than Victor's, with a thin layer of dust across the top. Parchment and books were scattered across the surface. They clearly hadn't been touched in years. Like Victor's room, there was a door that adjoined another room and a fireplace.

An identical ebony door overtook the opposite end of the room. Shadows danced across it in the light of the flames. Lane's throat tightened as Tripp crossed the room without a word, placing his hand on the silver handle. Shepherd hovered over his shoulder nervously, standing on her tiptoes.

"Are you. . . alive?" Tripp asked, his eyebrows raised. His hand hovered on the handle, the door open barely an inch.

Shepherd smirked. "I like to think so."

He narrowed his eyes. "A witch?"

"Depends on who you ask."

Tripp tsked as he swung open the door. "Lane, what have you gotten yourself into?"

If only he knew.

"She's kidnapping them, Tripp. Killing them. They aren't like what we were taught. They're. . . good. Some of them."

Lane looked past him where the door had revealed a dark, stone passageway. Unlike Eurydice's office, it was clean, devoid of cobwebs. She hoped she was right about this.

She turned to Tripp, Shepherd at her side in the doorway.

"You're really going to do this?" Tripp asked. "Help the witches? You don't even know them! What about us? What about Perry, Victor, your friends?"

Lane reached toward him. "Tripp," she said as he pulled his arm away.

She looked at the hurt on his face, chewing the inside of her lip. She'd never even seen him upset. Cracking jokes, maybe. But hurt? When she'd left, she hadn't even thought about how it would affect him, especially after Perry had turned into a nochtra. That just wasn't who Tripp was. Or so she had thought.

What could she even tell him?

"Tripp, there's not—we don't have a lot of time. We have to help them before it's too late, we don't—"

He cut her off. "You don't have a lot of time. I get it. You don't have time to explain. You don't have time for me."

Lane pulled her hand back like she'd been stung. But what could she tell him? He was right. So much had changed. She had changed. But that wasn't fair. He was still her friend, no matter how much had changed.

She reached for his wrist, tightening her grip as best she could so that he couldn't pull away, looking up into his eyes.

"Fine. Tripp," she said. "Here's the deal."

Lane quickly explained everything that had happened, from finding Shepherd to Haven Hall to the nochtra. She exhaled, trying to catch her breath, having said everything as fast as she could.

Tripp blinked. "All—all right."

"I'm sorry I left you," Lane said. "But I have to help these people. We already got to live our lives. They should get to live theirs."

Tripp nodded, his eyes still glazed over, processing everything she had said.

Her chest heaved. The dark hallway behind them blew cold air on her back. She tapped her fingers on her leg worriedly, itching to retie her hair. There was no clock in the room, but she could tell it was nearing midnight. The party would end soon, and with it, the last chance they had.

"I don't know that I understood half of what you said, but I do know that we're a team," Tripp said. "What can I do?"

Lane grinned. "We need to go. Can you go back to the ball and find Deryck and Victor? Meet me underneath the clock. And whatever you do, don't draw any attention. Eurydice can't know what's going on."

Tripp nodded.

Lane turned to Shepherd, motioning to the dark hallway beside them.

"Ready to find your sister?"

Together, Shepherd and Lane stepped into the darkness.

She tried not to look back as the stairs steadily declined. There were no sconces, no torches, no lights, and her eyes struggled to adjust. There was only the sound of their steps, crunching against the rock and stone, step after step after step.

Slowly, the stairs turned into a slope, and her calves burned as the stone turned to slippery ground. Bracing herself, her hand grazed the wall. There was no light, but she could still see Shepherd's face in the black jewel of its scarab-like surface. A backwards smirk reflected on her face.

"I'm sorry about your friend," she said, kicking a loose stone. "He seemed. . . nice."

"Tripp?" Lane asked. "He'll be fine."

She hoped.

Shepherd twisted her mouth. Before them, the hallway stretched into a long, cave-like darkness that seemed to have no end.

"So, are you going to tell me what you're hiding or not?"

Lane tensed. She felt the keys in her pocket, her hand instinctively going to them, tapping her fingers along her side.

"I didn't mean literally." She could almost hear Shepherd's eye roll. "I know you didn't tell everyone the entire plan. I know you better than that."

"You barely know me at all."

"That's what you think."

They turned a corner in the dark as they came upon a dead end, finding another set of stairs. The air turned colder as they descended. How much deeper could these halls go?

Lane turned toward her.

"I'm not hiding anything. You know as much as I do. If I had a better plan, I would tell you."

Shepherd held her hands up defensively.

"All right," she said. "I just. . . Don't do anything stupid. I know you think you're expendable because you're dead, but you're not. I don't need you risking your entire existence."

Lane fought a smile as the stairs enclosed around them, the space growing tighter and tighter in the dark. Her shoulders nearly scraped against the walls. Shepherd's hands found her shoulders, following her through the passage.

"Don't you know that as soon as you tell someone not to do something stupid, they end up doing exactly that?"

Shepherd laughed. "Sounds familiar."

Somewhere ahead, the sound of water echoed as it dripped like rain on a tin roof. Lane exhaled as the narrow passage opened, the stale air suddenly clear and cool. Shepherd looked at Lane with a strange intensity in her golden brown eyes, as if there was something she wanted to say, but bit her tongue instead.

The unlit passageway split into two, one leading back up into darkness and the other ending in a gleaming black door. It stood out against the wet cave walls, the antique wood adorned with brocade hinges and a large, silver lock. Like most things at The Academy, it looked out of place, the strange combination of something modern in a place that seemed more myth than real.

Lane paused. This had to be it. It didn't seem that the levels went any deeper. Shepherd reached for her arm, her fingers wrapping around her elbow.

Something twisted in Lane's stomach. When she touched Shepherd, she felt like she was being pulled underwater, and all she wanted to do was drown. The feeling was a puzzle to her, something she couldn't decipher, like notes to a song she didn't know. Something pressed against the inside of her chest, something she couldn't place, but made her heart feel like it was straining to survive.

"You didn't have to do any of this," Shepherd said. "You didn't have to help me. You didn't have to find my sister. You didn't have to help the witches. You could have left whenever you wanted to. It wasn't your fight, but you made it yours. So, well, thank you."

That's what Lane had told herself when they met, hadn't she? It would have been easier if Shepherd had never forced Lane to bring her. She told herself for days that she could leave whenever she wanted, go back to The Academy and prove that she was innocent. But what would have happened to Shepherd? What would have happened to her?

No, she didn't need her. Not at first, anyway.

"I knew I was growing on you," she smirked, repeating Shepherd's words back at her as she opened the door.

If it was usually guarded, they were lucky that it was All Hallows—only one guard stood on the inside of the door. It was a new development since Lane had escaped, if they were in the right place. His undead form barely seemed to register as Lane entered the hall.

"This area's off limits," he said, in his double-voice, one echoed and faraway. His clear eyes flicked to Shepherd in her uniform.

"They thought you might want to join the party," Shepherd said. "I've come to take over your shift."

The ghost guard looked up and down, then to Lane. "They did?" he asked, his voice suspicious. He took two steps away from them, backing himself against the wall.

"No," Lane said, bringing her elbow into his ear with as much force as she could. He fell to the ground, and she slammed his head into the wall behind him. He slumped to the ground.

"Hurry, he won't stay unconscious long." Not while they were in The Academy, anyway. The undead's connection to death magic was too strong.

They pulled the guard into a corner, tucking him between the columns of a carved alcove. Shepherd crossed his arms and ankles.

"He could almost be sleeping." She smirked, laughing silently.

No alarms had sounded, but Lane knew it would not be long. When Lane escaped, it was only minutes before the shades had attacked her. Eurydice wasn't stupid enough to not have increased her defenses since then.

Twelve doors lined each side of the hallway, almost eerily ordinary in their appearance. They could have been regular classroom doors if not for the small, rectangular slat that was barely large enough to be considered a peephole. Unlike the secret cave hallways they had traveled down, the walls and floor were aged white limestone, just like the rest of The Academy. Arches lined the hall between each door, carved with fleur de lis and other brocade patterns, a vestige from whatever The Academy might have been before. Victor had told her once that the school had been built to match the prestigious universities in Life, but to Lane, it almost looked like it had been stolen.

Lane took two steps forward and knelt to the ground. Red-brown drops of blood scattered across the floor, leading the way down the hall to another identical, black door. It must have been the way Lane had come the first time.

"Ivy?" she called out, a whispering, hissing shout. "Ivy?"

"Ivy!" Shepherd shouted.

There was no response. Behind one of the doors, someone let out a low, animal-like groan.

Lane glanced over her shoulder at Shepherd. "Step back."

Reaching into her pocket, she pulled out the bag of amperes she had stolen from Victor's room.

She tried to recall what Victor had done when he had broken through her cell wall. Her fingers ran across the surface of the coin, flipping it between her knuckles. The magic pulsed into her arm like hot water running over her skin. Her scar stung in response, as if greeting an old friend. Still in her pocket, the keys sang a high, shrill note in recognition.

She held the coin to the nearest door, pressing her palms flat against it. She thought of all the times she had to use death magic to send back drifters, or to fight an escaped ghost, or even just in class, sparring. The keys in her pocket screeched louder and Lane shoved the energy forward, out of her body, and into the wall.

Her eardrums thrummed as she was thrown backwards, the wall exploding with an echoing bang. She rolled into the opposite wall, her elbows skinning against the floor as rocks and debris landed all around her.

"Lane!" Shepherd ran toward her.

She gave her a half-hearted smile as she sat up.

"It worked," she said, dizzily.

"I don't think 'it worked' if you knock yourself out in the process," Shepherd said.

Shepherd dusted off her sleeves, covered in rock and dirt as Lane hurried to her feet. She stretched her jaw open and closed, trying to banish the buzzing. The cell door had been blown backwards into the cell.

No one emerged.

An alarm began to ring out overhead, piercing in Lane's still aching eardrums. It was a strange sound, not like any alarm Lane had ever heard on missions. It was a thousand violins strung incorrectly, playing out of harmony, accompanied by the familiar cry of ghosts.

This is what she had been afraid of. They would likely only have minutes to get out. It would not be enough time.

Everything seemed to slow—Shepherd motioning to the noise overhead, mouthing something at her as Lane pushed herself away from the wall.

Her thoughts zeroed into focus. Hurry. Hurry. Hurry.

"Block off the doors on either side."

She was running before she finished her sentence. Shepherd broke into a sprint in the other direction, not bothering to respond as she moved to block off the door they had entered through with the rubble.

The cells were eerily silent next to the screeching of the alarm. Lane ran up and peered through each eyehole, hoping to find one with someone inside.

Empty. Empty. Empty. 12, 11, 10. . . she thought of the pictures on the wall. Only nine doors were left.

A strangled cry came from the cell to her right, the very sound a struggle, barely audible over the howling alarm.

Lane rushed to the door. A weak, rasping voice said, "Took you long enough."

Lane wrapped her fingers around the lower half of the eye slat, peering into the cell.

Ivy laid across the floor, her arm twisted at an odd angle overhead. Lane's stomach dropped. She was shackled to the wall. Her shoulder was yanked out of its socket, whether by someone else's hand or her own, Lane couldn't tell. Her arm dangled loosely at her side, the bone protruding like a horn in her shoulder. She was covered in bruises, blue and black that circled her arms and neck. Puncture wounds dotted her skin with rust-red scabs.

Acid bubbled in Lane's throat.

"Is Seren with you?" Ivy croaked, trying to sit up.

Lane shook her head. "No. I'm going to take you to her. Let's get you out of here."

Ivy nodded. She tried to speak, but no sound came out.

She didn't want Seren to see her like this, Lane realized. Bruised and jabbed for Hades only knew what purpose. Lane pulled another ampere coin from her pockets, sliding it between her fingers.

As she ran her fingers down the seam of the door, she knew they would not have enough time to get to every door. They would have to leave someone behind.

If there was anyone else there.

There was no point in telling Ivy to step back.

"Cover your ears." Lane said. Her hands shook, and she ordered them to be steady as she pushed energy into the wall.

Footsteps bounded toward her. She turned her head to the side to see Shepherd's long legs, sprinting down the hall. Lane's hands reached to warn her, but it was too late.

"Shepherd!" she cried out.

The door exploded, knocking Shepherd into the air. She flew backward, her back slamming into the floor as she was showered with debris. Lane ducked, shielding her face at the last second as rocks flung toward her face.

Thunder clapped in Lane's head, followed by the sound of suction and whooshing air. Pain split through the side of her head, her eardrum ruptured.

Her vision tunneled as the pain in her ear screamed. The dust settling around her, she crawled to Shepherd across the floor.

"Shepherd?"

Her dark skin was covered in a light layer of dust, eyelashes fluttering with bits of rock. She coughed, the wheeze wet and desperate.

"Warn a girl next time," she said.

Lane grabbed her arm, pulling them both to their feet. "Maybe look where you're going, next time."

Shepherd grinned at her. Lane rolled her eyes, turning toward Ivy's cell.

Climbing over rocks and the destroyed door, she pushed a boulder out of the way. Ivy was covered in dust like Shepherd, a layer of debris covering her auburn hair. She fingered the shackle at her wrist, leaving fresh bruises as she pulled against it.

"Let me," Lane said. She wrapped both hands around the chain and pressed her feet against the stone wall. The other woman pulled backward into a small ball as Lane pushed her body weight against the chain. Bracing her feet on the wall, Lane pushed as hard as she could, sending a small bit of magic into the cuff. Lane fell backward as the metal hinge ripped from the wall, still holding it in her hand as she fell to the ground.

"Show off," Shepherd said. She took a cautious step toward Ivy, extending her hand to help Ivy stand. Next to Shepherd's tall form, she seemed even more fragile.

"I'm Shepherd," she said. "And you must be Ivy."

She nodded, running her hands over her face as if she couldn't believe it was still there. Or perhaps she was wondering if she was in a dream and she would wake up any second, still in a nightmare.

"We need to keep moving," Lane said, the alarm still screaming in their ears. "We probably only have a few minutes, and we have more people to get out."

Ivy rubbed her dislocated shoulder. "You should have left me for last—I won't be much help," she said. "I'm only human."

Lane frowned. She hadn't known. Her eyes flicked between Shepherd and Ivy. Two humans with no abilities, no defenses.

How did they end up in a place like this?

"I'll just have to be twice as fast," Lane said. "Shepherd, take her and check the other cells. Figure out which ones actually have people."

She nodded, turning to the next cell over with her arm supporting most of Ivy's weight. Lane turned in the other direction. Eight more doors to go.

Down the hall, there was an angry grunt.

"Did someone say Shepherd?" The voice was hoarse, as if it hurt to speak.

Lane turned to Shepherd, her breath in her throat.

Shepherd's eyes went wide. To her surprise, she didn't seem worried to hear her name in this place. She should have been. Lane would have been.

Shepherd's expression was trapped between shock and a grin that would have put the sun to shame. It sent a thrum through Lane's entire body.

"I will kill her," the voice said, louder. "Shepherd, you better not be out there!"

Shepherd broke into a run.

"Addie?" she shouted, slapping her hands against the door. "Addie!"

They had done it. They'd actually done it.

Every nerve in Lane's body turned rigid. A part of her hadn't believed they would find her, and that part of her was electric with relief. But the fear of finally meeting Addie—the person in the world most important to Shepherd—was there too.

Shepherd's hand clung to a smaller, darker hand, their fingers interlaced as they whispered to each other through the window.

Shepherd blinked at tears that brimmed along her lashes. Her knuckles turned nearly white, her mouth twitching as she fought to keep her face calm. Lane had never seen Shepherd look like that. She had never seen anyone look like that. It was a face so full of love that Shepherd had literally gone to Hell for it.

She swallowed, acid filling her throat. As happy as she was for Shepherd, there was a tinge somewhere in her that was also sad for herself, sad that she would never have that, and probably never had.

"What are you doing here?" Addie snapped.

"I'm your big sister," Shepherd said. "It's basically written in blood that I'm supposed to look out for you. Even if you are smarter and stronger than me."

"That's for little kid stuff like bullies," Addie said. "Not literally going to Hell."

"Potato, potah-to," Shepherd said with a shrug that Addie likely couldn't see.

The alarm rang overhead, muffling their conversation. With each shrill cry, her heartbeat a little faster. They needed to get Addie out—they would have to come back for everyone else.

If they could.

Lane couldn't bring herself to interrupt them, but she had to. They had to go.

"How did you find me? I mean, you don't know anything about magic." Addie said.

"I learned a thing or two," Shepherd said. She looked back at Lane. "And I had help."

"Oh my gods. Are you dead?" Addie gasped.

Shepherd laughed.

Voices shouted in the distance, barely audible over the screeching alarm. The torches at each end of the hall flickered.

"We've got to move," Lane said, pushing Shepherd out of the way as she started to rub an ampere between her fingers.

"Shep?" Addie called through the door. "Do you happen to have my necklace? The one grandma left me?"

Lane's hand froze. Her fingers twitched, suddenly feeling the key alongside the muscle of her arm, next to the other key and the small bone shard.

Of course Addie wanted it back. She could feel the hum it released when Addie spoke, like a whistle signaling in the dark.

"If you have it, I can help." Addie said. Her words were hoarse, full of cracks, like a wanderer stranded in the desert. It didn't sound like she'd be able to do much of anything.

Lane looked at Shepherd, watching her hesitate. Her hand floated between them, the ampere still gripped between her fingers. With

321

a heavy exhale, Lane reached into her pocket, her fingers wrapping around the now familiar metal chain.

She handed it to Shepherd without looking. Footsteps bounded overhead, cascading down the staircase. Lane counted five, six sets of steps.

"Hurry," Lane said, as she walked past Shepherd to the entryway. If she had successfully blocked the door, they might have an extra minute at most.

Shepherd shoved her hand through the small window, dropping the necklace between the gap.

Lane's breaths grew heavy as she focused on the sound of the approaching footsteps. With each bark and shout, her heart grew quiet, the distance between seconds growing. She glanced over her shoulder at Addie's cell door.

The ground beneath their feet shook, letting out a guttural groan, as if After Life itself was splitting open. Shepherd sprinted toward her, dragging Ivy by one hand. She grabbed Lane with her other hand, pulling her into a run so quickly that she tripped over her own feet.

"What are you doing?" Lane shouted.

Without warning, Shepherd threw them both to the ground. One arm landed protectively across Lane's back, the other draped over Ivy. An angry boom resounded through the hall, the sound ripping through the pain in her eardrum like a crack in the Earth. She felt blood pool in her ear, her mouth filling with dirt as Shepherd pushed her against the ground.

The floor rumbled underneath them like a wave. The entire Academy was going to collapse, trapping them beneath it. That was not exactly how Lane wanted to spend the rest of her existence.

Another crack resounded behind them, rocks peppering their backs.

Lane peeked from underneath Shepherd's arm, waiting for the ceiling to crush them. The wall split in two and then flew across the hall, exploding outward in a thousand pieces of metal and stone. But it was not just the wall—the rock itself was separating on both sides of the hallway. A fog of debris rolled toward them as the wall collapsed, revealing the cells, now completely open.

Addie's hands were outstretched in front of her, a bead of sweat on her brow. Her hair was full of debris, tiny pieces of sand-colored dust clinging to long strands of jet black hair. Her hands fell, revealing the bruised inside of her arms. Shepherd ran to embrace her, pulling her into a tight embrace. She was shorter than Shepherd, but not by much.

Rolling her shoulders, she placed the key back around her neck, still trapped in Shepherd's arms.

Ivy crawled to her knees, staring at Addie. Lane rubbed her face, trying to wipe the dirt from her eyes.

"What the hell?" Ivy said.

Addie shrugged. "Normally, I could do that without the help, but—"

She gestured to everything around them. She'd been down here for weeks. Of course she wasn't at full strength.

Lane reached up to her ponytail. She understood why Addie had been worried. With that kind of power. . .

Addie held her hand out to Ivy, helping her struggle to stand. Around them, people started to exit their cells, the walls blown to pieces beneath their feet. Lane recognized a few of them from the photos—a satyr and six more witches. Each of them were covered in bruises around their necks, wrists, and ankles. Each of them had needle marks up and down their veins, their sleeves ripped open.

"All right, let's get out of here."

Lane turned to Shepherd, Addie standing at her side. She met the other girl's eyes for the first time and tried to smile, despite the alarms and collapsing rock around them. Looking at Addie was like looking at a haunted reflection of Shepherd. In place of Shepherd's smirk, like sunsets, her eyes were flat, and empty, frown lines etched in her face.

Addie opened her mouth and screamed.

She grabbed at Shepherd, her fingers frantic as she pushed and pulled at the same time, as if she was unsure if she should hide behind Shepherd or hide Shepherd behind her.

Lane stood frozen in place next to the others, unsure what to do.

Addie's chest heaved as her scream calmed.

"You," she growled. Her steps were wobbly as she rushed toward Lane. "You!"

Lane sidestepped as the girl bulldozed toward her, confused. Shepherd was on her heels, trying to stop her.

Behind them, the door at the end of the hall shook, as if being hit with a battering ram.

Lane's eyes flicked from Addie's angry, frightened face to the door, wondering how long it would hold.

"Addie, what are you doing? That's Lane—my friend. She's the one that found you. She helped me." Her voice trailed off as she looked at Lane. "She saved all of you."

"No," Addie spat, wrestling her hand from Shepherd's. "She's the one who took me."

CHAPTER TWENTY-NINE

The world dropped out from underneath Lane.

"What?" Lane asked. "No. What? I've never seen you before."

She bit her tongue, suddenly aware of dozens of eyes appraising her. The man next to her took a step away from her, as if she would attack him at any moment.

Her fingers went numb.

"Shep, listen to me." Addie pulled on Shepherd's arm. "She's one of them. *She did this.*"

Shepherd stared at Lane, her brown eyes circled with shock. Her mouth opened and closed, her hands clenching at her side, trying to find words.

"Addie, you must be confused. She's my friend."

Her voice stuttered, and Lane felt the odd sensation that she was watching the scene playout from above. She was an actress in a play, a muse in a myth. Nothing was real.

Addie pulled Shepherd away, giving Lane a glare that felt like being dunked in cold water.

"You can't trust her." Addie yanked on Shepherd's arm, pulling her further away in the hall. Ivy stood between them, looking at Lane with pleading eyes as the door shook again.

"It's not true," Lane whispered. But she knew there was no point. They needed to leave.

There was only one thing Lane could do.

She took a step toward Shepherd, trying not to look at Addie as she glared at her, her breath still shaking. Lane's mouth was a thin, forced smile as she took Shepherd's hand. Addie took two steps backward, into the crowd of witches.

Lane took a shuddering breath as Shepherd blinked down at her. Her expression was burning, her eyelashes wet with confusion and fear. *Is it true? Tell me it's not*, her eyes seemed to say.

Lane shook her head.

"We're running out of time. We didn't get all these people out just for them to get captured again," she said. "Get to Deryck's bar. He will help you get them back. Hide until you see him, don't come out for anyone else."

Shepherd's mouth hung open. "What about you?"

Lane looked down at her feet. She didn't ask if it was true. Lane wasn't sure if that was a good thing.

"I've got to go back," she said. "This is how it's got to be."

Shepherd's grip on her hand tightened. Behind them, the freed witches gathered behind Addie, as if she might protect them from the threat of Lane.

Her moment as a hero had been short lived, it seemed.

"What are you going to do?" Shepherd asked. She wrapped her fingers in Lane's, as if holding Lane tighter would make it harder for her to leave.

Howls carried through the hallway.

"Give them Hell." Lane smirked.

It was always going to be this way. She was dead, and Shepherd was not. There were never two things meant to be more separate.

She gave Shepherd her best devilish grin as she backed away. Shepherd's hand floated between them, frozen in time.

Nails scratched at the door as it finally gave way, the hinges snapping. A hellhound's face filled the space, black teeth snapping at the metal.

She pushed Shepherd back toward the prisoners as hard as she could.

"Get out of here!"

She turned to run the opposite way as Shepherd grabbed her wrist, pulling Lane toward her. Before Lane could stop her, Shepherd wrapped Lane in her arms, pressing against her as tightly as she could. Warmth radiated from her arms onto Lane's skin, melting away the armor she had built against their goodbye.

Without a word, Shepherd's mouth crashed onto hers, furiously, hungrily, desperately.

Electricity fired across her nerves. Feeling returned to her fingers, heat swelling in her chest. Her heart seemed to stop beating as Shepherd closed her arms around Lane's neck. Lane pushed herself tighter against Shepherd's chest, pushing her mouth harder onto hers as static jumped back and forth between their skin.

She had been struck by lightning.

Shepherd pulled back, her lips red and raw.

The kiss had been full of so many things—that hunger, but also betrayal, anger, and somehow, forgiveness. They had crashed into each other as if it was their last moment, and then split apart with the realization that maybe it was.

It was the bloom of something that could have been and never would be.

Shepherd gave Lane that same summer smile.

"See you soon," she said. "Don't die. Not again, anyway."

Lane smiled back. It seemed that joke would never get old.

She turned away, ready to face the guards and whatever else awaited her as she listened to their footsteps. Her heart thudded in time with each foot fall, her mouth still raw from Shepherd's kiss.

Lane braced herself as the door exploded outward. Blurred, uniformed chests came into view as the guards ran toward her.

Growls and shouts overtook the sound of the alarm. There were two hellhounds, two nochtra, and four guards. She couldn't fight them all and survive. She couldn't face Eurydice bloodied and broken. But she did need to fight them all long enough to give Shepherd a chance to escape.

The first hellhound reached her, leaping to bite into her neck as they were trained to do. It soared overhead as she dropped to the floor in a tuck, rolling away from its claws as it landed behind her. Lane kicked out her foot as a guard jumped off the broken door. His foot caught on her leg, his face hitting the floor with a thwack. The smell of blood and broken bone filled the air.

Two more guards and both nochtra barreled toward her.

The doorway stood empty behind them.

Lane held her breath. In moments, the hellhounds would have their jaws on her ankles.

The hellhound she had ducked under scrambled to its feet, turning to face her with an angry growl. It broke back into a run, claws scratching into the stone floor.

She was surrounded on all sides.

Now would be a good time to pray, she thought, if she believed in anything other than death itself. And praying to Death to avoid getting the life beat out of her seemed too on the nose.

Lane hoped it would work as she tensed every muscle in her body. She closed her eyes, letting the energy wash over her. She fell into the darkness as she Blinked.

The darkness disappeared as her feet landed on solid ground. The guards stood several yards away from her, turning in confused circles. In the span of a breath, she had crossed the room, landing behind them and on the other side of the passageway, inside the door they had broken down.

And she had landed on her feet.

Looking around the room, their gazes finally found her, surprised. Had they known she could Blink? If they remembered her from The Academy, maybe. But it certainly wasn't supposed to work like that.

Whatever was happening to her ability, she was more than happy about it.

With a smirk, she broke into a run up the stairs. Her legs flew toward the end of the hallway. It ended in a spiral staircase, like the one that connected to Eurydice's office. Where that one had been old and gray, dusty and dirty from disuse, this staircase was polished and shining. She didn't remember it from when she had escaped, but she didn't trust her memory. Not anymore.

She could hear the guards rumbling footsteps chasing her, like low thunder, as they finally realized what had happened. Her chest heaved as she leapt to take the stairs two at a time. The barely healed wound in her stomach throbbed as she forced herself to go faster. She pushed forward on pure adrenaline, circling the staircase as it went up and back into the school.

Turning corner after corner, flight after flight of stairs, Lane finally slowed her pace when she heard music in the distance. The unfamiliar halls turned familiar again, the library coming into view. She finally felt comfortable enough to pretend to casually stroll when she passed two ghosts floating absently outside of Victor's room. They didn't even give her a second glance as she entered the entryway ballroom.

The music had turned into a fast-paced waltz of competing string quartets battling from opposite sides of the room, although there were still no musicians to be seen. They hit alternating high notes as the ghosts circled the room in pairs, switching partners as the instruments crescendoed and then flatlined, like lovers meeting and crashing into one another. The dancers' hands met, and then drew apart, and then together again, the strings matching them in time as the ghosts were pulled by the song itself. It was beautiful and eerie, as if they were being led by some unforeseen force. Some of the demons wore masks of gold and black as they watched the performance unfold from around the room, glittering eyes sparkling as the gray ghosts drifted and glided across the floor, more weightless than any ballerina. As if in unison, all of their necks rolled in time to the music and then snapped up, facing their partners as the violin strings plucked a single, strapping note.

At the center of it all, Victor gave Eurydice a final spin. They were still dancing, just as Lane expected them to be.

The guests all clapped, pulled from their reverie. Some shouted their excitement, turning to the other undead beside them. Lane took the moment to slip in among the crowd. Across the room, she saw Tripp, leaning against the wall with his eyebrows furrowed and a drink in his hand. The clock hung over his head, the hand slowly ticking toward midnight. Lane smiled.

She scanned the room as she moved between the guests, trying to stay out of sight. Her hands brushed the tails of her velvet coat, rubbing off the rubble and dust. Overhead, the song changed. The middle of the dance floor raised into a dais, the floor shifting beneath their feet as an entire band and orchestra crashed cymbals together, drums beating a dramatic introduction. Lane scurried to the edge of the room as the audience gasped in awe, breaking into thunderous applause. Her back hit the edge of the room as two undead visitors in front of her clapped with champagne flute in hand.

"Bravo!" they shouted.

Lane's hands felt for the wall behind her as she stretched her neck, searching the room for Tripp and Victor. On the platform, the orchestra began to play again. The ghosts danced around them, their gray forms trotting in time.

A hand grabbed Lane's arm.

"You might want this," Deryck said.

He slipped a mask onto her face as she gasped.

"Deryck," she sighed, as he spun her toward him. Behind her, the crowd clapped again.

"And this."

He slipped a knife into her hand. It was the same, scalpel-like blade he had used to remove her obols.

Lane held her breath as she slipped it into her sleeve.

"Tripp is waiting for you," she told him, pointing her chin at the clock. "Get to the bar."

She couldn't say more, not with so many people around. She hoped she didn't have to. Deryck knew the plan.

"Lane," Deryck said. His voice was barely audible above the music as he looked down at her. "You don't have to do this alone."

A knot twisted in her stomach. She had lost Shepherd, poor Addie twisted and convinced that Lane was a part of Eurydice's machinations. She'd lost Perry. She'd even lost herself and come out the other side.

"I'm not alone," she said. "Don't forget. All of After Life is here."

She turned away from him as she made her way through the masked crowd toward the dais, unrecognized by the other Academy students, demons, and ghosts. Eurydice still danced with Victor at the center of the dais, surrounded by the musicians and unaware that Lane was making her way toward them.

A woman in a glittering gold gown and matching gold mask laughed as she was dipped by her partner, her skirts swishing. Lane stepped around them, her own coat swinging around her knees as she walked slowly in time with the beat. On the other side of the room, the guards that Lane had escaped in the prison appeared, their eyes searching the room. Just in time.

The music slowed as Lane made her way to the dais. The dance ended, Eurydice curtsying to Victor and he clapping to her with a forced smile. The room applauded them as if it had been a performance, but Lane could only hear her only thundering heart as she pushed two of the bystanders that circled the stage out of the way.

She was on the platform, inside the ring of the orchestra. The audience's eyes fell on her and Victor followed their gaze, his eyes wide.

"Eurydice," she said, her voice loud over the dying music. "May I have this dance?"

CHAPTER THIRTY

"Lane," Victor hissed, the violins crawling to a quiet lull. Thousands of eyes stared up at them.

"Explain yourself, girl," Eurydice said, as she motioned for the guards.

"Actually, I think you should explain yourself, Headmistress." Lane looked at the crowd. "Eurydice has told all of you that the witches are after death magic. None of that is true. Eurydice has lied to all of us. The witches are not hunting us—she is hunting them. The witches have no means and no motive to attack us. She was keeping them prisoner here, in this very building, and draining them of their magic to make herself strong. Because they have what she doesn't have. Their lives."

Blank stares.

"Eurydice has been lying to us and keeping us all here. She told all of us that After Life isn't safe, that the witches would destroy us if we tried to leave this world for even a second. That is why you're here, isn't it? Why you can't leave the afterlife? Why she throws this party? Because she is protecting you from the witches. We were all told that without her, none of us could leave After Life. But that was a lie. She wants all of us trapped here, under her control. And if you wanted. . . I think all of you could leave."

"They would all die within days," Victor said, barely loud enough for the first row to hear.

"But she won't even let them leave at all," Lane said. "It's All Hallows. The veil between worlds is thin. Why not let them see?"

Lane turned to the audience that surrounded the stage like the ripples of a wave. They watched her intently now, thousands of eyes like beads in a gown.

"I'm not asking you to care about the witches or about me. But what she is doing to them—what she is doing to us—is not right."

Her eyes glanced from face to face, mask to mask.

Seemingly all together, the demons threw back their heads and laughed. Some of them turned to the person beside them, grinning madly, buckling over at the waist. The gray ghosts stood completely still, as if set to pause.

"This is Death, darling. Nothing is right," one of them shouted, still laughing.

"What do you say?" someone close to the stage shouted. "Should we try it? Let's go see what Life is all about." The demons around him laughed, and they scurried toward the exit, laughing and spilling pink champagne on their gowns. Most of them simply turned away, back to the party, as if nothing had happened at all.

The world seemed to freeze around Lane as she watched them laugh. Her head spun, her legs threatening to buckle beneath her.

None of them cared. Not a single person in After Life cared about any of it, about anything. . . but themselves.

It was truly Hell.

"No," Lane shouted. "Don't you all understand? She's been working with The Keys, taking power from the witches, stealing it for herself! I have the Keys; I can prove it!"

"I think we've heard enough," Eurydice said. "Victor, get her out of my sight."

Victor appeared at Lane's left, grabbing her arm and pulling her backwards off the stage with a litheness she had never seen before.

She opened her mouth to protest, but he shook his head. It was a slight movement, a jerk of his chin—but there was a warning in it.

The guards followed them from the room as Victor pulled her through the crowd, the demons laughing and pointing. Lane barely noticed. Her head felt like it was beneath water, the demons and ghosts blurred and faraway. She tripped over her own feet as he pulled her into the hallway, trying to force her vision to clear, force her lungs to breathe. Her entire body was trapped inside a tunnel with no air and no way out. Her heart beat outside of her body, droning from the follicles of her hair to the bones of her feet.

It was all over. Her plan. Everything.

"Lane. Lane!"

Victor waved his hand in front of her face. She tried to focus her eyes.

They were in the library, outside of his room. The guards lined the wall behind him, standing along the bookcases. She was sitting on one of the long study tables, Victor hovering over her.

"Vic, you have to listen. . . everything I said is true. She's kidnapping Vis, draining their magic. She's using the Keys of Persephone to steal their power. There were dozens of them in the dungeons—"

He placed his hands on her knees, his hair falling into his eyes.

"You really made a mess this time around, didn't you?" he asked. "A dozen times, I ask you to leave it alone, and you never can. And now you've done it in front of all of After Life!"

Lane leaned away from him in surprise, her back pressing into the wooden table.

"You knew?"

"You did say once that I know everything." He shrugged. And that was that.

Lane closed her eyes in disbelief. He had warned her to stop asking questions. He had begged her not to go back and try to help the witches. When Perry had been injured, he hadn't been shocked— because he already knew what was happening, just not how it had gotten that far.

He reached for her, and she yanked her face away.

"Where are they?" His eyes flashed in a way she no longer recognized.

"What?"

"The Keys. You said you have them. Where are they?" His voice was urgent. "Do you have all seven?"

Lane didn't answer, slowly sliding away from him on the bench. Her pulse was racing, her skin sweating under the intensity of Victor's stare.

"You knew, and you didn't say anything to me?" she spat. "What about Perry? Did you let her die?"

He ignored her.

"I know you have them." Victor placed one hand on her shoulder, pulling her back toward him on the bench. "At least, the one you found when that drifter went nochtra."

She shook her head slowly. In her pocket, the Key's song was disturbingly silent, as if it was hiding.

"What are you talking about? Why do you even care about the Keys?"

Cold washed over Victor's face. His dark eyebrows arched, casting shadows across his steel eyes as they pierced into her. He dug his fingers into the table.

"I'm trying to be patient, Laney."

It was like they were having two different conversations. Lane didn't understand—either because her mind was still reeling or because of something else.

Victor looked over his shoulder at the guards as he snapped his fingers, twisting his hand in the strange way Lane recognized as spellwork.

Tripp stumbled into the library, his footsteps seeming forced and awkward. He held Addie by the collar of her shirt, dragging her across the floor as she clawed at his hands, kicking her feet into the stone, screaming at his face. Tripp did not react. He barely seemed to see her. He didn't even seem to be breathing.

Lane looked from Tripp to Victor, her mouth hanging open. "Tripp?"

Two guards followed them into the shadowed entryway, Shepherd slumped across their shoulders.

Lane screamed, jumping to her feet.

No, no, no, no, her mind cried.

Each had Shepherd by one arm, holding her in place so that she could barely move. They had tied ropes around her wrists and crossed them down to her ankles, like an animal ready for slaughter.

"Victor?" Lane's voice cracked.

Everything sharpened into focus.

I know you have them.

Perry, turning into a nochtra.

Victor, telling Eurydice about their mission, and then telling her to run.

The hellhounds finding her right after Victor had appeared.

The nochtra finding Haven Hall.

Addie, screaming.

Her skin flashed white hot with anger. Jumping away from the table, she wheeled toward Tripp.

"Tripp?" she asked.

A smile grew at the corner of Victor's mouth. "To be fair, he doesn't have much choice."

As if to prove his point, Victor raised his hand. His obols glowed as he turned his wrist.

Like a puppet, Tripp's hands lifted. He dropped Addie's shirt and, with a flick of Victor's knuckles, he wrapped his hands around Addie's throat. As she began to struggle, Tripp's face turned purple. His cheeks swelled, the veins in his neck popping, as if his own throat was being choked.

Victor was controlling him, not just to strangle Addie—he was forcing him to not breathe.

As quickly as it began, Victor dropped his hands. Tripp's hands fell from her neck, but he did not fall to the ground. Addie sputtered for air as he caught her by the wrists. He had no choice. Victor wouldn't even let him catch his breath.

Tripp's eyes glanced at Lane, pleading.

Lane took two steps toward them, but Victor held up his hand. Addie's necklace dropped from his hand.

"It took me a while to find this one. But when I heard she had trapped all her power in it herself—and managed not to die in the process—well, I knew I had to see it for myself. Just fascinating, don't you think? Brilliant, excellent work."

He nodded his head toward Addie, as if he was complimenting her. It only made her thrash harder, kicking at Tripp's legs, scratching at his flesh. Even when she drew blood, he didn't move.

The thoughts she had hidden in the back of her mind swam to the surface.

She turned to Victor.

"It wasn't Eurydice," she said. "It was you."

He laughed, running his fingers across his forehead, pushing back his bangs. The image of him mussing his hair brought Lane back to memories that now felt sour, tainted.

"How could you do this? Lie to me, to us?" Lane said.

Victor cracked his neck. "We've been here before, and frankly, it's exhausting." He looked to the ceiling, twirling Addie's necklace between his fingers. "How many times are we going to repeat the same conversation? If I didn't like you so much, I wouldn't go to so much trouble to continue having you around."

He smiled at her, as if he thought it was a compliment.

They had this conversation before. She had forgotten so much. . .

The blank spots.

They hadn't happened because something had gone wrong, and they hadn't stopped because she was away from After Life. They'd stopped because she hadn't been near him.

He was the one erasing her memories. He was the one that had erased her identity, her entire life.

They had done this before. She had found out the truth before.

"You've been making me forget. Everything. My name. My life. This."

"And I will again," he said, casually sitting on the library's desk.

He waved his hand at the guards. They charged at her, grabbing her arms before she could fight back. They pushed her to the ground.

"I wish it didn't have to be this way," Victor said. He spoke toward the bookshelves, unable to look directly at her. At least that small piece of the Victor she knew was still there. "But this time, with how public you've made everything. . ."

"Why?" she asked him. "Why would you do this? Erase our memories? Why do you even care about any of this?"

Lane tried to reconcile the two Victors. The one she knew: smart, bookish, quiet, even sheepish in some cases. All he wanted to do was be with his books, to learn, to help them, to find new and exciting things. And this Victor: confident, angry, a liar who seemed desperate for the strongest power she had ever known.

"Take her away, and we'll see if we can salvage this," Victor said to the guards. "Although I doubt it."

The guards yanked her to her feet, pulling her toward the towering library entrance.

He was going to do it again. Her heart raced, her eyes flitting from guard to guard, from Shepherd to Addie. She had to think of something, anything to stall him.

"Tell me," she said, as quickly as she could, "and I'll give you the keys. All of them."

He turned toward her, an eyebrow raised. She had his attention now. "I could just take them off of you."

"They aren't here," she said.

He rolled his eyes. "Of course."

Victor stood up, pacing back and forth. He walked toward Shepherd, placing a finger beneath her chin. She snapped her teeth at him, and the guard yanked her backward, almost knocking into a shelf.

"I was a little like your friend here when I was alive. A sad excuse for a witch, really. I have been working on this particular problem for hundreds of years. You know how I am, Laney. A scientist at heart. Even when I was alive, it bothered me. Why did magic need to be separate? Why did a witch have a skill? And then I died, and Vis was lost to me. It doesn't seem fair, does it?"

Lane stared at him. She didn't have to ask.

"Yes, I remember my life. I am sorry about that."

Her knuckles tightened.

"Eurydice was more than happy to let me experiment over the years. I think a part of her wanted to know what would happen if we could harness the witches' magic too. Could we do it safely? And if so, what did that mean? But of course. . ."

"The nochtra. All these years, all the history books, that was you," Shepherd said. The guard yanked her again.

Victor ignored her. "Everyone said it was impossible, that living and death magic would eat at one another. The nochtra are proof of that. I had started to think they were right. . . until you."

Lane's vision blurred.

"The Academy presented an opportunity to slowly drain the power over time, rather than all at once. And it was working. I chose you all carefully, hoping that you would be—pardon my pun—the key to unlocking the next phase."

He had been using them. Nothing mysterious had happened to Perry. Victor had happened. She cried out, unable to stop herself.

"But we were so close. Look at what we've accomplished! I can finally control the nochtra. They answer to me now. The guards and the ghosts follow us like puppets. I knew we were just one break-through away from what had evaded us for so long."

Tears brimmed at Lane's eyes. The sound of her breath echoed in her ears. Nothing he was saying made sense. It was like someone had possessed Victor and replaced him with a person she had never met, but at the same time, everything he said began to fill in the blank spaces. Her time at The Academy had been a puzzle of questions that was suddenly fitting together, and she didn't like the picture.

Victor had picked them, one by one, to be a part of his little experiments. He had erased their memories and used them to try and figure out how to harness the witches' magic—by kidnapping them, or worse. Whatever he needed. Lane couldn't even think of it, couldn't even imagine the things he had done. And he had hidden it all behind The Academy. Had he been working with The Keys all this time?

"So that's it, then? That's why you've been doing all of this? To make yourself all powerful, collect as much power for yourself as you can in these keys?"

Victor turned toward her, his head cocked to the side. "No, Lane," he said. "*You're* the key."

She stumbled back, the guards catching her and tightening their grip on her elbows. She glared at them, their silvery faces as blank as walls. She should have known they were being controlled.

"I thought it was obvious," Victor said, matter of factly. "It worked with all of you, at first. Slowly having Nil and Vis run through your veins, with obols, with the missions, going back and forth between Life and Death. Some of you didn't last long. Like poor Perry. Unfortunately, she was not a good candidate, it turns out. But you! I knew you were a success after you were able to go to Earth and survive for so long. I had only meant to use you as a distraction when Eurydice began to become suspicious. I almost can't believe my luck. And you tracked down another key in the process!"

His tone was smug, delighted, almost delirious. He took two steps toward her. He glanced down, taking her hand in his, even as the guards still pinned her arms at her sides. She couldn't so much as kick at him as they held her back.

"Together," Victor said, "I hope that we can finally finish what I have been trying to do, all these years."

"And what's that?" Her voice shook, trying to hide the fear and anger that trembled beneath her skin.

Victor turned to her. "Cheat death, of course."

Lane pulled away from him.

"Isn't that what you've always wanted?" he asked "A second chance? Imagine being dead for years, knowing it was just within reach. I could have a life—not this empty, sad imitation. A better one than your friend over there has; certainly, I could be powerful. I could go back to Earth, like you have, and breathe fresh air."

It couldn't be.

"It was all a lie," Lane said. The Academy had promised them a graduation, a second chance, a reincarnation. It had been a lie. A lie that none of the students would ever truly see.

Victor had never been on a mission. He had never been to Earth. Because he couldn't.

A second chance at life hadn't just been a lie. It was impossible.

The dead couldn't go to Life.

"I'm alive."

Shepherd mouthed something at her that she couldn't read.

"Lane," Victor interrupted. "I never wanted to hurt you. I never wanted any of that. That's why I needed to keep erasing your memory—I didn't want you to have that burden."

She whipped her head to stare at Victor, her vision blurring. "The burden you gave me! You did this!" she spat as she yanked against the guards' arms.

"But don't you see? I did it. We did it. You're proof. Nil and Vis both run through your veins, surviving. You could have ended up like Peregrine, but you didn't."

Her fingernails dug into her palms, drawing blood. "You said that I had a choice," she said. "You let me believe it was my choice. You sent us on your little missions because you couldn't go. You *needed* us because you couldn't do it yourself. Because you were weak."

Victor's eyes flashed. She had always known how to hit someone's pain points.

"You don't understand. I wish you did. I wish we could work together, now that you know the truth." He paused, looking at the ceiling. He looked at her, his expression both angry and sad. "I don't know that you'll survive another mindwipe. We could work together instead. Me and you."

He stumbled over his words, the same shy, awkward Victor she knew and cared for piercing his calm veneer. But that person didn't exist. He had been a lie.

"Lane, I care about you. I don't want to hurt you. Think of the things we could do together, Laney."

"Lane isn't even my real name!" she yelled. She thrashed against the guards' arms. "You were my friend, and you betrayed me. Go ahead and wipe my memory. It's the only way you'll get me to do anything for you ever again. Come on, do it!"

Spit flew from her mouth. Forgetting again scared her, chilled her deep in the knuckles of her spine. But forgetting was so much better than this.

His fingers twisted in the same position he had used when controlling Shepherd. His eyes glinted as a small smirk pulled across his lips. He flicked his wrist.

Nothing happened.

He repeated the motion, turning his hand toward her. His hair fell around his face as he reached toward her, grabbing her by the wrist. She was surprised at his strength—he had always said he was weak, not suited for the field. He lifted her like a paper doll as he pushed her sleeve up to her elbow.

"What did you do to your obols?" he yelled. He dropped her to the ground with a crash.

The obols. That was how he controlled Tripp. That was how he was pushing Nil into them and pulling it out like a syringe in a lab rat.

And she had cut them out.

"The obols," she said. "They siphon our power."

Her power. Not his power. Not the Nil that The Magistrate doled out like scraps. She hadn't felt weaker since they removed her obols. She had felt stronger. She had been able to Blink objects, entire trees, and she had brought Shepherd and Deryck to After Life. She didn't just feel stronger—she was stronger.

That was why he had chosen her and Tripp and Perry. They were Vis. He had used them as his experiments, connecting them to him through the obols to trickle away their power rather than drain it.

All her veins froze. Her hands shook at her side.

And then, she laughed.

"You can't control me without them, can you?" She flicked her chin toward Tripp. "You can't drain my power and you can't control me, wipe my memory."

She twisted her body against the guards, dropping her weight so that their hands dropped in surprise.

"I was your puppet. Not anymore."

An angry growl escaped her mouth. The foundation beneath her feet cracked as she cried out, her growl turning into a scream.

She was an empty vessel. She was nothing. She had nothing. She was empty spaces, blank spots in memories. She filled all the holes inside her with rage. And then she exploded.

The guards flew backwards as she Blinked, barely noticing the darkness in that fleeting movement as she appeared at Victor's side.

Her hand flew to the dagger at her waist, the blade on his neck within seconds.

His face was the picture of calm as she held the silver blade to the pale skin of his neck. He lifted a single finger, wagging it back and forth.

His eyes were flat, bored. "Do you really want to put your friends in danger like that? I am already dead, after all. What would be the point?"

With another flick of his wrist, Tripp's hands went to Addie's throat. Her eyes bulged as he lifted her off the ground. At the same time, his own face turned purple and blue, as if every second of air he deprived her of was ripped from his own lungs at the same time.

Victor smiled as Lane realized.

"Addie!" Shepherd thrashed, kicking at the guards' legs. She tried to use her height against them, pulling away, but they only tightened their grip on her bonds.

"Stop!" Lane shouted. "Just stop."

She dropped the knife from his throat, letting it clang to the ground.

He was right. She couldn't risk their lives for revenge.

Victor smiled. "You were always smarter than people gave you credit for," he said.

He held his arms out like a circus master, showing the crowd all that belonged to him. "You saw the nochtra. You know how close I've come. I only need the Keys, just a last bit of power to make my experiments a reality. I'll finally be able to cross and live again—a true life." He paused, taking a half- step toward her. "You could come with me. We could find your family. I could tell you your real name."

He glanced up as he heard her breath hitch. His chin tilted down so that his eyes stared at her over the top of his glasses.

"But if you don't give me the keys—well, let's say I have already found your replacement. It will take longer, but luckily she is already more powerful than you'll ever be."

Victor waved his arm, and Tripp pushed Addie forward. She fell, stumbling over her own feet, but his hands remained locked on her arms like manacles.

Behind them, Shepherd screamed. She threw her weight into the guards, her face red as she struggled against the bonds at her wrists. Her voice carried across the room as it turned from a scream to a desperate cry.

Tears streamed down her face, and Lane felt her own eyes stinging. She clenched her fists at her sides.

It didn't matter if she was alive. It didn't matter what could have been, with Shepherd, with her life. All that mattered was that she did what she came to do.

The fire inside her grew from a smolder to a wildfire.

"No," she growled. "Let her go."

Victor cocked his head to one side, Addie's key swinging from his fingers.

"Take me," she said. She reached for her pocket, unzipping the hidden sleeve on the back of her arm. "Take the keys."

Her eyes flashed to Victor's, her gaze burning like embers. She opened her fist, revealing the key that the drifter had left behind and the shard of bone.

"It's mine, isn't it?" She brought the shard between her forefinger and thumb, lifting it to eye level. It was small, small enough that if you took it from the right place, the person might not even notice, other than a slight tinge in their side. "You tried to make it a Key." She laughed. "You saved me with something that always belonged to me."

Victor's face fell, his eyes on the floor. He did not respond. It was more confirmation than she needed.

"You know what the worst part is? I was yours, Victor." Her words were acid in her throat. "I would have done anything for you. But you've stolen that from me. You've stolen everything from me."

She tightened her fist around the two keys. In her hand, they hummed, electric and shrill, a harp played out of tune. Inside her, the sound grew louder, a cacophony of haunted voices calling for a reckoning.

"I won't let you steal my life too," she said.

She broke into a run, her body a blur of rage and grief as they collided. The impact knocked the wind from her lungs as they fell to the floor.

Lane grabbed for his fingers. She locked her hand around his, shutting it tight as she shoved the point of her elbow into his forearm. He shouted as she pushed the nerves into his arm to go numb.

"Lane, no!" Shepherd cried out from across the room. Lane barely threw her a glance as she locked her other hand across Victor's, holding his arms in place with her own.

Behind him, Tripp dropped Addie from his hold, freed from Victor's control.

Her eyes locked with Addie's. She wouldn't let what happened to her happen to Addie. She wouldn't let Victor hurt her or anyone else.

"Lane, please," Shepherd called out again. She couldn't look at her.

She had been annoying. A pest that forced herself into her life. And once there, she had opened doors inside her that she hadn't known existed. She had been the darkest corners in the middle of the night. And Shepherd had been a candle.

Together, they had gone through the darkness.

She shoved her knee into Victor's leg, pinning him beneath her as their gaze met. She had so many things she wanted to say.

All Lane had wanted was a life. And she had gotten it or something like it, anyway.

Victor had wanted more. He had wanted to touch the sun.

And Lane would see him burn.

Pain shot up her arms as she dug her nails into his flesh. He twisted underneath her weight, wrapping his fingers around the grip she had on his hands. Static traveled up her arms, pin pricking the pores on her face. Victor's inky black hair stood on end. Her own curls leapt from her face as the current poured through them.

He was trying to suck the power out of her—and from the Keys—by force.

She screamed as a shock rolled through her body. Her vision went white as they flew from the ground and came crashing down as if blown by an invisible bolt. Around them, the air crackled, the smell of cooking flesh filling her nostrils.

He was going to kill them both.

Lane wrapped her hand tighter around her shard of bone, clasping it against the other two keys—the first in her hand, and Addie's in Victor's. As their ivory surfaces met, she felt a high-pitched scream rattle through her, like a tuning fork struck by lightning.

Black and white rays exploded from their interlocked fingers, spraying the room in darkness and light.

Lane pulled at the Keys, begging them to give her their power. She felt the electricity running through them, that first strange key, empty and cold, and Addie's, shining. She imagined them running through her skin. She imagined the power jumping from the keys.

She did the only thing she could think to do. She Blinked.

The darkness unfurled around them like a rushing tide. In her arms, Victor screamed. He had never Blinked before. He had never passed through that space of nothingness between worlds, that true, infinite darkness where all things ended.

The black and cold rushed across her skin, pulling them down, and down into the depths. Lane did not think of a place to land, a place to reappear.

This was exactly where she wanted to be. In the Nether. The place where all things ended.

With a final sigh, she released Victor's hand. She imagined she heard him call out her name as he disappeared, falling backward into the darkness.

CHAPTER THIRTY-ONE

Lane ended it like it began.

Alone.

The darkness of the Blink returning inside her, her back hit the floor with a slam. She closed her eyes once, twice, trying to adjust from the infinite blackness. The blurs of the library appeared around her, leather bound browns and the stone grays.

Victor was gone. He was not next to her, slowly waking up on the ground. He was nowhere at all, and always would be.

Nochtra flooded the room, confused and out of control with Victor gone. Their shadowed outlines flickered like poltergeists, thrashing into walls and tearing stone from the floor. The guards shouted in confusion, unsure of what to do, whose orders to follow.

Lane's hands went to her throat. A metal collar was cold against her skin. Her fingers grabbed at it desperately, but she could find no clutch, no opening. What was this thing? Where had it come from?

A guard ran toward her. She didn't have time to worry now. She scanned the room.

Tripp was on his knees, his palms facing the ceiling as if in confession. His jaw hung open and heavy. Lane crawled across the floor to him, her eyes still searching the library. Two hellhounds lunged at a guard, his gray form disappearing to dust beneath their jaws.

"Tripp," she shouted. "You have to move. You can't stay here."

She pushed him, but he barely glanced at her as the guards rushed toward them. They grabbed his arms, yanking him off the floor. He half-heartedly fought back, throwing elbows toward their faces. But Lane could tell. He had given up. Even if they were alive, something inside him had died.

She skittered away across the floor like an insect. The guards lunged for her, their hands just missing her ankles as she spun away.

Beneath the chandelier at the center of the room, she turned in a circle. The hellhounds attacked the guards, and the guards attacked the nochtra, and the demons from the party flooded the hall, excited by all the chaos. The library was torn to pieces, books flying in the air, white pages falling to the floor like winter leaves.

Lane didn't see Shepherd, not anywhere.

Finally, her eyes landed on Addie screaming as two guards lifted her from the ground. One threw her over his shoulder, the other holding her legs, trying to carry her down a back hallway.

Across the other side of the room, someone yelled her name.

Shepherd.

Lane spun on her heel. She was in the opposite corner from Addie, backed up against the archway that led back toward the dormitories. The two sisters could not have been further apart. Two nochtra cornered Shepherd against the Fiction section, surrounding her like wolves.

"Shepherd!" Lane broke into a run.

Behind her, Addie screamed.

She needed to grab both of them and Blink out of here.

Lane closed her eyes, letting the darkness surround her one last time.

A guard grabbed her, yanking her to the ground. She kicked him away from her. Again, she closed her eyes. With an inhale, she imagined herself returning to that darkness between worlds.

And nothing happened.

She closed her eyes again.

And again.

Her heart racing, Lane looked around the room with panic in her eyes. Her hands went to the collar at her throat.

"No, no, no," she said, the room crashing around her.

A guard grabbed Shepherd by the shirt, wrapping a rope around her neck, her hands, her feet. The nochtra circled them, flapping their wings and swooping down, scratching at her face with a cackle.

Addie screeched as the two guards carried her further into the hallway.

Lane's eyes met Shepherd's, the guards pulling her into the dark archway that led deeper into the school.

White noise filled Lane's ears, blurring the world around her. The room was too big for her to get to them both. She might not even be able to get to one of them in time, even if she hurried.

"*Go*," Shepherd mouthed. "*Help Addie.*"

"No," Lane shouted, not even hearing her own voice. "I won't leave you!"

But the guards were already pulling her further and further away. With each step, Shepherd disappeared into the shadows of The Academy.

Lane knew what Shepherd wanted her to do. She knew why, and she even knew that if their roles were reversed, she would be asking Shepherd the same thing.

She listened, her ears straining over the violence around her, as Shepherd's shouts quieted until she heard nothing at all.

Before she could turn away, before she could do anything, Shepherd was gone.

Addie struggled in the guards' arms, flipping her body in a circle so they lost their grip. One of the guards grabbed at her shirt, pulling at it with angry, hastened hands as he lifted her off the ground. She threw her weight back down against his wrist, falling to the floor once again.

Lane didn't have time to think about what might have happened to her, why she couldn't Blink. She had been on plenty of missions. She broke into a run, barreling past the guards and jumping over a hellhound as she leapt onto the library tables, vaulting from one to the next across the room.

"Tripp!" she shouted as she ran. He was still kneeling on the ground with his head in his hands. Somehow, even like this, he had fought off the guards. "Get up, I need you!"

Something in him snapped. Lane reached for him, holding out her hand as she ran past.

"Help me grab her!"

He nodded, red braids falling in his eyes.

They took off together, side by side. For a moment, it was a regular mission.

So much had changed, and nothing had changed at all.

"Get her away from the guards!" Lane pointed at Addie. Tripp thrust more force into his run, charging ahead of her as she jumped from table to table. A group of demons screeched as they moved out of his way at the last second, almost knocked over by his sheer size.

He reached Addie before Lane did, grabbing one of the guards by the forehead and cracking his face into the table. At the same time, he kicked to the side, shoving his foot into the back of the other guard's knee. Addie fell to the ground as they dropped her.

The guards rose to their feet as Tripp tried to pick Addie up, but she screamed, scrambling away from him. One of the guard's tried to take advantage of it, but Lane leapt off the table as he reached for Addie, tumbling into him and knocking him to the floor.

Tripp gathered Addie into his arms, trying to be calming as he said something into her ear that Lane couldn't hear. Lane didn't try to soothe her or say anything. There was nothing she could say that would help.

The room was a storm around them. The nochtra screeched, their monstrous forms thundering as the guards and demons cried, trying to get out of their way. The hellhounds ran circles around the room as some of the guards left the library, possibly deciding they no longer cared about the job they had been forced into.

The floor beneath their feet shook, threatening to give away under the strain of destroyed columns and ripped apart foundation.

Lane grabbed Tripp's shirt. Behind them, something boomed, shaking the walls. The room filled with screams. The building was going to collapse. She glanced over her shoulder as the ceiling began to cave in, mosaic crashing to the floor.

"Tripp, get us out of here!" Lane screamed, wrapping her arm around him. He nodded, closing his eyes, tucking Addie into his chest.

Silence enveloped them as the chaos around them disappeared, replaced with darkness.

All they left behind were their footsteps in the dust.

CHAPTER THIRTY-TWO

Lane walked across the lawn of Haven Hall—or what was left of it. The formerly grand, sprawling estate had been reduced to just a few stone walls and a field of dirt and rubble. It wouldn't be like that for long. The students and refugees had returned, and they had already started to pile together the rock that could be salvaged. The Salvagers had already started to rebuild some of the walls.

That was what they had taken to calling themselves. The Salvagers, the Salvaged. It was a sort of inside joke with the people they had been able to rescue from After Life—they had been salvaged, saved by the skin of their teeth, like treasure hewn from the Earth, like rubbish, discarded, that turns out to be valuable. It was an admission that something kept them as outsiders, apart from everyone else, from the ones who had never experienced it and from the ones who hadn't made it out.

After Tripp had Blinked them out of the library, they had gone back to Deryck's bar, where the rest of the prisoners waited for them. Shepherd had told them to wait for her while she went to look for Lane, and Addie had refused to let her go alone. They had been captured shortly after. Everyone that had stayed in the bar made it out, with Tripp and Deryck's help.

And Eurydice's.

Deryck had made a deal with her that she would let them all go, and they wouldn't come after her for what part she had played in Victor's plan. She claimed she hadn't known, and Deryck told Lane not to ask. Maybe to him it had seemed like a worthwhile trade. Lane wasn't sure she agreed. Some days, as she watched families reunite at Haven Hall, she couldn't blame him. Other days, the only emotion she did feel was blame.

Lane crossed the courtyard, the stone steps blown to pieces that slowed her pace. Perry had done that, she realized. Lane still had so many questions about what had happened to Perry—and to herself, her own power. Her hands went to the collar at her throat. But the only person that could answer them was lost to the dark.

She thought about Victor sometimes. It had already been a few months, but everything felt as raw as a new wound. Maybe it would always be like that. Every day she woke up and had to remind herself she was alive. They had given her a bedroom at Haven Hall, alongside Tripp, although she was rarely there. The others still acted like she was the reason for all their pain.

And they were right.

She hurried to the stairs, hoping not to run into anyone on her way to what she had to do. The main hall was always full of people now, scrambling to plaster this or that so that they could have a ceiling again.

Lane cursed as Ivy saw her. She and Seren were sitting on the bottom step, as if they had been waiting for her. Or at least, Ivy was. She waved excitedly as Seren walked off, barely glancing at Lane. Things between them hadn't warmed up, even though she had invited Lane to stay there. Lane was a witch, after all. Even if she didn't have powers temporarily.

Ivy jumped to her feet, wrapping her arms around Lane's shoulders. She was no longer the skin and bones Lane had found, pink in her freckle-covered cheeks. And she was a hugger. Lane hated it.

"Penny for your thoughts?" Ivy asked.

"I still don't know what that means."

"You were dead for a year, not a century."

Lane laughed. It did feel that way sometimes. But really, she had never been dead at all.

It was one other thing she couldn't bear herself to think about, questions she would never get the answer to since she had chosen to kill Victor. Who was she? What did the collar around her neck do?

When she, Addie, and Deryck had first gotten back to The Haven, they had tried to figure it out. Ivy had run tests on it, Deryck had asked all the demons he was friendly with, and even Addie had tried to blow it off—although Lane suspected she was using it as an excuse to kill her. One thing was clear, though—she was no longer able to Blink.

Lane cleared her throat. "I'm here to tell her something."

"She's in the same place as usual." She nodded her head toward the stairs.

They had been blown to pieces, creating a happenstance landing that looked out over the acres of destroyed earth. A perfect overhang created a balcony-like effect, so that when you stood at the edge of the stone, it felt like you were looking out a window to the end of the world.

Addie sat off to one side of the broken opening, her legs hanging over the cliff-like edge of the floor. It abruptly ended as you stepped off the top of the stairs, so that if you weren't paying attention, you would plummet straight to the rubble of the courtyard below. Addie was always there, staring off into the distance.

She jumped to her feet when she saw Lane walking toward her. Unlike Ivy, she did not look like being at Haven Hall was helping her. She refused to go home without Shepherd, to face their parents. Her shirt had stains on it that Lane couldn't identify. Purple bags sagged under her eyes, turning her once beautiful, earth-colored skin to the ashen color of a dry desert.

"How are you?" Lane shoved her hands into her pockets, reminding herself too much of Shepherd.

Addie shrugged. She might not be afraid of Lane, but they had never spoken about the fact that Lane had been the one to capture her, even if it was under some kind of mind-control. It left an awkward, betrayal-sized hole between them.

Still, that hole was not as large as the one Shepherd left behind.

"Did you find her?"

She already knew the answer. It was routine between them now, for her to ask and for Lane to disappoint.

Addie turned away from her. Several minutes passed, the sun setting over the school and Lane listening to the students screaming in the distance. Somehow, it felt like a semblance of normalcy, at least compared to the rest of her life.

"What do you think she's doing, wherever she is?" Addie asked.

"I'm going to find her," Lane said. Her voice came out soft, a whisper, when she wanted it to be strong. "I just want you to know that."

"I know you will," Addie said.

Lane smiled. "You do?"

Addie looked up, feet swinging over the edge. She smiled, her canines barely showing at the edges.

"Of course. Or I'll kill you myself."

ACKNOWLEDGEMENTS

Writing this book was an interesting journey in self-flagellation during the worst parts of the COVID-19 pandemic, one that I would not have undertaken and survived without so many people. There are so many people who have supported and encouraged me along the way, and I am deeply grateful to each and every one of them.

First and foremost, I want to express my heartfelt gratitude to my partner, Ryan. I know you will never read this because you don't read books, but your support means everything to me. Without you, I wouldn't have believed I could do something like finish a book after trying to for so many years.

To my editor, Jamie Ryu, thank you for your keen insight, invaluable feedback, and tireless dedication to helping me shape this book into the best possible version of itself. Your expertise and guidance have been instrumental in bringing my vision to life, and I am profoundly grateful for your expertise.

To my family, thanks for the childhood trauma that led to me wanting to be a writer.

To my friends, both near and far, thank you for always supporting me and not pushing me to go to brunch when I said I needed to meet a deadline.

To my writing group, thank you for pushing me to keep going, for your beta reads, for your feedback, for your time, and for continuing to inspire me every day. Thanks, OWLs.

And finally, to my beta readers, thank you for taking the time to read and provide feedback on early drafts of this book. It has been a labor of love, and I think the final draft looks almost nothing like the first.

To all of you, thank you for believing in me and for being a part of this journey as I publish this first book, hopefully the first of many.

Love you, mean it.

Kate Gray Glass is a lover and writer of stories, many of which include magic and the supernatural, but not always.

Glass received a BFA in Creative Writing and studied as a Fellow in Writing and Linguistics at Oxford University. Nine to five, she works as a Creative Strategist at Warner Brothers Discovery. She splits her time between LA and DC with her partner and their two crazy goblin dogs. *The Keys of Persephone* is her debut novel.

Visit her online at kategrayglass.com.